Digging with a Spoon

By Anne Main

The Streets of Cardiff Series

Book 1

This book is a work of fiction. Names, characters, and incidents are a product of the author's imagination. Certain locales, public names and historical references to incidents that occurred at certain times, are used for atmospheric purposes only and have been interpreted by the author, they are not meant to be a true or factual representation.

Any resemblance to actual people living or dead or to places of business, companies, events, or locales is completely co-incidental.

1

DIGGING WITH A SPOON

Anne Main

Chapter 1

Ely, Cardiff 1951

"Damn you Ivy!" He snarled, circling her like prey.

She flinched as his fist collided with the wall next to her head.

"How in God's name did this 'appen?" Spittle flew out of
Jimmy's mouth and landed on her chin. Terrified she daren't
wipe it away. He towered over her, filling the small kitchen
with bulk and fury.

Ivy hated his foul mouth; cruel words hitting her like hammer
blows. His slack blubbery lips spitting venom and lies.

2

"You're kidding me!... a problem!" Jimmy hissed, his face redding with rage.

"Well .... this is your fault you stupid, mare! You know that don't you? ... Your fault! I always said you should never have had her; you should have got rid when you had the chance... now look at the trouble she's caused!" He raged.

Ivy gave a small whimper. "Oh, please don't say that Jimmy. June's a good girl, really she is." She feared the gathering storm threatening to crash over her; she had contradicted him.

Jimmy thrust his face within an inch of hers. Ivy tried not to inhale the sour reek of his teeth. He glared at her daring her to move away; she stood transfixed in his cobra like gaze. *She must not cower, it riled him when she showed fear, tonight she must be brave.*

"Well, it is true isn't it! You could have got rid of *it,* but oh no, not you. You come over all Catholic on me. *Please Jimmy don't ask me to...it's a mortal sin,"* he whined in a mocking, sing song voice.

"And now this!... Well, whatever's 'appened ... it's your fault an' you'd better sort it!" He quivered with rage.

Ivy shook her head from side to side, *no this wasn't her fault.*

According to Jimmy it was *always* Ivy's fault… *look what you've made me do Ivy.* She knew that even this one small act of defiance could earn her a punishment. Jimmy would not be contradicted or crossed. *Yes Jimmy, no Jimmy… three bags full Jimmy.* His word was law in the Benson household.

Ivy cringed; Jimmy raised his hand. The vicious slap from the flat of his meaty palm caught Ivy hard on the side of her head. He always aimed for the area where Ivy's hair covered her ear and cheek, the sweet spot for bruises. Sly he was, didn't use his fists; Jimmy didn't like to leave tell-tale marks.

Once, when Ivy had dodged a blow, she made him split her lip by mistake; obliged to stay inside for days until the swelling subsided.

"So careless of me Norah…. I slipped over in the garden putting the washing out." She lied to Nora Ashworth, her friend and neighbour from across the road. Ivy was used to lying. The tighter Jimmy's control became the better liar she became.

"Goodness me Ivy, you look like you've been in the wars. I

said to Jack the other day that I hadn't seen you for a while....
What have you been up to?" Nora couldn't hide her shock
when she saw Ivy in the street. Norah peered at Ivy's injuries.
"That lip looks dreadfully sore, perhaps you should have seen
a doctor about it?" The sight of her friend Ivy looking black
and blue from nose to jaw raised her suspicions.

"Just tripping over in the garden; well, you were lucky not to
lose your teeth if you ask me falling flat on your face like
that!" Nora peered at the puffy swelling and black crust on
Ivy's top lip, a yellowish, green bruise travelled down Ivy's
neck.

Norah Ashworth was a kindly woman and she'd been a good
friend to Ivy over the years. "You certainly came a cropper
Ivy."

"It's not that bad Nora, really it isn't...looks worse than it is,
not worth bothering a doctor about." Ivy dipped her face a
little, her auburn hair flopped over her cheek. She hated lying
to her friend; but visiting a doctor with his probing questions
and doubtful stares would be impossible; Jimmy would forbid
it.

Jimmy would be furious if he thought Nora was sticking her

nose in again. He'd warned Ivy before about telling Norah
Ashworth the family business. She didn't dare visit Norah as
often as she used to. When Jimmy caught her "gossiping" too
long with the neighbours there was always hell to pay.

Norah didn't look convinced. She reckoned she'd got the
measure of Jimmy Benson a long time ago. "You need to look
after yourself my girl!"

"Yes…. It was silly of me… rushing about, not looking
where I'm going…. I had my arms full of washing at the time
and I just couldn't save myself. Jimmy said I needed to watch
my step." Ivy lowered her lying eyes, couldn't meet Norah's
gaze.

"Hmmmm." Norah could spot a bare faced lie when she saw
one.

Ivy was fond of Nora; a motherly soul who clucked and
fussed around her large brood of children, like the proverbial
mother hen. She'd taken Ivy under her wing when baby June
was born and had been her rock during Ivy's struggles in
those early sleep deprived days. Jimmy thought Norah was an
interfering busybody.

Nora had a reputation for generosity amongst the local kids for doling out treats; scraps of cooked pastry with jam and hunks of bread and dripping to feed the gaping mouths of children playing in her garden. Norah couldn't bear to see a hungry child and Wilson road was full of them.

The Ashworth household was the most popular, exuberant one in the street, and from the day Nora and Jack moved in, their door at number 7, Wilson road, was always open.

"Hmm... if you say so Ivy," Nora Ashworth raised a sceptical eyebrow but left it there.

Even from the road it wasn't difficult to hear Jimmy's raised voice coming out of the Benson household, especially on a Saturday night when he rolled home three sheets to the wind. The informed gossip in Wilson road was that poor, little Ivy Benson had a lot to put up with from that bullying husband of hers. The men in Wilson road gave Jimmy a wide berth.

Not long after the Benson family had first moved into the new Council house at number twelve there had been *talk*. Ely had its share of hard men and Jimmy Benson revelled in his reputation as a hard man.

7

Lesson learned, today Ivy stood and took her punishment for defying him. Tonight, of all nights she needed to look him in the eye and be brave and she would.

"What do you mean by telling me *we've* got a problem Ivy....*You've* got the problem and *you'd* better sort it. Use your brain for once; come up with something!... An' you'd better keep that stupid, half-wit of yours out of my sight until it's sorted... do you hear me!" Jimmy snarled.

"Please don't call her that Jimmy," Ivy pleaded, she adored their flaxen haired, little girl, "June can't help being the way she is.... really, she can't."

Jimmy's fury was stoked by Ivy's defence of June.

"What's the matter with you Ivy... Look at me when I'm talking to you!" He raged.

"I'm out there working my arse off trying to get money together to put food on the table, and then you've got the nerve to tell me *"We've got a problem Jimmy."* He whined in a sing song voice, mocking her.

Jimmy hammered his huge fist down on the wooden kitchen table. Ivy shuddered and waited for the next blow to land.

8

"Well, I'm off to the pub and when I come back *this* had better be sorted!"

Jimmy grabbed his coat and hat and left the threat of retribution hanging in the air. The door juddered in its frame as he slammed it furiously behind him.

Jimmy would be drunk when he came back. Jimmy Benson did three types of drunk; the rare, maudlin "I love you my little, darlin' Ivy," drunk, that used to appear when they lived in Bute street. The exuberant "treat -the-whole-pub-to-a-round" drunk when he'd had a good win on the gee-gees and, more often, the mean, spiteful drunk that hated the world and used his fists to put it right. This was the drunk Jimmy usually brought home to Ivy, the one to be kept within the four walls of their home in Wilson road.... The one Ivy loathed.

Ivy had grown to hate Jimmy, she hated who he was and most of all, now she *knew* what she knew... she hated *what* he did.... He was vile... a monster.

He was right about one thing though; she *was* a stupid fool. A stupid, blind fool. In the few years they'd been married he'd made her life a misery, so nervous she jumped at the sight of her own shadow, unable to make the slightest decision without seeking his permission. Cut off from friends and family and kept on a leash so short it was finally strangling her.

She had tried to be a good wife to him; kept the house spotlessly clean, his meals always ready on the table when he got in and if the housekeeping was short, he always had his portion and she'd go without … She had turned a blind eye to his failings and overlooked his lies and excuses to keep the peace.

When they'd got married that fearful day in 1949 she trusted him to look after her, to do the right thing, after all he was the one who'd got her in trouble. She had been so naïve; so wrong.

It wasn't an escape from Bute Street when Jimmy Benson had agreed to marry foolish, pregnant Ivy Benson, it was the start of a life sentence.

Ivy waited until Jimmy was out of sight. He would be heading for the Red Lion on the Grand Avenue; she had about three hours, if his money didn't run before then. Like a lioness protecting her cub, all she could think about was June now.

Ivy had enough time to do what she had to do, and she would stop him... she wasn't afraid of Jimmy Benson!

CHAPTER 2

Bute Town, Cardiff. August 1947

Over a pint of ale Jimmy often learnt things to his advantage and today he learned about Betty Jenkins.

Early that lunch time Jimmy had strolled into the bar of the Rose and Crown, one of the many pubs clustered around the busy Cardiff quays. The trade was slack in the mornings, with an almost empty bar to tend, the landlord Bill had plenty of time for a natter; especially if the customer stood him a drink.

Bill knew all the regulars and all the local gossip. Jimmy was a fresh face in this neck of the woods and Bill was happy to pass the time chewing the fat. You never could tell what you might learn from a new face on the patch.

From a glance the landlord could tell this Irish lad had something about him; a confidence that spoke of a man who knew his own mind. Not a man to cross either, by the looks of him..

Jimmy's quest for cheap lodgings was a common refrain amongst drifters around Tiger Bay. In the cosmopolitan cauldron of the dock lands, land ladies weren't too picky about who paid the rent; down at heel Irish and Blacks thronged into the area looking for work. Money was money wherever it came from, everyone wanted a piece of it.

Bill didn't like Betty Jenkins much; she was a bit too mouthy for his liking; inclined to upset his customers if she was in her cups. Betty could be bad for business if she was a bit short of the readies; cadging drinks and offering a "goodtime."

Bill had to admit though that Betty supplied him with the best and cheapest brawn he could get his hands on, so he cut her a bit of slack.

Betty's daughter, Ivy, was a quite different kettle of fish; a reliable, hardworking girl who could be trusted to turn up on time if ever he needed a bit of extra help cleaning. You could count on sweet natured Ivy, which was more than could be said for Betty.

"Well, if you're looking for a room hereabouts, you might

13

want to see if Betty Jenkins still has one available. I hear she's got one going spare, least wise she did last week." Bill ventured.

Betty Jenkins was a widow down on her luck; lifting her skirts when the bills were due. Bill wasn't too sure he believed her convenient yarn about being a "widow." He wasn't even sure that the mythical Mr Jenkins ever existed except in Betty's imagination, but one thing for sure Betty was always looking for ways to earn a shilling.

"She's not a bad soul, is Betty. It's tough when you're on yer own like." Bill admitted grudgingly.

"Betty's always trying to make ends meet; might be worth you checking it out Jimmy, she won't be asking too much rent. Knowing Betty, it won't be too fancy, but then what is around here?" Bill guffawed.

"Well, I'm none too picky Bill and I do need a room. What is it they say, about *any port in a storm*? Is it far from here?"

"Just follow your nose," Bill the landlord had joked; "you can't miss Bute Street-we could roll you home from 'ere if ever we had a need to.... an' there's usually a friendly prozzy on the corner to make sure you don't lose yer way like!"

Jimmy rewarded the landlord with a hearty chuckle and the offer of a half pint of best bitter for his good self.

Bute street was a long and straggling thoroughfare hugging the railway line. The area was bustling with people from morning until night. At the dock end clusters of small shops displayed their wares; chandlers, grocers and ironmongers spilled out onto the pavements; goods balanced in boxes and stacked up against the narrow fronts. Butchers with open-sided windows displayed bacon, offal and rabbits hanging on hooks. Everything you wanted was to be had in Tiger bay.

Jimmy Benson had no trouble finding the narrow, terraced house, it really *was* only a couple of hundred yards or so from the Rose and Crown.

Gradually the shop fronts on the terrace had petered out and scruffy houses and dingy back alleyways started to appear like rotten teeth.

A cardboard sign hung drunkenly in the front window of number twenty-two:

"*Clean Room to let.... Washing done and meals made.*"

15

The grubby, net curtain gave lie to the boast of cleanliness. But the niceties of clean net curtains didn't worry Jimmy Benson, Bute Street was just his sort of neighbourhood. A place where no-one asked awkward questions and where there was always an opportunity to make a bit on the side.

Jimmy believed in making his own luck in life; *grab it while you can* was Jimmy's motto.

In his younger days Jimmy had been considered a bit of a looker; not exactly what you'd call handsome, but he certainly had an air of swagger and confidence about him with a cheeky grin, a mop of golden hair and a soft Irish lilt that seemed to charm the girls. And Jimmy certainly had an eye for the girls; he liked them fresh, and he liked them young, the younger the better.

When problems caught up with Jimmy, he'd either wheedle his way out of them or he scarpered, often with an angry father close on his heels. The magnitude of his crime usually dictated the distance he needed to put between himself and the Dublin Garda. For the time being he'd decided a lengthy trip to Cardiff was probably for the best.

Jimmy's strong hands found him work as a labourer and paid

16

testament to his reputation for being a bit of a "scrapper," a lad who could look after himself.

Jimmy had a hot temper that often got him into trouble, especially when the drink was upon him. He could be a charmer if he had a mind to but often as not he was mean and moody drunk, picking a fight with his own shadow.

As a young man he'd damaged the sight in one eye in a bar brawl in Dublin leaving one green eye with a milky film creeping over two thirds of the eyeball. The lack of this Irish Eye didn't stop the other good eye roving over the young factory lasses that frequented the bustling Dublin docks. It did mean however, that he wasn't fit to serve his country when the call up came, which was fine by Jimmy.

As far as Jimmy was concerned over the war years, the more of his mates that were out of his way serving their King and country the better, it left all the more for Jimmy Benson.

There were plenty of opportunities to be had for a strapping Irish chap with the gift of the gab and work to be had for able-bodied men. Jimmy had spent the last couple of months labouring and dossing about here and there; now he'd scraped a bit of cash together and he wanted a room of his own.

Betty's place might just be the ticket.

Jimmy mounted the grubby steps, straightened his tie, and rapped at the front door of number twenty-two with a meaty fist.

The green, peeling paintwork and dirty front steps of number twenty-two hinted at a lack of money and care; but nobody was too picky about such niceties in Bute town. If it was cheap, close to the docks and didn't have fleas then it would suit him down to the ground.

Jimmy was surprised when a slight, fresh-faced young girl with thick red-brown hair twisted back in two short plaits, tucked under a headscarf, a dusting of freckles and large grey-blue eyes answered the rap. She peaked her head around the door and leaned on the door frame.

"Mam's out." She said flatly.

Despite being sixteen the girl looked years younger; a fresh-faced child with a bibbed pinny tied tightly around her tiny waist. Jimmy ran a practised eye over her.

The girl might be quite a looker when she was older; the slight swelling beneath the bib hinted at a budding bosom, but to Jimmy's eyes she looked perfect just the way she was.

The savoury aroma of a boiling pig's head and onions drifted out into the street. Jimmy's stomach rumbled. It was past noon, and he hadn't eaten yet that morning.

"Morning Darlin'.... I've come about the room," Jimmy pointed to the sign and flashed a winning smile.

The girl regarded him with a doubtful stare. Ivy knew her mother needed to let the room.

Betty was out on "business," and Ivy was alone in the house, watching the pig's head and doing chores. There would be hell to pay if Ivy let the man walk away. At least this chap was reasonably well dressed and even wearing a tie.... By Bute Street standards that almost made him respectable. The last man to enquire about the room had reeked of piss and booze.

"As I said, me Mam's out...Mr?"

"The name's Jimmy, darlin'… Jimmy Benson. I really need a room, could I just take a quick look? I won't take long." He wheedled.

19

Reluctantly Ivy decided she should take the risk.

"Well, I suppose you'd best come in and take a look at it then." Ivy moved aside to let Jimmy into the dark hallway.

"Mam said I could show the room if anyone asked about it," Ivy said by way of explanation. "It's upstairs.... I'll show you the way."

"Thank you kindly, darlin'.... I'm obliged to you." Jimmy removed his cap and flashed her a warm smile.

Jimmy decided to turn on the charm, a bit of Irish flannel always worked its magic.

"An' what's your name then my lovely.".

"Ivy.... Ivy Jenkins," she muttered over her shoulder.

She knew her Mam would kill her if she got too chatty with a man, but her Mam needed the rent.

Jimmy watched her hips wiggle from side to side as she led him up the steep flight of stairs. When Ivy reached the top of the landing, he saw the reason for the wiggle; Ivy had one leg fractionally shorter than the other, the effect was a gentle, almost seductive, rocking gait when she walked. Normally

20

Ivy wore a slightly stacked shoe to correct the defect; house slippers gave the game away.

"In here." Ivy held the door open for him to look inside. "The bath's opposite and the lav's out back.... we don't have to share it." Ivy added as an afterthought.

The room was no better, nor worse than he'd expected. A lumpy looking mattress covered in a faded eiderdown and two saggy pillows covered in navy ticking sat on top of the old-fashioned iron bedstead. A thread-bare rug graced the floor, and there was just enough room between the bed and the window for a small wardrobe and chest. Barely room to swing a cat, but it would do.

Through the grimy window Jimmy could glimpse the tiny yard stacked high with bits of broken packing case for firewood. The yard backed onto a small, cobbled alleyway that served the privies behind all the terraces. The alleyway joined a web of similar rat runs behind the houses and shop yards. *Always good to have an escape route Jimmy lad!*

Jimmy could see that the room and the household offered all sorts of opportunities. "Yep, I think this'll suit me just fine darling." He made a play of bouncing on the bed.

21

"Oh yes that feels all right.... Grand! I'm a man that likes a good set of springs."

The front door slammed downstairs. Ivy jumped.

"Ivy.... where on earth are you Ivy.... Ivy!" A voice screeched up from below.

"Up here Mam...." Ivy's eyes darted nervously towards the hallway, she backed out of the room towards the landing.

Heavy footsteps thumped up the staircase. A blowsy, hard-faced woman, running to fat; probably only in her late thirties, but looking a decade older, clattered into the room.

"What on earth are you doing up here Ivy? That bloody pig's head was nearly boiled dry.... Oh!" Betty scanned the room.

Jimmy flashed her his best smile.

"And just who might you be?" Betty Jenkins softened her tone and regarded the stranger with a calculating stare.

"Jimmy Benson, Mrs Jenkins. I'm here about the room" he extended his hand.

"Your Ivy kindly showed me up."

Ivy stood shrinking against the doorway, unsure if she would cop it later from Mam.

It only took Betty Jenkins a few moments to cast her business eye over Jimmy. She took in his worn, but serviceable corduroys, sturdy work boots and the half decent tweed jacket sporting a red flannel handkerchief in his top pocket.

She'd seen his type before hanging round corners in Bute town paying for girls when their pockets were full on pay day or flirting with bar maids in the pubs hoping to get it for free. Still if he had brass, then Betty Jenkins would like a bit of it.

She had a bit of a soft spot for the Irish lads that swept into Cardiff with their cheeky comments and generous wallets. "Well, if it's about the room, you won't find better round here Mr Benson." Betty flashed a winning smile.

"My Ivy keeps the house nice and tidy. She's a good hard-working girl. An' it's quiet... none of that noisy trash you get in Loudoun Square... just me and my Ivy; no other lodgers to bother about."

Jimmy liked the sound of the set up more and more. "I'll take it then.... and I think we can come to some sort of arrangement Mrs Jenkins, Jimmy winked.

Yes, just as she thought a typical Irish charmer. Betty patted her jet-black tinted hair and smiled back; wrinkles, garnered from a life of disappointment already tipped down the corners of her mouth. A faint whiff of Gin and cigarettes perfumed the air.

"Oh, I'm sure we can Mr Benson."

"Please call me Jimmy."

"And you must call me Betty," she simpered through smudged red lips.

Jimmy flashed her a cheeky grin. He understood women like Betty.

CHAPTER 3

October 1947

It was 8am Friday morning and despite the early hour Betty was already out on "business." Exactly what Betty's business was, Ivy was never too sure, and she knew better than to pry. Sometimes Mam was out cleaning floors or pulling pints behind the bar in the local pubs and clubs. Other times Mam just went out on *business*. Today it was business.

Jimmy had settled in nicely to the Jenkins' household. He'd certainly fallen on his feet; he came and went as he pleased with no back chat from Betty. Betty was just Jimmy's sort of landlady-not too many questions and happy to turn a blind eye so long as his rent was paid on time.

Betty minded her business, and she kept her snout out of his; there was always the added bonus of young Ivy about the house to brighten Jimmy's day.

In only six short weeks since chatting to Bill the landlord,

Jimmy had established a very comfy billet for himself and things were certainly looking up. Ivy's cooking was usually tasty, the girl kept the place on just the right side of clean and best of all, she was easy on the eye.

Apart from the odd errand or cleaning job, Ivy wasn't allowed out much, she was usually stuck at home doing chores and making Betty's brawn to supply the pub orders. Yes, as far as Jimmy was concerned, things were looking up.

Ivy laughed at his jokes, blushed when he called her *darling girl* and was as fresh and innocent as any man could wish for. A completely untouched canvas; perfect.

Betty kept the girl on a short leash; frightened to say Boo to a goose. But best of all, as far as Jimmy was concerned, there was no Mr Jenkins to worry about when he flirted and charmed the girl, no watchful Da to take him to task.

Ducking and diving around Bute town Jimmy soon learnt all the short cuts and back alleyways like the back of his hand. He kept his ear to the ground, learnt who to trust and who to avoid; Jimmy was a player, a man making a name for himself.

On his wanderings Jimmy often spotted Betty hanging

around some of the rougher pubs on the wharf front, some distance away from Bute street. If he caught Betty's eye standing in the shadows or hanging about in doorways down on the wharfs, he just tipped his hat.

Jimmy could be discreet when it suited him.

The weather had turned bitterly cold on the greasy streets of Tiger Bay; a crippling wind from the North set all the windows rattling and wove its spiteful way under doors and through cracks. Bitter, icy blasts swirled around the rows of terraces, nagging away at people and chilling them to the bone. It wasn't even November yet, and already the weather was turning vicious.

In January that year, seven weeks of unrelenting snow had piled up in drifts ten feet high and brought the mighty dock yards to a complete standstill and now the year was threatening to end the same way as it began.

The big freeze was still fresh in peoples' minds. Sheep had died in their hundreds in mountainous drifts on the Welsh hillsides. Dozens of dockland street dogs were found dead weeks after the snow had receded, a grim, pathetic tangle of paws and fur frozen solid; unwanted animals huddled against

27

each other in desperate heaps under railway arches.

 The bone-chilling cold spared neither man nor beast. A few
miserable scarecrows down on their luck and covered in
newspaper for blankets had been found lifeless in shop
doorways. Scraggy men and old soldiers numbed with booze,
unable to leach any warmth from the bricks they crouched
against.

 Jimmy went out early this Friday morning on his rounds, like
a foraging dog he got up early to sniff out his quarry. Stalking
the dockland streets to get the lie of the land; catch up with
the gossip.

"Morning Jimmy," a deep voice shouted from behind him.

Jimmy turned to see Jack, a burly Pole lounging in a doorway.
Jack had some bizarre Polish name that Welsh tongues just
couldn't or wouldn't master; everyone called him Jack.

"'An a good mornin' to you Jack," Jimmy tipped his cap. Jack
worked as a stevedore and kept his eye on the comings and
goings in port, always on the lookout for work. "You got any
news for me this morning?"

"Aye Jimmy, they say a Liberty ship arrived in this morning, fully laden from Argentina. Might be worth heading over to Queen's dock to take a look at her.

If I'm going to be in with a chance of any work today, I'd best be off over there myself." Jack took one final drag on his pencil thin roll up that threatened to singe his fingers and tossed the fag end onto the cobbles. "See you around Jimmy."

The Radnor, a massive Liberty ship had arrived in port fresh from delivering coal to Argentina and returning via the River Plate grain route with a full cargo. She was a huge ship that regularly docked in at Newport. Her appearance in Cardiff that morning was an unexpected bonus. Opportunities beckoned.

"Thanks for the heads-up Jack!" Jimmy shouted after the retreating figure.

The bustle surrounding the arrival of a big cargo ship brought the dockyard to life. A cacophony of voices shouting instructions, massive ropes and chains pounded onto the quayside securing gangways, men scrambled over rails opening hatches.

Jimmy made his way to the store sheds where the deals were

done.

A gaggle of men stood huddled in a corner of a cavernous grain store; deep in discussion, money changing hands. All talk stopped as Jimmy appeared. Suspicious faces turned his way; hard eyes evaluating the newcomer.

"Top of the morning gentlemen," Jimmy flashed a bright grin and tipped his hat respectfully.

"There's nothing to see here Paddy… so sling your hook," a hatchet-faced crew member, a mate from the newly arrived Radnor warned.

"Now then lads, I'm sure there's enough business to go around, no need to be hasty." Jimmy soothed.

"Says who?" the man growled as he started to advance towards Jimmy, muscles flexed and menacing.

"Jimmy, Jimmy Benson."

"Well, what's *our* business got to do with you Jimmy Benson? People who put their noses into places where they're not wanted, find themselves in trouble." The mate snarled.

"Calm down Sam," a small wiry Chinaman grabbed the mate

by the sleeve. "No need to be unfriendly. I recognize Mr Benson here. He may be able to help us with that little problem we were discussing."

"Thank you kindly" Jimmy held his gaze, "and you are..?" He regarded the Chinaman with interest.

"People call me China Joe; friends call me Joe." He stretched out a wizened hand; nicotine-stained fingers. "Nice to see you Mr Benson," China Joe gave a polite bow. "I am a good friend of Mr Harry; I know that he would like to make your acquaintance. Come to see Mr Harry tonight in The Feathers."

Jimmy nodded; this was good news.

"Eight o'clock then." Joe said in a tone that brooked no argument.

Mr Harry was a legend in Bute town and Jimmy was keen to be admitted into the golden circle. It seemed as if he'd just got lucky.

"Why that would be champion… and what was that little problem you thought I could help you with Joe?"

31

Joe pointed in the direction of the grain store office. "Him!"
Joe jabbed a finger towards a fresh-faced chap, checking off a
complex stock sheet at the entrance to the depot.

The man was guarding the entrance to the office and store
with all the intensity of a keen Jack Russell terrier, his beady
eyes scanned the depot area guarding the goods as if his life
depended upon it.

"That guy…. He's new, and he needs to be taught a lesson,
he's making it his business to see too much." Joe said
smoothly. "Old Alf used to know when to turn a blind eye,
knew what was good for him did Alf. It seems the company
decided to part with Alf's services and brought this whipper
snapper in. He needs a little lesson in manners Mr Benson."
China Joe inclined his head and smiled.

"It will be my pleasure."

"Nothing too obvious, so long as he gets the message," Joe
advised.

"Consider it done." Jimmy strolled in the direction of the
unsuspecting new official.

Twenty minutes later a shaken, but uninjured, Dafydd Price

emerged from behind the grain store. He wore the look of a wiser man. Fearful of his home, his wife and his kneecaps Dafydd was quick to learn the correct ways of conducting business on Queen's dock. Dafydd Price would not be troubling Joe or Mr Harry again.

All in all, it had been a profitable visit to the docks for Jimmy.

Now, it was getting cold, Jimmy shivered, scanned the gloomy skyline and picked up his pace; he needed to get back to Bute street before the weather closed in. From the look of the leaden sky hanging over the docks it was threatening snow, the start of another cruel winter.

Ducking down the piss reeking alleyways, Jimmy soon found himself back home at number twenty-two. He slipped in through the yard.

Jimmy took refuge from the biting chill in the fragrant, steamy fug of the kitchen, all warm and cosy from a morning's cooking. He could see Ivy was hard at work.

"How do's Ivy,"

"Oh, Jimmy you startled me!" She said with a jump. Ivy never ceased to be amazed how Jimmy could come and go so silently like Irish mist.

"I can't stop to chat; if Mam catches me standing around nattering she'll go berserk. That kettle has just boiled if you'd like a cuppa Jimmy."

"OK Ivy love I can shift for myself. Tea would be grand, I'm freezing." He said as he added some fresh hot water to the remains of a lukewarm pot of tea.

He sat with a cigarette dangling from his mouth and mug of stewed tea steaming between his fingers, a contented man. It had been a very profitable morning.

He watched Ivy pick the flesh from half a boiled pig's head.

Ivy peeled back the gelatinous skin, removed the eyeball, cut off the tops of the ear for next door's cat and set about dicing the warm white meat from the skull. She worked her way methodically around the bones to find every scrap and morsel. She shredded the meat between two forks before eking it out with as much finely chopped skin, soft gristle and onions as she dared.

The liquor pan sat steaming outside the back door waiting for the fat to rise and set. The pink bristly tongue would be skinned and pressed later in a bowl. Betty was very partial to a bit of cold, pressed pig's tongue surrounded by lots of tasty jelly.

"Nice bit o' meat on that one," Jimmy said approvingly as he eyed the growing pile. "I bet he was a fair old size.... Go on pass us over a bit Ivy darlin', I've not had any breakfast this morning.... I'm absolutely starving."

"I mustn't Jimmy, I've *got* to get three large basins of brawn out of this one or Mam will have my guts for garters.... she's got orders for this lot from the Rose and Crown, the Nag's head and the Fighting Cocks.... she'll skin me alive if there aren't three full basins to deliver."

Jimmy quickly reached across the table and snaffled a choice piece of meat. He popped the moist, greasy morsel into his mouth before replacing his cigarette.

"Oi.... Keep your fingers out Jimmy.... that was a *huge* piece too," Ivy grumbled. "An' watch your ash, I can't have bloody fag ash in the brawn, I'll have complaints."

"Needs salt," Jimmy said ignoring Ivy's moaning. "When a man has got a drink in his hand, he likes a bit of salt in his meat," he handed her the condiments.

"Plenty of salt and pepper that's the ticket.... and watch that mouth of yours my girl. If your Mam catches you swearing like that, she'll tan your cheeky hide."

Ivy kept her head down looking for bristles and any other stray bits and pieces that had no business being in "Betty's Best Brawn." Ivy knew she was being watched.

A blush crept over her throat.

Ivy was shy; lacking in confidence she wasn't used to attracting attention. Hard work and a lack of money meant there was no spare flesh on Ivy. Unlike her buxom best friend Alice Tranter, Ivy's own budding breasts had barely advanced from the two pink, swollen nipples that appeared along with her period when she was twelve. Every night she willed them to grow.

When Ivy looked at herself in the pocked bathroom mirror a scraggy, child-like frame stared back at her. Ribs and hips poked out; her clothes hung off her. Ivy didn't feel pretty at all.... she had never felt pretty, especially with her gamy leg.

Last month she'd turned sixteen and the pot boy, John, from

the Nag's head had flirted with her when she'd delivered the brawn, said she had pretty eyes and offered to buy her some winkles.

Ivy liked John Price, it was flattering to be complimented, most of the other boys barely noticed she was there, John was different... kinder. John lived around the corner in Crichton street, and he made her laugh.

When she told her Mam that John Price had called her pretty, Mam had clipped her ear for hanging around and chatting to lads, especially lads from the Price family. *Couldn't afford a pot to piss in could old man Price.... you can do much better than that trash my girl when time's right, and remember, no man wants soiled goods!*

Ivy longed for a better life, a life far away from the docks. She didn't want to end up poor and harassed by bills and debts like her Mam, scraping around to make ends meet.

At least now, with Jimmy as their lodger, money was a bit easier, and Mam was a bit less snappy. Jimmy's work around the docks meant there were plenty of tit bits and trinkets to be had and sometimes a few pretty things even came Ivy's way.

It was thrilling to be to be spoilt just a little. Jimmy was fun and he made her laugh.

"Here you are Ivy darlin', a nice packet of hankies for you.... Now don't go telling your Mam, there's a good girl.... 'cos I've only got the one set.... Are you going to give Jimmy a little kiss to say thank you?"

All sorts of things just seemed to "fall" off vans and pallets into Jimmy's pockets; cigarettes, rum, nylons, chocolate, even a side of smoked bacon once passed through Mam's yard and if Jimmy didn't need them, then he always knew a man who did.

Times were hard and money was to be made; debts were called in and favours were to be had in the tangled wharfs of Tiger Bay.

Jimmy made sure he kept Betty sweet as well, he knew which side his bread was buttered on. Spreading a bit of grease always oiled the wheels, so Betty found plenty of little treats came her way just to keep her sweet.

"I've got a couple of pairs of nylons and a bag of sugar for you Betty Darling... now don't you tell me Jimmy doesn't know

how to treat a girl right." Betty blushed at being called a girl.

Ivy didn't have time to stop and chat to Jimmy. She kept to her work, greasing three large pudding basins ready for the meat. The brawn needed time to set if it was to be pressed and turned out in time for Saturday morning.

"Don't 'spose you could do me a favour could you Jimmy and bring me in that stew pan...?" Ivy held up her greasy fingers, "save me washing my hands again.... please Jimmy," she wheedled.

"Course I can Ivy love and as I always say one good turn always deserves another doesn't it?" Jimmy winked and set off to the yard.

Ivy blushed. Lately Jimmy had been taking liberties, especially when Betty was out-a quick squeeze of her breasts when he gave her a hug, a snatched kiss on her neck, or even whispering a dirty word in her ear. She knew her mother would be furious if she suspected Jimmy was messing about, but as Jimmy said - *Mam didn't need to know it was their little secret.*

Ivy didn't really mind not with Jimmy being so nice and

generous to her and Mam. He might be a bit free with his hands, but he wasn't really doing any harm was he? Mam was much happier now Jimmy was their lodger; it would be silly of Ivy to rock the boat and make a fuss over nothing.

Jimmy carefully placed the brimming stew pan on the scrubbed deal table next to Ivy. Her hands stirred and mixed the greasy meat.

 "I've put in some more salt in for you, just like you said Jimmy." Ivy kneaded the mixture together, spatters of goo coating her slender arms.

"Well, I'm obliged, my darling girl, thank you kindly, "Jimmy gave a low mock bow. As he started to rise, Jimmy ran his practised hands up under Ivy's skirt, giving her buttocks a fondle.

"Hey there...!"

 He quickly removed his hands and snatched a quick kiss from the back of her neck. "Now don't you go tempting me again you little madam," Jimmy chuckled. "I've got work to do. Places to go, people to meet see you later Ivy. Be good, an' if you can't be good, be careful!" He chuckled at the old joke.

Jimmy grabbed his coat and hat and left by the back door. He'd taken to using the lane entrance; he found coming and going through the yard suited him. Jimmy wasn't keen on people knowing his business.

Ivy could hear him whistling as he disappeared through the back gate and down the lane.

Thick gobbets of congealed fat floated on top of the golden liquor. As Ivy strained off the pig fat to be used for dripping, she pondered Jimmy's antics. Ivy did like Jimmy, and she was flattered he seemed to like her. But his wandering hands were a bit of a shock; Ivy's cheeks and neck were still flushed with embarrassment.

Oh yes, Jimmy Benson certainly had a silver tongue on him that dripped compliments like honey off a spoon. It did give her a warm feeling inside to be called my darling girl, my angel, my pretty lass. Nobody had ever called her that before, but then nobody ever stroked her arse before either! She reddened with shame at the thought of his hands slipping up her skirt.

The world of men, boys flirting, courtship and sex was a complete mystery to Ivy. Ivy was woefully ignorant, and she knew it. *Mam never lets me out of her sight, how am I supposed to know anything?* she thought ruefully, pressing down the thick ooze of brawn meat that threatened to spill over the edge of the first bowl. Everything Ivy knew about *anything* she'd learnt by asking her friend Alice.

Alice said she thought Jimmy was quite handsome with his dark blonde hair and cheeky grin; she thought his dodgy eye made him look mysterious. Ivy could see Alice's point, even if Jimmy was twenty years older than her, he did have a bit of Irish charm.

It certainly was a mystery to Ivy why on earth Jimmy, or any other lad for that matter, would even want to look at her let alone flirt with her.

It was her best friend Alice with her sexy wiggle, tumbled golden curls and slash of red lipstick, who always caught the admiring stares of local lads. Ivy felt invisible when standing next to the buxom Alice Tranter; a curvaceous eighteen-year-old who could easily pass for twenty if it suited her.

Despite doing her exercises every night, vigorously flinging her arms back and forth like a barn door caught in the wind, and no matter how many times Ivy chanted *I must, I must improve my bust* at her boyish reflection in the mirror, it was all to no avail. Ivy's bust refused to be "improved," she was as flat chested as the proverbial ironing board and could easily pass for a thirteen-year-old... life just wasn't fair!

Ivy had known Alice for a lifetime, well that's what it felt like. When Mam moved them both to Bute street, twelve years ago, she was a lost, lonely little five-year-old until the day Ivy took Alice's hand on her first morning at school.

Despite their age difference the two girls had occupied the same crowded classroom under the watchful eyes of Miss Leonard. The two forms were taught side by side, and as the classroom monitor for the girls, it was Alice Tranter's job to look after the new girls, help them find their coat peg, show them the ropes.

From the moment Alice took Ivy's hand and promised to look after her, Ivy had worshiped at Alice Tranter's feet. From that first momentous day onwards, they sat together at play time; shared Alice's sugar sandwiches, shared secrets and even shared nits.

43

Perhaps she ought to try and get some advice about boys from Alice, just in a roundabout way like, no need to let Jimmy down and break her promise.

The two girls had agreed to go for a walk on Sunday afternoon to watch the spectacle of the fishing fleet unloading on the quayside. Ivy and Alice loved the bustle of the quayside on a Sunday when the fishing trawlers landed.

The jaunty boats were a refreshing change from the lumbering, noisy coal containers that frequented the quays. Many of the trawlers were owned by the same local families for decades; some saw dangerous service during the war defending the beleaguered food convoys. It was good to see the boats were now bringing in the herring and mackerel, unloading the Icelandic cod and bulging crab pots for market.

On Sunday, families out for a stroll and lads, on their day off, gathered to watch the glittering catch being landed and haggled over by the market traders looking for stock.

Yes, Ivy would talk to Alice on Sunday, that would be best.

Decision made; Ivy breathed a little easier. She ladled meat and liquor into the other two basins; they were full almost to the brim and there was even enough meat left over for Ivy to squeeze in almost another half pint pudding basin for Mam. Bunce!

Ivy tied grease proof paper lids over the top of the basins and put dinner plates on to act as weights. The brawn would be ready for turning out in the morning when the jelly had set. Ivy was proud of her handiwork.

Mam would be pleased with her morning's effort; she would not be pleased with Jimmy's antics. Still Mam needn't know. He was only being silly; Ivy was sure of it.

Alice would know what to do.

CHAPTER   4

That Sunday afternoon the weather was distinctly chilly; a stiff breeze swept through the docklands numbing fingers to the bone. November was shaping up to be the start of another bitter Welsh winter. The two girls had agreed to meet by the Norwegian church before heading off to East quayside to see the catch being unloaded.

The little Norwegian church with its corrugated, tin roof and grubby white walls was a hive of activity on Sundays, a magnet for hundreds of sailors and their families. The sharp, needle-like church spire piercing the skyline could be seen from every vantage point on the docks. No sailor worried about his soul could miss it, the spire stood like a beacon calling them in.

In the colder months, a brazier sat outside the church; the pavement piled high with broken fish crates and disused fruit boxes ready to keep the fire stoked up. Today the brazier glowed brightly, showering sparks as the wooden slats collapsed.

Alice warmed her hands and waited for Ivy. Alice didn't mind being a bit early; it gave her the chance to preen a little in her Sunday finery. Alice's sage-green woollen coat was a cast-off, courtesy of her older sister Phyllis who'd run to fat after having the twins last year. The coat had certainly seen better days, but it still had a lot of wear in it and on Alice the snags and rubs just seemed to disappear. The muted green suited her fair colouring. By mending the small tear on the sleeve; and moving the buttons across on the waist Alice had created a very fetching, hour-glass silhouette.

Alice looked pretty and she knew it. Alice stamped her feet and craned her neck looking for Ivy.

A cacophony of chatter and noise in strange languages floated around and gave the church forecourt an exotic air. As the church doors swept open, sailors from Scandinavian ports and harbours across the globe, poured out jabbering away.

The Norwegian church was a good place to see and be seen.

Alice certainly drew admiring glances from the young men as they tipped their caps in her direction.

Soon Alice spotted Ivy scurrying along in the distance, struggling to make headway through the bustling crowd; crushed by the throng elbowing her aside.

Ivy wore her old, crumpled gaberdine mac in lieu of a proper winter coat; Mam didn't run to winter coats. Ivy had tried to soften the rather utilitarian look with the addition of a pretty headscarf tied over her auburn curls. Even so, Ivy always felt like a drab pigeon next to the glorious peacock that was Alice Tranter.

Ivy saw her friend as she fought her way through the throng, she waved. Alice noticed Ivy's bobbing head, a bright dot in the crowd and beckoned furiously.

The silky headscarf had originally been a gift to Mam from Jimmy, a little sweetener, but after only a few outings Betty refused to wear it again, she said that the busy floral pattern of turquoise greens and sugar pinks didn't suit her. Well, that was a version of what Betty heard Mrs Thomas saying to Mrs

Price as Betty passed her open window one morning.

The words *mutton dressed as lamb* and the ensuing gales of mocking laughter had smarted. Betty threw the pretty scarf in the coal scuttle. In an unexpected fit of generosity, Mam relented and gave the scarf to Ivy. Ivy treasured it.

"You hoo…Over here Ivy," Alice called, her voice carrying over the heads of the crowd.

"Get a move on Ivy," one cheeky sailor teased. His friends roared with laughter and joined in the fun.

"Come on Ivy! Over here Ivy!" the lads shouted in unison.

The priest, standing to greet his flock as they were leaving the church, shot the boisterous young men a withering glance; he tutted loudly.

"Sorry I'm late, Alice," Ivy panted.

Alice stood surrounded by her admirers, like a queen holding court.

Ivy blushed fiercely as the lads teased her with a chorus of jeers "it's about time too Ivy!"

"Oh, come on now lads give it a rest, you've had your fun!" Alice turned to face the cat chorus.

"Not fun enough, with you love," one brave anonymous voice muttered just within earshot.

Alice shot the offender a withering glance, grabbed Ivy by the elbow and turned on her heels to go. "Come on Ivy, let's get out of here; these lads can find someone else to annoy."

Alice tossed her golden curls, thrust out her bosom and walked loyally away arm in arm with Ivy.

The girls headed straight for the East quay. Greedy herring gulls were already gathering; circling and wheeling high above the quayside. The raucous, squawking and screeching heralded the approach of the fishing fleets into harbour. Any time now the catch would be unloaded onto the granite cobbles.

The hungry birds started to settle on the roof tops of the nearby warehouses. Neat rows of beady -eyed sentinels waiting to snaffle some discard.

"Ivy let's head over to the far side. Look, over there! I can see the Thomas brothers, waiting with their Da." Alice pointed to a gap towards the end of the quay where buyers for the catch were starting to collect. "If we hurry, we can stand next to them as they get their crate... come on!" She grabbed Ivy's sleeve and dragged her in the direction of "The Jacqueline" moored up on the quay.

It was no secret that Alice harboured hopes for George Thomas the older of the two Thomas brothers. If Alice failed in her quest to marry a famous movie star before she was twenty-one, then the handsome George Thomas might just have to fill the gap.

The Thomas family ran a marvellous fish and chip bar in Caroline street, people came from miles around to get the best and cheapest fish supper in Cardiff from old man Thomas. Apart from a rather overpowering whiff of cooking fat from serving behind his father's counter, George was everything a girl could wish for; polite, handsome with good teeth and good prospects. He'd been sweet on Alice for nearly a year now, and occasionally she gave him a few crumbs of hope to keep his flame of ardour alive.

Alice had decided to keep George Thomas simmering on the back burner just in case the required movie star did not emerge over the horizon to sweep her off her feet. Alice certainly didn't want to end up an old maid and as her mother pointed out on a regular basis, *she could do a lot worse than George Thomas*, Alice favoured him with just enough attention to keep the lad keen.

Alice hadn't seen George for a few weeks recently, she decided that a few running repairs were probably needed in their relationship. Today George Thomas would feel the full effect of the Alice Tranter charm.

"I'm coming as fast as I can Alice," Ivy stumbled a little on the cobbles, her stacked shoe slowing her progress. "You run along and keep my place… I'll soon catch you up." she puffed.

"Oh, I'm sorry Ivy I forgot about your shoe, it's alright we will get there soon enough. Here, you take my arm."

As the two girls made their way over to the "Jacqueline," Alice spotted Elsie Evans, a petite red head who lived next door but one to the Tranter household in Angelina street. Elsie, was welding herself to George's elbow, flicking a piece of lint off his shoulder, simpering and giggling flirtatiously.

"Well, I never, just look at that Elsie Evans... she's all over George," Alice snorted in disbelief. "The brassy little madam, she's barely fifteen! Her Mam would skin 'er alive if she caught her pawing George Thomas, she's got a cheek!"

Alice quickened her pace.

"Good morning Mr Thomas," Alice called to Les Thomas, as she came within range "morning George, morning Billy," she flashed the two brothers a dazzling smile. Her gaze landed on George and with a flutter of her lashes he was her faithful hound again; George's leash instantly yanked back to Alice.

"'Morning Alice." He tipped his hat, the warmth of his smile caused his eyes to twinkle, he nodded a polite *good morning to* Ivy ... Alice had George's full attention.

Alice imperiously ignored young Elsie who'd slunk back a few discreet inches. She would be having a few words with that little madam later!

Fish crates were now starting to pile up on the quayside. Showers of iridescent scales coated the cobbles like drifts of silver glitter.

"Looks like a good catch Mr Thomas," Alice said

knowledgably as the old man inspected the various crates. "I hope you have a good morning; there do seem to be rather a lot of buyers today."

Alice was wise enough to keep old man Thomas sweet. Les Thomas had developed a soft spot for Alice. He'd said on more than one occasion that George ought to try courting the decorative Alice Tranter; they'd make a handsome couple serving behind his chip shop counter. The lad had turned twenty-two the other month, so it was high time he started to think about finding the right lass. His wife Nora was getting a bit long in the tooth to spend hours standing serving customers; someone needed to take over the shop and it needed a husband-and-wife partnership.

The throng tightened; men pushed to the front eager to inspect each crate as it landed.

"Good fish is getting harder to come by Alice and prices are getting ruinous 'aint they George?... 'ere look at the other side of that crate for me lad. What d'you reckon to that one?" Les jabbed his thumb in the direction of particularly glossy crate of medium sized cod with fresh bulging eyes. "They look like they'd suit."

Les had a reputation to protect, freshly fried cod and haddock were his best sellers.

"Looks good to me Da…. Crate six it is then and that crate of haddock over there next to the hake… if we can get both for a good price that is." Aware of the need to impress his Da in front of Alice, George made a big show of checking and evaluating the fish crates with a knowledgeable air.

Alice gave George a little nod of appreciation.

Of late Les had been letting his eldest son do the bidding on his behalf, if George was to take over the running of the family business, then he needed to know the ropes. The fish auction, when it got started, was rattlingly fast with only seconds for decisions to be made; George needed to master the art of buying. Fish couldn't hang around spoiling on the quay. In under an hour the whole quayside would be deserted with only a few scraps left for the waiting gulls.

Ivy stood next to Billy Thomas and looked on with interest, the throng of the crowd and fresh salt tang of the catch was invigorating. It was so good to be out of the house, away from Betty's critical gaze and the endless list of chores. Ivy liked Billy Thomas, he was a good-hearted lad and had been in the same year as her at school, kept back a year for missing nearly six months with whooping cough. He'd always been a quiet lad, but now Billy was painfully shy.

At nearly eighteen, Billy was a strapping young man, four years younger than his handsome brother and with the bit of dark fluff already gracing his top lip, he already looked a man. With only one exception Billy shared all the same captivating, good looks of his big brother; the same strong black wavy hair and striking blue eyes but, unlike George, from the age of thirteen an angry rash of painful acne ravaged poor Billy's face and neck. Billy's fingers gravitated to the angry boils and yellow topped pustules, his cheeks already bore the pits and scars of frequent picking.

Ivy felt so sorry for the poor lad, he was regularly taunted and mocked; girls didn't lust after Billy Thomas and other lads didn't include him. Ivy knew what it felt like to be different, left on the outside.

"How's things Billy?" Ivy noticed nosey Elsie Evans edging nearer to eavesdrop. "Do you work for your Da an' all now?"

"Yeah… Well, I work out back like, you know chopping spuds, making the batter, preparing fish. Da doesn't like me

56

serving behind the counter Ivy, he leaves that to Mam and George." Billy looked embarrassed by the admission. A red flush crept up his neck, inflaming his spots. A particularly angry pimple appeared to chafe on his collar.

"Oh well, that's not so bad Billy, I reckon I'd prefer that job if it were me… you know not having to work slaving over hot fat all day, up to my elbows in grease, ending up smelling like a bit of crispy, old haddock!"

Billy and Ivy laughed so loudly that Alice turned to see the source of amusement.

George was busy watching the auctioneer waiting to place his bid. Craven's Auction House operated a Dutch auction; the callings were fast and furious; George couldn't afford to be distracted from his task by chatting to Alice.

The noise of the bidding and chattering was deafening; Alice moved over to join Billy and Ivy.

In the distance George gave a triumphant thumbs up. He'd secured his fish crates.

"Isn't this fun Ivy," Alice slipped her arm through Ivy's blocking Elsie's view of the proceedings. "Nice to see you

Billy, is your Mam keeping well?"

"Yeah, not too bad thanks Alice, you know our Mam, always busy with the shop." Billy mumbled avoiding her gaze.

"Looks like George has sealed the deal on some good fish, your Da will be pleased."

"That he will, and I'll be busy filleting," he gave Ivy a wink. "You an' Ivy ought to pop along to the chippy some time, bag of scrumps on the house," he added, the likes of the Jenkins family didn't often run to fish suppers.

"That's a kind offer Billy, perhaps Ivy and I could come over some time." She gave Ivy's arm an encouraging squeeze.

Ivy knew in her heart Mam wouldn't allow it; but maybe the offer of free scrumps would sweeten the deal, the piles of tasty fried batter scraps with plenty of salt and vinegar were Betty's favourite.

The auction was over, crowds on the quayside were starting to disperse, a leaden grey bank of cloud threatened the horizon. A fine drizzle was damping the cobbles and the afternoon light was starting to fail, it would be getting dark soon.

George left his father to settle the bill; he walked towards the girls with a pleased look on his face.

"Are you off then girls? Looks like rain coming in," George eyed the skyline, the clouds were grey-green and rolling over the headland into the bay, a sure sign of rain. "If it gets much colder this drizzle just might turn to sleet tonight." George blew on his cold hands.

"Yes, I think you're right we've got to get back now any way. It's been grand today George; watching how things are done. It can't be easy doing deals at speed, you're just so clever George." Alice flattered shamelessly.

George basked in the praise and the sunny disposition that was Alice Tranter. His Da was right Alice would be an asset serving customers behind the counter. She could charm the birds off the trees. He would have to try even harder to win her over.

"We must come again, mustn't we Ivy, an' maybe we'll take you up on that offer of yours Billy."

Billy beamed. "Bye Alice, bye Ivy, see you then," he said hopefully.

Alice and Ivy turned to go, Elsie was still hovering behind them, earwigging.

"Haven't you got a home to go to Elsie Evans?" Alice's tone was caustic. "Just wait 'til your Mam hears you've been getting fresh with men down on the quay!"

"No, I never!" Elsie looked appalled, ashen faced. "Oh no Alice, don't say anything like that to me Mam. Da will take a belt to me if you say that! Please Alice, I wasn't doing anything honest." Elsie Evans looked as if she was on the verge of tears. With five children to bring up and number six on the way, old man Evans ruled his household with a rod of iron.

"I see…Well that's not what it looked like to *me*." Alice eyed Elsie suspiciously. "If that's the case then you'd better run along before I change my mind; go on be off with you."

"Thanks Alice," Elsie gasped and scuttled off as fast as her legs could carry her.

Alice rearranged her face into a beautiful smile, bid George goodbye, and arm in arm the two girls headed for home.

"I think Billy fancies you Ivy," Alice gave Ivy's arm a

squeeze.

"No, he doesn't, he was just being friendly. I think it's mean, the way he gets teased all the time. Billy can't help his face being the way it is, he's a nice lad." Ivy rallied to Billy's defence.

"An' it sounds to me as if *you're* keen on him too!" Alice teased.

"Stop teasing Alice! Anyway, you're being mean to young Elsie." Ivy chided her friend, rapidly changing the subject from Billy Thomas. "You know her Da will murder her if he thinks she's flirting and carrying on with lads. You're not going to say anything to her Mam are you?"

"Course I'm not you daft ha'p'orth…I'm just teaching her a bit of a lesson. young Elsie's going to get herself in trouble the way she's carrying on. I'm doing her a favour Ivy. Not all lads are respectful like George, she's playing with fire, an' if she's not careful she'll find herself in trouble one day."

Ivy pondered this turn of events. She had to admit, Alice was certainly wise where affairs of the heart and men were concerned.

61

"You saw what she was up to Ivy, she couldn't keep her hands to herself, pawing away at George Thomas like that. She's asking for trouble that one, an' it would break her Mam's heart if Elsie got herself into trouble because of some lad she'd led up the garden path."

The concept of Elsie's wanton hands provided Ivy with just the opportunity she had been looking for all afternoon.

"Alice, can I ask you something, you know private like?"

"Course you can, ask away."

"Well, it was something Mam, said, that I had to *watch out for wandering hands*... you know lads an all." Ivy felt tongue tied.

Alice looked intrigued.

"And what Ivy?"

"Well, that's just it, Alice she didn't say much else, Mam never does say much where lads are concerned." Ivy took a deep breath. "So, I was wondering what you do if a lad... well you know... had wandering hands?"

"Ivy Benson, has some lad being trying something on?" Alice laughed.

"Not really," Ivy lied. "I just need to know about *"things,"* and I could never ask me Mam all she ever says is don't do stuff."

"Oh, Ivy lads try things on all the time with girls, pinching bottoms, copping a quick feel if you bend over, stuff like that. One chap in the Coal Exchange office pats my bloody behind whenever I go past him with my trolley; says he can't resist a pretty girl in uniform… the cheeky beggar!"

Alice was immensely proud of her new job as tea lady in the Coal exchange, jobs were hard to come by, working in the kitchens and taking around the tea trolley was certainly a step up from cleaning and skivvying.

"So, what do you do?" Ivy was all ears.

"Nothing! I tell him to keep his hands to himself and he just laughs. The thing is Ivy I'd be more worried if *no* lad wanted to pinch my behind!"

Ivy digested this nugget of wisdom.

"It's a sort of game we all play Ivy. They do it and we protest but really we like it, because it means they fancy us… So long as it doesn't overstep the mark, most lads know how far they can push it; the better looking they are the more they try it on, makes them look like players to their mates. Does that answer your question?"

"I think so Alice, but where do you draw the line?" Ivy looked puzzled.

"It's simple Ivy. No should always mean no! If you're giggling and squealing that's just playing along with the game, even pushing them away or slapping a hand is still showing a green light unless you say No! and mean it."

"Oh… I think I see,"

"In the end it's a law of averages Ivy, eventually some silly girl will let them go all the way. I'm getting a ring on my finger before some lad has me." Alice looked at her slim fingers and imagined a sparkling ring on her wedding finger.

"It's a fact Ivy… Most men will try it on, it's what lads do if they find you attractive, or…" Alice added darkly "if they

64

think you're easy, and that's why young Elsie Evans needs to watch her step."

Alice turned up the collar of her coat. "Come on Ivy let's get home before my hair is as flat as a pancake with all this drizzle, at least you've got that pretty scarf to protect yours from the damp you lucky devil!"

The two girls scurried away from the East dock; clouds were gathering fast squashing the last of the daylight.

The two girls hugged each other at the end of Bute street, Alice still had a short walk home to Angelina Street.

"You take care now Ivy, you know you can always tell me *anything*, you're like a sister to me… always remember that."

As Ivy strolled the last few yards home. Alice's words certainly gave her a lot to think about she was such a good, wise friend.

I must have led Jimmy on somehow, given him encouragement…the only problem is I didn't think I'd been doing anything. Ivy was perplexed.

Ivy had to admit that she didn't say No! So perhaps it *was* her fault. Jimmy had accused her of being *a little madam tempting him*, that day in the kitchen. But ivy didn't know the rules to this flirting game!

Mam would be furious if she thought Ivy was encouraging him, she would try to be more careful next time.

*

"You're late Ivy where've you been? You should have been back hours ago; it's nearly dark!" Betty was in a foul mood. Jimmy hadn't paid his rent for nearly two weeks and earlier that afternoon they'd had a row. It would be December soon, Betty needed the cash to pay her rent, else they'd all be out on their ears.

She wasn't a bloody charity; bills were piling up, and she needed the money!

Jimmy had tried to make amends with four crisp pound notes, and a gift of an ox heart that had come his way. He promised her faithfully that the balance of the money would be paid by the end of the week, but Betty was having none of it. Jimmy was getting too free with letting the rent money slide.

66

Betty had accepted the meaty ox heart as a gesture of good-will, but she needed that rent money paid on time, in cash, not payment in kind. Jimmy was on notice to find a way of paying his rent regularly. Or else!

What's more, now someone needed to tackle that blessed ox heart; they were devils to prepare, all caul fat and veins to sort, not to mention making the onion stuffing. *Where was Ivy when she was needed, out late gallivanting with that Alice Tranter no doubt?*

Offal didn't keep even in this cold weather, that heart needed doing today. Betty had been on the verge of tackling it herself when luckily Ivy walked back in through the door.

Ivy spied the ox heart sitting on the kitchen table in a pool of bloody juices that were oozing through the grease-proof paper. A fly looped lazy circles above the packet.

"What's that Mam? Is it for us?" The question deflected Betty from quizzing Ivy about her where abouts.

"Yes it is, Jimmy was short with his rent again," Betty said crossly. "He's left us an ox heart, but I'm none too sure it's as fresh as it should be." Betty gave a dramatic sniff in the direction of the package. "It needs sorting today if it's going to be fit to eat. It'll need soaking in milk for a good hour and make sure you get all the tough tubes out of it before you stuff it and braise it." Betty ordered.

"You'd best get that apron on Ivy and get started, an ox heart takes ages to cook unless you want us to chew on a bit of old shoe leather. I've got "business" to see to tonight."

Betty tossed a grimy pinafore in Ivy's direction and stamped upstairs to freshen herself up for the evening. She hated what she had to do, the pawing, desperate men and dark smelly alleyways. But she'd always kept a roof over Ivy's head, kept her daughter safe and she wasn't having freeloader taking advantage. *Someone's got to pay the bloody bills, she fumed.*

Chapter 5

December 1947

Jimmy was on the lookout. He stood, tucked inside the dark entrance of the alleyway. Jimmy's vantage point was away from the shops, houses and prying eyes of Bute street and gave him clear view in all directions. The road to Queen's wharf stretched ahead.

Jimmy was stamping his feet to stop the intense cold creeping up through his boots, the soles were painfully thin, and he felt every stone and pebble. The day before Jimmy padded out the insides of his boots with thick wads of newspaper to help protect his feet, but, despite all his efforts, his toes were still numb with the cold. He felt sure that chilblains were coming on.

Jimmy's coat collar was turned up to his ears in a vain attempt to keep the icy draughts off his neck. His cap was pulled down low over his face, but that was nothing to do with the weather. Jimmy liked to keep a low profile.

A small dew drop kept gathering on the end of Jimmy's

reddened nose, he wiped it away on the sleeve of his coat.

It was nearly a quarter to 8 o'clock and he'd been standing outside in the cold for best part of an hour watching who came and went in Tiger Bay.

Bloody brass monkey weather.

Jimmy was desperate for a fag, but he knew better than to light up. *Don't draw attention to yourself Jimmy boy, not long to go now.*

Two months of intense freezing conditions meant that during the day the docks were now almost at a standstill; cranes and haulage gear sat idle, festooned with garlands of icicles. Deep snow had already hit the South Wales valleys interrupting the mining and clogging the roads for the haulage lorries.

The mountains of anthracite that usually dominated the Cardiff wharfs had dwindled to small, lumpy mounds hidden under a coating of snow like frosted burial cairns.

A vicious, choppy swell buffeted the few small fishing boats brave enough to venture out to sea and desperate seagulls harried and dive bombed the quay as the meagre catch was unloaded. Songbirds died in their hundreds that month and their small corpses littered the gardens and parks throughout Cardiff like so many frozen pinecones.

The radio spoke of a vicious European freeze that had been sweeping across Britain for weeks with no end in sight. Clusters of idle men stood about the wharfs, all waiting for the chance of a day's labour. There was little work to be had and even less opportunities to make a few honest shillings. Clearing snow was a lowly paid, thankless task. Jimmy Benson had bigger fish to fry.

He'd missed his rent for the last couple of weeks and Betty was on the war path. She'd made herself clear that he was on notice. *I'm not a bleeding charity Jimmy Benson. I've got my Ivy to think of.... there are bills to be paid, an' you'd better cough up soon...no more excuses else we'll all be finding ourselves out on our ears.*

He'd earned a bit of leeway by slipping her a few quid and that ox heart had helped sweeten the deal, but he needed cash if he was going stay in Bute street.

71

Luckily for Jimmy his meeting with China Joe had borne fruit and now he was in the employ of Mr Harry. Jimmy needed some readies and tonight he was going to get paid in hard cash, at least it would get that shrew Betty off his back for a while.

A dog fight had been arranged by Black Harry in a vast disused shed off Queen's Wharf at 8 o'clock. Any dockers and factory workers would be long gone by then. The wharf should be deserted.

Black Harry had the reputation for being a cautious man. Jimmy and two other men were covering the roads leading into the wharf on the lookout for trouble and ensuring punters found their way. The night watchman had greedily accepted a ten bob note to ensure he took a different route that night when he went about his rounds. The coast was clear.

Bute town and its alley ways were eerily quiet with only the moaning of the wind to keep Jimmy company. Decent folk had no business being out on the wharf after dark.

Queen's Wharf was the farthest wharf away from the main drag into the docks. The disused cattle shed, complete with metal stock pens, had the advantage of being tucked away from the streetlamps. It boasted a large concrete area for the dogs to fight on and a small landing jetty to chuck any dead and dying dogs off.

If the police were spotted in the area there were plenty of escape routes. Men could scuttle away down back alleyways and disappear into the shadows like so many nimble and hungry rats.

Negroes and whites alike sought out the thrill of a dog fight in Tiger Bay. The screaming punters, the sheer raw brutality of it acted as a powerful draw. If a fight was rumoured to be on there was always a good crowd ready to part with their money; row upon row of scraggy men urging their dog on. No matter how skinny and hungry a man looked, his dog was always well fed.

At a good dog fight the betting was heavy. Stakes were high and plenty of money changed hands. If a man was caught cheating, he would most likely end up with his throat cut, floating out with the tide. If a man couldn't settle his debts, he would find himself in a dark alley with heavy punches seeking out his face and numerous boots kicking the lesson home when he hit the deck.

Black Harry didn't accept excuses, only payment and hard men like Jimmy were sent in to collect.

Three men with collars turned up and mufflers wound tightly around their faces turned down Bute street. One man, a thick set chap in a heavy pea jacket had a powerful, brindled Staffordshire bull terrier on the end of a heavy chain lead. A piece of blanket was fastened over the dog's back forming a makeshift coat. Even so Jimmy could see it was a huge beast with a massive, chiselled head. The scars on its muzzle spoke of victories in past fights. The dog looked like a champion if ever Jimmy had seen one.

"Nice evening to be out for a stroll," Jimmy drawled in his soft Irish accent, as the group drew nearer. "Nothing like taking the dog for a good walk before turning in for the night.... Are you heading anywhere in particular?" He eyed the men up and down taking in key identifying features, he might need them later.

"My friend Harry suggested we might want to take a walk along Queen's Wharf, tonight," the man with the brindled dog said as he fixed Jimmy with a fierce glare. He was a huge man, standing a good three inches taller than Jimmy with thick set eyes and massive slabs for hands that glistened with chunky silver rings; he looked every inch the stevedore he probably was.

Jimmy could tell from his accent the man was Polish. His two companions regarded Jimmy with suspicion. They whispered something unintelligible between themselves and started to move off. They would not want to keep their dog hanging around long in the cold wind. The punters liked to take a good look at the dogs before placing their bets; this dog had a date in the show ring.

"Then have a good evening my friends.... be lucky." Jimmy tipped his hat and stood by to let the men pass.

The dog growled a deep and throaty rumble and the men hurried along the greasy street before slipping down a dark alley that led to the shed. They knew where they were heading.

Just after 8 o'clock Jimmy aimed for the disused cattle shed. The deep inky gloom of Queen's wharf was only broken by a thin crescent moon out on the bay and a faint, sulphurous yellow glow streaking out through some cracks in the wooden shed.

Two men stood guard at the doors to the front and back entrances of the sheds. Jimmy recognized the man outside the front entrance, Joe Ferrari.

Joe was a small man of Italian extraction, what he lacked in height he made up for in attitude. Joe's hot and feisty nature was backed up with the reputation for always carrying a deadly stiletto- nobody messed with Joe.

"Evening Joe. All's quiet.... Night watch knows not to come this way tonight," Jimmy said as he sidled up to Joe.

Joe acknowledged Jimmy with a slap on the back, he peeled back the wooden door and let him in. Jimmy was needed inside to mingle and watch out for trouble.

The intense heat hit Jimmy as he entered the cavernous shed. There must have been nearly a hundred men milling about inside. The babble of voices and accents reflecting the melting pot that was Cardiff's Tiger Bay added to the excitement. Hot damp air mixed with the stench of tobacco, beer, sweat and piss. The atmosphere was electric.

In a far corner of the shed Jimmy spotted the man he was looking for- a tall, imposing Kenyan with skin so black it looked almost indigo. Under the glare of the sulphurous lanterns illuminating the sheds the man looked like he was carved out of polished jet. Kayfe Ramrakha- Black Harry.

Black Harry was surrounded by a huddle of men, last minute bets were being wagered. Shifty looking individuals were passing over money they could probably ill afford to lose and collecting their stubs. Jimmy skirted the makeshift ring that dominated the centre of the shed.

The iron bars of the cattle pens had been reinforced with wooden pallets and boards, blocking all gaps. There would be no escape for a dog once the fight was under way. The ribbed concrete floor was thickly coated in fresh saw dust to give the dogs' claws better purchase and to sop up the blood.

Black Harry caught Jimmy's eye, and with a slight toss of his head he gestured for Jimmy to make his way towards the back entrance of the shed. Jimmy was to bar the way if anyone sought to escape without settling their debts.

As Jimmy wove his way through the crowd, he overheard two men talking animatedly. The men were tucked in a corner near the back of a shed out of the main view of the ring. One was arguing about which dog looked the better bet. The man looked scraggy; he had the feverish look of a desperate gambler down on his luck.

"Oh, come on Gino.... e's a champ that dog. It's sure-fire bet, I mean…" he gestured towards the brindled dog snarling at his smaller opponent. "Just look at 'im for God's sake, he's a monster, that other white dog doesn't stand a chance against 'im.... I've going to 'ave a bet even if you aint."

The small swarthy man with a grubby red neckerchief tied around his throat grasped his friend roughly by the coat sleeve. He kept his voice low as he cupped his hand over his mouth. "Look I'm telling you my friend for the last time, don't waste your money betting on that brindled dog... I've heard word that Ludwig is going to prick his heel tonight."

The scraggy man's eyes widened with shock as he digested the information.

Jimmy could tell from the heavy accent the man with the neckerchief was Italian. He shuffled a little nearer to catch the rest of conversation.

"Aye is that right now Gino?......You're absolutely sure man? So, who tipped you the wink then? Can you trust 'em Gino?"

Owen hissed. Jimmy watched the scraggy man hesitate; unsure of risking his money now on the favoured brindled dog.

"Look Owen, let's just say that Joe Ferrari and I are cousins, an' we look out for each other" Gino gestured his head towards the front entrance.

"Take my advice Owen, keep that money in your pocket tonight take it home to that pretty wife of yours. Let's just watch the fight and then we go." Gino urged.

So, the men knew the fight was rigged.... Joe Ferrari had tipped them off... Jesus, if word got out there would be a lynching. Black Harry had a reputation to protect.

Joe made his way across to Black Harry. Black Harry stood in the corner watching the spectacle of the two dogs being paraded around the ring. All eyes were on the competitors.

The barking and snarling reached fever pitch. Pink slavering mouths and faces coated with flecks of spittle as the two dogs worked themselves up to a blind frenzy.

The massive brindled dog Jimmy had seen earlier was straining at his leash; pulling so hard his front legs pawed at

79

thin air; Ludwig struggled to hold him back. The dog's eyes were rolling dramatically, his tongue lolling and mouth foaming; he strained to get at his prey.

The challenger, a white Staffordshire bull terrier with a black head looked smaller, younger and leaner. His bodyweight would be no match for the bigger dog. What the dog lacked in weight he might make up for in agility, but the odds looked stacked in the larger dog's favour. The white dog was barking and snarling aggressively, spoiling for the fight. His handler paraded the dog with a cocky attitude that said, whatever appearances might say to the contrary, he had confidence his dog would be the victor.

Either that or he knows the fight is being rigged in his favour. Jimmy thought.

Jimmy sidled up to Black Harry,

"I need a word Harry... it's important." Jimmy tipped his hat out of deference.

The tall Kenyan regarded Jimmy with a degree of irritation. The timing was bad. The dogs were due to be set.

"It had better be Jimmy," Black Harry drawled in a voice so

rich and deep it sounded like liquid molasses.

Jimmy put his mouth close to Black Harry's ear and relayed his discovery.

Black Harry's eyes narrowed to deep slits as he processed the information.

"Thank you Jimmy my man. It will be dealt with, make sure the two men in question are ejected now before the fight starts, if they're not betting then they have no business being here." Black Harry beckoned forward a burly black man.

"Jimmy take Ajo with you to give you a hand. No fuss mind just put them out of here. Once they are outside my lads will remind them who sets the rules around here. I'll deal with the rest."

Jimmy and Ajo slipped through the crowd to where the two men were standing. Each grabbed a man firmly by the elbow. Gino's eyes registered Ajo as one of Black Harry's men and tried to wriggle free.

"Let's be 'aving you lads, I think you ought to be leaving now," Jimmy said as he tightened his grip on the small Welshman.

"No fuss now, evening's over.... just head for home boys."
Jimmy and Ajo propelled the terrified men through the back
gates.

The two men stumbled out into the night relieved to be
released.

"I'd go straight home if I were you boys, it can get pretty
dangerous on the wharf at night." Jimmy called. "Safe
journey!"

The two men started to run hell for leather, ducking down the
nearest alley way. Arms pumping, desperate to put as much
distance as they could between themselves and the cattle shed.

"Come on Jimmy, the Boss will need us inside," Ajo turned
to go. "Don't worry about them all the alleyways on this side
of the wharf end up on Quay street... the Boss will have it
sorted."

Ajo and Jimmy slipped back inside the shed.

Black Harry saw them arrive and gave a nod to the ring man
standing on a small podium on the outside edge of the pen;
the fight could begin.

The crowd sensing the action was about to start hushed a little and jostled for the best view.

"Right, you know the rules. When I give the word, both handlers must release their dogs and leave the ring immediately," the ring master warned the two handlers who struggled to hold their dogs back.

Leads were unclipped and the barking, slavering beasts strained at their collars.

Jimmy watched the brindle dog's handler. Meaty ring-clad hands restrained the animal.

"Get ready...."

Both men crouched low, hands grasping thick leather collars ready to propel their dog forward as soon as the word was given.

"Go!"

Then it happened in the blink of an eye. If he hadn't been looking for it, Jimmy would have missed it.

The Pole knelt slightly and as he pushed his dog forward, his ring-clad hand swept over the base of the dog's hind leg.

A hidden blade in the base of his ring sliced deep through the sinew and blood vessels. The dog's yelp of pain was lost in the howling, baying of the crowd.

Propelled by the instinct to fight and maddened by pain the brindled dog leap towards his opponent. The scuffling dust of the sawdust obscured the trickle of blood running freely down the dog's hind leg. Within moments more blood and saliva spattered the ring as both dogs reached for folds of flesh, ears, neck, shoulders. Lips drawn back as fangs searched for a deadly grip.

Jimmy could see the brindled dog buckling as his weakened hind leg repeatedly gave way. The white Staffie pushed home the advantage executing a roll. Using the weight of the bigger dog against himself, the white dog aimed for the soft under belly and throat.

Once down the brindled dog with his crippled leg was powerless to push himself back off the floor. The white dog powered in straddling his victim; teeth ripping deep into flesh. Scenting blood the screaming of the crowd was at a crescendo. The yelling and roaring deafening. Screams of encouragement drowning out the brindled dog's screams of agony. The fight was going out of him.

The stricken dog lay, eyes glazed and twitching on the sawdust, his life blood pooling around him. The victorious dog bloodied and panting with exertion grew calmer as its prey lay before him; all resistance gone. The white dog, with one final shake of the limp brown heap in front of him, backed off and stood four square to his audience. Victorious!

The crowd erupted.

The man on the podium beckoned for the handlers to collect their dogs.

Jimmy watched as a grim-faced Ludwig picked up what remained of his dog. A brown Hessian sack was chucked into the ring. Ludwig stuffed the still twitching body in the sack and slung it over his shoulder. With a brief nod to his companions to join him they made for the back gate to dispose of the dog off the jetty. Black Harry, surrounded by his men, watched them leave.

Jimmy would deliver Ludwig's agreed payment in the morning.

In the weak, grey early morning light the mangled body

bobbed about in the harbour, buffeting up against the thick wooden posts of the jetty, snagging on the ropes that dangled off the sides. The tide was on the turn.

Snow was starting to fall thick and fast and the quayside was deserted. The empty cattle sheds bore no trace of the night before. Bloodied sawdust had floated on the grey froth of the harbour before getting lost in the churning water swirling around the jetty legs.

In an hour, the tide would retreat, and the bloodied corpse of Joe Ferrari would drift far out to sea, dragged out by the fierce rip tide that cut across the Tiger bay.

CHAPTER 6

Jimmy slipped into Betty's yard through the back gate a warm glow spreading over him. He felt particularly good and more than a bit drunk. He patted what remained of the half bottle of rum that nestled in his pocket; he'd certainly earned a drink tonight. The intensity of the evening had left him on a high and Black Harry had been grateful.

Jimmy had proved himself to be loyal in more ways than one. Joe Ferrari hadn't stood a chance.

When Joe joined Black Harry and the others after the dog fight to collect his payment he had swaggered into the room like a man without a care in the world.

"Eet was a good night? Eh Boss?" Joe smirked.

Stony faces stared back at him. At the slight flick of Black Harry's head, Jimmy barred Joe's exit and Ajo bolted the door.

The smile slid off Joe's face. The little Italian now had every care in the world on his shoulders.

When Ajo and Jimmy had pinioned Joe's arms behind his back and handed his stiletto to Black Harry, Joe knew that he was in trouble, big trouble.

Joe tried to rack his brain-what had happened? Whatever it was, from the look on Black Harry's face he knew that he probably did not have long left on this earth. Beads of sweat broke out on Joe's forehead. There was no escape. Joe tried to wriggle and bluster "Hey lads... Come on now... there must be a mistake.... I can explain....I... No!"

That was the last thing he would ever say as Black Harry sliced off his tongue. "No explanations Joe... no one talks about my business.... ever!"

When Jimmy and Ajo chucked Joe off the jetty he had struggled for a while against his fate. The freezing cold water and ties around his wrists and ankles meant his doom was sealed. The thrashing soon stopped.

Joe was the first man Jimmy had ever been directly involved in killing and it gave him a rush like no other he'd felt before. Looking a man in the eyes as you throw him to his death was a powerful feeling.

Jimmy let himself into the kitchen. The range fire was smouldering under the thick coating of small coal and dust that would keep the embers alive until morning. The kitchen felt warm and comforting.

Jimmy put two one-pound notes and a ten bob note on the table to cover last weeks and this week's rent. *Betty could whistle for that extra shilling.... bad tempered old cow that she was... she should be grateful he didn't just skip off owing.*

Jimmy sat by the fire swigging the rest of the dark rum. The more he drank and thought about his night's work the more restless he became. He thought about Ivy.

Betty slept in the double bedroom above the kitchen. Jimmy always knew when Betty was asleep; her grunts and snores could be heard rumbling through the ceiling, especially when she'd given the Gin a good pasting. *It would take an*

89

earthquake to rouse the old cow. Out for the count!

Ivy slept at the front of the house in a small room on the half landing next to the bathroom. Tonight, he wanted Ivy, he'd wanted her for months.

He'd been working on her for weeks, treating her nice, softening her up so to speak. He was willing to bet, she wasn't going to make a fuss if he upped his game a bit.

She well past sixteen for Christ's sake. Ivy wasn't exactly a baby even if Betty did treat her like one. Besides, he'd had them younger. He liked them young; all dewy skinned and malleable. In Jimmy's eyes Ivy owed him a few favours, and to Jimmy's way of thinking favours ought to be repaid.

Jimmy reckoned being almost seventeen was safe enough to chance his arm...after all the police weren't going to be interested in the antics of a lass above the age of consent from Bute, even if she did cut up rough, especially one that had a prostitute for a mother and no father around to be on the war path.

Jimmy crept up the stairs. He stood outside Ivy's door listening to the small creaks and groans of the house. Jimmy let himself in.

The thin bedroom curtains allowed the faint, silver blue moon light reflecting off snowy roofs to filter in. It was freezing in her room. Ivy's small, tousled head was just visible above a huddled mound under the eiderdown.

Jimmy edged stealthily over to the bed. He stood looking for a few moments at the ruffle of reddish-brown hair that spilt across her pillow. Ivy's face looked like alabaster with only her nose peeping out above the covers. Jimmy liked watching.

He stroked her forehead; fingers tracing the delicate arch of her doll like eyebrows with the lightest of touch. Her skin was warm and soft. Ivy sighed in her sleep.

Jimmy knelt on the floor beside her bed. He gently stroked her hair easing the coverlet away from her face. She was wearing a winceyette nightgown that buttoned at the neck, Ivy murmured and stirred a little and then rolled onto her back.

He needed to be careful, mustn't have Ivy crying out and risk rousing Betty.

Jimmy's hand was warm from the rum and kitchen fire, he

slid it under the bed clothes, edging his way softly towards his goal.

He placed his hand on her thigh and left it there for a while. He watched her face twitch a little, small flickers running across her lips. She was dreaming.

He moved his hand a little higher and left his hand there.

"Urmmmm..." Ivy was starting to rouse to consciousness.

He used his free hand to stroke her face "Ivy... Ivy.... it's only me Jimmy.... don't you fret my darling girl." He whispered. His fingers placed on her lips "Shhhhhh now." he said. "It's only me."

All the while his hand stayed still on her thigh as though it were part of her.

"Oh Jimmy.... is something the mat...." she mumbled still caught in the half world of waking and dreaming. Drowsy and disorientated. His hand rested unnoticed.

"Shh Ivy.... Nothing's the matter...it's all right.... just relax.... pretty, pretty girl." He crooned. His fingers stroked her face, whisper soft caresses fluttering down her cheek. His hand wandered gently across her soft skin.

Ivy was awake now. She tensed a little as she felt the flickering of Jimmy's fingers. *What was he doing?*

She felt sure she should be afraid, but his low rhythmic voice seemed to hypnotize her. She was his darling girl, a little princess. Words trickled into her ear like fairy promises. The stroking of her face soothed her, she felt frozen, rooted to the mattress.

"You are such a good girl Ivy... so good.... Oh yes …. So good. Shh now…"

In the dark it seemed surreal, as if it were a dream. She didn't notice when he stopped caressing her face all her focus now was on the stroking fingers wandering over her thighs, travelling higher.

"You're so good Ivy....sooo good!" His grunting was guttural. A spasm raced through him and he quickly removed his hand from under the eiderdown. In a few moments it was all over.

"Are you all right Jimmy?" she whispered urgently. Those strange noises…She was worried he might be about to vomit.

93

"Yes Ivy.... my darling girl you've made Jimmy happy." He whispered.

"Shh now Ivy and go back to sleep." He soothed.

He bent over to tuck her in. "Sleep tight, remember this is our little secret Ivy.... Just between us."

The next morning Jimmy slept in late. It was nearly 9 o'clock before he ambled downstairs in search of his breakfast. He was hungry, ravenously hungry.

The kitchen was thick with the smell of carbolic soap and blue bag. A grey steam fogged up the small windows. Snow had piled in small drifts up against the panes outside. It was another freezing cold day.

Ivy stood at the Belfast sink, up to her elbows in swirls of wet bedding and underwear. A mountain of dripping laundry sat on the draining board waiting to be rinsed out. Ivy mashed and pulped the laundry before wringing it out and slapping it on the ever-growing pile. She swept her sweaty forehead with the back of hand.

"Morning Ivy darling," Jimmy chirped through pursed lips as he drew heavily on a cigarette and plonked himself down at the kitchen table. "Fancy making me a nice cup of tea and a bit of toast?"

Ivy looked over her shoulder. She hadn't heard Jimmy come in. Her hair was tied into a loose bun at the base of her neck. The steam had caused soft tendrils of red gold to curl around her heart shaped face. Her cheeks were pink with exertion.

Jimmy gave her a broad grin and held her gaze. He could see she looked flustered like a ruffled hen. He slowly blew out a thick stream of cigarette smoke. "Come on Ivy, there's a good girl... I'm fairly famished."

"I can't Jimmy.... I'm up to my eyeballs in washing." She eyed him nervously. "And Mam will be back soon, I'm late already."

All morning she'd been tormenting herself about his visit to her room last night. By the time she'd run the impossible events through her mind for the umpteenth time, she was beginning to think it might all have been a very odd dream.

Ivy felt conflicted, confused and more than a little embarrassed. She *knew J*immy shouldn't really be creeping about the house at night, coming into her room, touching her.

But there he sat at Mam's table, bold as brass smiling and smoking as if nothing important had happened at all.

What did it all mean? Ivy wished she could talk to Alice about it, but Jimmy said it was to be *their* secret and she didn't want to cause any trouble. Jimmy said it would be her fault if he got in trouble with Mam, upsetting her over nothing.

Ivy had to admit that Jimmy was good to her and to Mam. Her Mam had been a lot less bad tempered and stressed since Jimmy had helped pay the bills.... *Perhaps she was just being silly after all.*

"Oh well if that's the way it is, I suppose I'll just have to help myself to breakfast then Ivy darling.... And there's me thinking you liked me." Jimmy made a small pout, as if his feelings had been mortally wounded.

"I do Jimmy, but..." Ivy raised her dripping hands in exasperation, she was confused and just a little scared of him.

"No buts.... Well, that's settled then -you're forgiven for *not* getting my breakfast." He gave her a broad wink. "I'm only teasing you Ivy, don't look so worried over nothing." He saw

96

a nervous tightening of her mouth. He knew he'd had to play her gently, reel her in like a fish on the line, coaxing her into his grasp.

"I know! When your Mam comes back how about I ask if I can take you *both* out to the flicks? Humphrey Bogart is playing Phillip Marlow in "The Big Sleep" at The Ninian."

"Really Jimmy! You'd take me *and* Mam to the pictures?" Ivy hadn't ever been to the picture house. This was so exciting!

The Ninian with its Art Deco façade and neon lights had always appeared to Ivy to be the height of sophistication; a picture palace in every sense of the word, even the boarded-up windows to prevent blast damage during the war hadn't dulled its allure. Mam didn't run to such fripperies and extravagances.

The very thought of going to The Ninian drove her troubling thoughts away.

The prospect of walking up the steps into the foyer was beyond exciting- She couldn't wait to tell her best friend Alice. Alice would be green with envy.

"But of course, if you'd rather not come with me?" He drawled.

"No, no really.... I mean thank you Jimmy, I'd love to. Oh, my goodness.... Humphrey Bogart!" Ivy beamed with excitement.

"And later if you're a *particularly good* girl Jimmy might just run to a nice fish and chip supper for everyone as well.

CHAPTER 7

"Honestly, Alice, I could've died it was just all so beautiful. I wish I could go again. The carpet was this deep," Ivy's fingers illustrated a generous inch of pile.

"It was this lovely red colour with yellow golden swirls, your shoes fair sunk into it they did, it even went all the way up these huge stairs. It looked like red and gold velvet!" Ivy's eyes glistened with rapture as she paused for breath; the memory of that glorious December evening as fresh in her mind as if it were only yesterday. All over Christmas, week after week Ivy re-lived the delicious experience.

"And the lights were like diamonds- a huge ball of diamonds," Ivy enthused awestruck by the glamour of it all. Even after months Ivy still couldn't forget the thrill of walking up the hallowed steps of the Ninian.

"Yeah so you've said," Alice was getting a little bored with the endless details about Ivy's fabulous first, and indeed only, trip to the Ninian picture house.

Alice *had* been green with envy when Ivy announced her cinema visit, but now the repeated recounting of the event was beginning to grate on Alice's nerves.

Discussing film stars was another matter entirely; it was worth a few minutes indulging Ivy's fascination with picture houses if they led to Alice's favourite topic…film stars.

"So, Ivy what was the film like… you know Humphrey Bogart, I mean he's quite dishy isn't he?"

Alice had a major crush on most of the screen heart throbs and the rugged Humphrey Bogart was one of her favourites. On a good day she reckoned she even looked a bit like the glamorous Lauren Bacall with blonde hair!

Alice was fond of the attention she attracted from the local lads, but her dream was to nab a film star. She didn't plan on spending the rest of her days having her bottom pinched as she served tea in the Coal Exchange. Alice planned on being famous; and *when* she was famous, she'd be able to waltz into all the top places on the arm of some gorgeous hunk.

"He was pretty gorgeous." Ivy admitted. "Mam's a big fan of Humphrey Bogart an' all. He's a good actor." Ivy observed briefly. She didn't really want to open the whole, *who's your favourite film star conversation;* indulging Alice's impossible dream of being swept away by a glamourous actor who draped her in fox furs and diamonds and swept her off to the bright lights of Hollywood.

It was a lazy Sunday afternoon; early, sugar-pink blossom garlanded the Bute Park cherry trees and drifts of cheerful crocus spread out across the lawns. After the bitter winter, Spring was well underway.

The two girls sat gossiping in the gentle warm sunshine on a bench in Bute park. The girls were casting in breadcrumbs watching the ducks dabbling for weed on the Dock feeder canal. A convoy of small drab ducklings cheeped and squeaked to each other as they paddled furiously to catch up.

"So, you sly thing Ivy you never actually said but how come *you* got to go to the flicks as well as your Mam? Playing the gooseberry, were you?" Alice teased.

"I thought Jimmy Benson was making eyes at your Mam-leastwise that's what my Da says." Alice nudged her friend and laughed.

"Don't be stupid Alice. My Mam would wash your mouth out with soap if she heard you gossiping about her like that!" Ivy said.

Alice looked mortified by the accusation of gossip. "I was only asking about Jimmy Benson."

"What do you mean *asking about Jimmy?*" Ivy blushed. Jimmy had been taking liberties more often lately. Ivy squirmed when she thought about some of the little secrets Jimmy expected her to keep.

"Well *why* did he take you along? It doesn't make sense to me." Alice crossed her legs inching her skirt a little higher and flipped her hair suggestively over her shoulders as two lads strolled past the bench; she was rewarded with a low whistle.

"Cheeky monkeys," she called after them.

"Well, it stands to reason doesn't it, Ivy?... You know the old saying. *Two's company three's a crowd.* Most men don't want an audience on an evening out with a lady. So, what was he up to?" Alice used the word *lady* in the loosest sense of the word.

Ivy was very loyal to her Mam and wouldn't hear words said

against her.

"You've got the wrong end of the stick Alice Tranter, it's not like that at all. Jimmy's been good to us; pays his bills regular and helps Mam out. It's not been easy for her you know being a widow. This was just Jimmy's little treat in return for a favour…There's no big secret to tell."

The lie slipped off Ivy's tongue like castor oil off a spoon. She knew Jimmy Benson had plenty of secrets and she was one of them.

"But Jimmy's got a temper on him Alice and he doesn't like people talking about his business; so, can we just drop the subject." Ivy lowered her voice conspiratorially; her face took on an anxious air. Ivy didn't need Alice making loose comments about her Mam or Jimmy. He would blame Ivy if any gossip reached his ears.

"Suit yourself then!" Alice got up from the park bench and fluffed out her skirt like an indignant hen. "It's time I was getting back anyway."

Ivy looked miserable. She hated quarrelling with Alice.

"Oh, come on Ivy don't be mardy…Tell you what there's a

big jazz dance on at the Odeon in two weeks' time. Bryn Williams has asked me to go with him." Alice smirked. She gave Ivy a hug.

Brynleigh Williams was a handsome young lad of twenty-two with the gift of the gab and a cheeky grin. He worked in his father's butcher's shop on the corner of Bute Street; he was a bit of a Jack the lad, flirting with all the local girls, but he'd set his cap at Alice. Brynleigh regularly slipped a few ounces extra onto the Tranter order if Alice was collecting. He'd been chasing after Alice for weeks and she found it flattering to have such an ardent suitor giving George Thomas a run for his money.

Alice had become a little bored of doting George with his cow eyes and gentle ways; she had decided to play hard to get; have a bit of fun before she had to settle down. George needed to know that he wasn't the only game in town, especially when George was being kept busy by his Da serving chips most Saturday nights, he couldn't expect her to sit around waiting for him to have an occasional night off. She was young and she wanted some fun, if other lads asked her to a dance then she didn't see why she shouldn't accept. If George really wanted her he was going to have to try a bit

104

harder.

Brynleigh was Alice's latest devoted slave wrapped around the end of her little finger.

"Come on Ivy. Enjoy yourself for once! Why don't we make it a foursome? He's got a nice friend, Gary Jones, who isn't courting, you know the blonde lad, he works in the green grocers, we could all go together. It doesn't mean anything; it would just be a bit of fun for once!" Alice enthused. "Surely your Mam must allow you to have a bit of fun sometimes," she cajoled.

Ivy felt tempted; she'd never been to a proper dance. The Odeon was rumoured to be the place to go on a Saturday dance night, but Mam didn't approve of courting at her age, and she certainly didn't approve of girls like Alice Tranter.

"I'd love to but…"

"But what?" Alice was getting exasperated with Ivy's excuses. One day Ivy was going to have to stand up to that overbearing mother of hers.

"But I know my Mam won't let me that's what. You know what she's like." Ivy looked crest fallen.

"Oh, for heaven's sake Ivy, she can't keep this up for ever you know. She can't tie you to her apron strings for the rest of your life, can she? Just tell her you're going out!"

Alice made no effort to disguise the irritation in her tone; this was a regular battle whenever Alice suggested going out with Ivy. Ivy was her best friend, but Alice was starting to lose patience with her. What was the point of having Ivy as her best friend if they could *never* go out together! It was getting awkward, she couldn't exactly go out on her own with lads to the Odeon, even her own Mam drew the line at that, but that meant she'd always have to go with other friends. She wanted to go with Ivy.

"You've turned seventeen now; you're not exactly a baby now Ivy… you are going to spread your wings at some point. She can't keep you under lock and key for ever. Promise me you'll at least ask her? Who knows your Mam might just say yes this time." Alice wheedled.

"I promise. I will, really I will Alice" Ivy mumbled.

Ivy didn't dare look Alice in the face; she knew she had no intention of keeping that promise. Last time she'd mentioned wanting to go out to a dance with Alice Tranter her mother had locked her in her room for the evening with threats to tan her hide if she tried to sneak out.

  Her Mam said it was all for Ivy's own good, but Ivy was fed up with being good.

CHAPTER 8

"Well, you really take the biscuit this time Jimmy Benson, sitting there like you own the bloody place.... Who the hell do you think you are?" Betty's eyes swept the small room absorbing the scattered newspaper, dirty teacups and overflowing ash tray.

It had been nearly seven months since Jimmy Benson had bounced up the steps of twenty-two Bute street and settled into the easy rhythms of the Jenkins household, even so Betty's shrewish temper and sharp comments still caused his hackles to rise.

Too free with her bloody opinions and criticism for his liking.

Betty was certainly in a foul temper and spoiling for a fight.

She'd been drinking since noon at the Nag's head. Copious amounts of brown ale and glasses of gin had sharpened her tongue.

When Betty had been ejected from the bar by the landlord Victor at five o'clock, her temper had rocketed to boiling point. *Bloody barred from the Nag's Head .... and all because of that stupid, mouthy Price boy.*

She tottered home from the pub spoiling for a fight and Jimmy Benson was in her sights. By the time she found Jimmy sitting at her kitchen table lounging about as if he owned the place, she was incandescent with rage.

Jimmy could see she was swaying as she stood in the kitchen screeching at him like a demented fish wife, demanding answers, jabbing her finger at him. Her eyes looked glazed, and her mouth was set in hard line, Betty was a mean and mouthy drunk.

Earlier that afternoon in the Nag's Head, Betty had sat in a booth sipping gin with one of her regular punters, snippets of conversation and cackles of laughter from the other side of the booth caught her attention. Her name and Ivy's were being bandied about and obviously proving to be the source of great amusement.   Betty leant a little closer to hear more.

 Apparently, Ivy had spurned John Price's attentions again and he wasn't taking it well.   John had his views on the matter of *stuck-up* Ivy Jenkins and the likely goings on in the Jenkins' household.

 Nettled, John Price was holding forth to another customer sat at the bar.   His willing audience was one of the Nag's Head regulars: old Bob Griffiths.

 Old Bob used to spend his afternoons nursing a half a pint of bitter at the bar, sifting through morsels of gossip and tittle tattle like a whale sifts plankton.   When a particularly juicy morsel came to Bob's attention he would pocket it, to be used later as currency when another punter was buying at the bar. Bob managed to trade quite successfully off his reputation of being in the "know".

  "Jailbait that's what they used to call it in my day John... trashy young girls no better than they ought to be, batting their eye lashes and hoping for a good time, but there again you can't blame a red-blooded fella like Jimmy Benson, or any other man for that matter, trying it on… 'specially not if it's right under his nose, served up on a platter so to speak."

110

Bob sipped the remains of his beer.

Old Bob could make a drink last all afternoon especially if he thought another might just wing his way courtesy of another generous drinker. But today the bar room was quiet, and he was nursing the last two inches or so of amber ale. "Mind you, if there's them that puts it about, there's always going to be some man willing to take them up on the offer." Bob eyed John and wondered if there was any chance the lad would add an extra inch to his glass. He angled the glass hopefully towards the pump.

John ignored the hint.

"Well, now don't get me wrong Bob, I'm not actually saying I blame Ivy or anything .... not with that mother of hers. I mean everyone around here knows what *she's* like." John said as he polished glasses with his barman's apron. John might be spurned but he still had hopes that Ivy would relent; it wouldn't help his chances if he blackened Ivy's name. Much safer to run down Ivy's Mam.

"Her mother? Oh, you mean that old slapper Betty Jenkins?" Bob cackled. "Oh aye, I don't think there's a man in the whole of Tiger Bay that doesn't know what Betty Jenkins is

111

like." Bob winked suggestively. "I think half the royal Navy has had Betty at some time or another.... *Seaman's mission* used to be her nick name!" Bob chortled loudly at his own joke.

John collapsed with laughter. The two men guffawed loudly until John caught sight of a furious Betty Jenkins stomping towards him. She had an empty glass in her hand and a face like thunder.

John backed away behind the bar as Betty pushed herself forward. Bob Griffiths shrank into his coat and regarded the last two inches of ale at the bottom of his beer glass with intense interest.

Betty swiped Bob's glass and chucked the dregs over John's apron closely followed by her own glass hurled as a missile at his head. John ducked and the tumbler shattered into smithereens on the counter.

"Hey....Hey! What the hell do you think you're doing!" Bob was outraged at losing the last of his ale.

"'And you can fuck off Bob Griffiths, you randy old sod," Betty pushed the startled man off his bar stool. He landed heavily on the floor.

"And as for you John Price.... Just ask that useless father of yours why your little brother looks nothing like the rest of your trashy, no good family... your mother Mary is well known for turning a few tricks on the front! I'm only surprised your little Billy didn't come out black! You can tell him from me that everyone round here knows your Dad's raising a cuckoo!"

Responding to the commotion the landlord, Victor, skittered out of the back office and pushed his way through to the bar. He grabbed Betty by the arm before she could aim another glass.

Betty Jenkins was famous for her hot temper. Victor had had to tell her to button her lip on more than one occasion. Throwing glasses was beyond the pale.

"Right, *you*.... that's enough of your mouth. Go on get out of here Betty.... You're leaving right now!"

Victor hustled her out through the bar door before she could do any more damage.

"And don't you come back," Victor shouted after her,

113

"You're barred Betty Jenkins, do you hear me…. barred!"

When Betty eventually made it home, she was determined to get some answers. Bob Griffiths was a nasty old devil with a spiteful mouth. What had she ever done to him?

Until the moment Betty barged into Jimmy's consciousness with her cursing and screaming he had been feeling quite mellow and at one with the world. He had money on the hip; the proceeds of nice little win at the dog track the night before and a generous back hander from the landlord of the Queen's Head for delivering a case of misplaced whiskey. Yes, life had been feeling rather good, until storm Betty had turned up in the kitchen making enough noise to raise the dead.

"So are you going to tell me then Jimmy Benson. Is it true? have you been sniffing around my Ivy? Go on have you? Because that's what that bloody John Price was saying to anyone who'd listen at the Nag's!!"

Jimmy drew on his cigarette and gave Betty a stony stare. He was beginning to get rather bored of her tantrums and mood swings. Draping herself all over him one minute like some cheap suit, and then screeching blue murder about the rent being overdue the next.

Betty's hair was dishevelled, and her lipstick smeared across her cheek. She looked old and raddled; it was hard to believe she had just turned forty. Women like Betty revolted him with her thick make up, slack tits and age-mottled hands.

Maybe it was time to move on? Jimmy had been giving some thought to the next step and it certainly didn't involve hooking up with the likes of Betty Jenkins.

The only trouble was what to do about Ivy?

Little Ivy was shaping up very nicely; he'd got her very well trained and just where he wanted her. Ivy was like a timid puppy. He'd moulded her, trained her until she was biddable, grateful and just a *little* frightened of him…Perfect.

He'd still not gone too far; he'd learnt the value of caution over the years. He'd always been careful not to raise Betty's suspicions about Ivy. If the stupid cow had plenty booze to keep her happy, she never seemed to notice anything, even if it was going on right under her nose.

That sneaky, weasel John Price had certainly thrown a

spanner in the works, roused Betty's suspicions. That lad needed to learn to keep his mouth shut.

Jimmy continued to stare at Betty as she stamped around the kitchen venting her rage. He resisted the urge to slap her. Mustn't be too hasty Jimmy, you've got a comfy little billet here and life is full of possibilities around this neck of the woods. He couldn't let Betty queer his pitch by making trouble, giving substance to rumours. After all he hadn't really done anything.

Betty waved her arms and shouted abuse, raging at the world. *Didn't he know how hard it was for a poor widow like her to make ends meet. Hadn't she trusted him whilst all along he was sneaking around Ivy behind her back.* He watched her blow herself out like a storm at sea before she collapsed onto a kitchen chair and burst into tears of frustration.

"You *quite* finished?" Jimmy drawled as he drew on the remains of his Woodbine. "You and that no good mouth of yours?" He held Betty in his gaze.

"Well, I'm not having you, or anyone else for that matter, taking liberties… not with my little Ivy. She's a good girl. I've always done my best for Ivy; kept her safe." She sniffed.

The fight had gone out of her. Under the fuzz of alcohol Betty was becoming maudlin.

Jimmy placed five one-pound notes on the kitchen table. Each note was carefully peeled off a thick wad in his wallet and spread out in a tempting fan. He leaned back on the stick back chair, stretched out his legs in front of him and waited for her reaction.

Betty's eyes narrowed; *he must have at least a hundred pounds there ....* Her hand slid across the table towards the five, crisp green notes in front of her.

"My little Ivy is as innocent as the day is long and that's the way she's going to stay understood!"

Jimmy's eyes narrowed.

"Perhaps I should talk to her?" Betty's fingers edged towards the money.

Jimmy slapped his hand down hard on top of Betty's paw before she could pick up the notes. His grip on her hand was vice like.

"Don't push it Betty," Jimmy growled.

"All I'm saying Jimmy is that a Mother has to look out for her girl, I can't have my Ivy taken advantage of can I now?"

Jimmy gave a brief tip of his head. "Oh, I think we understand each other Betty, don't we? Now you've got your rent money an' you've got a bit extra this week, but *only* 'cos I'm in a generous mood, it's nothing else; do you understand me Betty? Nothing!" He snarled.

She nodded. He released his grip. She snatched the money off the table and stuffed the notes down into the cleft of her bosom.

"Well, let's say no more about this little…er…misunderstanding shall we Jimmy? That Price family always were a load of lying, no-good troublemakers." She stood up to go.

"It *is* a pack of lies Betty…is that understood?"

Jimmy grabbed her by the wrist and twisted the skin so tight it burned. "Oww...you're hurting me.... let me go Jimmy." She whined..

Betty struggled to pull her hand away, but there was no escape. She was rooted to the spot like a bird stuck fast on

118

quick lime.

"Understood Betty?" Jimmy menaced; his face thrust within inches of hers.

"Yes.... yes", she gasped.

He released his grip. "No-one messes with me Betty....no-one!.. And if you know what's good for you, you'll watch that mouth of yours, making accusations, passing on gossip else it'll get you into big trouble!"

Betty scuttled out of the kitchen like a scalded cat.

Later that evening, after closing time in a dark alley way behind the Nag's Head, Jimmy enjoyed knocking out John Price's front teeth and flattening his interfering nose halfway across his face.

Chapter 9

"Here he is lads, 'ees made it... Over here Jimmy... we're here!" Sean Riley shouted over the sea of heads jostling to get to the bar. Sean gestured to a small stool tucked in the corner alcove, a prime position next to the bar's radio.

"We've got one in for you," Sean held a creamy pint of Guinness aloft, he tried in vain to make himself heard over the excited babble of Irish voices.

A young girl, Noreen, muttering her *excuse me's* balanced four dirty glasses, one on each of her tiny fingers. Fighting the tide Noreen pushed her way across the room towards the kitchen. Terry would need the empties washed up else he would soon run out. Noreen had never seen the bar so busy. The air was laden with tobacco and hope, slopped beer tacky on the boards as men jostled for position.

"Make way for the young lady, lads... let the lass through," some wag yelled. The crowd parted a little to let the girl through before swiftly closing behind her like the biblical Red sea. No-one wanted to lose their place. Noreen wriggled her way through the crush, ignoring a few lewd comments as she brushed up against thighs and backsides.

Jimmy Benson fought his way through the forest of elbows and green ribbons. The Duke of Edinburgh was rowdy, overflowing onto the pavement, doors wide to the street disgorging a thick beer laden fug. It was as if every Irish man for miles around had converged on the Duke for the historic event.

"My God you're cutting it a bit fine Jimmy, I was beginning to think you'd got lost, here take a seat" Sean patted the stool. "I've already had to kill four men defending this bloody thing" he joked.

The tiny pub table was littered with dwindling glasses of beer and sodden, cardboard beer mats frayed into layers by nervous hands.

"We've got a round in so get this down you," Sean thrust a pint in Jimmy's hand "I can't see us getting anywhere near that bar until half time."

"You're a pal," Jimmy supped the froth off the top greedily. "I popped into the Nag's Head on the way over…I needed to speak to someone," he didn't elaborate, Jimmy didn't like people knowing his business. "An' it's just as mad over there an' all… full of Welsh lads, a sea of red it is." Jimmy pinned his green ribbon on his jacket. "Not the place to be wearing one of these though unless you wanted to start a riot!"

Behind the bar festooned with green and white drapes the radio crackled into life. Terry, the landlord twiddled and fiddled with the dials, a scream of static screeched and fizzed. A clamour of eager hands reached for beer; men needed a drink when battle was being waged. Noreen scuttled about helping the land lady Joan with the orders, the till clinked and chimed as money rattled in, it would be a profitable day.

Terry was a contented man but if he didn't get the blasted radio tuned in he'd have a riot on his hands.

"Come on Terry let's get that thing going, it's already gone past a quarter to three…kick off is in just over ten minutes!"

"Hold your horses, it's coming don't rush me… just get your singing voices on boys we need to make a good noise for our lads across the water, make sure they can hear *"Irelands Call"* over in Belfast," Terry twiddled the knob delicately, ear close to the radio like a safe cracker listening out for tumblers.

The radio commentary sprang into life. A tumultuous cheer ran across the room.

"Turn it up Terry," a voice roared from the back. A hush gradually draped itself over the bar room, only the chink of coins in the till, muffled orders whispered across the bar ruffled the hallowed walls of the Duke, the match was about to start.

As the anthems played, voices were raised in song, thirty-two thousand Irish men in the Ravenshill stadium, joined by several hundred brothers in Newton, willing them on. All the power, all the pride was with Ireland.

The game began in a fury, the ebb and flow of play drove the bar to a frenzy. Ireland had the Welsh on the run. Mistakes were being made on both sides; the game was close but by half time the Irish crowd dared to dream of winning. Ireland had the bit between their teeth.

"Bloody hell lads, there'll be some drinking tonight if they can pull it off," Jimmy gasped after prop John Daly led a

123

tremendous race for the Welsh touchdown.

"Yesss!" The pub erupted. It was now 11v10 to Ireland, all hopes rested on surviving the last few minutes.

"Wales might have denied us eight times before but if our boys can just hang on," Sean could hardly dare to listen as the clock ticked down to the final whistle.

When the blessed relief came Sean and Jimmy jumped out of their seats. Everyone was embracing, clapping friends on the back. They were all brothers in victory. "We've only bloody well gone and done lads…Daly should be made a saint!" Sean gasped. I intend to get *very* drunk tonight!" He beamed from ear to ear.

"There speaks a happily unmarried man," Jimmy joked. "But if you're buying the next round Sean Riley, then mine's a pint."

The whoops screeches and general hullabaloo emanating from the Duke could be heard all over Newton. Little Noreen was lifted off her feet and kissed, grown men cried and Terry the landlord beamed from ear to ear as money poured over the counter.

There would be a lot of sore heads in the morning, but for now it was time to celebrate.

Chapter 10

On Monday morning Ivy decided to start on spring cleaning, beginning with the kitchen. In the sharp, early April sun the small kitchen looked greasy and grimy; smeary windows hindered the sunlight, dust clung to thick cobwebs in the corners of the sloping ceiling where gossamer legged spiders made nests.

The tin lampshade above the stove wore a fuzzy coat of fat and dust testament to steam from numerous pigs' heads, boiled to gelatinous perfection and the red quarry tiles were blackened to Bisto brown by the tramp of mud and coal dust that coated the lane.

With her pinafore wrapped tightly around her waist, and a headscarf to protect her hair Ivy rolled up her sleeves to tackle her mornings work. She eyed the clock…it was nearly eight o'clock, Jimmy was out for the morning and Mam was still in bed, she had plenty of time to get the job done.

A bucket of hot soapy water steamed up the kitchen

windowpanes, they would be the last on her to do list with crumpled newspaper and vinegar. Ivy decided to tackle first the ring marked, pantry shelves before moving onto the wall shelves. She had a strict rota for cleaning to get as much value out of the hot soapy water as she could from each bucketful. Food surface areas tackled first, then cupboard fronts, then finally the floor tiles. Each heavy bucket load took ages to heat, it wouldn't do to waste precious hot water. Two more pans were simmering on the hob for when Ivy needed to change the dirty slop.

It was a beautiful April morning; Ivy sang as she worked, rubbing and scrubbing at the wooden pantry shelves, getting in the grooves of the blocked wire mesh vent.

For a few weeks now the household felt happier, and Ivy felt happier with it. It still worried her that Jimmy took liberties, but she thought she understood why now. He'd explained it all, said that she was his favourite girl and that it was a *special* thing you did, so *special* people kept it a secret, didn't tell. He said there would be trouble for Mam if she told tales and made a fuss. She didn't want to do what Jimmy said but she felt that she had no choice, not if she wasn't to upset the applecart.

127

Jimmy was always good to them afterwards so she reckoned she could put up with it for Mam's sake…as Jimmy said it was Ivy's way of helping to pay the bills, part of her duty to help her Mam.

Best of all Mam had been in a much better mood of late, less shouty, less critical; less drunk. Ivy had even caught Betty singing to herself sometimes, strains of "*Keep young and beautiful*" could be heard coming from behind Mam's bedroom door. Mam's makeup, always slapped on, seemed to be applied with a little more care now.

After two hours on her hands and knees the grimy floor tiles now glowed a warm terracotta red. Ivy worked her way backwards out of the kitchen doorway and through to the hallway, dragging the bucket as she edged along the hall tiles and skirting boards. Finally, Ivy reached the front door and tipped the bucket down the steps and into the street gulley; scrubbing brush in hand, she got into all the mossy crevices on the steps.

"Well now that's a fine job you're doing, young lady."

Ivy raised her head to see a short, fat balding man with a neat toothbrush moustache, inspecting her work. He wore a loud tweed jacket sporting a jaunty bluebell threaded in his buttonhole and brown corduroy trousers supported by natty blue braces. He looked a man dressed for an occasion.

"'Ave I found number twenty-two lass?"

"You have," Ivy pointed to the tarnished numerals above the knocker, the green-black Verdigris demanded some Brasso.

"So, this is where Mrs Jenkins, Mrs Betty Jenkins lives then?" The broad South Wales accent grabbed her attention… a local man.

"Why whose asking?" Ivy narrowed her eyes suspiciously. She had learnt over the years to be cautious about giving away information about Mam's personal affairs. The man looked nice enough, in his early sixties she would guess, but you never could tell; looks could be deceiving, he might be trouble, might be looking for money.

"Mr Williams…Gerald Williams, and you must be young Ivy?"

"What do you want Mr Williams? Mam's rather busy at the moment, but I can give her a message if you like?" Ivy barred the step as she stood up, blocking the view of the hall. Arms

129

crossed defensively across her bosom; Ivy would not invite him in.

"I just thought, since I was passing like, I'd bring her these," he produced a small bunch of daffodils bound with raffia from behind his back. His face broke into an amiable grin that showed the lack of a front tooth.

"Here take them," he thrust the cluster of tight buds towards a stunned Ivy.

A man bringing her Mam flowers, well you could knock her down with a feather!

"They're nice early ones and fresh buds so they should open up a treat, they need putting in water pretty sharpish though… Please say Gerald sends his regards." Gerald Williams lifted his cap and strode off down the terrace whistling.

"Thanks Mr Williams," Ivy called, she clasped the green bundle, goggle eyed at this remarkable turn up for the books. What on earth would the neighbours think seeing a man with flowers on their doorstep and who was this mysterious Mr Williams?

Ivy quickly cleared away and headed to the kitchen on the

hunt for a vase. She couldn't remember ever seeing a vase in the house, still if all else failed she could always use an old jam jar, there were plenty of those stored in the pantry awaiting pickled onions.

She carefully trimmed the seven slender green stems. Having failed in her quest to unearth a vase she selected the nicest jam jar she could find for the daffodils and set it in the centre of the newly scrubbed kitchen table.

"There we are perfect, these are going to look very nice in day or two." Ivy stood back to admire her handy work.

"What are?"

Her mother's voice echoing from the hall passageway nearly made Ivy jump out of her skin.

"Mam... look Mam these are for you!"

"Flowers, Oh Ivy we can't afford to..."

"They're from Mr Williams Mam; a Mr Gerald Williams, he called about an hour ago. I was out front cleaning the step when he just turned up and said he'd brought these for you."

Ivy noticed her Mam blushed a little, for a moment her

131

careworn face lifted; she looked younger and pretty. She still had her hairnet on over her rollers, smears of mascara smudged under her eyes but at that moment her Mam looked happy.

"Oh an' he also said to give you his regards, those were his very words, Mam," Ivy could see that her Mam looked quite overwhelmed.

Standing in her threadbare, felt dressing gown with a belt that barely made it around her thickened waist and the blue piping hanging off the collar Betty looked every inch of her forty years, and she knew it. The pretty girl of yesteryear when hope was bright, was long gone. The sight of the simple daffodil posy made her heart skip a beat.

"Well, that was kind of Mr Williams, I must thank him when I see him next." No explanations given Betty busied herself putting the kettle on for a pot of tea.

"I tried to find a vase Mam, but I wasn't sure if there was one, so I used that jam jar instead,"

Betty ambled off into the sitting room. A few minutes later she came back with a battered shoebox. She carefully unwrapped the tissue paper and produced a small pink glass vase with a clear fluted rim and an intricate cut base. Even in the dull kitchen the delicate ruby glass seemed to glow with a lambent beauty.

"That's so pretty," Ivy gasped. She'd never seen the vase before.

Betty started to arrange the stems in a spiral along the frill. "It belonged to Nanna Patterson, my Mam gave it to me for my twenty first birthday," Betty carefully folded the tissue paper back into the box, "I've kept it all these years an' it's the first time I've ever had cause to use it." She stood back to admire the effect, "They do look very nice, bit wasted in the kitchen though." Betty headed back into the front room to place the arrangement on the black slate mantle-piece.

The kettle whistled for attention. The arrival of Mr Williams had sparked her curiosity.

Mam never mentioned her family… it was the first time she'd ever heard of Nanna Patterson. Mam was so close about her younger days. When Ivy asked her questions as a little girl, sometimes Mam got angry, sometimes upset. Even her father was destined to remain a sad mystery filed away in the too difficult box.

Betty sat with her cup of tea dunking a biscuit. "You've done a good job with the kitchen this morning Ivy, it looks very nice." She sucked the drooping biscuit.

Ivy was lost for words Mam never usually noticed her good work, only her failings.

"I've been thinking Ivy, you're getting to be a young woman now and perhaps I should let you have a bit more freedom, let you go out and about a bit?" Betty stirred in the remains of the drowned Rich Tea.

"How would you like to go out for a few hours this Saturday evening, perhaps go around to see that friend of yours Alice…er".

"Alice Tranter? Oh yes please Mam that would be wonderful…thanks Mam." Ivy couldn't believe her ears she was being allowed to go out, and Mam was the one suggesting it! Only just that Sunday afternoon Alice had been nattering on again about wanting to go out with Ivy on Saturday night. Now she could stop making excuses, and say *yes*, so long as Mam didn't change her mind.

134

"So, you mean I can go *this* Saturday Mam?"

"No boys or funny business mind!" Betty felt a jolt of concern.

"Of course, not Mam," Ivy crossed her fingers. Ivy beamed. She couldn't wait to tell Alice.

"And you'll back by ten thirty sharp or there'll be hell to pay, you understand me!" Betty fixed her daughter with a hard stare. Ivy looked so happy.

"Yes Mam, thank you Mam," Ivy gave her mother a hug.

Betty flapped her away, stifling a sob. "You daft thing; just remember I'll find out if you get up to something. Your Mam only wants what's best for you Ivy, you know that don't you?"

"Of course, Mam."

Betty knew that *one* day she would have to let Ivy spread her wings; she couldn't keep the girl out of harm's way forever. She could see a lot of her old self in Ivy, the same willingness to please, the same trusting, sweet nature that thought the best of everyone, the same vulnerability… and it terrified her.

Betty knew she was often too snappy and critical with Ivy.

135

But the fierce love she had for her daughter made her afraid of what the future might be for a poor girl in the broken, dangerous world of Tiger Bay.

Even now Betty could remember the pain of her mother weeping hysterically as her father threw her out of their "respectable" home in disgrace.

You're dead to us, Elizabeth! He'd yelled aiming her shoes at her head, throwing her clothes on the floor in a rage that caused veins to bulge in his neck. Your brother John died fighting for his country and you…you tramp! What do you do for your country?… Put it about like some trashy tom cat with any man that will have you. Won't even tell us his name… you trollop! Well, you've made your bed, now go lie on it, Madam! You've been a fool and your name will never be mentioned in our house ever again. Never! Both my children are dead now… Get out of our house Elizabeth and don't come back!

It would be the last time she would ever see her Father. She had cried bitter tears the day she left her home Alma road. She was only just twenty-one years old and for her sin her father had thrown her out into the street and slammed the door

136

behind her, so hard it nearly broke the glass. Forced to leave in disgrace with only a few possessions she could call her own.

Her mother, Iris, watched the walk of shame from the upstairs bedroom window. Elizabeth knew that Mam was sobbing her heart out, but Iris would not defy her husband.

Elizabeth was labelled a slut and a tramp on that fateful day in June when she announced her pregnancy. From that day onwards Elizabeth Evans vowed never to go back to number twenty Alma Road. Sweet, naive Elizabeth Evans died that day and Betty Jenkins was born.

As widow Betty Jenkins, she fought hard to keep both their heads above water, used whatever means she had to pay the bills. The school of hard knocks taught Betty one thing at least, she had to sink or learn to swim fast if she and the baby were to survive. Betty became good at swimming.

Living in Tiger Bay, people didn't ask too many questions, didn't notice a woman on her own with a child. Whatever she made of her own life she vowed never to let her own daughter be labelled *spoiled goods*. Betty vowed to watch over Ivy like a she-wolf; stopping the dirty world she moved in from

137

contaminating her precious daughter.

Betty knew she may not have been the best of mothers.

There were times when, Ivy was left asleep alone in the house whilst she stood shivering in city doorways plying for trade. Times when Betty was so fearful of the child turning wayward that she had slapped the girl hard…maybe too hard. Times when she stole from Cardiff market because Ivy needed something warm to eat for supper.

And the dark times, when the booze was on her, when Betty had considered holding Ivy in her arms and jumping into the swirling waters of the Taff…ending it all, only the thought of her own poor mother stopped her from being yet another poor wretch lying waiting to be identified on a post-mortem slab.

Over the years Betty had narrowly escaped the clutches of the law and wrath of angry landlords; dodging her debts, until she found safe haven in Bute street and the haunts of the Tiger Bay. Streets where she could hide from her past.

Could Betty ever slough off the hard shell she had covered herself in?

By going into Gerald's world, she risked shame and derision.

She was a survivor; she had made it in *this* world… could she make it in his?

Chapter 11

The next day at a quarter to five, Ivy waited outside the Coal Exchange; soon workers would start to stream out into the street. She kept her eyes peeled for Alice. Ivy couldn't wait to share her good news.

"Yoo Hoo…over here Alice," Ivy waved frantically. She could see Alice strolling arm in arm with another girl, hips swaying, drawing the eye. Both girls looked so confident, self-assured, pretty. Ivy felt a tremor of doubt she wasn't like Alice; she didn't look pretty like the other girl. She didn't even have anything smart to wear and what about her gamy leg? She felt like one of those drab and dreary, crippled pigeons with toes lost to fishing wire, she'd seen hobbling around the quayside.

"Ivy!" Alice's face lit up. She bid a quick farewell to her friend and raced over to envelope Ivy in a hug.

"What are you doing here?" She took Ivy's arm, "I've just finished, but I mustn't stop long, Mam's expecting me back for tea, I can walk part way with you… so come on, tell me how's tricks?" Alice was curious, Ivy had never met her from work before.

"I just had a bit of news, that's all and…" Ivy hesitated it suddenly seemed an impossible venture. "But perhaps you've already got plans for Saturday?" She'd said *No* so often, she wouldn't blame Alice if she was already committed to another date.

"You can come with us after all?... Oh, Ivy that's fantastic news, you mean she's *actually* gone and said yes?" Alice gasped.

Ivy nodded her head, beaming from ear to ear, thrilled with Alice's generous reaction.

But who was Us?

"George suggested we go to go to the Splott Welfare club…you know the one in Portmanmoor road. They call it The Bomb and Dagger now. They've got a jazz group playing most Saturday nights," Alice's eyes shone with excitement. "You must come with us Ivy it will be such fun."

Ivy looked dubious, The Bomb was a few streets away in Splott, a pub with a certain tough reputation and even tougher lads who called it their local. It certainly wasn't what she had

141

in mind for a dance.

"Oh, I couldn't play gooseberry to you and George Alice, and I'm not sure Mam would like me going *there*." The more Ivy thought about it the more impossible it seemed.

"You daft thing… your Mam doesn't have to know *where* you're going, just tell her there's a good dance on at the Odeon if she asks. You don't have to say that's where you're going, just let her *think* it's where you're going. And you won't be playing gooseberry either, Billy is coming with us so it will be a foursome!" Alice demolished Ivy's objections.

"Say you'll come Ivy and don't worry about The Bomb, I've been heaps of times, and they have a dance floor as well, so you are going to a dance; it's simply the best fun!" Alice was positively fizzing with excitement.

The two girls strolled along, making their way to the corner of Bute street.

"Alice?" Ivy was in a turmoil.

"What now? No more excuses Ivy it's decided we are all going."

"The thing is Alice…I don't have anything to wear. Mam never allows me out, all I've got is my work clothes and my old shoes," Ivy's eyes started to fill with tears. She would be ashamed to be seen in her scruffy old frock and battered black shoes with the clumpy, ugly heel.

"Oh Ivy," Alice gave her a hug. "I'm sure we can find you something. My sister Phyllis has some pretty things she's outgrown; she'll never fit into them again after having those twins. My Mam wouldn't mind if you borrowed something. I'm certain there's a blouse that would fit 'cos I tried it on the other day,… it was too tight across the top, if you get my drift." Alice laughed and puffed out her impressive breasts.

"I think the skirt might be a bit loose though," Alice eyed Ivy's slender frame, "but I could nip a temporary dart in the side seams, that would sort it, and you could just give those shoes a bit of spit and polish and nobody would even notice. All sorted!"

Ivy looked doubtful but admitted defeat, "Do you really think so Alice?"

"I don't just think so, I *know* so. Come around to our house at quarter to seven and we can get you dressed; this is going to be such fun."

Ivy lived in dread until Saturday came around, treading on eggshells in case permission was removed. Mam could be capricious at the best of times but of late she seemed to have mellowed.

Betty had been out every evening that week. Each night Mam left the house looking smart; her hair just so, new rainbow glass beads glinted on her twinset, a tang of rose water and lavender lingered in the hall and each night Ivy heard her bidding Mr Williams goodnight on the doorstep.

Even Jimmy noticed Betty hadn't been hanging around the bars recently, he'd not seen her down on the docks of an evening. Something was up.

"You scrub up well Betty, so who's the lucky fella then?" Jimmy came bounding down the stairs. He sniffed the air, noticed the glass beads. Betty had an admirer.

It was Friday evening and Betty was preening in the hall mirror, adjusting her hat before going out.

"Get away with you Jimmy Benson… just mind your own beeswax," Betty smirked girlishly. Red lipstick slicked over plump lips.

"I'm off then; see you later Ivy," Betty called, she shut the door leaving a trail of perfume in her wake.

"Well, well, I wonder what your Mam is up to then?" He gave Ivy a wink.

"Shush Jimmy," Ivy eyed the hall nervously, Mam might come back.

"All I know is Mam's in a good mood, she's even said I can go out tomorrow. I don't know what's up exactly but if it means I can go out then I don't care!" Ivy pouted.

"I see, you're off out gallivanting then...where to?" Jimmy dragged on his cigarette, eyes narrowing. This was a new and unexpected development.

"Umm..I'm not sure, it's only a dance with my friend Alice," Ivy mumbled. Mam hadn't said a word all week about Ivy's plans, too busy caught up in her own business. *What Ivy was getting up to, was not even on Mam's radar thank goodness.*

She'd kept her Mam sweet all week and now Jimmy was quizzing her, it wasn't fair. She wished she'd kept her mouth shut.

"Now why don't I believe you, my chicken?" Jimmy moved closer, fixing her with a hard stare that seemed to pierce her soul. "So, be a good girl and tell Jimmy what's really going on Ivy."

"Nothing!" Ivy trembled, tried not to cry. "Nothing's going on, please don't say there is to Mam, else she'll stop me going," Ivy pleaded.

"You know me Ivy… we have our little secrets, don't we? Tell me what's really happening tomorrow night and I promise not to tell your Mam."

He eyed her suspiciously, fixed her with a snake like gaze, that commanded her to tell him the truth.

"I'm going to a dance with my friend Alice Tranter, honest we are Jimmy. It's just that it's over in the Splott welfare Club," she glanced to see his reaction.

"I see," Jimmy knew The Bomb only too well and he knew the lads that liked to hang out there.

"Bit rough isn't it for two young girls out on their own?"

"We're not going on our own Jimmy, well that's to say Alice is

146

seeing a boy George,…George Thomas, his Da owns that nice fish shop in Caroline street. George's bringing his brother Billy, so it will be the four of us. We'll be safe, Alice says she's been loads of times."

"Hmm, so you like this lad Billy then do you?" Jimmy didn't like the idea of his Ivy being the object of Billy's attention. Nobody sniffed around Jimmy's goods.

"Billy's nice enough, we've known each other since school, he's a friend nothing more. He's ever so shy; poor lad gets teased 'cos he's got this terrible skin. It's not his fault, but even his Da won't let him serve the customers fish suppers, in case he puts them off!" Ivy shook her head sorrowfully.

This piece of information gladdened Jimmy's heart. The lad was ugly and shy, perfect!

"You take care young lady, even if your Mam has her thoughts elsewhere, just remember *I'll* be watching you. I'll find out if you get up to any mischief." Jimmy wagged his finger.

"I'm off now Ivy, and remember what I said, I get to know *everything* that goes on around here… so I *will* be watching you." I gestured to his eyes and tapped the side of his nose.

147

Ivy heaved a sigh of relief as he turned to exit via the yard and lane. She was in no doubt, Jimmy did have eyes and ears everywhere, he would make it his business to know what she got up to.

Jimmy walked along the cobbles lost in thought, nicotine drifted deep into his lungs, sharpening his mind. Betty's behaviour was a turn up for the books, the old bird was fluffed up like a spring chicken of late. Betty had something up her sleeve, he needed to find out what she was up to and more importantly *who* she was carrying on with.

He made a mental note to have a word with Tudor, the doorman on The Bomb. He'd soon find out if Alice was being led astray by Alice Tranter.

Ivy belonged to Jimmy.

Chapter 12

Ivy got up extra early that Saturday morning to tackle the chores; she wanted the house looking immaculate, securing a place in Mam's good books and, more importantly, her date with Alice. It was vital to preserve Mam's sunny mood, if Mam got up prickly and scratchy, probing Ivy for details there could be trouble; the longer Mam stayed upstairs, out of Ivy's way the better.

At eight o'clock Ivy continued the charm offensive and took Mam up a cup of tea in bed served up in her best bone china cup covered in forget-me nots.

"Well, well Ivy, this is a nice surprise," Mam, sat up in bed painting her nails, she spoke through tight lips, face freshly slathered in a liberal layer of Ponds Cold Cream, a hairnet covering regimented rows of rollers. Two dark eyes blinked

149

out of the white mask.

"Just put it down over there, Ivy," Betty flapped a crimson paw in the general direction of the bedside table, "I'll have it in a minute when these are dry… don't want to risk smudging them now."

Ivy glanced around looking for a free surface to place the tea.

"Thanks Ivy darling,"

Mam never called her darling.

"Oh, and Ivy, whilst you're at it give the front room a bit of a going over this morning with the Bex Bisell make it look nice like."

"Yes Mam," Ivy turned to go.

"And make up the fire an' all, in case I want to sit in there with…er my friend this evening,"

"Course I will Mam,"

Ivy clomped back down the stairs, flicking a duster over the spindles as she went *…so that was why Mam was letting her go out tonight.*

By twelve o'clock all the kitchen surfaces were scrubbed, the hall front steps were swept, the front sitting room fireplace cleaned and laid ready for a match and the coal bucket filled.

Ivy worked up quite a lather running the carpet sweeper over the hall and the sitting room rugs, now her hair looked greasy and unkempt where her grubby fingers had trailed through it. She felt hot and sweaty.

Damn, she wouldn't have the time or the hot water to wash her hair this afternoon, it would never dry in time and she didn't want to rouse Mam's suspicions primping her appearance on a Saturday. A good brush would have to do.

Mam trailed downstairs in her dressing gown and curlers at one o'clock. Mam's face looked remarkably shiny and plumped up, three fat curlers marched across her hairline. She flopped onto a kitchen chair.

"Fetch us over that crusty bread and the chopping board Ivy," Betty gestured to the enamelled bread bin, "second thoughts you'd better cut me two slices, I can't risk chipping these," she waggled her nails in Ivy's direction. "Got to look my best," she winked at Ivy. "Stick a bit of that pork dripping on it and get some of the jelly too… plenty of salt mind."

151

Betty glanced around the kitchen, "you've been busy Ivy." She lit a cigarette, "you're a good girl for your Mam."

She dragged deeply on the cigarette. "Make us another cup of tea, I'm parched," she regarded Ivy through a scrunched-up left eye evading the plume of smoke she blew out of the corner of her mouth.

"So what are you up to this evening Ivy, off to one of those dances you keep going on about?"

"Yes Mam, I'm going with Alice," Ivy crossed her fingers; prayed her Mam wouldn't start to probe.

"Well, I'm trusting you to behave yourself. Make sure you're back home by ten thirty on the dot my girl or this will be the last time you'll be out." Betty gathered up her plate of bread and dripping and the hot strong tea. "I'm just going upstairs to have a little lie down for a couple of hours, my head's killing me, sleeping with these blasted rollers in all night, I barely got a wink of sleep, it's like sleeping on a log pile! The things we women have to put up with to look pretty." Betty grumbled and ambled back upstairs.

Mam eventually disappeared out of the house at six thirty.

152

With her new roll-on Betty had shaved pounds of her waist
and hips so her skirt clung in all the right places and the drape
of her blouse disguised the bulge at the top of her girdle. Her
curls were arranged to perfection and her make up applied
with particular care -Betty looked ten years younger than she
had of late and she felt a happy woman. *Gerald would
certainly notice, he often complimented her.*

Ivy clattered through the few dishes left in the sink from
Mam's tea and scrambled to give her shoes a quick polish
before she left for the Tranter's house in Adeline street.

She grabbed her battered handbag, an old cast off from Mam,
and ten shillings she had scrimped and saved in a jam-jar
under her bed. The thought of the night ahead made Ivy giddy
with excitement.

When Alice opened the door to Ivy, Alice's face fell. She
dragged Ivy indoors.

"Good Lord Ivy… what on earth have you been up to? Your
hair looks like you've been through a hedge backwards.
They'll never let us in with *you* looking like that!" Alice
shuffled her friend up the steep stairs to her bedroom. "Come
on we've only got half an hour to fix you up!"

"Sorry Alice I was so busy doing the chores I didn't have time to…." Ivy explained, tears prickled in her eyes. She caught sight of her scruffy appearance in the landing mirror. She did look a fright; no wonder Alice was cross.

"Get undressed, we need to get a wriggle on" Alice ordered. "Now bend over while I rub a bit of this stuff through your hair,"

Alice started sprinkling powder through the back of Ivy's hair, parting sections to add more powder, then rubbing it through.

"What are you doing" Ivy's voice was muffled as she stood bent at the waist.

Alice couldn't help but notice that under Ivy's slip she was still wearing just a vest. The young girl's knobby backbone and prominent ribs visible on her tiny frame.

"I'm using some Mini-poo. Stand up, now close your eyes." Alice brushed Ivy's hair vigorously one way then another.

"What is it?"

"It's a dry shampoo, only in your case we best hope it's a miracle worker…there that's looking better already." Alice

154

expertly teased Ivy's auburn hair into soft coppery waves framing the girl's delicate features. "It's my Mam's so I'd better not use too much, else she'll skin me alive."

Alice regarded her handiwork. "Here let's put your fringe over to one side Ivy…there we go, that's much nicer," Alice slipped a long hair grip in to secure the draped fringe in placed, "see it's almost like Veronica Lake's," she handed Ivy a small vanity mirror to admire the effect.

"Now let's get your make-up done."

"Make up!...My Mam will kill me if I get all painted up" Ivy looked terrified.

"You won't be *all painted up*! See I've got some on, just a bit and I'm not *all painted up*," she peered into Ivy's face. "now sit still and look up, I haven't got all day."

Alice spat onto the small black mascara block and scrubbed the little brush over the paste. "Now hold still… no fluttering else it'll be everywhere."

Ivy sat, statue like, gazing at the ceiling, controlling an overwhelming urge to blink. Alice slicked black paste onto Ivy's sandy lashes and from nowhere a glamorous feline

155

sweep appeared. Ivy's grey blue eyes looked almost pale turquoise against the rich black.

"Wow Ivy that looks fantastic… now the lipstick."

"Oh, not lipstick please Alice, if anyone was to see me and tell Mam," Ivy's heart was racing, Jimmy's warning etched in her mind.

Alice shot her a withering gaze. She dipped her finger in a pot of Vaseline and slicked Ivy's eyebrows into a tamed arch. "Honestly, Ivy, I don't know who you think is going to be watching us; still have it your way, *no* lipstick."

Alice started to undo the buttons on a short sleeved, sprigged green cotton blouse. It was a little old fashioned and even a little summery for the time of year, but it was very pretty. "Here put this on,"Alice handed it to Ivy.

Ivy shivered a little as the blouse slipped over her thin arms.

"That colour suits you Ivy, it sets off your hair, we can't help the short sleeves, but I've got a cardie you can borrow, anyway once we're in the club it will be warm enough."

The club…that sounded so glamorous.

"Now this is the tricky bit," Alice held up the green, tweed skirt to Ivy's slender hips. "You are such a skinny minx Ivy, still let's give it a go. I've already taken in the two seams at the side with a bit of running stitch and I've got a safety pin as well, just in case, we can't have the blessed thing falling around your ankles can we?"

Ivy stood obediently as Alice dressed her, she allowed herself to be pushed and prodded into shape. The skirt was pronounced *good enough if a little long* and when the same scruffy little Ivy Jenkins glanced in the landing mirror an attractive, groomed young woman looked back at her.

"Gosh thanks Alice," Ivy turned her head this way and that. Even she had to admit she looked quite fetching, not exactly pretty but still fetching none the less.

"Just call me a miracle worker! You do look nice Ivy, you're a very pretty girl you know." Alice beamed.

"We can roll your old dress up and if we squash it down it will get in that handbag of yours and then you can let me have Phyllis' things back next Saturday. Luckily for you, with me having an older sister there's always some hand me downs around the house."

Alice rummaged in the drawer and unearthed a light grey knitted cardigan. "Here this will do, now we better get a wriggle on." Alice looked at her watch, "heavens its nearly quarter past seven already, we've only got five more minutes else we'll be late meeting George and Billy."

Alice expertly outlined her lips with carmine pencil and slicked on a matte blood red bow before dabbing on a Vaseline gloss. *Mw, Mw*, she pressed her lips together. "Right, that's done, I'm ready Ivy…let's get our coats and we're ready for the off,"

Ivy gazed in amazement and awe at the glamorous creature who stood in front of her. She was humbled that Alice chose to be her friend.

The two girls rushed out of the house, anxious to avoid any questions. Alice called a brief goodbye to her Mam and Da before ushering Ivy out the front door. "Come on Ivy before Mam comes out and sees my lipstick," Alice yanked Ivy by the hand and linked arms. "It's only about fifteen minutes from here, with luck the boys will have saved us a seat."

Once out of sight around the corner, Alice whipped out a packet of Craven A and lit up, Ivy's eyes widened "I didn't

158

know you smoked Alice,"

"Oh, I don't really… I only smoke on weekends, I can't afford to smoke more often than that" she said airily, "an' it's just for the look of it really, film stars always look so mysterious and sophisticated when they do it," Alice gave a small cough, and cleared her throat, "I'm still getting used to it… here *you* have a try. It can make you feel a bit giddy at first."

Ivy took the proffered half smoked cigarette and sucked tentatively on the lip stick coated tip.

"No, not like that Ivy, … you've got to draw right through the filter! Here let me show you… like this," Alice took a deep drag and exhaled slowly, tilting her head backwards to dramatic effect. "Just imagine you're Rita Hayworth, now you try it."

Ivy held the cigarette between shaky fingers. This time, as instructed, Ivy took a deep drag, felt her head spin a little and a massive rush of nicotine course through her.

"Good?" Alice laughed.

 Ivy exhaled deeply; two pink roses had bloomed on her cheeks. "Gosh that made me feel proper light-headed, I

159

thought I'd float away."

The girls exploded into giggles and quickened the pace.

Even from across the street the girls could hear the hubbub. The club on the corner of Portmanmoor road had thrown its doors open, a snake of customers was weaving its way into the crowded bar.

A large doorman was waving some through and holding his hands up to others.

"What's going on Alice?" Ivy looked worried, perhaps they wouldn't be let in… she would just die if she wasn't let in.

"Don't worry Ivy they are just making sure the right people get in, we'll be fine; they always let pretty girls in then, if there's space the doorman lets in the others, that is if he likes the look of them." Alice strode confidently to the front of the queue; Ivy glued to her side.

"Evening Tudor, our friends are already inside," Alice flashed her best winning smile at the burly doorman, he gave both girls a hard stare and with a flick of a hand they sailed straight in.

"There they are," Alice waved wildly to George and Billy, she dragged Ivy over to where the two brothers had secured a small table near the stage and dance area.

A black Jazz singer accompanied by a small backing band was tuning up and just about to start his first number.

"Good evening Alice... evening Ivy, take a seat." George gestured to two stools tucked in the corner.

Billy smiled shyly at the newly transformed Ivy. He was nursing a half pint of beer out of the gaze of the watchful barman on the look-out for under-age drinkers.

"I got you girls a half of shandy each, it will be so full in here soon that we won't stand a chance of getting a drink in and remember if any-one asks you're *both* over eighteen." George fixed Ivy with a beady stare as he rose to let the girls move into the corner seats.

George was grateful Ivy had tried with her appearance; the girl looked quite pretty... very pretty in fact!

When Alice had said Ivy Jenkins would be joining them he'd worried the girl would draw a fuss from the doorman. Ivy never looked much older than fifteen at the best of times,

161

running around looking scared of her own shadow. But Alice had insisted she would not come without Ivy, so George had backed down.

"Thank you George," Alice purred. She plonked herself on the stool nearest to George's elbow. Ivy noticed that mysteriously another top button on Alice's blouse appeared to have popped open since leaving the house. Alice lit another cigarette, crossed her legs seductively and looked every inch the femme fatale.

Ivy didn't like to say that she didn't drink. The clothes and make up made her feel brave, a far more grown-up sophisticated version of her usual mousy self... it would be silly to make a fuss over shandy.

For the first time in a long time, she was having fun. The sins were piling up, but Ivy didn't care, tonight was going to be one to remember and nothing was going to spoil it. She felt happy and it was the best feeling in the world.

From the moment the rich, fruity voiced singer started to belt out his version of the hit "Near You," Ivy was floating in heaven.

Chapter 13

Gerald Williams sat waiting in the saloon of the Golden Cross public house... waiting for Betty. He was wearing his best shirt and his tie sported his lucky tie pin complete with a small diamond, bought as a gift to himself after a good win on the horses. He'd given his shoes a thorough polish front and back and trimmed his toothbrush moustache to perfection. He was early.

Gerald loved the old pub with its intricate tiled design that flared all over the exterior; the green and gold tiles caught the sun so that the walls glowed emerald on a bright day, a beacon that could be seen from yards away. The proximity to Betty's house suited them both and the spacious saloon bar meant they had some privacy.

Gerald nursed a whisky and a bottle of Mackeson and kept his eye on the door.

Gerald was not a stupid man; he knew Betty had been barred from the Nag's Head and he knew why. He knew what people thought of her, had heard them judge her... call her "slapper," heard them joke about her shrewish temper and drunken rages. But that was not the Elizabeth he knew.

The minute he first saw her that night, standing on the wharf, hovering in a shadowy doorway near where the working girls stood, his heart bled for her. Even under the fizzing orange lantern he had recognized her... it was Elizabeth Evans!

He'd been looking for trade that night, of course he had, anything to help quell the hungry loneliness within him just for a brief while. The sight of Elizabeth Evans hustling for business jarred him to his senses. Janet would be so disappointed in him seeking out prostitutes on the wharf.

Gerald was a simple man, but he did have faith in God. As the weeks wore on he began to believe he was meant to meet Elizabeth Evans that night and that he was meant to help her. God did move in mysterious ways.

Of course, Elizabeth didn't recognize him at first, she'd accepted his money just to have a drink with him, easy money for Betty. It took a long while before the penny dropped, then she was shamed.

To him she would always be sweet natured Elizabeth Evans,

the little girl who came into his shop with her mother Iris on a Saturday morning to buy vegetables. The polite young lass full of pleases and thank you's when his wife Janet gave her a toffee apple and made a fuss of the pretty girl...the one they never had... the one his Janet had so desperately longed for. He didn't know this hard-faced creature called Betty Jenkins.

It took some courage to let her know that he knew her secret over ten weeks ago. He could have used her like all the others did, but he didn't. Now she placed her trust in him, relaxed a little, safe in the knowledge he would respect her secret and he was grateful for it.

It had been over ten years since his wife Janet had died of cancer, he had nursed her as best he could, but his life was very lonely without her. He still lived in the old house in Inkerman street, their three sons had flown the nest long ago; married now with lives and families of their own. Rattling around in the old house, his days felt long and lacking purpose. After his Janet died the heart had gone out of him.

When Gerald had turned sixty, he'd handed over the reins of his green grocery business to his sons; Jack, Peter and Dafydd. They were running the profitable little shop now and had no real need of him. Sometimes he helped out when the shop was particularly busy, but Gerald felt put out to grass...redundant. He was lonely.

Gerald Williams just wanted someone to spend the rest of his time on God's earth with. He was short, fat, balding and sixty-three for heaven's sake, but he had his own home, most of his own teeth and a tidy amount of savings from his business in Wellfield Road and now if only Elizabeth would *let* him make her happy, *let* him look after her then, he would end his days a contented man.

Betty sashayed in through the swing doors. A jaunty felt hat perched fetchingly on her freshly curled hair. She gave him a warm smile. Gerald noticed that she had tried to look pretty for him. She was still a striking woman even after all this time. He stood up for her.

"Good evening Elizabeth." He took her coat and placed it neatly on the spare chair. Ever since their discussion all those weeks ago, he did not call her Betty when they were alone.

Betty coloured a little at the courtesies. Only Gerald ever treated her like a lady.

166

"You're looking lovely tonight," He noticed she was wearing his string of graduated pearls around her neck. They'd belonged to his Janet, he'd given them to his wife for their thirtieth wedding anniversary, it was such a shame she had only enjoyed wearing them for three short years before she passed away. The trinkets were wasted now... pretty things just lying in a box, it was good to see them being worn again. The pearls glowed against Elizabeth's neck.

"Would you like your usual Elizabeth?"

"I think I'd like a Port and Lemon please Gerald,"

He liked the way his name sounded on her tongue. "Coming up."

As the evening wore on he took her hand, he willed himself to be brave.

He cleared his throat. "Hmm...Elizabeth...I think there are a few things you should know, and I have a few things I need to say to you. Please hear me through." He kept his voice low.

"Of course, Gerald," she looked worried, things had been going so well. When she was with him the casual profanities and coarse expressions didn't drip off her tongue; the urge to

167

do battle with the world, seeing slights and snubs around every corner stilled for a while. With him she could relax, be Elizabeth.

"Your Da, Evan, was a hard man Elizabeth and in my opinion an old fool. When he threw you out, carrying that baby of yours it was the worst day's work he ever did… and I told him so. He bit my head off for my pains, cut me dead in the street after that he did, sanctimonious fool that he was. He fair broke your mother's heart, poor woman."

Betty looked shocked.

"My Janet sometimes asked your Mam how you were, asked about the baby. But Iris wouldn't say a word, said your Da had forbidden her to talk about you." Gerald shook his head sadly.

"It cut Janet like a knife it did to see your poor Mam so sad, but your Mam wouldn't go against him. Pig headed that's what Evan was."

Betty had always wondered why her Mam didn't try to get in touch, now she knew.

"When Evan died of heart attack a five years later, I said to my Janet that there was some justice in this world after all."

"Oh, please Gerald, don't say…"

"Shh Elizabeth I'm having my say," Gerald raised his finger to quieten her.

"If you cast a poor girl out on the streets what did he expect you to do? How did he expect you to live, there aren't many options for a girl in trouble especially if she doesn't try to do away with it?... Call himself a Catholic!"

Betty started to cry softly; raw wounds started to gape. She thought by now she was beyond hurt. The fact that this good, kind man had taken her side all those years ago touched her deeply.

"Don't cry Elizabeth, you mustn't upset yourself" he gave her his handkerchief. "What I wanted you to know is that I hold no blame on you whatsoever for the things you had to do to survive. To *me* you will always be Elizabeth Evans and I shall always be proud to know you."

Betty sniffed silently into his handkerchief. "You're a good man Gerald, but why are you telling me now? This is all water under the bridge." Her face was blotchy, all the careful artistry when she applied her make up washed away. Red and black smudges stained his handkerchief.

"I'm telling you because I want to look after you Elizabeth." He looked straight at her, held both her hands between his and kissed them.

"Elizabeth I know I'm not much to look at; too fat, too bald, too old," he laughed as she smiled at him. "You know I'm right! ... And some, in fact many, would say I'm a stupid, sentimental old fool, old enough to know better and they're probably right an' all."

Gerald nailed his courage to the sticking post.

"But you see I don't care what other people think, at my age I'm past caring on that score, I only care what *you* think. Please will you let me look after you Elizabeth?"

His voice was tender, she could see the look of hope in his eyes.

"But your sons?"

"My sons and their wives had better respect my wishes Elizabeth...they don't need to know the ins and outs of everything in my life. Your business is your own affair. If you wish to introduce yourself as widow Betty Jenkins then that's fine by me, but otherwise I'll always be proud to call you Elizabeth Evans and if other folk have a problem with that, then they can go hang for all I care."

Betty gathered her thoughts. Gerald was a good, kind man, and she knew that when they were sat together he looked old enough to be her father, or her customer! She never thought there would ever be a way back for her, back to respectability, back to being treated like a lady, but perhaps, even after all this time, there was a glimmer of hope?

"Gerald thank you, you're so kind, I er… I don't know what to say?" She had worn the hard-faced impenetrable armour of Betty Jenkins for so long now it had become part of her; a carapace that protected her from hurt and slights. Could she ever be Elizabeth Evans again?

"Elizabeth I'm not asking you to say anything, not *yet* anyway. I just want you to know I have a deep affection for you and if *you* wanted I could give you and of course Ivy a home with me." He looked flustered. He willed her not to turn him down.

"I wouldn't ask anything of you Elizabeth not in *that* way. You could start anew, leave this difficult life behind. You and Ivy can both start a new life, turn over a fresh leaf! … I just want you to think about it please. I'm a lonely man Elizabeth, if we can both help each other then, where's the harm? All I'm asking tonight is that you will *think* about my offer." He caught the startled look on her face.

"I know this is out of the blue Elizabeth, but if you promise me you'll consider it and then in a few of months, after you've got to know me, when you've had time to weigh things up… I'll ask you again." He willed her not to say no.

"Thank you Gerald, you're a kind, generous man and I *promise* I'll think about it."

Gerald looked at his watch, "I think it's time we went back now, I'll walk you to your doorstep Elizabeth."

As they walked arm in arm down Bute street Gerald felt content, a happy man. Elizabeth hadn't turned him down flat; he had hope.

They stopped outside the shabby front door; the house looked dark, empty and un-inviting. One light burned in the hallway;

172

it was only a quarter to ten.

"Would you like to come in for a little while Gerald. I could light the fire… maybe have a cup of tea?" Betty felt nervous, girlish even, she wasn't used to being treated with respect and it unsettled her. Betty Jenkins made deals, traded and she never brought men home.

"Not tonight thank you Elizabeth, maybe some other time," he kissed gently her on both cheeks.

"Thank you for a lovely evening." He raised his hat in salute. "Perhaps I could call for you on Monday, maybe we could go for a stroll, perhaps to the park?"

"I'd like that Gerald."

"Excellent, shall we say two o'clock on Monday then?"

Betty closed the door behind her. She caught sight of herself in the hall mirror, in the yellow glow of the hall light she looked deflated, fragile and old; the perky bounce and glow of only three hours ago had evaporated. She felt stripped back and vulnerable.

All those years dodging her past, hiding her true self, closing her mind to the disgusting things men did to her in exchange for money. Here was a man who wanted nothing more than companionship from her, who wouldn't use her, who didn't judge.

As Betty she had learned to survive, to overcome, to be fearless. Could she shake off Betty and take what Gerald had to offer; start caring again?

She heard the click of the back-door latch being raised. It was Jimmy, he was back early. Elizabeth couldn't face him tonight…nothing escaped Jimmy's snake like gaze, he had a knack for ferreting out secrets. She didn't need him asking questions, prodding and probing her for information. In the morning, after a night's sleep, Betty would be a match for anything Jimmy Benson had to say, but tonight Elizabeth wanted to be left in peace with her thoughts. She scuttled upstairs to her room before he could catch her in the hall.

Jimmy hung his heavy coat on the back of the door. He heard the creak of the stairs; Betty was back.

Jimmy's stomach growled; he was hungry, he rummaged around for something to eat. The heel end of a cob loaf was in the larder and the remains of a plate of cooked pig's chitterlings under a dish, it was a meagre supper, but it would have to do whilst he waited for Ivy to come home. The girl couldn't slip upstairs without him noticing; Ivy was not allowed a front door key yet.

At exactly twenty-nine minutes past ten Ivy let herself into the yard. Through the kitchen window she could see the back of Jimmy's head. Jimmy wasn't usually home on a Saturday evening; he was waiting for her.

Ivy's face was pink from running the last few hundred yards home and from the shy kiss Billy had given her after he had held her hand and walked her home. She stopped for a moment to catch her breath and composed herself. She let herself in.

"Evening Jimmy," she kept her mac wrapped around her, hoping he wouldn't spot her borrowed plumage.

"Evening Ivy," he scattered a liberal amount of salt on his supper. "Have you had a good night?"

"Yes thank you Jimmy," she kept her eyes low.

"Tudor tells me it was a busy evening at The Bomb."

So, he *had* been checking up on her!

He fixed her in a piercing stare, "you'd best scrub that muck off your face before your Mam catches you."

Ivy stood her ground, "it's only a bit of mascara Jimmy, Alice did it…it's just a bit of fun, it doesn't mean anything, plenty of girls my age are wearing it, I'm sure Mam won't mind, not this once."

"And do plenty of girls your age sit drinking with a pair of lads in a rough club in Splott of a Saturday night?"

Ivy stood lost for words, furious, she'd obviously been spied on all evening. Jimmy really did have eyes and ears everywhere.

"Always remember I'm watching you Ivy and I *will* find out everything that goes on, now you'd better scarper, your Mam is back already," he pointed to her skirt drifting below her mac, "and if she catches you wearing clothes you don't own she might have a few questions about the matter an'all."

Chapter 14

Weeks went by before Betty saw Jimmy, his rent money appeared on the kitchen table with pleasing regularity, and he usually came home after she and Ivy had gone to bed. Sometimes she heard the tread of his footstep up the stairs, and sometimes she heard him moving about on the landing, but otherwise they were like ships that passed in the night. Even Ivy seemed a little more elusive of late; she'd have to keep a closer eye on that!

Gerald Williams called at Bute street, three times a week, dependable as clockwork. The couple went for walks arm in arm together, he took her for tea and cakes to the Lyons tea house in Queen street and every day he grew a little more in her estimation; Betty was getting very fond of Gerald.

As the days and weeks passed they talked about this and that, but his offer was never raised. Sometimes he insisted on pressing a few pound notes in her hand *to help with the bills*, it was left unsaid between them that he recognized if she was out with him then she wasn't earning money. She had to live and provide for Ivy and he didn't judge her for it. Ultimately she would have to make choice and he hoped she would choose a life with him.

As the weeks went by Betty began to warm to the idea that maybe she *could* make a new life with Gerald, a better life for both her and Ivy. As he said why shouldn't they all be happy.

When Gerald called he always waited respectfully for her on the doorstep, one day when the weather was particularly inclement he stood just inside the hallway, but he never entered her domain.

He did not wish to enter the world of Bute street, he wanted her to walk back into his world.

It was to be another six weeks before Gerald met Jimmy Benson.

Jimmy was mending a broken fixing on Betty's front door. A stiff breeze, heralding the approach of autumn, had wrenched the rotten door off its hinge; chisel in hand Jimmy was attempting a repair.

"Good afternoon," Gerald tipped his hat. "Is Mrs Jenkins about?"

Jimmy recognised Gerald in an instant, he regarded him with interest. *The old boy was certainly making a lot of effort, he must have some intentions towards Betty.*

"Good afternoon Mr?"

"Mr Williams and you are Mr Benson, Betty's lodger, I presume?"

The men shook hands.

"Seems that this old door has seen better days, it's getting on a bit," Jimmy grinned. *A bit like you Mr Williams he added spitefully in his head.*

"I told Betty I'd do my best to patch it up. Her landlord doesn't keep the place up, never sorts any of the niggles out. Mrs Jenkins needs a man about place really, it's not easy for a woman on her own is it Mr Williams?" Jimmy glanced slyly at Gerald.

"Could you please give Mrs Jenkins a call for me." Gerald ignored the pointed comment. He didn't like the cut of

179

Jimmy's jib. From what Elizabeth had said Jimmy hailed from Dublin and could be unpleasant when he had a mind.

"Betty," Jimmy bellowed, "Mr Williams is here."

"Thank you. It's nice to meet you Mr Benson, and which part of Ireland are you from, I've got relatives in Dublin... perhaps you might know them?"

"Oh, I shouldn't think so. I'm from just outside Dublin Mr Williams...I don't really know many people in the city."

Gerald could recognize a lie when he saw one.

Betty positively skipped down the stairs. "Afternoon Gerald." She turned to Jimmy, "thanks for fixing the door Jimmy, the blasted thing has been threatening to break off that hinge for ages."

She took Gerald's arm, "Ivy's got some pig's liver and cabbage for dinner tonight, tell her to make sure she gives it a good going over before she cooks it for you Jimmy. I don't want any tubes left in, fair turns my stomach if liver hasn't been treated right," Betty gave a shudder. "I'll have mine a bit later on."

Jimmy gave a mock salute," I shall follow orders Mrs Jenkins."

Gerald narrowed his eyes "Ah a military man I see, and which regiment did you serve in Mr Benson?"

Jimmy gave him a calculated stare. Gerald Williams was being a little too nosey for his liking.

"Oh, Jimmy wasn't fit to serve," Betty chipped in quickly. She knew Jimmy's lack of military service was a sore point. "Shall we be off then Gerald?"

Betty felt that having the two men side by side on her doorstep was like a collision between her two worlds and it unnerved her. Tension bubbled up in her chest.

Away from home she slipped between the two worlds effortlessly, separate compartments. When the two worlds came together it frightened her.

Could she hope to leave this life as Betty behind for good and start anew with Gerald?

As Betty her language coarsened, she felt her suspicious, grasping nature roar to the surface. She could spot an opportunity to make money a mile off, sniff out a fool in moments and pick a fight in a paper bag.

Betty knew she presented a hard, calculating face to the world, *a don't mess with me* attitude that warded off trouble. She might have created Betty Jenkins to survive but all the years of having to lie and scheme, drowning her miseries in booze to rise above the jibes and slights had shaped her into what she was. Was Elizabeth Evans still under this armour?

When Betty lay awake at night pondering what to do she was terrified. In some ways it was easier being Betty; nobody expected her to act well or achieve much. She didn't care what people thought; if they didn't like her then they could go hang. Betty answered to no-one! All that had ever mattered to Betty was keeping Ivy safe, saving Ivy from a life like hers.

Today Gerald wanted her to see his home in Inkerman street for the first time. It was a big step for them both. She would be entering his world.

Part of her was desperate to leave her life in Bute and sample the simple pleasures of a decent home again. She was getting too old to be selling herself especially when she had a chance to abandon that life for good. Part of her was terrified about

182

trying to go back to acting respectably, minding what the neighbours thought; playing by the rules.

She had a decision to make; Gerald deserved an answer.

Betty knew it wouldn't be plain sailing if she decided to go ahead with his proposal. Some of his neighbours might recognize her, might ask awkward questions. Even if they didn't ask questions, they looked such an odd couple together it was bound to provoke comment, get the net curtains twitching.

Betty had been relieved and saddened to hear that her Mam Iris had moved away from the area years ago. Relieved she wouldn't run into her mother and saddened she had lost her. All she knew now was that Mam had gone to live with a spinster Aunt in Canton. Betty had no idea if Mam was alive or dead, she kept a small hope alive that one day she might find her.

Gerald said she needed to hold her head high, if he could cope with sneers and comment then so could she. But could she? Stripped of her "Betty armour" she was as soft and quivering like a newly cracked snail waiting to be pecked out of its shell by a sharp beaked thrush.

183

In her heart she knew there was only one sensible decision, each day the house in Bute street got a bit more decrepit, each day it didn't make any sense that she was struggling to make ends meet. If today was a success she would have to make some changes, give Jimmy his notice and most importantly, tell Ivy her plans.

The only cloud on her horizon would be telling Ivy, she wasn't too sure how much to tell the girl about the arrangement without unpicking her past as Elizabeth Evans.

Ivy was such a good girl, Betty felt sure the girl would do as she was told...surely Ivy wouldn't rock the boat.

Betty still wasn't certain if she could go back to the streets of Roath; seeing Gerald's house today in Inkerman street was to be the first step.

CHAPTER 15

The year was wandering along at a sedate pace, mornings were still soft and warm; an evening chill had not yet arrived.

Betty was still seeing Gerald Williams as far away from Bute street as she could. She rarely bothered about what Jimmy was up to these days. Even when he was a bit late with the rent she seemed not to care so much, the ferocity of Betty's tantrums had calmed, Jimmy's life became easier.

Ivy, much to the girl's delight, was being allowed out more often, which didn't suit Jimmy at all. Sometimes he would follow Ivy to see where she went, who she met with, or he had reports sent back to him about her whereabouts. He was determined to bring Ivy into line. She needed to know he was in charge, even if Betty was taking her eye off the prize he certainly wasn't.

A lack lustre August had slithered away in a squall of rain showers but the Autumn was showing great promise. The day had been hot, and Jimmy sauntered along Bute street heading for the Nags' Head. He needed a pint of beer.

Jimmy Benson was beginning to feel well and truly at home in his adopted City of Cardiff, his youthful exploits and sins in the bars and parks of Dublin was another world away.

In Cardiff when men walked past Jimmy in the streets around the docks, they tipped their hats. Jimmy Benson had earned a reputation that demanded respect, he was a friend of Black Harry now.

Betty frequented other pubs now, Victor had not relented, she was still barred from the Nag's head which suited Jimmy. Jimmy could drink in peace and mind his own business without worrying about Betty's nosey snout keeping an eye on his dealings.

The more they kept out of each other's hair the better, as far as he was concerned.

If Jimmy needed to talk to people, then a quiet booth tucked away in the Nag's head became his office. People knew where Jimmy Benson could be found if there was a deal to be done.

When Jimmy entered the bar of the Nag's Head stools were vacated. He'd assumed the mantle of an important man in Tiger Bay. Even better in the convivial smoky fug of the Nag's Head bar Jimmy was now shown all the respect that John Price certainly owed him.

John had learnt his lesson about gossiping the hard way, his nose would always have a crook in it. When invited to gossip, particularly about Jimmy Benson John kept his opinions to himself.

"Yes Mr Benson… No Mr Benson…if you say so Mr Benson, is there anything else I can do for you Mr Benson? Thank you very much Mr Benson."

The humiliation of John Price was nailed to the mast like the proverbial albatross for all to see.

Word had got around that Jimmy Benson was not a man to be

crossed.

But today, apart from looking forward to a well-deserved pint, Jimmy was on a mission. It was business. Black Harry's business.

Black Harry had come into possession of a large quantity of cigarettes and Jimmy needed to find buyers. Jimmy needed to keep his eyes and ears open, couldn't afford to attract the wrong sort of attention when he was going about his business. Black Harry was particular about keeping business private.

In this cocoon of comfort Jimmy felt cock of the walk, Lord of the neighbourhood, but behind the doors of twenty-two Bute street he had to admit he'd become a little reckless of late.

Jimmy and Betty it seemed had reached an amicable agreement; they stayed out of each other's way and the household rubbed along fine and dandy. Betty collected his rent and with Betty's thoughts elsewhere, he had a lot of time to himself with Ivy.

The other evening, after being stood several rounds in the

Nag's head and feeling like a king, Jimmy had broken his own house rules. Whilst Betty snored like a navvy in her bed, he'd gone too far with his sweet little Ivy. Crossed a line.

The drink had been upon him and he'd made her go all the way. If it hadn't been for all that whiskey it wouldn't have happened, he'd told himself. He was stupid but thank God the girl hadn't called out and roused Betty.

Still, he reckoned Ivy owed him; he'd done plenty for her over the weeks, it was a return on his investment.

Okay, so she'd said *No* a few times, when he told her to lie still, but she hadn't really objected much. For days before he'd showered Ivy with treats and trinkets, called her *Princess* and promised to take her to "flicks" next week.

She must have known something was up; must know he'd want something in return. Jimmy convinced himself Ivy was willing, well at least not *un*willing as far as he was concerned she was just learning a lesson about the way the world worked.

 He did feel a twinge of regret the next day, when he caught Ivy crying in the kitchen over the bowl of dirty laundry, tired

189

eyes testament to a sleepless night.

But what did she expect? The girl might be young, but surely not such a fool as to think men just shelled out for nothing. How did she think her Mam earned her money? If it wasn't for *his* rent money, then Ivy would probably be out standing in doorways herself, alongside all the other poor girls earning their living in Tiger Bay.

The girl was scrubbing away at a bed sheet as if her life depended upon it, trying to erase the stains of shame she'd found that morning.

Ivy knew her Mam's suspicions would be aroused if she was caught washing bed linen on a Wednesday. She'd have to say it was her *monthlies* if Mam asked; she couldn't possibly admit the truth.

He'd given Ivy a wink and told her she looked pretty but the girl still looked subdued and miserable, cowed even, like a beaten puppy. He'd have to be extra nice to her; get back into her good books.

Shouldn't piss on your own doorstep Jimmy boy, first rule of survival.

190

He'd make it up to Ivy. Keep her sweet; she'd be right as rain in a few days.

That night two bars of chocolate appeared on Ivy's pillow.

Jimmy kept out Ivy's way and took his urges out on the working girls that hung around the docklands and alleyways at night. There were plenty of skinny, young girls with hard eyes and old faces trading themselves for a man with money. Some of the girls hanging around the seedy haunts of Tiger Bay were younger than Ivy; girls barely out of school with empty bellies and hungry siblings waiting back home.

Girls helping to pay the rent.

Jimmy always sought out the freshest faces on the quay; he was getting a name for himself amongst the working girls in Tiger Bay as a man with certain tastes.

At a price there was something for everyone in the melting pot of the Cardiff docklands. For a while Jimmy would pay other girls to satisfy his desires.

Chapter 16

Jimmy was sat on a bench in the watery sunshine next to his friend Sean Riley smoking his fourth cigarette. Dragging deeply on the short stub, Jimmy used the dog end of one cigarette to light his next. "D'you want one Sean" Jimmy, in generous mood, proffered the open packet.

"Thanks Jimmy, and if it's all the same to you I'll keep it for later." Sean tucked the Woodbine neatly behind his ear.

Sean was visiting Jimmy's patch for a change. Jimmy wanted a quiet chat away from the regulars in Sean's usual local, the Duke of Edinburgh. The Irish Bar in the Duke was too gossipy sometimes for Jimmy's liking for doing business.

The two men leaned against the wall of the Nags Head pub companionably sipping their pints of ale in the warmth of the late autumn sunshine, the stone wall warming their backs. The pub was one of Jimmy's favourites, especially now Betty was barred- at least he could have a drink there without her sticking her nose in.

Sean Riley was a chatty amiable man, liked to share his thoughts and opinions on the world with anyone who would listen. He was a gang master on Queen's dock; a Belfast lad, he had docking running through him like words through a stick of rock. Sean was a popular man with a ready wit; he was known to be firm but fair.

The men took Sean into their confidences, tipped him the wink if trouble was brewing; he was one of them. If ever Jimmy wanted to find out a nugget of information or to test out some dock yard gossip, then Sean was the man to ask.

Nearly three years ago Sean had been honourably discharged from the Royal Navy after being diagnosed with hearing loss in his left ear thanks to coming under intense shell fire off the coast of Dunkirk. Sean counted himself lucky to have come out of his Naval service with nothing worse than a bit of deafness and all four limbs intact. Too many of his mates never made it back.

After Sean's discharge he gravitated from Belfast to the bustling Cardiff dockyard and never looked back. At thirty-three years of age the chirpy Belfast man was lean, well-muscled and as fit as a butcher's dog.

Sean was currently living in a single, cramped room in a draughty, three bedroomed house, part of *Bute villas* in Ellen Street. The street was at the heart of the Irish community of Cardiff known as Newtown to the locals, but *Little Ireland* to sniffy outsiders who despised the poor immigrants. Newton was chock full of his fellow Irish Catholics living in equally cramped unsanitary conditions.

Ellen street, like many others around the dockland area had suffered during the nightly bombing raids on the docks. The pockmarked, grubby rendered facades, and cracked brick work were testament to the nightly punishment meted out in the bid to destroy the vital coal port. Ellen street was a ribbon of drab grey terraces not bothered by trees or even so much as a blade of grass, and it housed huge Irish families all crammed into tiny rooms. Children, often ten or twelve to the house, spilled out into the streets playing until it was too dark to stay out longer. Girls without shoes playing hopscotch and scraggy lads throwing pebbles at the train that rattle along the end of their street.

Sean was staying in the box room of number twelve with widow Isla Murray and her fifteen-year-old son Craig. Isla just about scraped by with rent from her lodger Sean and

194

young Craig's wages. The battered house, once part of a long, skinny terrace, had lost its companion during the Blitz. A Luftwaffe bomb had destroyed the end house in 1941 leaving only a mound of rubble and a small bedroom fireplace hanging drunkenly mid-air, ribbons of floral wallpaper still clinging to the chimney breast. Number twelve Bute Villas was now promoted to be last in the row with only four thick wooden props to support it.

"Can't say I'm looking forward to another winter in that bloody, freezing house, not if it's as vicious as last year. Draughts 'ave got fifty ways to get in, I can tell you Jimmy it's torture, sheer bloody torture living there." Sean said by way of introducing his piece of news. "It's fair to say on a windy night that it's a marvel the whole bloody terrace doesn't just collapse like a set of dominos, there's only a couple of bits of wood holding the dam thing up."

"I thought you navvies were used to just a few pit props holding things up!" Jimmy chuckled.

"Bloody cheek, I'm not a navvy, and you know it-you're a cheeky sod Jimmy Benson!" Sean whistled. "At least the Council had a bit of sympathy for a former serving man, when

I talked to them about living in that shit hole last week," Sean caught Jimmy's offended look and realized he'd struck a low blow.

"No offence Jimmy like. It's not your fault you didn't serve, I know you've got your injuries too mate."

Jimmy had allowed the myth to grow up that he'd been savagely beaten up after defending a young lass from some Dublin bar room drunks and that his gallantry had cost him the sight in his eye.

"I mean, I know as much as any man," Sean said rubbing his left ear. "If the Brass say you're not fit to serve, then you're not fit to serve so, no shame there."

Honour settled Sean moved swiftly on "Any way, as I was saying to that Council man, something ought to be done about getting decent housing for those poor beggars who got bombed out like the Kelly family who copped it at number fourteen... an' he gave me this." Sean unfolded a small well-thumbed leaflet from his trouser pocket and passed it to Jimmy.

"Here just you take a look at this."

196

Ely Taff Vale and Cyfartha Housing Development Area

COUNCIL HOMES FOR HEROES

COUNCIL HOMES FOR FAMILIES

"Massive so it is!   Apparently, they're putting up hundreds of new houses. First they're building some of those temporary ones. Prefabs he called them, and later in the New Year, it'll be proper brick built, family homes with gardens as well. Council owned they'll be with low rents."

The snippet of information caught Jimmy's interest.

"They're planning a second phase now, and they're starting a waiting list.   Don't reckon I'd be paying much more for a proper little house to rent with the Council, than I would for a few scrubby rooms around here." Sean enthused.

Jimmy started to read the leaflet. At the back was a long list of qualifying criteria.

"Just imagine Jimmy, having a *whole* bloody house instead of just one crappy room.... an' maybe a garden." Sean sighed. "I'd love a little garden, so I would. I'd grown my own

197

vegetables; perhaps a few potatoes, and broad beans with some marigolds in amongst them to keep the black fly off and some nice, sweet leeks.... and maybe even keep a couple of chickens if there was room - just think about it! It's been itching at me for days now Jimmy, so it has. Any way I've decided I'm going to give it a go. What do you reckon?"

"Says here you've got to be married to qualify." Jimmy pointed to the list on the back page.

"Well, that part of it will be sorted, in no time at all," Sean chuckled. Sean fancied himself as a bit of a lady's man, but he'd set his cap at Eileen Murphy; a twenty-one-year-old, green eyed, beauty with raven hair from an old Dublin family who worked in a fruit and vegetable packing warehouse on Queen's quay.

Eileen was a kind, sensible girl with a smile that lit up the room and Sean was smitten. They'd been courting for six months now and Eileen being a good Catholic girl hadn't let Sean get past first base.

"It's about time I settled down anyway. Last night I asked Eileen to marry me. My old Mam is always telling me to find a nice, decent Irish girl to keep me in order. Scruffy bastard that I am." Sean joked.

"That you are!" Jimmy laughed. "Many congratulations." He shook Sean by the hand. "But it says here priority given to families, so you'd better get a move on."

"That's the bloody bit I've been wanting to fix for months now!" Sean said ruefully, "my Eileen was having none of it without a ring on her finger. So now she's said *Yes* I suppose the quicker the deed is done the better. An' the quicker I can get her in the family way!" Sean sipped his beer as he warmed to his theme of married life.

"Breed like bloody rabbits the Riley's do, I'm one of six myself. My Mam used to say that just a look from my Dad was enough to fetch another baby on her. Oh, aye once Eileen becomes Mrs Riley she'll catch soon enough." Sean guffawed.

"Any way I decided to ask her last night after I read that notice, no point hanging around now, especially her being Catholic. Quicker we can get ourselves on that Council housing list the better I reckon."

"Well good luck to you Sean." Jimmy shook him by the hand. "I only hope Eileen doesn't have the good sense to run a mile before you get her to the altar!"

Jimmy ran his eye over the list; *married former serving men with families and possibly other dependants living in cramped or unsanitary conditions* were most likely to get allocated housing.

"Says here if you have a dependant relative living with you that helps with your application. Fancy getting Eileen's Mam to come in with you to boost your chances?"

Sean rolled his eyes, "Come on Jimmy! Have you ever met Eileen's Mam? She's like a bloody battleship that woman, she might only be a scrape over five foot, but God help us if she's riled. She's like a massive unstoppable force, comes out with all guns blazing she does. I've seen less fire power on a frigate!" Sean shook his head.

"I reckon old man Murphy couldn't wait to hop into his grave for a bit of peace and quiet! No Jimmy I couldn't live with Ida Murphy for all the tea in China."

"Well in that case, you'd better hope Eileen cops for twins to help push your score up!" Jimmy quipped. He didn't think it would be helpful to point out that as the old Irish saying goes, before wedding a lass you'd best take a good look at the Mother. Apples rarely fall far from the tree.

A soft peal of church bells drifted across the roof tops chiming the end of Friday midday mass for the faithful at the Holy Church of St Paul's. The church, with its tall bell tower still intact despite best efforts of the German Luftwaffe, was three streets away on the corner of Tyndall street but the chimes carried right across the mean terraces of Tiger Bay.

"Oh my God is that the bloody time already! I best be off Jimmy, my Eileen wants me to go to see the Minister with her, discuss what I've got to do before he'll let us get wed. Apparently they've got to try and make a good Catholic out of me first." Sean joked.

"Well, that might take the poor old Minister some time," Jimmy snorted.

"I can't hang around all day gassing with you Jimmy." Sean stood up to go, he threw the last of his pint down his throat. "An' if my Eileen catches me smelling of booze when I'm meeting Father Malone, there'll be hell to pay." He grinned.

Jimmy ground his thumb into the table to show what he

thought of that. "You need to put your foot down Sean else who knows where it'll end. You don't want Eileen turning out like her mother do you?"

Sean laughed, grabbed his jacket and dashed down the street.

Fool. No bloody woman will be telling Jimmy Benson what to do; bossing him around and telling him what time he had to be home of an evening.

The housing pamphlet lay abandoned on the bench; Jimmy tucked it in his pocket; it might come in handy if he could pull a few strings. If some bleeding heart in the Council was willing to provide a nice little house in a fresh new area, then Sean was right, that prospect certainly had possibilities.

CHAPTER 17

Ivy was working for a few weeks in the Duke of Edinburgh pub. Terry Flanagan had offered her the job at short notice; she was keen to make a good impression. It was only 10am and she'd already given all the shelves and glasses a good polish and now she was starting on the tarnished brass work around the bar area. It felt good to be away from the usual pubs in Bute and her mother's beady eye. Mr Flanagan seemed pleased with her work, she hoped it might lead to better things.

Her Mam had been none too pleased that she was working over in Newton, she preferred to keep Ivy closer to home where she could keep an eye on her, but Jimmy's assurances that Ivy would come to no harm had swayed her.

Fifteen-year-old Noreen Nolan who usually cleared up and washed the glasses for Terry was off sick with a bad case of Scarlatina. The poor girl had picked the infection up from one of her nine younger siblings and was confined to the same crowded bed, that she probably caught it in in the first place, until she and the rest of the brood recovered.

Terry Flanagan the landlord of The Duke, had been desperate to find a temporary replacement, honest hardworking staff were hard to come by. Sean Riley had tipped Terry the wink about Ivy Benson.

"She's a cracking good lass Terry, comes from Bute street; she's a hardworking girl with a good way about her, she'll turn her hand to anything."

"How do you know her then Sean, you've not been flirting with Bute street girls have you? Cos Eileen will have your guts for garters if you have," Terry joked, he was fond of the jovial Irish lad.

"Get away with you Terry, I'm soon to be happily married man! Na…it was Jimmy Benson's idea- he has rooms over there with Ivy's Mam, he suggested her when you said you were shorthanded; said Ivy was a hard worker."

Terry cast a glance over in Ivy's direction. The girl was cleaning out the pump slop trays. "She's not a bad looking lass either, despite that limp of hers; a bit too skinny though for my liking. I must admit I found it hard to believe the lass was seventeen. You could have knocked me over with a feather when she first came in. Noreen is fifteen but you'd swear it was Ivy who were the younger."

"Well, Terry she's certainly showing willing, however old she looks," Sean saw Ivy get down on her hands and knees to polish the brass footrest that circled the wooden bar. "Jimmy says her mother Betty works the girl pretty hard, so she's used to grafting and she keeps her on a tight leash, no going out or messing around with lads. I reckon you've fallen on your feet with that one... perhaps you ought to keep her on."

"Hmm, perhaps I ought...at this rate she's certainly giving Noreen a run for her money. I'll think on it." Terry knew the Nolan family needed the money, but he'd never seen Noreen put her back into it like Ivy was. After all business was business.

He'd told Ivy the job was hers for the next four weeks until New year was over, so he didn't need to rush the decision.

Chapter 18

January 1949

Even in January on any given Saturday evening the atmosphere in the Nag's Head was lively, but this Saturday evening the pub was so busy it was humming. Several boats had docked during the week and there were plenty of men from all over the globe roaming the City bars looking for a good time. Raucous laughter drifted out into the street.

Jimmy had spent most of his evening in the company of three sailors fresh off a cargo boat from Belfast. Over foaming mugs of beer, the men cracked jokes and told tales of his homeland. Jimmy was enjoying himself enormously. In the company of his fellow countrymen his accent deepened, and they embraced him like a long-lost brother.

The bar room was hot, smoky and jammed with customers. Victor the landlord was pulling pints and holding court behind the glossy wooden counter, surveying his domain. He liked the Irish lads; they were heavy drinkers and good for business.

Just so long as they behaved themselves, they were welcome at the Nag's.

Victor prided himself on running an orderly pub, any hint of trouble and the culprits were out on their ears. He kept a weather eye out for any tensions or rowdy behaviour. So far, the evening was passing amicably; lads queued at the bar jostling good humouredly as empty glasses vied for attention from the landlady Daisy.

Daisy, Victor's wife of some twenty years, spent the evening pulling pints and encouraging the sailors to part with their money. "Right, you are then my 'andsomes… Who's next? Come on lads speak up."

A forest of impatient hands waggled tankards over the bar.

"Just put another pint of Worthy in there Mrs and why not have a drink for yourself while you're at it." A clatter of coins skittered across the counter and secured Daisy's attention.

"Why thank you kindly Paddy. I'll take for a half then and I'll have it later, if it's all the same to you" Daisy fluttered her eye lashes at the gormless young sailor who leered at her over the bar. Daisy didn't drink.

Daisy adjusted her ample bosom and drew the pimply faced lad a fresh pint. "Here's your change then my 'andsome.... mind how you go now." Daisy winked.

The lad blushed and his friends cackled with laughter.

Some old boys sat in the corner nursing their pints, playing a quiet game of Cribbage. As the bar filled up a lively crowd of young locals had challenged the sailors to an impromptu darts match. Nags Head locals against visitors. To balance the numbers Jimmy was playing on the Irish visiting side. Out of sight of Victor's eagle eyes, bets were being placed on the outcome of the game.

"Double top again! God's teeth Jimmy, you might have mentioned you were an ace darts player. I'd have placed a few sovs on you myself if I'd known! Bloody hell you're smashing us!" Sean Riley grumbled from the side-lines; he was beginning to regret loyally backing the Nag's Head lads. Sean's team were on course for a crushing defeat.

"Talk about hiding your light under a bushel you sly old dog!" Sean watched the score creeping towards the inevitable defeat. Jimmy had only one dart left and needed twenty-seven to win.

Despite his bad eye Jimmy was proving to be a demon with his arrows. The Irish sailors roared him on. "Come on Jimmy lad.... you can do it!"

Jimmy composed himself, planted his right foot forward, took aim and let loose his final dart. The dart arched slightly before hitting the board with a mighty thump just inside the treble nine.

"Yessss!" Jimmy punched the air triumphantly. The visiting Irish crowd erupted. Jimmy took a bow, soaking up the roars of victory.

"Well done Jimmy lad. Go on give us your glass then, you must have worked up a thirst with all that arm lifting. I think this round of drinks is on me!" Sean patted his friend on the back.

"Just remember, you're on *our* team next time." Sean joked. He trotted off to buy the pints leaving Jimmy to savour his victory.

A throng of triumphant Irish sailors headed for the bar, eager to beat the crush.

Jimmy decided he needed a sit down and headed for the far

corner of the room to nab a newly vacated bench. As he made his way through the bustle, for a fleeting moment, his eyes were drawn to a brawny figure propping up a pillar next to the bar.

Dressed in blue overalls the thick set man stood slightly apart from the crush supping his pint of stout. The throng heaved and scrummed in front of the bar area. Thirsty men jostled to get Daisy's attention. As she handed out some glasses a few lads gave way leaving a small gap for some new customers to fill. In the moment that the space opened their eyes met, and for Jimmy the recognition was electric. *Seamus O'Malley!*

The last time Jimmy had seen Seamus it had been on a dark wet night in a back alley in Dublin. Jimmy was being taught a hard lesson for his sins against the O'Malley family, particularly for his transgressions against the youngest of the family, Deirdre O'Malley.

Deirdre was a sweet natured, impressionable, thirteen-year-old with porcelain skin, ice blue eyes and chestnut hair that tumbled down her back in soft waves. A good Catholic girl, Deirdre was the apple of her father's eye and being the youngest in the family, she was the darling of her three protective brothers: Seamus, Craig and Donal.

At her school, the only useful things that the elderly nuns had managed to teach young Deirdre was to love Jesus and to keep herself pure for her future husband by keeping her legs firmly together at all costs.

That fateful Saturday afternoon Deirdre and her friend Kathleen had been strolling through Phoenix Park hand in hand, laughing and giggling. The two girls had been flattered when the smiling man on the park bench called them over them and offered them both cigarettes if they would sit with him. They had laughed when he told them a dirty joke about a fat lady and a priest. But when Jimmy tried to put his hand up Deidre's skirt the booming voice of sister Annunciata echoed in her head and reminded her of her duty.

Deirdre had jumped up like a scalded cat, screamed blue murder, and kicked Jimmy hard on the shins. The two girls had streaked home, as fast as their legs would carry them to tell her Da about the dirty man lurking in the park.

That evening Jimmy didn't spot he was being followed until it was too late. Herded into an alleyway the punches rained down. Despite his own skills with his fists, Jimmy was powerless to defend himself from the bruising. He was pinned against the alley wall, his arms held in the vice like grip of Donal O'Malley, Deidre's protective brother.

Donal was the younger, smarter and meaner of the three O'Malley brothers. If Donal was the brains, then Seamus was the brawn and Seamus hammered home his advantage on Jimmy's gut. Craig O'Malley kept watch at the entrance of the alley way to ensure no-one came to Jimmy's rescue.

Jimmy was trapped, like a rat in a sack and without any means to defend himself, Jimmy's face and abdomen sucked up the blows like a punch bag. All protestations about mistakes being made and no offence being intended fell on deaf ears. The O'Malley brothers were in no mood to listen to excuses. Their father Brendan had sent them on a mission to teach Jimmy Benson a lesson and they were delivering the message loud and clear.

This is for Deidre you filthy bastard.... if we ever catch you sniffing around schoolgirls again, you'll live to regret it, you pervert! As Jimmy had slumped to the floor Donal rammed the message home with his boot.

"Stay away from our little sister Deirdre! Now get out of here 'an if you know what's good for you, you'll sling your hook. We don't want the likes of you around here, nobody does!" Seamus snarled as he planted a well-aimed boot on the retreating backside of Jimmy Benson.

Jimmy winced as the memory of that brutal night came back to him. Seamus held Jimmy's gaze across the bar room; his eyes squinted in the fug of the bar; a flicker of recognition crossed his face. The crowd suddenly surged and swirled in front of Seamus blocking his view, creating a wall of bodies between the two men.

Jimmy spotted his opportunity to escape. Before Seamus could make a move, Jimmy grabbed his coat and eased towards the rear entrance. In a trice he slipped out the door to the toilets in the back yard and legged it.

Jimmy vaulted the fence, jinked to the left and in a bid to put as much distance as he could between himself and Seamus O'Malley, he dived down the first alley in the road behind.

Once away from the immediate danger of the Nag's Head Jimmy could scarper onto safer territory. Jimmy knew the twisting, dark lanes of Bute town like the back of his hand. His feet pounded the cobbles, dodging left and right. Legs

213

and heart pumping, driving him further and further away from the bar. Not daring to stop and catch his breath until Jimmy was certain there was no chance Seamus, and his mates would be able to follow him. Jimmy wasn't taking any chances, he scuttled back to the familiar comfort and anonymity of twenty-two Bute Street.

He'd be keeping away from the Nag's head for a while; best keep his head down and lie low for a bit. Jimmy crept stealthily; cat like he felt his way up the pitch-black alleyway behind Bute street. He kept close to the wall dodging the greasy puddles and uneven cobbles.

In the distance a squawking cat fight sent bins clattering, a few dingy lights sparked on. Only the red, pin prick glow of his cigarette gave him away in the inky blackness.

Jimmy was dragging heavily on the last couple of inches of his Woodbine, the harsh nicotine flooding into his system. He sucked the smoke deep into his lungs to quell the jitters. *Damn you Seamus O'Malley an' those no-good brothers of yours.*

As Jimmy calmed his nerves before slipping through the back door to the yard, he pondered this latest turn of events. The

214

sight of Seamus O'Malley in the bar had thoroughly rattled his nerves. He thought he'd left all that behind him in Dublin and now Seamus turns up just like some bloody bad penny, large as life and drinking in Jimmy's local.

It would be just his luck if Seamus started a bit of rumour and gossip about him.

Use your brain Jimmy boy, that's the answer... come on use your brain! The bar had been dark and crammed with sailors. It was over five years ago when they last met in that dark alleyway, Seamus wasn't the sharpest knife in the drawer, and he didn't have his brothers with him now as back up. Jimmy was probably panicking over nothing.

After a few slugs of Whisky to calm his nerves Jimmy managed to talk himself down, but just to be on the safe side, he vowed steer clear of the Nag's Head until all the latest boats had left dock and there would be plenty of blue water between himself and Seamus O'Malley.

Chapter 19

Ivy loved working in the Duke of Edinburgh. January had come and gone and no more was said about young Noreen Nolan coming back any time soon.

"She's a cracker that little lass Ivy" Terry observed. "Really good with the customers…Old Donald there thinks she's an angel, told me as much the other day."

Whilst wiping down the tables Ivy was chatting to the elderly Donald Potter who liked to nurse his pint of Guinness and warm himself by the pub fire. Old Donald was such a fixture in the Duke he was like part of the furniture. No-one ever joined the old boy for a drink though and Ivy took pity on him.

Every day about lunch time, without fail, eighty-year-old Donald came into the bar with Scamp his Jack Russell terrier. He headed straight for *his* chair next to the fireplace and settled in for the afternoon with his magazine and a slow burning pipe that he sucked and nurtured. Donald, a keen pigeon fancier, and former President of the Welsh Homing Pigeon Union, spent his afternoons studying his pigeon magazine, comparing form and breeding lines over a pint.

"Well, that lass must have the patience of a saint listening to Donald witter on about his pigeons every day." Sean chuckled. "Before she knows it she'll be an expert on pigeon racing!"

"It certainly was a good day she came our way Sean; she's hard working and reliable, which is more than can be said for some lasses these days. She's still a bit shy especially with lads, but that's no bad thing! "Terry ventured. "That mother of hers has been in a few times though trying to get an order for her brawn… won't take no for an answer, she even got a bit mouthy about it the other day when I said my Joan prefers to make her own. Talk about Chalk and Cheese! It's hard to believe such a nice, well-mannered lass has that harridan for a mother."

"It were Jimmy who suggested the girl Terry. Apparently the mother makes the poor girl's life a misery, Betty's bit too fond

217

of her drink and all. Apparently that woman can be as sour as crab apples when she's in her cups… Jimmy keeps an eye on the lass, tries to look after her a bit, it's good of 'im really." Sean said.

"Come to mention it, I've noticed that Jimmy Benson drinks in here quite regular like, these days, I thought he usually favoured The Nags Head," Terry observed.

"He says he prefers it over here in Newton now, likes the crack and says there's a better class of customer." Terry and Sean chortled at the thought that Newton might have a superior drinking clientele.

Ivy sauntered over. "I'm off now Mr Flanagan, unless there's anything else you want doing?"

Terry shook his head.

"Will you want me to come in again next week as well?" Ivy asked.

"Course Ivy lass, the job's yours unless I say otherwise, you're doing a grand job."

"Thank you Mr Flanagan," Ivy removed her pinafore and

headed for the door.

"Talk of the bloody devil Terry, here he is, the man himself!"
Sean whistled. "We were just talking about you Jimmy."

Jimmy strolled in just as Ivy was leaving. He gave her a broad
wink and tipped his cap. "Afternoon Ivy, mind how you go."
She blushed; she hated being singled out.

"Talking about me you say, all good things I hope," Jimmy
joked "An how's our little Ivy getting on then Terry?"

"She's a diamond Jimmy, does whatever is asked of her,
works hard and is cheerful when she's about it, she'll make
someone a cracking little wife one day she really will. Talking
about wives how are *your* wedding plans coming along
Sean?"

"Oh, don't go there," Sean grimaced. "On top my religious
instruction with Father Malone every Friday for three more
weeks, we've now got to attend Catholic marital instruction
every Monday evening with Father O'Leary for three weeks
and we both have to attend St Paul's for six Sundays in a row
whilst the banns are read. Six bloody Sundays in a row," Sean
muttered gloomily. "I'll be so prayed over, and instructed, I

219

wouldn't be at all surprised if St Peter himself hasn't already found me a comfy slot in heaven! I thought we'd have got wed weeks ago, but oh no there's a system and we 'ave to go along with it whether we like it or not." Sean looked hang dog.

"And so how *is* the marital instruction going from Father O'Leary?" Jimmy guffawed.

Devout seventy-five-year-old Father O'Leary was firmly of the purist Catholic view that all sex was *only* for the procreation of children and that it was a mortal sin to try to prevent any more of God's little angels entering the world.

"All I can say Jimmy is that it's no wonder there are so many huge families of hungry children in Newton if their parents listen to advice on family planning from Father O'Leary. He might tell you that God expects his Faithful to go forth and multiply, he doesn't tell you how God expects them all to be clothed and fed. That man's a positive liability." Sean grumbled. "Eileen and me won't be 'aving ten or more kids and that's a fact… I've got a stock of those French letters and I intend to use 'em, Catechism or no Catechism!"

Terry and Jimmy roared with laughter.

220

"So, when's the happy day then Sean?" Terry asked.

"It's on March 30th, that's the earliest 'ee could fit us in after the classes. It's only going to be a quiet do, just my brother and Eileen's family, mind you there's still eight of them, including her Mam."

Jimmy and Terry exchanged a knowing, *just you wait,* look.

"My brother, Connor, is coming over from Belfast but Mam and me three sisters won't make the trip what with my Dad being so sickly, and both Mary and Breda being in the family way" Sean sighed. It was a blow when his Mam announced his Dad was ailing; cancer the doctor said. The question of his own father's mortality had spurred Sean on to propose to Eileen, he promised his Mam to bring his blushing new bride back to visit as soon as possible after the wedding.

"So, it will only be a small affair no real fuss, even so I was hoping you'd do me the honour of being my best man Jimmy."

"Why Sean I'd be honoured to," Jimmy felt quite touched. Sean was the nearest he had to a proper friend. He didn't take Sean into all his confidences, some things Jimmy would never

221

share, but they did get on. Over the years in Dublin old friends had deserted him and here he was a feared man, on the margins. Sean was the closest thing he had to a mate. "Consider it done Sean."

"Champion Jimmy, but there'll be no kissing Eileen's bridesmaid though. She's asked her youngest sister Moira to do the honours and she's only nine!" Sean joked.

Terry and Jimmy chortled.

"I'm a happy man to be sure. Eileen's a wonderful lass and I know she's going to make me a happy man."

"Even better," Terry teased, "not only do you get the old shackle around your finger, if the boys keep playing rugby like they have been then Ireland look set to win the Five Nations again!"

"Hold your horses, they've got to beat Wales first; so, don't go hexing them!" Sean wagged his finger. "I reckon this has got all the makings of being an incredibly good year... the best in fact! So, let's all drink to that. I'll buy us all another pint and you take one for yourself Terry," Sean fairly glowed with pride.

"To a Sean, Eileen and to Ireland winning the rugby," they chorused and chinked their glasses for luck.

Chapter 20

March heralded Spring and a welcome influx of trade to the docks; the quays were bustling with work and ships. The start of 1949 had been the wettest January on record. Sheets of driving rain had turned the Taff into a raging torrent, farmland turned into treacherous ooze and farmers struggled to save their livestock from starvation and drowning.

Three hapless, mud laden sheep washed miles downstream from Pontcanna fields, their bloated, coal washed corpses bobbed around in the docks trapped in the scrubby bushes near the bay mouth. Perkins the local rag bone man and his son fished them out to render down, so they said, rumour had it the ewes went into faggots for Cardiff market.

 January and February had been particularly lean for trade, men had been laid off for weeks waiting for work, belts were tightened with families struggling to make ends meet. Now things were picking up, more prosperous times beckoned.

The raucous noise of ship's horns sounding off echoed across Bute town, the low, mellow *harrump* came as welcome rallying call to the men searching for work. Long lines of casual workers that once queued around the labour exchange building now dwindled to a trickle as the docks filled up with trade.

With so many ships needing unloading and turning around, ready to leave port in double quick time, plenty of hands were needed. Casual labour flooded in to take advantage of the pickings.

Several large ships had recently pulled in to be fettled, in the vast dry dock, others were backed up waiting to be shown into berth on the quaysides by the flotilla of doughty tugs lined up patiently waiting in the bay mouth. Sean and his team were working at full capacity. All morning hundreds of boxes of cargo had been disgorged onto the quayside, stacked and sorted into orderly rows like regiments of soldiers, before being directed off to cavernous warehouses. The afternoon was dragging on, men were getting tired, concentration slipping.

The lucrative coal trade into Cardiff docks had been

dwindling since the War and amongst many ship owners there was a notion that the mighty port of Cardiff was ill-fitted to handle a more general cargo.

Harbour authorities had meetings with the City Council; fears were raised that the docks were on a slow decline and something needed to be done about it. Questions were even being asked about the problem in Parliament. Plenty of other ports were vying for trade, Cardiff was struggling to stay ahead of the game.

The historic discharging of coal dust into the estuary meant that some areas were rapidly silting up making it hazardous for the deeper -hulled, general cargo boats to enter. Already some shipping lines were threatening to take their trade elsewhere into less tricky ports. Valiant little Tugs battled against the fierce Taff cross-current to navigate the treacherous humps and banks created in the port's inland channels. The legendary, roaring race current that gave the Tiger Bay its name had been the nemesis of many an unwary vessel over the years.

The dockland authorities were desperate to encourage new business. Sean and his crew were expected to turn around ships in record time. If Cardiff was to secure the lucrative general cargo trade then the dock workers needed to pull their weight.

"Shift those blasted crates lads… get them out the way now!" Sean roared at a group of Polish dock workers, cigarettes in mouths lounging in front of pile of packing cases discarded from an Argentinian beef consignment. It appeared that they were taking a break.

"Oi… you lot, move yourselves. Oh, for God's sake! I'll swing for that idle bunch if they keep cluttering up the quay and don't get a move on." Sean growled to his friend and right- hand man; Jack "Cappy" Thomas.

"Cappy you keep an eye out here and if needs be, kick those sloppy bastards into the drink if they haven't moved their arses and those boxes out of here in the next two minutes, we haven't got all day! I'm heading over to the East Quay; seems they've got a bit of a problem over there."

"Gotcha boss," Cappy grinned. "Will you be long?"

"Hope not, some tugs are having a bit of difficulty navigating the "Prince Edward" into dock due to the low tide and now the wind is starting to pick up as well. I think they might need a bit of a hand lining her up to the quay before the light starts to fade. I'll check in with the Harbour Master, see what's what. He's the boss around here." Sean winked.

Sean strode off across to the East Quay in search of the "Prince Edward" leaving Cappy in charge of the dry dock quayside. Sean was spread too thin, running around fixing problems like a demented puppy chasing its own tail. The Port authorities were always breathing down his neck wanting everything done yesterday.

By the time Sean arrived at East Quay a sizable crowd was gathering, watching the drama. Harbour Master Jack Phillips was shouting instructions to the captains of the two tugs straining to keep the unruly ship on course. A babble of languages calling instructions hither and thither added to the sense chaos.

"Is there anything I can do for you Sir," Sean tipped his cap respectfully in the direction of the Harbour Master.

"Get down there and see what the matter is Riley. Looks like they need more men helping with those capstans. Something's up, they're struggling to bring her in." The

228

harbour master frowned as he watched the disorganised melee. "There's going to be an accident at this rate, get over there and tell them to halt whilst we work out what the problem is." The Harbour Master gestured to the scene at the end of the quay.

The two struggling tugs seemed unable to get the ship level with the quay despite several thick metal hawsers being fastened around the two huge quayside capstans. Three crewmen on board were pushing on the ship's capstan mechanism, to help ratchet the vessel nearer to the quay, the notched backplate helped prevent backward rotation and the line grew increasingly tense. All the men on deck strained to put their backs to the job. Slowly but surely the ship edged a little closer into the correct position.

Sean sprinted down the quay. If the tide turned before the Duke was fully secured it would leave the huge boat on a dangerously slack mooring.

As Sean got to within a few feet of the capstans he instinctively knew something was wrong…very wrong; he could hear it. Over the shouting and groaning of the men and the roar of the tug's engines, a grating high-pitched whine started to build, jarring his senses like nails dragging down a blackboard.

The strange metallic hum quickly built to a frenzy, and before Sean could yell for the men to jump clear the hawser snapped like an enormous elastic band, each metal strand pinging away from the core.

Sean, the crew and the three other men stood on the quayside were all in the killer snap back zone. The pistol crack of the fractured hawser could be heard echoing across the docks, other lesser ropes, now unable to bear the strain also gave way adding to the mayhem.

The deadly hawser lashed around, whipping left and right zipping through the air with a razor-sharp cluster of fibrous steel. The first two men in its line of fire were aboard the Duke of Edinburgh. The sailors were carved almost in two, the vicious metal strands sliced across their backs, cutting through muscle and bone, their bodies dropped to the deck in a welter of life blood. Other sailors on deck were injured in the crush as men scattered away from the metal coil and flailing ropes. A man standing on the quay was catapulted on the hawser's recoil into the harbour, struck across his face by

230

the slashing line. His lifeless body sank quickly in a bloody wave that dragged him under.

Sean and two other men were smashed into the harbour wall by the flailing hawser line, each man walloped hard up against the huge granite block wall. Limbs splayed at drunken angles, blood oozing from head wounds. A man, his leg almost hanging off at the knee, was screaming piteously. The scene of carnage looked like a bomb had gone off.

The emergency dock klaxon sounded the alarm. The deep boom resonated across the docks. Dozens of men dropped tools and ran to the scene. In the distance an urgent bell heralded the ambulance.

"Oh Jesus!" Cappy exclaimed, "it sounds like there's been a major accident over at East Quay... And Sean's over there!"

Cappy started to run hell for leather in the direction of East Quay. He was overtaken by two ambulances, bells sounding furiously, streaking along the service road towards the casualties.

People started running towards the docks from every direction, women fearful for their men folk poured out of the warehouses and joined the crowd.

By the time Cappy reached the scene the crowd was standing back to give the medics room to do their work. Blood ran in rivulets on the cobbles, the first two men to be struck on the ship were laid out under sheets, no point tending the dead when the injured might stand a chance. Other sailors were administering first aid to crew members caught in the crush. There was no trace of the poor devil who entered the water.

The docker with the partially severed leg was being loaded on to the first ambulance, a tourniquet stemmed the blood flow, his screams quenched with ether.

Two unconscious men were being loaded on stretchers; dangling limbs carefully arranged by the medics.

The less injured men on the quay, pushed over by the crowd scattering away from the hawser, were being led away for first aid, handkerchiefs staunching blood from cuts and grazes; dazed and bedraggled men grateful to have escaped serious injury.

By now the word of the tragedy had spread, a low keening spread through the crowd; some of the injured men were local. Women wailed as they waited to hear which son or husband had been lost, wide eyed children clung to skirts, mothers beside themselves with grief.

"Where's my Johnny?" A desperate young woman with a care-worn, face and a toddler clasped in her thin arms pressed forward, she pleaded with the crowd for information. "'Ave you seen 'im mister?" She grabbed Cappy by the arm, "I can't find my 'usband…'ee only clocked on at East Quay this morning, said 'ee was going to work with bringing in the boats, first time in weeks he's 'ad any work, Johnny Evans. For the love of God…Someone must have seen him," her eyes were wild with panic. The toddler started to wail, snot trailing down his lip.

"Now calm yourself missus, let's try and get to the bottom of this" Cappy soothed. Cappy's eyes scanned the throng for Sean.

"What did he look like, your Johnny?"

"Short, about my height… and a moustache," the woman racked her brain for some definitive detail, "'and ee was wearing a red neckerchief this morning."

233

The crowd collectively took a sharp intake of breath.

"They say the bloke in the water had a red neckerchief on," a voice from the back of the crowd shouted.

"That's right 'ee did, I saw 'im go under." Another yelled, soon a clamour of voices added to the certainty. The man thrown in the dock *was* wearing a red neckerchief.

She looked puzzled, as the voices built her terror grew, her heart hammering in her chest... *what did they mean in the water? ... Johnny could swim... please God he could have got out.*

"One of 'em got thrown in by that hawser, missus, hit him straight on it did" an old man at her elbow informed her, he jabbed his thumb in the direction of the shattered metal coil, "he 'aint been seen since, don't reckon the poor devil stood a chance. 'Tis a bad business." The man sucked thoughtfully on his pipe.

The women let out a scream and fell to her knees. Other women rushed forward to comfort the bewildered child clutching at her skirts.

Cappy looked over to the stretchers being stowed in the

234

ambulance. In an instant he felt sure that he recognized the check jacket and crumpled body of Sean Riley. Sean was out cold, a medic was stabilizing his neck and bandaging a gaping wound on Sean's head, the activity gave Cappy cause to hope. If his time in the army taught him one thing; Doctors only work on the living.

He pushed his way towards the ambulance, desperate to get a closer look at the man being loaded, aware of the need for certainty. By now two young police officers were ordering the crowd to get back.

"Let me through…let see him, "Cappy yelled to the officer as he elbowed onlookers aside. "That's my best mate Sean!"

The crowd parted and let Cappy through to the front.

"Sean!" Cappy yelled, but the body on the stretcher didn't stir.

"He's out cold; no point shouting sir, he won't hear you. Come away now, let them do their job," the police officer guided Cappy away from the ambulance.

The medics locked the doors and prepared to leave. The chiming of the ambulance bell caused the crowd to part and

235

the van hurtled away.

"They'll be taking him to the infirmary Sir." The police officer got out his note pad. "Now could you please give us your friend's full name and address so we will be able to start investigating the matter. His family will need to be informed of course."

Cappy felt numb with grief. Poor Sean, he loved that man... everybody did. Worst of all, how on earth would they break the news to his Eileen?

"Sir, could you give me his details," the police officer tapped his pencil on his pad.

"It's Sean... Sean Riley. Oh God he was due to get married in ten days, who's going to tell his girl Eileen?" Cappy sobbed.

Chapter 21

PC Paul Evans knocked tentatively on the blistered blue door of number 5 Adeline Street. It was past five o'clock and the early evening light was fading to murky dusk. The sitting room curtains were already drawn against the evening chill and the presence of an upstairs light showed some-one was home. He took deep breath and composed himself. He loathed being the bearer of bad news, especially for the second time that afternoon.

There was no doubt now about the identities of all three men taken to the Cardiff Royal Infirmary for treatment.

The older man with the injured knee was Jack Jones a forty-five-year-old father of four from Splott. Of the three men caught in the bloody carnage on the quayside he was the lucky one, his leg had been amputated just above the knee, but Jack was expected to make a full recovery. He and his family were just so grateful that he had survived the accident, buoyed up with morphine and good wishes Jack counted his blessings and was positively smiling in the face of adversity.

Fred Smith, a young lad of twenty never made it into the operating theatre, he passed away in the ambulance on the way to hospital. The unfortunate lad had suffered catastrophic multiple fractures and severe internal bleeding after his collision with the granite wall of the quayside. Poor Fred Smith was declared dead on arrival. That morning when PC Evans broke the news to his mother she fainted away with grief. Fred was her only son and after losing her husband to a bombing raid during the blitz Fred had carried all her hopes and dreams.

Cushioned by the body of the unfortunate Fred, Sean Riley had survived the collision. He now hovered perilously between life and death in the Royal Infirmary operating theatre. PC Evans had the unenviable task of breaking the news of his dire condition to his fiancée Eileen Murphy.

Not only was it uncertain if poor Mr Riley would pull through but if, by some miracle he did, then he would, in all likelihood, be a very changed man and certainly not in any position to be getting married to his sweetheart in ten days' time.

PC Evans dreaded his task and the tide of grief that would crash into the lives of the family behind the battered blue door.

I feel like the bloody angel of death.

He removed his hat and tucked it under his arm and waited for the drama to unfold.

He rapped a little louder. Across the road a curtain twitched in an upstairs window. Neighbours! The sight of a police officer on a doorstep was inevitably the harbinger of dire news or family disgrace.

In the neat, dreary front sitting room of number five PC Evans delivered the bad news with as much compassion as he could muster. Starched antimacassars graced the chairs, an image of the bleeding heart of Jesus, took pride of place above the mantle-piece and a small, slate mantel clock marked time as the lives of the Murphy household fell apart.

Eileen's mother, Ida, sat cradling a cup of weak tea to revive her nerves, the last of the tea leaves had been stretched too far for three decent cups. Every so often she dabbed at her eyes with the corner of her apron.

239

Eileen, white faced, was perched on the edge of the armchair desperate for news, "How did it happen?" She gasped.

"I'm terribly sorry Miss, it appears was a dreadful accident, an investigation into the circumstances surrounding the incident is already underway." PC Evans was struck by the girl's composure. When he broke the news, it was her mother who wailed and railed against the injustice of it all, bemoaning the cancelled wedding; the family bad luck, how her poor late husband would be turning in his grave. Eileen's focus was on Sean.

Eileen nodded, absorbing every scrap of information the officer could give her. "Will he be all right? I must see him...When can I see him?"

"I gather Mr Riley is receiving the best possible treatment at the Royal Infirmary. I'm not sure when, or if, you can visit yet Miss Murphy, but I shall ensure that information comes your way as soon as possible. If we get any news you'll be the first to know."

"Thank you officer, and what about his parents, will you tell them?" She knew his family would be bereft. Sean was the eldest, his father's golden boy.

240

"Can you help us with any information on that score Miss?" PC Evans started to take notes.

"All I know officer, is that Sean's family is from Belfast, his landlady Mrs Isla Murray, at twelve Ellen street, may have an address for them but I don't. Dear Lord, this will be such a blow to them both." Eileen shook her head sadly. "His poor father is gravely ill with cancer, that's why they weren't coming over for the wedding and now this, it will surely break his mother's heart." Eileen sobbed softly into her handkerchief.

It was the first tear Eileen had shed. PC Evans marvelled at her selfless demeanour; all her thoughts were for others. She was an admirable young woman.

"We'll do our best Miss, I'll be on my way to Ellen street then, see if I can find out an address for his family," PC Evans prepared to leave.

Eileen mumbled her thanks, she was incoherent with shock, words clagged into her mouth like lint.

His heart went out to the poor girl. "I'm sorry to be the bearer of such bad news, Miss, but, if you don't mind me saying, if

241

Mr Riley is a church goer you might consider letting the vicar know, ask for a bit of help from the Almighty, my Mam is a great believer in the power of prayer."

"Thank you officer…I'll let Father O'Leary know what's happened. We will all be praying for him." Eileen crossed herself.

PC Evans left the household to its grief and made his way to Ellen Street and Mrs Isla Murray.

The lowering grey skies threatened heavy rain, the light had faded now to a purple grey. Streetlamps on the corner of Ellen street flared a weak acid yellow on greasy, grey paving slabs, curtains closed along the terrace against the creeping night.

Number twelve Ellen street was easy to spot next to the derelict crater of what remained of number fourteen.

His shift ended at six, with any luck he would not need to trouble Mrs Murray for long, he wanted to be home in time for his dinner..

A lad answered the door, weasel faced and suspicious.

242

"Can I speak to a Mrs Isla Murray please?"

"Mam!..."

PC Evans craned his neck to see a small woman hastily removing her pinafore in the back kitchen.

"Just coming, Craig" she called.

PC Evans saw a careworn woman scuttling up the corridor her pinched face riven with anxiety.

"Oh, dear Lord it's the police! What's the matter now?" She rounded on the lad "have you been up to something Craig?"

"No Mam... honest!"

"It's all right, Mrs Murray, it's nothing to do with the lad. It's about your lodger Mr Sean Riley, he's been in a serious accident down on the docks this afternoon."

"I'm sorry to hear it officer, I did hear the klaxons," bird like she tilted her head in the direction of the docks.

"Mr Riley is receiving treatment in the infirmary, but he's in quite a poor way. We need to inform his family in Belfast as soon as possible. Do you happen have an address for his

243

family."

"That I do," she scurried off and returned clasping a scrap of paper. "Here, he told me this was where his Mam and Da lived if ever I needed to contact them."

"Thank you Mrs Murray, I'll take this with me if I may."

He turned to go.

"Wait officer!" Isla grabbed him by the arm.

"I'm sorry he's poorly, really I am, he's a nice, decent chap but ...." she hesitated, aware of the callous nature of her thoughts.

"But if Mr Riley's going to be in hospital a long time then I'll need to let his room go see?" Her face was anxious, shamefaced, hovering between compassion and poverty. "I can't pay the landlord without his money coming in. So, if he doesn't need the room then there's plenty that do and well... you understand me don't you officer?"

PC Evans understood.

"Tell 'im I'm sorry."

Chapter 22

News of the disaster spread quickly and by the next day every gruesome detail of the accident had been retold and evaluated. Everyone knew someone who had seen something. Fault and blame were being apportioned. There were even calls for James Callaghan MP to visit the area and get involved.

Callaghan, a former union official was popular with the dockers, if there was any hint of negligence the dockers were arguing Callaghan was the man they needed to raise the matter at the highest level.

In the Duke of Edinburgh, Terry the landlord was already organizing a collection for Sean. Sean was a popular man in the pub, chatty, good humoured, the very life and soul. Gloomy mutterings about his prospects cast a pall over the bar.

"Come on lads put what you can in that jar, every little helps."
Terry coaxed the spare change into the *Help Sean Riley* fund.

In only one day a steady stream of coins had built in the
empty pickled egg jar sat on the bar counter.

"Bloody dreadful news Terry, four men dead you say!"
Donald sucked on his pipe contemplatively. "An' him, poor
bugger fighting for his life they say," he jabbed his thumb in
the direction of the pickle jar.

"Just got engaged too, life's not bloody fair Donald," Terry
shook his head sadly.

"They say he'll be fit for nothing if 'ee do come round... If it
was me I'd want them to take me out and shoot me, put me
out my misery like."

"If I hear any more of that sort of talk in my pub Donald, I'll
take you out and shoot you myself!" Terry snapped. "The poor
lad's fighting for his life, give it a rest! You'd be more help
offering up a few prayers at St Pauls for the lad's recovery, not
preparing his shroud."

Donald retreated to the safety of his magazine and his
pigeons.

"Terry, put another half of Brains bitter in there when you're ready," Reg tipped his pint glass towards the pumps and put a shilling on the counter.

Terry pulled the pint and rang up 8d.

"As I was saying to Donald just now Terry…It's a blessing that health minister Aneurin Bevan got his national health service up and running last year, I always said it would take a Welshman to look after the working man, because it sounds like the poor lad's bills would be mounting up something shocking otherwise." Reg Reynolds sucked thoughtfully on his pipe. Sean drew a slow half pint; the barrel of Brains bitter was coming to its end.

"Glad to hear of your concern Reg, he's a good lad Sean. Would you like me to put this four-pence change in Sean's jar for you then Reg?" Terry's hand hovered over the pickled egg jar; Terry raised a questioning eyebrow.

Reg looked a little startled at being asked to part with his fourpence for the cause, on the other hand he liked Sean. "Aye …go on then. I reckon that lad's going to need it more than I am. I must say Terry the head's a bit lively on this glass o' beer put another inch in there please, the first few swigs

247

will be all froth else."

God that Reg was a canny old bugger. Terry shook his head and gave a wry smile. He topped up the glass.

When a grim-faced Jimmy Benson entered the bar half an hour later all eyes were on him. If anyone had any news of Sean Riley it would be Jimmy. The tap room chatter stilled a little as he approached the bar.

"Pint please Terry, I need it."

Terry raised a quizzical eyebrow.

Jimmy gave an almost imperceptible shake of the head. The news from the hospital was bleak.

Only an hour ago he'd come across Eileen Murphy in the soul-less waiting room of the Royal Infirmary. She had spent all night and day in vigil for Sean with Father O'Leary to help and comfort her. The exhausted girl looked bone tired with dark smudges under her pretty green eyes, her dry lips fluttered telling the rosary over and over. Hour after hour pleading with God for His mercy. Unable to be at Sean's bedside she must content herself with the spartan waiting room; she would not leave the hospital until there was some

248

news. Small shiny black beads passed rhythmically through her fingers as she mumbled countless prayers to the Blessed virgin Mary and St Jude.

"It's touch and go Terry...touch and go. They say the next few days will decide it." Jimmy shook his head. "The police are trying to get word to his Mam and Da, but I can't see his parents getting across from Belfast in the circumstances, perhaps his brother Connor might, he was due to come over for the wedding after all?" Jimmy mused.

"Poor sod... seems like all we can do for him now is hope and pray."

"True, true Terry. I think Father O'Leary is proving a great comfort to the lass. From what I saw there's plenty of praying going on already, although, as you know yourself, when you're invoking St Jude things *are* looking pretty bad."

The landlord chewed his lip thoughtfully. *St Jude!* Things must be awfully bad indeed. He vowed to pop into St Paul's and light a candle for Sean later. On second thoughts, perhaps he'd get his Joan to go along as well and say a few Hail Marys, add a bit of weight to the request so to speak.

249

Chapter 23

The quiet ordered nature of number 9 Inkerman street made
Betty cry the first time Gerald took her there all those months
ago.

She had walked up the street, certain that behind every net
curtain a curious pair of eyes was watching, a crafty gossip
collecting information. It was only three streets away from
where she grew up as a girl in Alma road...what if they met
someone she knew when they were walking arm in arm?
Everyone said she was the image of her mother Iris, someone
was bound to recognise her, after all Gerald had. Betty's panic
had grown to fever pitch that first time, as she waited for
Gerald to unlock the front door of a house with the same front
doorstep and with the same majolica tiles as all the other
houses in Alma road.

It was madness to think she could do this.

When Betty had finally stepped into the hall, a mixture of relief and sadness overwhelmed her; relief because the ordeal of walking to the house was over, and a sadness because the house and its hallway with black white and ochre tiles was the mirror image of her old family home.

The memories of that fateful day her father banished her from Alma road came rushing back as fresh as the day they were made. She collapsed crying in Gerald's arms; she wanted to run.

It would be another month before Betty would pluck up the courage to repeat the visit and another two months after that before she felt comfortable enough to allow him to make her a pot of tea served in his wife's best china teacup.

It chafed on her to be sat in his late wife's chair next to the fireplace, whilst an anniversary picture gazed back at her from the mantlepiece. A happy memory of a kindly woman, proudly wearing a row of graduated pearls next to Gerald in his best suit; smiling from ear to ear.

A woman who had cared enough to ask after Elizabeth all those years ago..

Everywhere Betty looked traces of the late Mrs Williams were preserved and treasured, Janet's winter coat still hung in the hall and in the hallstand drawer, balls of her rolled up gloves rested gathering dust. Everything in death preserved as if in life, it felt like wearing someone else's skin.

Today she felt sure she had the courage to be shown the whole of the house, she needed to see the upstairs rooms. The idea of seeing the bedrooms had tormented her. Did he expect her to share his bed…would it be the same bed he shared with Janet? Would all Janet's clothes still be in the wardrobe and drawers?

If she was to live in Gerald's house she needed to conquer her fears. That rising tide of panic no longer gripped her chest when Betty walked through the front door, but the thought of the upstairs rooms still filled her with dread.

Betty knew she owed it to Gerald to make her mind up, he'd been patient with her long enough. It had been over six months now since he first raised the matter…he'd hinted only the other day that he hoped for a decision soon.

Gerald had left the fire banked up, the house felt welcoming and warm.

"Come in Elizabeth dear, let me take your coat."

As he hung it up she noticed Janet's coat on the hallstand had gone.

"Come on through, I'll knit that fire together, get a bit of life in it, perhaps we can have cup of tea before you explore?"

As she went through to the back-sitting room she could see that Gerald had rearranged the room. Both chairs now faced the fire companionably, the framed anniversary photograph had been moved onto a small table in the corner and a new photograph of some delightful grandchildren had taken its place.

"I've had a bit of a sort out; I've been a bit of a thoughtless old fool. When I thought about it, it made sense really that you would feel awkward in here," he swept his hands around the room, "surrounded by all my...*our* things...I wasn't being fair on you Elizabeth. So, I made a few changes. I hope you approve?"

She nodded; she could feel tears bubbling up.

"Now don't go upsetting yourself Elizabeth, we can make a few more an' all, that is if you'll do me the honour...." his words tailed off. He'd never actually articulated a marriage proposal. Perhaps it would scare her.

Her heart melted, "Gerald you are such a kind man, I really don't deserve you." She gave him a warm smile. She would be a fool to turn him down.

"Let's have that cup of tea and then you can show me the rest of the house."

It felt like a dream climbing the stairs, in Alma road her old room had been the box room at the back of the house.

 "I keep this room for storage now… I'm still putting things away. My son Dafydd said he'll move some of these boxes into the attic for me next week, this used to be *his* old room, before he left home," Gerald creaked open the box room door. *Her* childhood bed had run along under the window, now his boxes were stacked along the same wall. The faded blue wallpaper and blue gingham checked curtains hinted at grubby fingers from a little boy long ago.

"I thought maybe this room could be for Ivy? The wall-paper is a bit old, but we could decorate the room… if you wanted to, any way what I mean is that *all* these things can be sorted."

He left the rest unsaid.

He clicked the door shut and in her mind the pink trailed roses of her old room were there again.

The middle bedroom in Alma road had belonged to her late brother John, Gerald led the way. In this room a single bed was tucked along the wall, allowing space for an arm-chair next to the tiny grate. A tall boy stood in the corner with a row of ties ranged along a side rail. She recognized Gerald's cufflinks and tie pin in the pin tray. "This is *my* room, I thought it was best if I moved my things in here, just until…" Gerald let her take in the simple room, neat and tidy with no concession to ornament. "Anyway, Elizabeth let me show you the front bed-room now and then you've seen everything."

He opened the front bed-room door; he stood back to let her through, he would not crowd her, he watched as she took in the immaculate room, as fresh and anonymous as any hotel room.

She could see the wardrobe doors had been purposely left open-the hanging rails were empty except for a row of wooden coat hangers. On the dressing table a small posy of

255

pungent lily-of-the- valley blooms in a tiny china vase perfumed the room. The expected hair dressing set was missing, only a small ring mark hinted that a lady's perfume atomizer had once stood there. A lace doily covered the fade mark where Janet's brush and hand-mirror had once stood.

The double bed was made up with crisp white linen and a feminine pink, sateen coverlet topped the bedstead. On the bedside table a small cut glass water jug and glass stood next to a lamp stand sporting a delicate pink and white shade.

"I bought a new bed-spread, it was about time this room had a bit of a freshen up. I hope you like it?" He looked nervous.

Betty appreciated how much it must have cost Gerald to pack away all of Janet's things. She was certain now that all those boxes piled in the back room were full of Janet's possessions. She gave him a hug and a kiss on his bristly cheek. "It's lovely."

Betty took a deep breath," I think we could be happy together Gerald if you still want me?"

"Of course, I still want you Elizabeth." He beamed with pleasure. "Let's go downstairs and have another cup of tea. I think we should start to make some plans, and you can decide when to tell Ivy all about it. It's only natural she'll have lots of questions, it's going to come as a bit of a surprise I'm sure."

"It *will* Gerald, but I can't rush things," Betty looked as skittish as a woodland faun.

"Of course not, we won't rush the matter. But, once we've sorted a few things out I'm sure we'll all be happy."

She gave his hand a squeeze. *Could she really find happiness after all this time?*

Chapter 24

It was a warm Sunday afternoon. The weather was
gorgeous for the time of year; even in Bute town the March
sunshine managed to brighten the darkest of dingy alleyways.
Washing flapped and fluttered on long lines strung across the
dingy terraced streets and yards. Women gossiped on
doorsteps and scrawny cats sunned themselves on shed roofs.
It was hard to believe the good weather was pretending it was
already summer. A lazy calm draped itself like soft lint over
the whole neighbourhood.

A soft, warm breeze stirred the leafless branches of the
avenue of majestic Horse Chestnut trees that lined the edge of
Bute Park and crocus were poking through the grass around
the trunks in a riot of yellow and purple. The railings had
been grubbed up in aid of the war effort, only the old trees
remained to mark the edges of the park boundary.

Ivy and Alice Tranter strolled through the park gates arm in
arm and headed for the wooden benches on the farthest side of

258

the park. "Come on Ivy tell me now.... you promised!" Alice pleaded. She'd been on tenterhooks since Ivy hinted that she had a big secret to share. Her patience was wearing thin.

"Let's go over to that bench by that hedge. We can talk there." Ivy pointed at a lone park bench tucked away in a quiet corner. It was usually a favourite spot with courting couples but today the bench was vacant. Shielded by a tall laurel hedge it would be safe from eavesdroppers.

Alice hurried over to secure the bench. "All right Ivy Jenkins, now you sit down and tell me all about it.... What on earth is this big secret of yours?"

Ivy twisted a grubby handkerchief between her fingers searching for the right words. She felt sure Alice would know what to do.

"Go on Ivy don't be sly. I know, let me guess- it's that Price lad isn't it? He's had his eye on you for ages, come on spill the beans." Alice teased. She knew Ivy was shy around the local boys and Betty was a tartar if Alice tried to keep Ivy out late. For all her own dubious morals Betty kept Ivy on a short leash as far as boys were concerned.

"You must promise you won't say anything Alice. Promise me." Ivy pleaded anxiously.

"All right-I promise-cross my heart and hope to die, now tell me what's up?"

"I'm in trouble Alice, I.... I think I'm going to have a baby." Ivy blurted out. She kept her eyes on her lap, not daring to meet Alice's gaze. Her fingers twiddled and turned.

"But you can't be! Can you?" Alice gasped.

Ivy nodded miserably. Hung her face, lank hair, greasy from worried fingers, covering her eyes.

"Oh my God. How? For crying out loud Ivy, what on earth's happened." Alice shook her friend by the shoulder. "Look at me Ivy," she demanded.

Alice knew her own behaviour often left a lot to be desired. Hard slaps from her mother had pushed that message home. Boys seem to be drawn to buxom Alice Tranter like bees around honey. Many a lad had tried their luck with Alice, but she never went all the way, she had more sense than that. She was gob-smacked; local boys and skinny little Ivy didn't mix, or so Alice had thought!

Alice had known Ivy Jenkins for ever, she never in a million years would have expected this to happen.

Ivy welled up and struggled to stifle her sobs. Her face was a picture of misery.

"Has a lad taken advantage Ivy.... you know, forced you" Alice demanded.

"No, no. It's not like that." Ivy didn't want to cause trouble. Jimmy had told her at the time that it would be her fault if Mam couldn't pay her bills because Ivy was being difficult, he'd said that she had to do what he asked.

"So, you *do* know who the father is then?"

"Of course, I do!" Ivy spluttered. Her face was beetroot.

"All right Ivy don't get upset; I'm only asking. And does this lad know he's got you in the family way?"

Ivy shook her head miserably.

"So, who is it then Ivy? Go on tell us."

Ivy hesitated. She knew if she told her secret then there would be no going back and Jimmy would surely do something awful, he'd hinted as much on many an occasion. She was frightened of what he might do. She'd promised him on her crucifix that she wouldn't ever tell.

Remember this is our secret Ivy.... you can't tell anyone ever; bad things happen when people break their promises!

She shook her head. "I can't tell. He made me promise I wouldn't tell Alice. Oh, what am I going to do now? Mam's going to kill me when she finds out, it'll ruin everything." Ivy wiped her nose on her sleeve.

Ivy hadn't told Alice about Mr Williams either, Mam had said to keep it private, but only the other evening Mam had hinted her relationship with Mr Williams was growing into something special. Ivy having a baby would certainly throw a spanner in the works.

"You've got to tell him Ivy! He's got to do right by you. It's not fair to leave you high and dry when he's had his way with you." Alice put her arm around Ivy's thin shoulder.

"Perhaps you could both get married- after all you're over seventeen now, the law says you can get married so long as you're both over sixteen. That is if your Mam agrees to it.... I

262

mean *he* is sixteen, isn't he this lad?" Alice probed, trying to guess who it could be. *Billy Thomas, he was sweet on Ivy? ... or John Price! Alice felt sure it must be John Price.*

"Yes, he is." Ivy mumbled.

"And you're certain you've caught, 'cos there's many a time a girl has had a scare.... you know, been late." Alice hoped her friend was just panicking about nothing.

The lack of her monthlies and the mounting waves of nausea that crashed over Ivy every morning left her in no doubt. She looked at her friend, "I'm sure Alice."

Despite all her hoping and praying Ivy *knew* she was in trouble. For over a week she'd tried to excuse the retching as a bad stomach but after days of heaving her guts up every morning the penny had dropped. Jimmy had gotten a baby on her. Ivy might be clueless about lots of things, but she did know how babies were made.

"Well then, if you're *sure* you've caught, you must tell him!" Alice said firmly. "Of course, there *are* other options as long as you don't leave it too late. That's not to say that you must consider them or nothing," Alice added hastily.

263

"They do say old Mother Creasy in Sebastopol Street might help you out, if you *really* had to. But she certainly wouldn't be cheap, or easy for that matter, I can't think it would be less than ten pounds, or maybe even more, to get you "sorted" and it'd be risky too Ivy." Alice cautioned; she'd heard tales about the likes of Mother Creasy.

Ivy felt she was teetering on the threshold of a world she knew nothing about, it was as if an abyss was opening in front of her waiting for her to fall in. She felt wretched.

Alice ploughed on, "they say she gives you loads of gin first and then she uses one of them long-handled marrow spoons to dig it out. They say that way is safer than the knitting needle some of them use.... but I don't know if that's true either," Alice said doubtfully.

Ivy shuddered at the awful prospect of Ma Creasy gouging out her sins with a long, slender, marrow spoon. She wondered who *they* were, the informed few who knew all about Mrs Creasey's dreadful trade.

"An' you'd be sworn to secrecy Ivy, no matter what happened. You could never tell who helped you out...never!" Alice left the awfulness of the process and potential for disaster hang between them.

Alice had heard rumours of desperate girls and women in trouble who'd visited practitioners of the needle. Some of the outcomes had involved huge loss of blood or worse with Doctors being summoned to a dying girl left in feverish agony.

"I couldn't get rid Alice, it's a mortal sin!" Ivy shuddered. "'An even if I wanted to do it, I haven't got any money anyway.... you know Mam keeps all my earnings. She makes me hand them over the minute I get paid on Friday. It takes me ages to save up even a few bob for myself. Where on earth would I get ten pounds from?" The figure was so impossibly huge Alice might as well have said the fee was a thousand pounds.

"Well then he must cough up, the lad whose got you in this mess! You've got to tell him. You've only got a few weeks to get this sorted one way or another Ivy!... Ask him what he's going to do to help. It takes two to make a baby, so he's *got* to do something." Alice put a comforting arm around Ivy's shoulders. · "God is forgiving Ivy, always remember that."

"I s'pose so." Ivy said doubtfully. Jimmy would be so

265

angry with her and when her Mam knew she would kill her. Or even worse maybe her Mam would kick her out on her ear. Where would she go then? What would she say when her Mam asked who'd got her in trouble, she was bound to ask?

Whatever she decided to do Ivy would need to speak to Jimmy. The trouble with Jimmy was you never knew when he would turn up, she could only pray he would be home this evening. Whatever happened it would have to be this week.

Ivy shivered a little, the whole dreadful mess made her feel sick with worry and shame. The wind was picking up and Ivy needed to get back, there were chores to do.

Mam had an order for three trays of faggots to supply the local pub, the very thought of peeling a mound of onions and mincing a vast slippery bowl of liver and pig fat with bunches of pungent garden sage made Ivy's stomach churn over.

"I've got to go Alice; my Mam will be expecting me back." Ivy said, her voice had a dull hopeless edge to it.

"All right Ivy, I'll walk part-way home with you. But promise you'll let me know how it goes," Alice gave her friend hug. "I'll try to help, honest I will. Remember you've always got me as a friend Ivy."

"Thanks Alice- but don't say a word to anyone please." Ivy's eyes were like saucers.

"Not a word, cross my heart and hope to die."

As Alice meandered her way home through the grey terraced streets, she pondered her friend's dilemma; Ivy was pregnant and very scared.

Poor little Ivy, who was hardly ever allowed to go out with Alice and never had any spare money for fun and fripperies. Shy little Ivy, kept virtually chained to the kitchen sink, slaving over laundry, doing all the cleaning and the cooking for Betty and her Irish lodger.

Stuck at home Ivy.

"He made me promise not to tell anyone Alice...."

The penny dropped.

Chapter 25

Betty padded down the stairs in her thick, felt dressing gown, carefully holding a brimming chamber pot in her hand. It was almost six o'clock, and a greasy dawn was just starting to break through over the roof tops. The roiling churn deep in her guts had driven her out of the warmth of her bed. She needed the outside lavatory urgently. *That damn beer Jack served last night must have been off.... I thought it looked cloudy; and I said so at the time. I'll be having words the next time I see him.* She fumed and, as if to prove her point, she emitted a smelly fart.

Every Friday evening, without fail, Gerald attended his weekly choir practice. He was a proud member of the Canton male voice choir, and the choir master hoped for a good result in the next Eisteddfod if they all put in their best effort.

Betty had spent her Friday evening drinking in the Rose and Crown with her friend Phoebe; she wanted to share her good news about Gerald and get some advice about how to break

268

the news to Ivy, weeks were dragging on and Betty still hadn't broached the subject.

Fifty-year-old Phoebe was one of the few people who Betty trusted with her identity and her life story. They'd first met when the newly created Betty Jenkins washed up on the rocky shores of the Tiger Bay street trade. Betty a fresh-faced young woman with startled Bambi eyes, stood out like a sore thumb amongst the seasoned prostitutes gathered waiting for customers. A group of foulmouthed brassy girls had tried to bully and chase this interloper Betty off their patch. Phoebe Horwat had come to her aid.

As a pretty, innocent Catholic girl, Phoebe had trusted her local parish priest rather more than she ought to and Father Edmund Roberts had conveniently forgotten his vows of abstinence. When the scandal broke the young priest found himself quickly shuffled off to a new parish. Phoebe labelled a temptress and a tart, no better than she ought to be, found herself out on her ear and resorting to the oldest business in town to earn her keep.

Older and wiser, that night when Phoebe spotted Betty looking like a lamb waiting to be led to the slaughter, she recognised a fellow abandoned soul, and took the girl under her wing.

Phoebe offered Betty her spare room to stay in until she'd got herself on her feet and mothered her throughout the difficult days of pregnancy.

Unlike Phoebe, Betty refused to give her baby away. *She owed it to James to protect their child it was all she had left of him.*

Betty named the baby Ivy and loved her with a passion so deep it hurt, the little girl had James' red brown hair and the same clear blue eyes and every time she grasped Betty's finger in her little fist Betty knew she could never let her go.

We'll get through this I promise you Ivy… I'll do whatever it takes to protect you.

And with Phoebe's help Betty just about managed to muddle through the mire she found herself in. Their friendship forged of tragedy and heartbreak welded the two women together and in the middle was baby Ivy surrounded by two women who loved her.

Over the years, through all their ups and downs, the two

women had remained firm friends and confidants.

Betty trusted Phoebe with her life.

"What shall I do Phoebe? I'm fond of Gerald, and he's a good man but he's years older than me and…"

"And what? For God's sake Betty why are you even thinking about this, stop dithering and tell him you accept. If it was me I'd seize the moment sooner rather than later!" Phoebe said over glass of stout. "It's not exactly as if your life is a bed of roses at the moment is it Betty love?"

Betty knew Phoebe was right. It wasn't so much that Gerald was old enough to be her father, or that she couldn't imagine sharing his bed, after all she'd shared her body with so many men, it was the fact that he wanted Elizabeth not Betty and she wasn't sure she could be Elizabeth again.

"Stands to reason Betty it's not exactly a match made in heaven but then plenty of marriages fall apart when loves young dream disappears, least this way you're both going into it with your eyes open, there aren't too many men around like Gerald Williams just waiting to scoop you up and rescue you. He's not going to wait forever Betty so tell him soon. You

271

listen to Ivy's Aunty Phoebe," Phoebe wagged her finger.

Betty nodded. She resolved to speak to Ivy the following day whilst her courage was strong.

What Betty hadn't banked on was feeling as weak as a kitten battling the effects of her insides complaining violently at both ends. Betty paused in the hallway. She heard a loud retching noise coming from behind the kitchen door. The tap was being run in the sink followed by more tortured heaving.

That bloody Jimmy Benson. Sounds like he's had a right old skinful. I'll be having words if he leaves that sink a mess like he did the last time he spewed his guts up.... the dirty hound. And blaming it on my home-made faggots as well.... bloody cheek of the man.

Her hand stayed on the knob; she heard bitter weeping follow the last guttural retch. So, it wasn't Jimmy after all. Her Ivy was being sick, sick as the proverbial dog by the sound of it. It was not like her Ivy to be sick; the girl was as strong as an ox. Betty said a silent prayer that it wasn't down to her latest batch of brawn, if she got a reputation for serving dodgy meats no one would buy from her ever again.

As Betty entered the kitchen, she saw her daughter hunched over the sink clutching her abdomen and groaning.

"So, what's all this about then Ivy?"

Ivy jumped on hearing her Mam come in. Betty normally stayed in bed until at least seven thirty or later. Ivy's morning battles with nausea usually took place well before the house started to rouse. She had not expected to be discovered.

Ivy's small, startled face looked greyish green with sickness and exhaustion. Tears sat on her cheeks. Her coppery brown hair looked greasy and lank; her eyes were two, huge dark smudges.

Betty, so used to floating about in her own world, had not noticed how pale Ivy had become of late.

"I...I... I" Ivy stuttered. Her brain raced to come up with credible explanation.

"Come on, speak the truth and shame the Devil." Betty eyed her suspiciously. She had to admit Ivy looked rough. What on earth could be the matter with the girl? Thoughts of tainted brawn pushed to the fore.

273

Betty knew Ivy ate all her meals at home. The warm weather of late had been turning the milk to curds, and the basin of dripping in the pantry was nearly liquid.

She'd better give that last slab of brawn in the pantry to next door's cat just to be on the safe side. Betty hated seeing food going to waste but she had a reputation to protect.

"I.... I just don't feel very well Mam, that's all." Ivy sniffed. She blew her nose into a grubby, handkerchief, desperately trying to swallow back the gorge rising in her throat. Keeping a balled fist in front of her mouth Ivy willed herself not to retch again. Her diaphragm bucked as it tried, in vain, to expel the last meagre contents of Ivy's stomach.

"What do you mean by *not feeling very well?* Do you reckon it's something you've drunk? 'Cos I've got a right old gut ache myself from some dodgy beer Jack Fowler's been serving at the Rose." Betty's guts grumbled audibly. "I reckon there'll be quite a few of Jack's customers not moving too far from the lav today."

Betty shuffled towards the door making sure not to slop the brimming chamber pot. "I'll just empty this gazunder and when I get back how about I make us both a nice, strong cup of tea and a piece of toast perhaps to line the stomach? From the look of you I reckon we could both use it." Her guts growled loudly. "Oh God no.... That bloody beer." Betty gripped her belly and shot out to the lavatory as fast as the chamber pot would allow.

Ivy's mind was racing. Her Mam would be back soon. What to do? Ivy was caught up in a lie of omission, Betty had provided her with an excuse for now, but it couldn't last.

Soon Ivy's sin would be obvious and too grave for the likes of Mother Hargreaves to dig out with her spoon.

Ivy knew she was stuck between a rock and a hard place. She would be eighteen next month and yet she felt like an old woman. She looked awful and felt even worse.

Ivy's head had been all over the place since she had shared her secret with Alice that Sunday. Every night she tossed and turned unable to sleep with worry and praying to everything that was holy her bleed would come. Hoping against hope that Alice was right, and it was just a scare. Every morning her sheets were clean, and her body was crippled with waves of violent nausea.

275

Nearly a whole week had passed; a whole week of the baby rooting itself ever more firmly inside her and she still hadn't found the courage to act. Now the decision was being forced on her. She couldn't wait much longer. Did she tell her Mam the truth first... or did she have to tell Jimmy?

Chapter 26

Ivy sat in the kitchen by the range and waited for Jimmy, listening for the creak of the back gate, the soft click of his boots in the yard. She knew Jimmy's habits; wending his way down the dark back lane, slipping in through the back door; and if the mood was on him…creeping up to her room.

Outside the comforting warmth of the kitchen the evening had suddenly turned to nasty. It was a surprisingly chilly, wet blustery night. Fat raindrops snaked down the window.

In the dark Ivy fidgeted, gathering her thoughts. She went over the words she needed to say in her head a thousand times. Her nervous fingers worried away at ragged cuticles.

Almost eleven o'clock, not long to go now. The pubs would be throwing out soon.

Mam had gone to bed long since. Ivy could hear the harsh, rasping snores drifting through the ceiling. All day Betty had trotted in and out to the lavatory clutching her guts; her bowels had turned to water, a martyr to colicky spasms and bouts of smelly diarrhoea.

"Oh God Ivy, this is getting worse.... It's been like a flight of larks coming out of my backside. I'm going to swing for that Jack Fowler, so help me I will" Betty moaned as she dashed outside for the umpteenth time. The deterioration in Betty's own health occupied her with such a ferocity it drove away any thoughts about her pale, sickly daughter.

A huge pile of wet washing draped over the clothes horse in front of the range, testament to Jack's bad beer and Betty's lack of continence. All afternoon Ivy had had to scrub away at the sheets and soiled smalls. All the while her own poor stomach heaved in protest.

Her mother eventually took to her bed with strict instructions to Ivy that her daughter would have to turn up for Betty's cleaning shift at the Trafalgar pub the following morning.

"You'll just have to do it Ivy, Now don't go all moon faced on me. I'm too poorly and there's nothing else to be said, we need the money. Just get there a bit early, six thirty should do it. Tell Cecil I'm too ill to get to work in the morning. Tell

278

him that bloody Jack Fowler at the Rose is serving bad beer, awfully bad beer if my guts are anything to go by. If word gets around there's dodgy beer on tap at the Rose there'll be plenty of customers coming his way, I can tell you. *"*

"But I can't Mam! You know I've got to "Do" for Mr Partridge in the morning." Ivy's heart had sunk at the thought of getting up extra early to clean for Cecil. Even worse the pub lavatories were always stinking piss holes after a hard Saturday night. It just wasn't fair. Her mother knew she had another job cleaning.

Ivy did chores for an elderly widower at one of the more well-to-do households nestling on the fringe of Grangetown. She spent her Sunday morning doing the heavy work, washing floors, scrubbing the lavatory and scouring the front steps. Betty turned a deaf ear and steam rolled on.

"Oh, for goodness' sake, don't fuss girl. A bit of hard work shouldn't bother a strong young body like yours. It just can't be helped Ivy so none of your whining. You've been lucky, you should have guts like mine then you'd have a bit more sympathy I can tell you." Betty felt wretched.

"If you put your back into it then you can still get over to

Old Man Partridge's in time to do his housework at nine, you'll have all afternoon to put your feet up; I wouldn't ask unless I had to."

Ivy looked resigned to her fate.

"Like I said, just get up a bit earlier an' have a nice bit of breakfast before you leave, and you'll be champion. There's some bread in the pantry for some toast. Oh, and now I think about it, you'd better give the rest of that brawn to next door's cat; just be on the safe side."

Ivy was left with no option, sickness or no, she had to get up extra early to fit in two lots of cleaning in the morning, and on her Sunday morning too. Life just wasn't fair.

In the dwindling light of the range fire, Ivy struggled to hold back the tears. She was exhausted; she feared the approaching storm when she told Jimmy about the baby.

Jimmy lifted the latch and slipped into the yard, a small light still glowed in the back kitchen, someone must still be up.

Bugger he wanted to think, not talk tonight. He certainly didn't want words with Betty.

280

He ground his dog-end into the yard flags and thrust his hands deep into his pockets. His fingers contacted the discarded Council flyer. Bloody hell he'd all but forgotten about this scheme. Well, Sean probably wouldn't be needing this now, the poor bastard was still stuck in the Cardiff Infirmary being treated for a stroke brought on by that bang to his head, lying in bed as weak as a kitten and Eileen at his side praying for a miraculous recovery.

He was surprised to see it was Ivy. "Oh, it's you... not like you to be up so late, what's up? "In the feeble light of the kitchen bulb the girl looked so pale, her skin was almost transparent, her eyes looked listless, her head flopped in her hands. Jimmy eyed her suspiciously.... *something was wrong.*

"Cat got your tongue?"

Ivy started to cry; fat tears rolled down her cheeks. She hung her head.

"I'm pregnant Jimmy" her voice was muffled, low and hesitant, as if the fateful words didn't want to leave her mouth. Now there was no going back.

"What did you say?" He moved towards the table, his face

only inches from hers. His voice menacing and low, sounds carried in the house at night.

Bloody hell he'd always thought he'd been careful. There had only been the odd occasion when he'd slipped up and now Ivy had caught; how unlucky could that be?

"I'm, I'm pregnant Jimmy," Ivy stuttered miserably, she didn't dare look at him.

"I see, well, well, that's a turn up for the books. Haven't you been a silly girl Ivy?"

Ivy wept into her hands.

"No use crying about it now, *you* should have been more careful. Whose is it then Ivy?.... Which of those pimply lads you like to hang around with on a Saturday night have had their way with you?" His face was within inches of hers. Anger made him cruel.

Ivy shrank as far back into her chair as possible; surely this couldn't be happening? She must be in a dreadful nightmare that would disappear if only she could wake up.

"So, tell me *who* was it? If you won't tell me perhaps I

should pay a few visits around to see the lads and their fathers, get them to face up to their responsibilities, give them a bit of encouragement like," he pounded his fist into his hand," that might help us get to the bottom of this mess." His eyes glittered and he paced up and down like a prison warder and she, his prisoner, sat pinned to the chair, terror mounted in her chest.

Ivy looked appalled, as if he'd slapped her. "No…no, I never did honestly Jimmy, I wouldn't let anyone do that" terrified of what he might do, she couldn't believe he was trying to put the blame on her.

She must be going mad. Apart from a few brief kisses no other lad had so much as touched her, she might not know much, but she knew enough to be sure the baby couldn't belong to anyone else. But it was Jimmy's word against hers now.

"Oh, but *you* must have Ivy. What have you been getting up to lately when you've been off out gallivanting with that friend of yours? Could have been all sorts for all I know. You've been a very silly girl and if you're asking me, or anyone else for that matter, to help you sort yourself out then you'd better face up to that fact." He rasped.

"Does your Mam know yet?" He lit a cigarette.

Ivy shook her head miserably.

"How long gone are you?"

"I don't know, not for sure…two months maybe a bit more?" she sniffed. "I don't know much about these things."

"Obviously *not* since you're in the club." He jibed. "Two months you say, well then Ivy, there's still time to get rid of it and nobody will be any the wiser. There'll be girls round this neck of the woods who know what to do and where to go. Get rid and that's the end of the matter. Problem solved."

"I couldn't Jimmy" she gasped. "I just couldn't, it's a mortal sin. Father O'Leary says women who do *that* burn in Hell. I couldn't kill a baby, please don't ask me to." She fingered a small silver crucifix that hung around her neck.

"*I'm* not asking you to do anything, *I'm* not the one with the problem…. You are!" He barked," I'm just trying to offer a bit of helpful advice and it seems it's not to your liking. It's your bed and you can lie on it as far as I'm concerned, if that's what you want, it's no skin off my nose what you do." He shrugged his shoulders dismissively.

Ivy started to weep uncontrollably. *How could this be all her fault?*

"Stop snivelling, that's not going to solve anything you silly girl."

Ivy tried to gulp back the sobs that wracked her frame, a pain was starting to form in her chest.

"For crying out loud Ivy what on earth do you think *is* going to happen if you go ahead and have this baby then? Do you think the angels will come and whisk it away? Maybe place it under a gooseberry bush for some nice family to find?" He sneered.

She shook her head, her hair hung in greasy sheets around her face, tears coursing down her cheeks.

"No of course not! I'll tell you what *is* going to 'appen Ivy. Your Mam will send you to one of those places for unmarried mothers, that's if you're lucky and that's only if she doesn't throw you out on the streets first."

Ivy gasped as if someone had punched her.

"I'm telling you the facts Ivy; if you won't get rid of it, you won't have much choice about what happens next" he jabbed his finger in the direction of her abdomen. "It will be off to the Mother and Baby home for you or, it's the gutter... one or the other so you'd better get used to the idea!"

"But I thought you'd help me Jimmy, after all you..." she moaned.

"Me! I've had *nothing* to do with this mess....and you'd better remember that Ivy or else. You won't be dragging *me* into this. If I help sort this out for you, it will be because I'm fond of you Ivy, and no other reason. Got that?"

Ivy nodded, she daren't open her mouth for fear of saying the wrong thing. She was such a fool where men and boys were concerned, she never knew the right thing to do.

"For your information Ivy, I could pack my bags and leave this place at a moment's notice if I had a mind to, and you'd better remember that! That would give your Mam something to think on as well. *You're* the one with the problem Ivy, not me." His voice was controlled, she felt like an insect under a microscope. Jimmy paced about the small kitchen; brows furrowed, deep in thought, smoking furiously on his cigarette.

286

Cowed, Ivy shook her head in misery and waited for his next move.

"Alright, *this* is what happens next…. *you* will keep your mouth shut and do exactly as your told, especially if you expect people to try and help and *I* shall be having words with your Mam tomorrow…. Make sure she knows the lie of the land. Understood?"

Ivy nodded.

"I shall tell her about your *mistake* and when your Mam asks you all about this you'd better come up with a good explanation my girl or, even better, just keep your mouth shut, especially if you're not even sure *which* of those lads it was!" He added menacingly.

Ivy moaned piteously.

"You're going to need all the friends you can get in the next few months and I am your friend aren't I?"

She half nodded unsure of her ground. "Yes Jimmy."

"Well, you'd better believe I am Ivy, because you need me! So, *if* you behave yourself, and *if* you do as your told

287

then….and only then I *might* find another way to help a girl in trouble, but that's only because I'm fond of you Ivy." He stroked her hair; allowed his fingers to trail down her neck.

He fiddled with the delicate silver crucifix around her neck. "Remember you've made promises before God Ivy and bad things always happen to people who break that sort of promise."

Terrified, she felt like a robin being pawed by a cat before it made the kill.

"Understood?"

"Yes, Jimmy," she whispered.

"That's my good girl," he released her.

"Now get yourself off to bed, it's nearly midnight….and you can count yourself lucky that old Jimmy always knows what to do in a crisis." His smile was like the gape of a hungry fox.

"Now are you going to stop telling those silly stories and accept you've been a bad girl?" He paused and waited for her nod.

"Good girl. And if you do *exactly* what you're told then we

288

might… *just might* be able to work something out. You're going to owe me Ivy. Always remember that!"

"Yes Jimmy." She trailed off to her room…. broken.

Poor cow he'd have to give this some thought, whatever happened Ivy needed to keep her mouth shut. He was sure Ivy had got the message, he wasn't having Betty shouting blue murder to anyone who would listen; creating a scene, he'd have to get steer Betty in the right direction of travel.

Anyway, if Betty did cut up rough, why should anyone believe a drunken old slapper like Betty! Like mother like daughter as they say."

The flyer rustled in his pocket. He spread it out on the table. Perhaps Sean had been right all those months ago, if he played his cards right then this scheme could be to his advantage.

He wasn't letting Betty get off scot free though. If Betty wanted to keep Gerald Williams on the hook then dragging a pregnant Ivy around like a ball and chain would certainly put a downer on the matter. Betty needed to know she had a big problem on her hands and if Jimmy helped take that problem off Betty's hands then she owed him big time.

Jimmy sipped whisky from his hip flask. A warm glow spread through him.

As the old saying goes Jimmy...When God shuts a door he opens a window.

Chapter 27

Ivy left for her cleaning job at the Trafalgar pub just as dawn was creeping over the yard wall. Birds were starting to call across the greasy, grey slate rooftops and the weak silver sun cast ripples of pink through the high clouds; rain would be on its way later.

Tossing and turning all night Ivy had barely slept a wink. Plagued with nightmares she dreamed she was walking the streets carrying a howling baby that she couldn't put down, faces loomed out of doorways leering at her *"What'll you do for a shilling luv?"*

 In the grey morning light, her sheets were still white, and her sin had grown a little bigger. Ivy was so sick with worry, so terrified about the reception she would get when she returned home from her jobs that morning that she contemplated running away…. But where was there to run to?

All she had was Mam, Jimmy and Alice. Probably not even Alice, not once the word got out. Like as not Alice's Mam would close the door in her face, cut her dead in case the contagion was catching.

There *was* only Mam and Jimmy and then *only* if she did as she was told by Jimmy. Last night he had frightened her into silence; Jimmy said he would look after her if she did as she was told. *She had to trust him; it was the only way.*

A flock of majestic grey geese flew high overhead. Ivy watched as the honking mass grew distant and wished she could fly away with them.

Betty padded downstairs at just before ten o'clock. After spending the previous day voiding her guts and existing on dry bread and weak tea she was starving. The appetizing smell of lightly singed bread wafted upstairs. Betty was partial to a thick slice of crispy, well-done toast, couldn't abide the pale flabby stuff that had been barely wafted under the grill. A bit of toast and home-made blackberry jam was just what the doctor ordered this morning!

 That Jimmy Benson had better not have used up all the bread and marge before she'd had a bit of breakfast else she would have something to say about it.

"Morning Betty, there's still some tea in the pot if you want it." Jimmy, feet up on a stool, and a newspaper scattered across the table, had a huge mug of steaming hot tea and a plate of toast piled high in front of him. He was studying the football results.

Betty ambled over to the pot to pour herself some tea, she was gratified to see there was still best part of half a loaf of bread resting on the bread board. *Ivy obviously hadn't bothered with any breakfast before she went out then, silly girl.*

Jimmy dropped his feet and folded his newspaper. "I'm sorry to say, but we need to have a bit of a talk Betty." His voice was calm and measured.

She lit a cigarette and regarded him with interest, *it was probably about money or being late with his rent again. Well perhaps today was the day she told him about her and Ivy moving out of Bute street; it was time for a new start, her mind was made up.*

"Take a seat Betty,"

She poured her tea and drew up her chair, the toast could wait a while.

"Sorry to be the bearer of bad news, but I've found out something you should know." He glanced over the top of his mug of tea. Noted with satisfaction, the look of panic spread across her face.

Her heart contracted a little, what had happened, what did he know about any bad news?

"You've got a problem. Or should I say, more to point, your Ivy's got the problem."

Betty's face fell. "What do you mean Ivy's got a problem? Spit it out Jimmy, what do you know about my Ivy?"

Betty's thoughts were whirling, possibilities raced through her mind. Surely Ivy hadn't been caught up to no good she'd taught the girl better than that.

"Whilst you've had your eye off the ball Betty, out with that gentleman friend of yours, I'm afraid your Ivy has been running a bit wild, getting in with a bad crowd so I've heard on the grapevine."

"My Ivy? Are you telling me my Ivy is in with a bad crowd? I just don't believe it Jimmy. Who told you this rubbish anyway? You know how people like to gossip around here!"

294

She puffed and blew her cheeks in disbelief.

She'd brought Ivy up to be a good girl. Jimmy must be jumping to conclusions, getting the wrong end of the stick.

"Nobody's just *told* me anything Betty, I've also seen her out and about with my own eyes, hanging around with that Alice Tranter at the Bomb in Splott with a group of lads buying her drinks all evening. I've *seen* her there all dressed up in borrowed clothes and make-up slapped all over her face like a tart. I even told her off about it one night when I caught her coming back in here all painted up. She said you wouldn't mind by the way, said it was stuff she'd borrowed from Alice Tranter."

Betty couldn't believe what she was hearing; Alice Tranter was certainly a bad influence.

"Course it's not up to me to keep the girl on the straight and narrow Betty, that's your job." He gazed at her pointedly and lit himself another cigarette; face dead pan as he delivered the awful news.

Betty was shaking her head in disbelief, she didn't recognize this picture of a deceitful Ivy sneaking around behind her back, wearing make-up, drinking with lads, up to no good.

"All I can say Betty is that she can't deny it, and there's plenty of others who will have seen her too. More to point, you know what lads are like when they've bought a girl a few drinks. They expect things, a bit of a return on their investment so to speak."

Betty gasped.

"Over the last few months, since being let off the leash, it seems your little Ivy has acquired a reputation with the local lads for being a bit…. Well shall we say, being a bit easy."

"Easy! I'll wring her neck when I catch her. God help her when she comes in this afternoon that's all I can say. She won't be going out again with that Alice Tranter or anyone else for that matter!"

"I'm afraid there's more."

Betty's face drained to a deathly pale, "more…what are you saying Jimmy?"

"She's pregnant."

"Oh no," Betty moaned.

"I caught her being sick several times in the mornings when I was going off to work so I tackled her about it, she's certain she's in the family way. Sorry to say Betty, she's *not* so certain which lad has got a baby on her." He dragged deeply on his cigarette and watched Betty crumple like a deflated balloon.

"The stupid little fool, so that's why she was heaving her guts up yesterday," Betty groaned and shook her head in disbelief.

"Can't she see how hard my life has been bringing up a child on my own? What on earth shall I do with her now? She's bloody ruined herself!" Betty gulped back the sobs building in her throat; her mind reeling.

"Well, I'm sure you will think of something Betty, but as I said to her, unless she gets rid of it then, you and I both know, she's going to find life difficult being an unmarried mother. It's a tough old world out there. It's a good thing she's got her mother to help look after her." Jimmy said slyly. He wanted Betty punch drunk with shock and worry.

"But she can't expect me to take responsibility and what about my friend Gerald? Gerald has asked me and Ivy to move in with him…. and I've said Yes." She buried her head in her

297

hands. "It's not fair we were supposed getting married soon. I can't ask him to take Ivy in now. Not now Ivy's in the family way, what would his neighbours think?"

Well, well, the crafty bird was planning on marrying Gerald Williams. He hadn't expected that, and it seems she had it all planned.... moving out, without so much as a thought about him. In a couple of months, he would have found himself out on the street and in need of new digs.

"She's gone and ruined everything. I'll have to tell Gerald it can't happen now. How I can keep a roof over our heads if she's got a baby to look after ...the stupid fool," Betty wailed.

Jimmy put his arm around her shoulder. "Listen Betty, Ivy *knows* she's been stupid, but we know she's a good girl at heart, the trouble is she's damaged goods now, an' there's not many men will want a piece of that."

Betty sobbed hysterically into her handkerchief, all her hopes and dreams of a better life for her and Ivy were disappearing into thin air. *Jimmy was right, it was exactly what Phoebe said about Gerald only the other evening, it was rare to find a man prepared to forgive a fallen woman, to take on another man's mistake.*

"So why are *you* telling me all this?" She eyed him suspiciously.

"Because Ivy's terrified, especially about telling you Betty; scared witless you'll throw her out. It's as simple as that."

Betty shook her head in despair and understood only too well. She remembered her own terror when she was certain she was pregnant, the bad dream that she hoped would disappear and never did, the reality she had to confront when prayers were not answered.

"She's even denying that she's let a lad go all the way though, but I told her babies don't just happen, so there was no point lying about it. Whatever she has done with these lads, it's been enough, and it has got her in the family way, she's the one left in the lurch."

Betty remembered that terrifying day she had to draw on every ounce of her courage and tell her father she was pregnant, the shouts and accusations the demands for answers, answers she refused to give. The tears and the ultimatums. The brutal resolution.

"She's very frightened now Betty, I felt sorry for her it's as simple as that. I told her she needed to come clean days ago, but she didn't. She needs to deal with this whether she wants to or not." He sucked thoughtfully on his cigarette.

"Course she lied a bit at first, tried to excuse the spewing up when I caught her with her head in the sink a couple of mornings ago; gave me some rubbish about eating dodgy faggots, but that nonsense couldn't continue for several mornings in a row. In the end she couldn't keep it a secret any longer that's why she pleaded with me to break the news. I said I'd do it, adult to adult like." He gave Betty a small smile that didn't reach his hard eyes. His tone trickled a compassion he didn't feel.

All this going on under her very nose and she hadn't spotted it. "And I thought I'd kept her sheltered and safe, I'm a damn fool letting her out of my sight," Betty muttered.

"You'd better know that she's adamant she's keeping the baby too…. Worried about burning in hell or some such superstitious nonsense. If that's the case we can only hope it comes out white."

Betty gave a sharp intake of breath. "

"I've got no trouble with the blacks myself, but you know how people are Betty if it's a coloured baby." Jimmy turned the screw a notch tighter.

Betty groaned in misery; each new dreadful possibility was like another dagger in her heart.

"The question is now that *you* know about the baby Betty, what are you going to do about Ivy?"

"I don't know" Betty wailed. Visions of young Elizabeth Evans traipsing the streets the night her father threw her out, flashed through her mind, it felt like the same horrible history repeating itself. *No matter how angry she was about the baby, she could never abandon Ivy in the way her Da had abandoned her.*

"If you want go ahead and marry Mr Williams and you say she can't live with you then I supposed you'll have to send her to one of those Mother and baby homes until she's had the baby?" Jimmy feigned compassionate interest, "all I know is that the ones we have in Ireland are fierce-some places, run by hard faced, shrivelled up Catholic nuns who have less compassion than the devil himself. I wouldn't want to put a daughter of mine in a place like that, still needs must as the

301

devil drives."

Betty shook her head miserably. *This was a scenario she'd explored and rejected for herself all those years ago. The harsh tasks and drudgery inflicted to atone for the sin of being a loose woman and then…. Worst of all, the expectation that she would just hand over the precious parcel she had nurtured, a child of shame that she had no rights over and that would never know her. Expected to abandon her baby.*

Jimmy looked at the kitchen clock, "Ivy will be back in a couple of hours, I told her I'd let you know about the baby before she got back so she'll be expecting to walk into a row."

"What shall I do with her Jimmy?" Her eyes were like saucers; two tears trickled down her face leaving sooty trails snaking across her cheeks.

"Haven't you got *any* family Betty that the girl could stay with, maybe your late husband's family could help if you spun them a yarn, just 'til the worst is over?" *Jimmy had guessed Betty's situation a long while ago, but it suited him to play along with the subterfuge.*

"You know there's no-one else Jimmy!" fury sparked in her

eyes. "Ivy's making the same mistake I did all those years ago and you know it! She's ruined her life, like I ruined mine."

"In that case," Jimmy unfolded the piece of council paper, smoothed it out and pushed it towards Betty.

"What's this supposed to be?" She pushed the flyer back towards him, irritated that he was changing the subject.

"Just hear me out Betty, go on read it! My mate Sean, you know that poor chap caught in that hawser incident, gave me this, ages ago. Said he was going on the waiting list as soon as he'd wed his sweetheart Eileen, course that's not going to 'appen now poor bugger. But the point is, I found it in my pocket the other day and it's given me an idea." He watched her reaction; he could see the pieces falling into place.

"If we can agree something then…" He jabbed his finger at the printed flier.

Ely Taff Vale and Cyfartha Housing Development Area

COUNCIL HOMES FOR HEROES

COUNCIL HOMES FOR FAMILIES

303

"Then *this* just might give us a solution to *all* our problems."

"Just so we understand each other Jimmy Benson, what exactly do you mean?" Her eyes narrowed suspiciously.

He knew this was delicate tight rope, he needed to tread with care. "I mean that if Ivy could persuade a man to marry her, then she'd have a chance of a new start in one these new council houses, the trouble is she doesn't have too many options on that score especially if she won't tell us who the father is."

"What are *you* proposing then?"

"I've been thinking about settling down ever since Sean told me about the scheme then what with his accident and everything it just slipped clean out of my head." Jimmy scrutinized the qualifying criteria.

"Trouble is, according to this, I don't qualify on any level; I haven't served, I'm not married, and I don't have any dependants."

"Go on,"

"I'd even thought about asking Julie, a girl I know from the meat packing factory, we've been seeing each other for a while on and off, I even sounded her out about it, but to be honest my heart's not in it. Julie's a girl that wants all that lovey dovey stuff, engagements, white weddings and spending her life moulding some poor sod into the perfect husband." Lies tripped smoothly of his tongue.

"You know me Betty I'm a free spirit, can't be told what to do by some woman with mother and father -in-law breathing down my ear. No that's not the life for me."

He dragged on the last of his Woodbine, before lighting the next with the glowing dog end. "You're on your own and so am I, no-one else to please but ourselves, so if we can come to some agreement about Ivy then it could kill several birds with one stone."

Betty shook her head doubtfully; *it wasn't as if he was promising her girl anything except a roof over her head.*

"I'm fond of Ivy, course I am, you know that don't you?"

Betty nodded. Jimmy did seem to make a fuss of the girl.

"She keeps a good house, and the girl is a hard worker, you've taught her well on that score Betty. She *would* have made

305

someone a cracking little wife if she hadn't gone and got herself in trouble. Terry the landlord of the Duke is always singing her praises on that score and he's not wrong." Jimmy watched Betty with his cobra gaze.

"So, what exactly are *you* saying about my Ivy," her face hardened, she never expected to be making a deal about her own daughter.

"What I'm saying is that in her condition Ivy could be.... Shall we say she could be *useful* to me. I'd take her on, look after her and if she played her cards right, did as she was told, she'd at least have a bit of a chance at happiness."

Betty flinched at his turn of phrase.

"Call it a marriage of convenience if you like. I get to put my name on a nice new Council house, you get to move in with Mr Williams as planned. Ivy gets to claim a "vestry conception" and, more important, she gets to keep a roof over her head, everybody keeps face. Unless of course you have a better idea? And if you have, well then we'll say no more about it." His face was crafty.

"I see, but Ivy is only seventeen and you're old enough to be

306

her father."

"The girl is nearly eighteen Betty, and Mr Williams is old enough to be *your* father, what is it…. twenty-two years between you two?" he raised a quizzical eyebrow.

"That's different and you know it!" Betty squawked, exasperated at being backed into a corner.

"I don't see it *is* different myself…I'm twenty-two years older than Ivy and the girl is old enough to be wed! Still suit yourself then Betty, it's no skin off my nose one way or the other, it was just a thought. I'll leave you sort this out then." Jimmy reached for the Council notice.

"Hey, hey just wait a minute," Betty grabbed his hand. "Don't be hasty, it's just this all such a shock Jimmy. I only want what's best for my girl."

"So, do I Betty! But I also want what's best for me an all, just the same as you want what's best for you with Mr Williams…. We all make deals when loves first young dream has flown out of the window. Like I said, I reckon Ivy and me could rub along well enough together. I've seen worse starts to wedlock and at least being young she will find it easier to

307

adapt. She'll need your consent to marry and of course your direction in the matter." He waited to let the idea sink in.

"She needs to know what her choices *really* are, whilst she's under twenty-one it's up to you to *tell* the girl what to do next Betty. The girl has got to be made to see sense; she's got to face up to the reality of her situation."

Betty nodded; the idea was beginning to grow on her. It was true, Ivy didn't have that many options open to her. The choice now was between a rock and a hard place.

"Don't get me wrong, I'm not saying it's a stupid idea Jimmy, if you're agreeing to put a ring on her finger?" She raised a questioning eyebrow.

He nodded. It was almost like playing poker and the stakes were high.

It was the best she could hope for. "It will just take me while to get used to the idea. I promise I'll talk to her, as you say, make her see sense."

"If you want to take up my proposal then *you've* got twenty-four hours to get this sorted Betty, I'm not being mucked about, else I'll just sling my hook and...." He hardened his

308

face. "And I have two conditions; it'll have to be done quickly so I can get those Council forms filled in before the list closes *and…* if that baby of hers is black it's being given up for adoption *or* Ivy will leave home with it and you can sort it out. *You* might want to welcome her into your household with it, but I'm not being made into a laughing-stock!"

Betty chewed her bottom lip, she lit a cigarette, thought for a moment or two and then nodded her agreement to Jimmy's terms. The deal was done, and Jimmy had won.

"Good, that's settled then Betty. I take it that you'll let Ivy know what will be happening and if she agrees I'll head off to the registry office first thing in the morning to get things underway." He gathered up the Council flyer and made to leave.

"But remember if she cuts up rough, then I'm off and I won't be back. I'll keep my side of the bargain and I'll expect both of you to do the same."

"Yes Jimmy."

"And then you can get on with your plans to move in with Mr

Williams."

Jimmy grinned, it was all going to work out beautifully and when Ivy was truly his he'd get her trained just the way he wanted.

Later that evening, just before ten o'clock, Jimmy came home to a grim -faced Betty waiting to greet him in the kitchen. She was wearing her house coat wrapped around her like battle armour.

He raised a quizzical eyebrow and waited for the verdict.

"I've talked to Ivy."

"And?"

"And she's still adamant that she hasn't let a boy go all the way. She didn't deny that she was pregnant and that she won't get rid of it *and* she admitted that she had been drinking with lads and wearing make up at the Bomb." Betty scrutinized Jimmy's face and moved smoothly on. "Even so I told her that, for your own reasons you were prepared to marry her under certain conditions." Betty waited to see Jimmy's reaction.

310

When Betty had told Ivy that Jimmy was prepared to marry her, Ivy had looked at her mother strangely. Betty tried to analyse the look it seemed to be a mixture of relief coupled with fear. Something *had* happened between Ivy and Jimmy, Betty was sure of it..

"I see, well, I might just withdraw that offer now since the girl is obviously a liar. Perhaps it's best just to leave it up to you to sort out, cos that list closes in a couple of months' time and then ....." Jimmy lit himself a cigarette and left the rest hanging in the air.

Betty flinched. "Let's not be hasty Jimmy. Ivy knows she doesn't have much choice about what happens next. I told her I expected her to accept your offer and that in exchange she will work hard and try to make a go of it, try to be a good wife to you."

"And the baby?"

"She swears it's not a black man's baby Jimmy. It's all she would say when I pushed her." It had been an ugly scene. Betty had even slapped Ivy when the girl obstinately refused to accept that she had allowed a lad to go all the way. Thankfully, after all the tears Ivy had agreed to do as she was told and marry Jimmy as quickly and as discreetly as possible.

Betty still couldn't push away the tiny nagging possibility that this baby might be something to do with Jimmy…. But there again, he was going to marry Ivy so what more was there to be done now even if the baby *was* his? If she wasn't careful the whole arrangement could fall apart, and Ivy would be left holding the baby just like she was all those years ago.

"She's just upset Jimmy but that's all, she swore on her crucifix, so we'll just have to take her word for it." Betty shrugged.

"No Betty, I'll believe it when I see it, the agreement is as I said Betty, if it's white then I'll allow her to bring it up, otherwise they're both out!" He jabbed his thumb over his shoulder to emphasize his point.

Betty nodded, she felt utterly wretched. "Understood."

Chapter 28

"He never did! Well, knock me down with a feather!" Alice's jaw dropped. "Jimmy Benson's actually gone and proposed!"

The two girls were sat on a bench on the edge of Mermaid Quay, the light was fading, a gloomy, heavy cloud bank was building on the horizon snuffing out the setting sun. Soon it would be dark. The girls did not have much time; Alice's mother would start to worry.

Despite being banned from seeing Alice by Jimmy and Mam, Ivy was determined to speak to her friend one last time. When Mam and Jimmy were out, Ivy seized her opportunity and collared Alice after work. It might be Ivy's last chance.

Alice had been anxiously awaiting news of Ivy's predicament ever since Ivy let her in on the secret. What her friend might do next had tormented Alice from the moment she knew; terrified that Ivy might tread the dangerous path to Mrs Hargreaves's backdoor, visions of Ivy laid out on a mortuary slab haunted her dreams.

Once Alice almost told her Mam, but Ivy had bound her to
secrecy; the sight of Ivy hanging around outside the Coal
Exchange looking rosy cheeked and healthy made Alice's
heart flutter with relief.

"Jimmy Benson is going to marry you?" Alice repeated;
dumbfounded.

"Shh, keep your voice down Alice," Ivy glanced around
nervously, in her world walls seemed to have eyes and ears.
Jimmy could be watching her even now; she didn't know
what the consequences would be for defying Mam and Jimmy.

"Well, is he? Either he's asked your Mam if he can marry you
or he hasn't? Come on Ivy, I want to hear all the details"
taking her cue from Ivy, Alice lowered her voice to a
conspiratorial whisper.

"Yes he has sort of" Ivy mumbled. "Mam has agreed it with
him, and I've said I will, so yes." Ivy's voice trailed off. She
was sworn to secrecy about the whole thing, only allowed to
say the absolute minimum.

After her row with Mam when storm of tears and shouting

had blown itself out, Jimmy went to the registry office on the following Monday morning. Jimmy filled in the forms, giving notice of their intention to marry. Mam and Jimmy completed all the documentation and Ivy's fate was sealed. She managed to place her spidery, scrawled signature on the dotted line and resigned herself to her fate.

What other choice did she have? Ivy knew the baby was Jimmy's and he was marrying her, who would take any notice about a young girl from Bute street who found herself in trouble.

In twenty-eight days, only one week after her eighteenth birthday Ivy would be Mrs Benson, for better or worse.

Alice thought getting married to Jimmy sounded impossibly romantic, she'd always thought Jimmy Benson was quite good looking in a roguish kind of way with his floppy blonde hair and cheeky smile.

"Well blow me. You really are a deep one Ivy Jenkins." Alice whistled. "They always say the shy ones are the ones to watch." She gave Ivy a friendly nudge. "You're going to be married and have a baby before me, who'd have thought it?"

315

Ivy sat twirling her handkerchief between nervous fingers, a vice like headache was forming around her temples.

 "Come on Ivy, stop being so secretive, surely the worst is over; now that they know about the baby? Why the glum face?"

Ivy looked as if she was carrying the weight of the world on her shoulders. She started to cry.

"Oh bless, don't cry Ivy, it's just your condition, it's usual for a girl to be a bit weepy when she's pregnant. My sister Phyllis cried buckets every day when she was expecting the twins. It'll all be alright."

Ivy gave Alice a fierce hug, clinging to her friend as if her life depended on it.

 "I can't tell you anything more Alice, I've promised not to. Mam and Jimmy would have my guts for garters if they knew I was here talking to you now, I'm only here to say good-bye Alice," Ivy sobbed.

 "What!" Alice squawked. "Goodbye. Why are you saying goodbye?"

"Mam and Jimmy have agreed that I must stay at home until the baby's born, I'm not allowed out anymore, so we can't see each other." Ivy's pinched, tear stained face was a picture of misery.

Ivy didn't want to describe the towering rage that engulfed her Mam when Alice's name was raised. Jimmy had ensured that a large amount of blame and fault for Ivy's predicament was apportioned to the brassy Alice Tranter. Her name was mud in twenty-two Bute street; it suited Jimmy and to a certain extent Betty, that flighty Alice should be blamed for leading Ivy astray. If the judge and jury found Alice guilty of being an undesirable, corrupting influence, then others were absolved of their failings. Ivy was banned from seeing her best friend ever again.

"That's not fair Ivy they can't keep you a prisoner," Alice was furious.

"I must go back home now Alice; I've been out ages. Mam would kill me if she knew I was here with you." Ivy's eyes darted around nervously.

"Wish me luck Alice, I just had to say goodbye, that's why I came in case I never see you again. Mam and Jimmy talked

317

about us all moving away; making a new start away from everything." Ivy couldn't bring herself to say amongst other things most importantly *away from Alice.*

Ivy gave her friend a kiss on both cheeks, "I'll never forget you Alice, whatever happens next and where-ever I end up; you'll always be my best and dearest friend. And who knows, maybe after the baby we could....?"

"Yes! After the baby, we'll find a way to see each other. And I won't ever forget you Ivy, I'll *always* be there if you need me. Remember that Ivy, if ever you need me, just find a way to let me know!"

Alice was devastated. Ivy was like a sister. She loved the delicate girl with her sweet, kind nature. Alice had never heard a nasty, bitchy comment pass Ivy's lips, Ivy saw the good in everyone. It was mean treating Ivy like a possession that could be parcelled up and sent away like an awkward package with no say in the matter.

"Write to me Ivy." Alice pleaded. "They can't stop you writing to me, even if it's just a few lines to let me know you're alright, or where you are." Alice rummaged in her handbag and pulled out two 2d postage stamps from her purse. "Here you take these and keep them safe for when you need them."

Alice's face took on a grim determination, she felt as if the prison gates were closing on her friend. Giving Ivy stamps was the least she could do. "I bought these stamps yesterday for my Mam, and I forgot to give them to her. I'll get Mam some more tomorrow. Go on you take them, keep them for when you need them." She thrust the stamps into Ivy's pocket.

Even if Ivy couldn't get to a post office for stamps she could post a letter, that was at least something. "There, now you can post me a letter. If you ask me for help, I'll find a way, somehow I will, I promise Ivy." Alice hugged her friend desperate not to let her go.

"Thank you, Alice, I'll keep them safe. I'm sorry about everything." Ivy kissed Alice for the last time, gulping back the rising tide of tears that threatened to overwhelm her. Alice was her best, her *only* real friend.

Ivy turned and ran home to her fate in Bute street.

"Write to me Ivy." Alice yelled after the tiny, retreating figure of Ivy. Her friend scuttled away as fast as she could; her

319

stacked shoe catching on the uneven cobbles.

"Please write!" Alice's voice carried down the long echoing street.

When Ivy turned the corner and disappeared out of sight, Alice broke down and sobbed as if her heart was breaking.

Chapter 29

Eileen had spent weeks on her knees at Sean's beside. It was all she could do. With the help of Father
O'Leary, she was going to pray her Sean better if it
killed her.

Eileen was a practical girl, and after the initial shock
and tears when she saw her poor fiancé fighting for
his life, she told herself to buck up and get on with
helping Sean mend.

No point snivelling and feeling sorry for yourself,
pick yourself up and do the best you can was Eileen's view on life. Now this comforting mantra of
not crying over spilt milk held her in good stead.
*Sean's relying on you she told herself every, you
can't let him down.*

Eileen set about helping. First she told the fruit
packing factory she couldn't come in for her job; her

job was at Sean's side. They thanked her for her consideration and gave her job to someone else.

She informed her mother that she intended to spend every waking hour at Sean's sick bed and that under Eileen's bed there was a small blue sock full of savings for her wedding, her mother was to use it to pay bills now that Eileens wages weren't coming in.

Eileen marched around to Ellen Street and secured an address for Sean's Mam and Dad from Mrs Isla Murray and wrote to his parents every other day with details of his condition and in turn she told Sean any news she received from back home.

 Her mind was resolute. She intended to marry Sean in whatever state God saw fit to release him from hospital and she would devote all her strength to getting him well. She brooked no argument about it. If people wanted to tell her she was a fool to waste her life on a broken man then she would send them packing.

If concerned friends tried to coax Eileen into seeing sense she sent them packing too. And if any doctor or well-meaning nurse had the temerity to suggest that Sean was a hopeless case and that she should get on with her own life, she simply put her shoulders back and prayed twice as hard; praying for Sean to get well and for the fool of a doctor or nurse to know the power of faith.

If ever Eileen was obliged by Sister to leave his bed-side she retreated to the waiting area and continued her prayers in there until she was given permission to resume her vigil at Sean's side.

"There's nothing more we can do for him now until he regains consciousness. He's holding on, which is a miracle but, Miss Murphy it's in God's hands now. All we do for Mr Riley now is hope and pray he will recover" Doctor Cradoc had said when Sean had de-fied the odds and been deemed well enough to leave the intensive care ward.

Taking Dr Cradoc at his word Eileen was doing exactly that. If hope and prayer was required then she was going to make sure Sean had the best spiritual assistance she could muster.

He mother Ida feared for Eileen's health and sanity as she watched her pretty, buxom daughter become a shadow of her former self. Pounds dropped off Eileen's trim frame until she became pale and gaunt, refusing all but the smallest of snacks to sustain her. *How can I think of food when my Sean is fighting for his life?*

Eileen was determined to pray Sean back to health. With Father O'Leary's help Sean was being prayed for night and day and no one was going to stop her.

Eileen invoked the highest order of prayers to help surround Sean with hope. She spent nine days on her novena to the Blessed Virgin and when Sean still failed to rouse from the depths of his dreamless sleep she turned to St Jude reciting his most Holy invocation as often as her strength allowed. She knew the words by heart and the very beauty of them comforted her.

Today Eileen ate a modest breakfast when she popped home to change into some fresh clothes, she'd felt in need of substance to recharge her batteries for the days ahead.

Pleas from her mother to look after herself fell on deaf ears, it was Father O'Leary's suggestion that she must bolster her support for Sean by looking after herself that hit home.

You're no good to Sean if you make yourself ill child, Father O'Leary had said one morning.

Eileen reproached herself for not considering Sean when she was running herself into the ground, going without food and rest, so she did just enough to keep body and soul together.

Eileen knew what she needed to do and would take no-one's counsel except Father O'Leary's. The kindly priest stayed by Sean's side whenever she had to leave him. He would sit holding Sean's hand praying to all the Saints to come to Sean's aid.

Now feeling refreshed she wanted to join him in their daily prayer to St Jude. She hurried back to the ward.

Through the glass of the doors, she could see Father O'Leary crossing himself and anointing Sean's forehead with Holy water, his devotion to his stricken parishioner touched her deeply. All her faith and hope centred on the small, wizened man sat at Sean's bedside. His frail bowed shoulders carried all her hopes.

"Thank you Father, "she murmured as she joined him at Sean's bedside.

"You're welcome my child," he gave her a twinkling, kindly smile that reached all the way to his nut-brown eyes. "Shall we share a few moments quiet reflection before we pray together?"

Eileen nodded and bowed her head, Father O'Leary laid his hand on her head and blessed her, then after a few moments he led the prayer to Saint Jude. *"O most holy apostle, Saint Jude, faithful servant and friend of Jesus,.....*

Eileen held Sean's hand and muttered the familiar words, willing Sean with all her heart to come back to her. The priest held his hands over Sean's broken body in blessing.

"....to bring visible and speedy help where help was almost despaired of.....

At first Eileen thought she had imagined it. There were so many dark hours she had wanted, prayed and hoped for something, anything... but there it was again! There

was no doubt. Sean had squeezed her hand!

"Oh" she gasped, "Oh thank you God,"

Father O'Leary looked up from his prayer. He could see she was crying.

327

"Father! Sean just squeezed my hand! He can hear us! Oh Father, it's a blessed miracle!"

His body was transformed with the power of prayer, he would later inform the Bishop as he recalled the incident and the events that followed. The scurry of nurses and doctors focussed all their attention on the patient surfacing back to consciousness from a deep chasm.

Father O'Leary was convinced he had witnessed a miracle of faith and it gladdened his heart; in all his seventy-five years he'd never seen the like of it…. *a miracle no doubt about it.*

Of course, the eminent Doctors attending Sean uttered platitudes about the power of the body to heal itself with the right treatment, *a body recovered in its own good time they said.*

But Father O'Leary would not be shaken from his belief that it was nothing less than a miracle and he went straight back to St Pauls to give thanks for it.

Sean Riley half-opened his right eye, his other eyelid still immobile from the effect of his stroke, barely twitched or fluttered.

The blank paralysis on the left side of his face continued into his slack, drooping, unruly mouth, but his right-hand side delighted Eileen with just the tiniest flicker of a smile. To Eileen it was as uplifting and beautiful as a sparkling rainbow after a storm.

Now she dared to hope. "I love you," she sobbed. "I love you Sean."

Chapter 30

"Sat up in bed you say Jimmy? Well Jesus lord have mercy!"
Terry crossed himself. "My Joan said a fair few Hail Mary's
on that lad's behalf I can tell you.... But who'd have thought
it? Sitting up!"

"Whoa hold your horses Terry that's *not* what I said" Jimmy
supped his pint and chewed the fat over the bar with Terry at
the Duke.

News of Sean's miraculous recovery had spread far and wide
and everyone laid claim to having a small part in in.

"What I said was that they *hoped* he would be sat up in bed
soon, he's still got a long way to go, some bits of him are still
numb from the stroke, not under his control like." Jimmy said.

"They say that girl of his, Eileen, never left his side;
marvellous she was. Her and Father O'Leary kept at it night
and day. Mark my words Jimmy if anybody can get Sean to
recover it will be those two!" Terry had almost promoted
Eileen to sainthood for her devotion to Sean.

"Oh, I reckon Father O'Leary wasn't letting Sean get off his Catholic instruction that easy, coma or no coma." Jimmy guffawed. "He's not letting one of his flock get out of marital instruction either! If anybody owes God and Father O'Leary it's Sean and I'm sure his Eileen will remind him of it if ever he steps out of line." The two men burst out laughing so hard Jimmy slopped his pint all over Terry's clean counter.

"Hey, you sloppy bastard, I just cleaned that! It's *you* that needs a woman running around after you an' all Jimmy Benson, a lass to keep you in order, a bit like my Joan," Terry teased as he mopped up the slops and added a few inches to top up Jimmy's tankard.

Terry's Joan had a reputation for being a rottweiler in a poodle's body, she might look all fluffy and inoffensive, a tiny woman who barely scraped five foot even when her permed curls added inches to her diminutive stature, but everybody knew Joan was a force to be reckoned with.

"Aye I know Terry, you're probably right there. All this business with Sean and Eileen got me thinking a few weeks back, you know, about settling down."

Jimmy didn't dare contradict Terry about the merits of his

lady wife Joan, but a feisty woman like Joan was *not* what he had in mind.

Terry pricked up his ears. People looked to him to have his ear to the ground and to know all the latest gossip.

"Oh aye, so what's up on that score then Jimmy?"

"It was Sean that got me thinking at first, he showed me that leaflet about applying for a Council house in Ely, he fancied thateas him and Eileen might get on the list, get away from here and make a new start, and I quite fancied the idea myself." Jimmy pushed an application form over the counter for Terry to read.

"Says here that the list closes for this development end of June 1949. Bloody hell, that's only about eight weeks away, you'd better get a shift on Jimmy."

"That's right and as soon as I can complete that section on the back of that form it will be going straight in the post."

"What?" Terry flipped over the form. "You mean, this section about marital status and dependants?" Terry looked puzzled.

"That's the one, now keep this to yourself Terry," Jimmy

332

tapped his nose. Terry nodded his agreement.

"I'm getting married on Wednesday,"

"What! This Wednesday?"

Jimmy nodded.

"Well blow me down. You sly old dog Jimmy Benson, you kept that quiet. So, tell us, who's the lucky lass? Anyone we know?"

"It's Ivy."

"Ivy? Do mean *our* Ivy Jenkins who used to work the bar until that mother of hers stamped in here about four weeks ago and announced she wasn't letting the girl work here anymore?"

"That's the one. In fact, it was you that gave me the idea of asking her Terry."

Terry looked flummoxed. *How had it been his idea?*

"You said she'd make someone a cracking wife one day and I reckoned you were right."

Terry shook his head in disbelief.

"What's more her Mam Betty has taken up with a "gentleman" friend and is packing up to go live with him, so that leaves me and Ivy out on our ears. Something had to be done. I got thinking about a few things and me and Ivy decided to give this a go." Jimmy folded his papers carefully and tucked them inside his breast pocket.

"As the form says, we need to be married to qualify, so that's what we're doing. It's going to be a quiet affair and if we're honest, we know it's not exactly a love match, but we have our own reasons for trying to make a go of it. So why not?" Jimmy shrugged his shoulders and watched Terry's reaction.

"Don't get me wrong Terry, I'm fond of the girl, she's a good hardworking lass and it seems that Ivy likes me. The deed will be done in two days." Jimmy flashed a crocodile grin. *Terry would spread Jimmy's version of the marriage lie far and wide.*

"Well, in that case congratulations are in order Jimmy," Terry shook Jimmy's hand and poured him a large whisky. "Here, have this on the house with my compliments and give Ivy my best wishes an' all. Good luck to you both."

Terry had to admit, it was quite a turn up for the books He'd

334

never heard the like of it before, people getting married just to get on a Council housing list, and Jimmy old enough to be her father too!

Shy little Ivy with hard man Jimmy Benson, well, who'd have thought it. Still, it takes all sorts as they say.... perhaps it was a bit like his relationship with Joan and that had worked well enough over the years.

Chapter 31

It was the oddest sensation, the water weed holding him down was beginning to lose its deadly grip.

The horror of his feet and arms tangled and entwined in slimy green fronds that grasped and tugged, caused a bubble of panic to rise in Sean's throat but he couldn't shout out. The strands had wrapped tightly around him in a deadly spiral, tying his legs and arms so tightly he could no longer move them. Now he felt one hand free itself just enough... and he reached for his mother's hand.

She'd told him not to go swimming in the river with his brother Donal, warned him of the dangers of currents and weed waiting below the surface to drag him under. When she pulled him out of the river that fearful summer's day she had slapped his legs hard in a mixture of fury and love. He'd promised her never to do it again, but he must have, because he was drowning again.... the weed claiming him a second time.

If he could just hold her hand he would be all right, she could pull him back… just a squeeze of her hand would rescue him.

He felt the weed drop away just enough to grasp her hand; it was there as he knew it would be. Her soft fingers; warm and sure.

Through the drowning green water, he could just glimpse her face, young and pretty. He could just see through one eye as he moved towards the surface, it was enough, she was there. *She was always there.*

This time the riverbank had crisp white sheets, the bright lights above his head were a different sunshine, dazzling his tired eyes and as he gasped onto this new shore, a sea of faces closed in on him. Where was he?

"Excellent Mr Riley," a voice that he didn't know said enthusiastically.

"Call Doctor Giles!" Shouts filtered through the depths.

Who? Who?

He could hear voices, clatter and bustle, shoes clicking on a floor running towards him. He tried to say he was sorry, but all he could manage was a sort of gargle through the froth that gathered in his mouth.

Shh, Shh, his mother said, "It's going to be alright Sean, shh, now." And he knew it would be.

As his leaden body gradually came back to him he knew that his mother was gone now. Her face was no longer in his mind's eye and it worried him. *Was she ever there?*

A pretty girl sat and held his hand now, but he kept forgetting her name. She wiped the drool that crept down his chin as he supped warm milky drinks, baby like, from a small china teapot held in her delicate fingers. *Who was she?*

His left eyelid refused to creep more than half open as if in sympathy with his numb left cheek, it refused to perform its customary duty.

Time dragged by in a foggy blur, faces came and went, names that meant nothing to him wished him well. Visitors with gifts came and went with perplexing regularity.

But *she* was always there.

Stern doctors and nurses, for now he knew who they were,

338

moved his limbs daily, worrying away at him. Hands turning and prodding his body, sticking pins in him until he gasped with the torture of it. *Good, good they said…Why was it good?*

But through it all *she* was there at his bedside.

Then one morning the fog clogging his brain lifted and a bubble seemed to burst in his throat. *Eileen?*

He looked at her, the girl in the chair. Her sweet, tired face smiling and willing him on as if to say, *you do know me.*

And he did.

"Eileen?" he whispered through his drunken mouth. *She was Eileen.*

"Yes, Sean, my love." Tears flowed down her cheeks. Hour by hour, day by day he was coming back to her, she squeezed his hand. "That's right Sean, it's Eileen."

He was tired with the enormous effort, but glad to have pleased her. She was *his* Eileen. It was all slowly coming back to him.

"Good Morning Mister Riley," a blue uniform drifted into

view. Silver watch and buckle glinting in the light. A face bent towards him to look in his lazy right eye. "And how are we this morning?"

"He just said my name Sister," Eileen's face flushed with fresh happy tears. "Clear as day it was. For the first time since the accident, he said my name."

"Well, I must say that is good news Miss Murphy. Dr Cradoc will be here soon and perhaps Mr Riley will do it again?" She checked his pulse with cool fingers.

"Let's see if we can sit you up a bit more, Mr Riley? Move Mr Riley please nurses."

Two starched white caps atop pretty faces put arms under his armpits and settled him higher in the bed. Pillows were plumped and straightened behind his head; his world expanded as his horizon grew.

"There that looks better, doesn't it Mr Riley? You can get a better look at things now. You can see Miss Murphy now."

Dr Cradoc strode into the ward. "Good morning Mr Riley. Good to see you're sitting up today," he looked at the patient notes. "You've made remarkable progress in the six weeks you've been with us. Exceptional."

"And he said my name this morning Doctor. Didn't you Sean?" Eileen beamed encouragement.

"That is encouraging news! In that case I think it's time we engaged Mr Riley in a course of physiotherapy. Let's get those lazy muscles working a bit don't you agree Sister Lewis?"

"Yes Doctor,"

"We can start a programme of manipulation this morning. Let's see how much you can do for us Mr Riley; we'll give those muscles a workout shall we?"

Sean smiled a small, weak lopsided smile.

"Good man...it's a long old road ahead of you, but with this lovely, lady at your side. I'm certain you're going to give it your best. It's progress Mr Riley. Progress!"

Eileen blushed at the compliment. Dr Cradoc was so inspiring, like her he saw the man not the broken shell. If Dr Cradoc had hope and plans for Sean, then she seized on them like a drowning sailor clutches on to passing wreckage.

341

"I'll see you tomorrow then Mr Riley. Keep up the good work; remember I'm expecting good things."

"Eileen" he croaked and squeezed her hand. *He'd be doing it for Eileen.*

Chapter 32

At just before two o'clock, sheltering from the April drizzle under a large black umbrella, Jimmy, Ivy and Betty trudged up the steep flight of marble steps that led to the magnificent porticoed front of Cardiff City Hall. Ivy had never been inside such an impressive building before, her stomach flip flopped with anticipation.

Ivy wore a small grey felt hat, cream gloves and a corsage of white roses and fern pinned to her frock. Betty had lent Ivy her pearl necklace, from Mr Williams, for the occasion.

Mercifully, clothes rationing had ended just a few weeks earlier and with Jimmy's help and contacts Betty had managed to buy Ivy a new dress for the occasion. The flattering grey-blue, floral cotton dress, had a boxed pleat at the front of the bodice, craftily disguising any hint of Ivy's growing bump beneath its folds.

For the briefest of moments Ivy felt quite pretty and dared to hope she could be happy in her own home with her little baby

343

to love.

Ivy had never known a man in her life, her father was never mentioned, and Mam never spoke of her own family either, there was simply *no* father figure for her to learn from; men were a mystery to her. Ivy just didn't know what to expect from this marriage, she'd never seen what living in a proper family was like. She must try to make this work for the baby's sake, and perhaps Jimmy would come to love their little baby and be happy too?

 Since the arrangement had been agreed an ordered calm had rested over the Jenkins household. Nothing was to rock the boat for the period of twenty-eight days before the wedding; Jimmy made sure of that.

Mam made her own plans to marry Mr Williams as soon as decently possible after Ivy's wedding. Betty and Jimmy had crafted a narrative to ward off any difficulty from Gerald Williams; any awkward queries about why Ivy would not be joining Betty in his home in Inkerman street. Ivy's wedding was painted as a surprise love match only declared by the couple when Ivy had reached her eighteenth birthday. It was hinted that Betty's own decision to marry Gerald had precipitated Ivy's decision to be with Jimmy.

Betty wasn't happy about keeping Gerald in the dark but then the alternative of exposing Ivy as some kind of easy slut, was just too difficult to contemplate.

Over the weeks Jimmy had settled down to wait for his prize like a cat waits for a soft bird to land within its range. He needed to be married if his plan was to work. The more Jimmy thought about it, the more it struck him as a stroke of utter genius on his part and Ivy must be kept sweet to ensure it all went as planned.

Jimmy had been kind to Ivy in his own way, like a man who nurtures a fowl he is growing for the pot. And just like the hapless fowl she had value, and he was going to look after it.

True Jimmy always kept a close eye on her, and she wasn't allowed out of the house without his say so, but otherwise Jimmy was back to his jovial, devil-may-care self, whistling as he went about his business, leaving little gifts for Mam, calling Ivy his *pretty girl* and reminding her how lucky she was to have a man to look after her. Ivy dared to hope all would be well; what else could she do?

345

Jimmy didn't visit her room now that he knew about the baby. Ivy often heard his tread on the stairs when he came in later than usual from the quays smelling of booze and cheap scent, but he left Ivy alone and she was grateful for it.

Reclaiming Ivy would come later as far as Jimmy was concerned.

Once inside the glorious white, civic building with its soaring domed roof, the small party followed the signs and shuffled off down a winding treacle-coloured wooden corridor. The dark panelled walls and herringbone floor led to the gloomy and less impressive official office with a brass plaque proclaiming: Births, Deaths and Marriages. A row of functional chairs sat ranged along the corridor wall.

Betty's friend Phoebe, who'd agreed to be their witness, sat waiting for their arrival.

Phoebe gave Jimmy a perfunctory nod, before clasping Ivy in a warm embrace.

"Good luck my little darling. Never forget your Aunty Phoebe will you?" She kissed Ivy on both cheeks. *Poor lass it's like a lamb to slaughter, she prayed he would be kind to the girl.*

Phoebe didn't trust Jimmy Benson one iota. Phoebe knew what the word on the street was and she didn't like it. Jimmy was a hard man with an explosive temper and tendency to lead with his fists.

You're a nasty piece of work Jimmy Benson, nothing but trouble! Ivy deserves better. Phoebe was more than a little cross with Betty for going along with the scheme when her friend told her of the plan and asked her to be a witness. What on earth was Betty thinking of?

All Betty would say when Phoebe challenged her on the wisdom of the marriage was, "needs must as the Devil drives Phoebe you should know that. We all have to do what we think is best at the time." Phoebe smarted at the subtle reminder that she had given her own baby up to an uncertain future.

Phoebe loved Ivy as if the girl was her own. In all the years Betty and Phoebe lived together Phoebe always remembered the day Ivy was born. She had helped Betty get through the gruelling home birth. She'd spent all night soothing and clucking, mopping brows and assuring the terrified girl that

347

she would survive the ordeal.

Ivy slipped pink and greasy into their world with her piercing blue eyes and a cap of soft, downy, copper coloured hair like the fuzz on an apricot. In the years that followed Phoebe laughed at Ivy's first smile and clapped her first hesitant steps. She loved Ivy like the daughter she had given away all those years ago and she would defend her like a lioness would protect her cubs.

Jimmy Benson might have played Betty Jenkins for a fool, but Phoebe wasn't fooled. She'd lay a pound to a penny that Jimmy was the father of Ivy's baby.

Wasn't man enough to admit it though was he? If Jimmy was marrying Ivy he would have his own reasons she was sure of it.. She was amazed Betty was so blinkered.

Jimmy stood next to Ivy waiting to go through to the registrar's office. Phoebe could see he barely glanced at Ivy who stood looking small and lost in the cavernous corridor. It was as if Jimmy was waiting in one of those interminable shopping queues that formed when treacle or tinned fruit came in the grocers; everyone staring resolutely ahead, waiting their turn in line, wanting to get on with more

348

important things.

Still, what was done was done now. There was no point in Phoebe rocking the boat and causing any fuss, *but she would be watching.*

The ceremony seemed to be over in a matter of moments, familiar words uttered in the expected order and when Jimmy placed the narrow gold band on Ivy's tiny finger the registrar proclaimed that Ivy Elizabeth Jenkins had become Mrs Jimmy Benson. For better or worse.

"Champion, now we've done the deed lass and got the certificate we can sign these and hand them in on our way out." Jimmy reached into his inside pocket and pulled out a fat wad of papers.

Phoebe watched the proceedings with interest. *So, he does have an agenda! I thought as much, the ink is barely dry on that marriage certificate and he's already using it to his advantage.*

"Just sign along the bottom Ivy darlin' and make sure you use your new name; we can't have any mistakes can we?" He stood over her, finger pointing to the correct box.

349

Ivy knew the importance of the Council application form; replies had been carefully crafted by Jimmy and Betty to stress her disability and her pregnancy. *It was a mystery to Ivy that she had asthma brought on by damp.* An accompanying statement about the couples' imminent prospect of homelessness, all added weight to their claim for a council home. The address in Bute Street spoke for itself.

Ivy signed her new name as instructed.

"That's a good girl…all done." Jimmy added his scrawl and sealed the documents in the buff envelope.

"Fingers crossed we get the right result Ivy. They say that the decisions will be made early in July. I reckon we stand as good a chance as any of a nice little house." He gave Ivy a perfunctory peck on the cheek for appearances sake.

"Congratulations my lovely. I hope you both will be happy." Phoebe gave Ivy a warm hug, tears trickling down her lined cheeks. She whispered in Ivy's ear, "remember that you can always come to me darling if ever you need me…. Always!"

Jimmy, out of earshot watched the tender scene with suspicion. He didn't trust meddlesome Phoebe Horwat and her interfering beak. Still, she'd served her purpose today and Ivy belonged to him now. There would be no need to see Phoebe ever again.

"Let's be off then ladies, we can't clutter up the corridor. Come along Ivy, we can leave this envelope at the reception desk on the way out." Jimmy took Ivy by the arm and marched her towards the exit leaving Phoebe and Betty to trail in his wake.

"I hope you know what you're doing Betty!" Phoebe hissed. The two women walked slowly arm in arm towards the exit.

"The girl didn't have a lot of options under the circumstances Phoebe, as well you know," Betty said sharply. Her conscience had worried at her for weeks, but Ivy seemed resigned to the arrangement. *What more could she have done?*

"We *all* have options Betty, you should know that as well as anyone,"Phoebe said levelly. "It may be a long time ago now Betty, but I remember scared young Elizabeth Evans; that frightened girl I met on the streets of Bute, lost and desperate." Phoebe turned and held her friend by the shoulders, "Ivy is going to need us, I'm sure of it…. and I will do my damnedest to keep an eye on her and if he isn't good to

351

her he'll have me to answer to!"

"Thank you Phoebe, you're an angel," Betty saw Jimmy gesturing for the two women to get a move on. "We'd best go Phoebe; Jimmy hates being kept waiting."

Chapter 33

Gerald felt giddy with excitement as he left the jewellers in Wellfield road. The delicate leather ring box, with its precious cargo of a gold band set with three, dainty, twinkling diamonds, seemed to burn a hole in his jacket pocket. Every few moments he patted his pocket to make sure it was still there.

He knew he was acting like a lovestruck schoolboy but the reality of Betty finally moving into his home in Inkerman street filled him with such joy, it was bubbling out of him like a water-fountain.

Gerald had agreed to continue paying Betty's portion of the rent in Bute street enabling Jimmy and Ivy to continue living there for a few more months. It seemed such a small price to pay have Elizabeth Evans walk through his own front door for good as his wife. With this last obstacle removed the date was agreed for a simple, civil ceremony on the last Wednesday in June. No fuss, no family, no explanations.

Gerald felt nothing but affection and compassion for Elizabeth. Her past was water under the bridge as far as he was concerned and if neighbours poked and pried and tutted or shunned them then they could go hang. Elizabeth had agreed to share his future, and he was looking forward to spending the rest of his life with her.

She'd told him about the baby, and the news delighted him, and if it was a "vestry conception" as Elizabeth implied, who was he to judge? "All babies are precious gifts from God," was what his dear late wife Janet had said when she heard about young Elizabeth Evans' fall from grace all those years ago and Gerald had believed she was a wise woman then. This baby, this "grandchild," was sure to be a blessing.

For weeks Betty had been fretting about Ivy losing her home, especially in her condition and she had ummed and ahhed about setting a firm date with Gerald for their own wedding. Impatient, he could wait no longer.

"Of, course I can't help put Ivy out onto the streets. Heaven forbid Elizabeth, what sort of man do you take me for?" His tone bristled with exasperation.

Betty looked sheepish. "I'm sorry Gerald, it's just as a mother

I don't want to pull the rug out from under their feet, they've had no time to plan and…" She left the rest un-said, he'd heard the refrain before.

"Come now Elizabeth, when you are my wife," he gave her a bashful smile, "I shall look after you in every way I can. I'd fully expected to look after Ivy too, now of course things are different." he cleared his throat, mindful of the delicate nature of his solution. "If you're so worried that Mr Benson can't afford to rent the property on his own until they can find somewhere else to go, then I'm more than willing to help out with Ivy's portion; especially if it means *we* can agree a date." He watched Betty's face.

"Unless of course you think Mr Benson might find the proposal of financial help, how can I put this… insulting?" He was unsure of his ground, he knew Jimmy was a proud, difficult man; Gerald didn't like the man, but he was Ivy's husband now.

Betty's heart leapt with joy, "Oh Gerald, thank you so much. If you're certain. I'm sure Jimmy will see the kind gesture for what it is." Betty spoke with a certainty that Gerald couldn't appreciate. Only the other night Jimmy had suggested Betty

355

approach Gerald for some money.

 At Gerald's insistence, Betty wasn't working now, and she relied on Gerald to pay her rent, if Betty moved out of Bute street then Jimmy would be left picking up the bills and he wasn't prepared to take on the burden.

It was the one hurdle to overcome, and Gerald had sailed over it with alacrity.

"Well, well, that's a turn up for the books Betty! The old boy has finally coughed up then. I told you he would if you laid your cards on the table." Jimmy drew heavily on his cigarette. Feet up in the kitchen, when Betty delivered the good news Jimmy felt a satisfied glow spread over him; another piece in the puzzle fell into place.

Betty flashed him a scowl, "Don't call him that. Gerald's a kind man, it was Ivy he was thinking of. And I told him it wouldn't be for long." She raised a quizzical eyebrow. "When did you say the Council decision notices were being sent out?"

"I popped in the office yesterday and some bloke in a suit said they will be letting people know in three weeks. The houses are all ready, it's just an allocation process now. That reminds me Betty, what's happening to this furniture of yours? You won't be needing it. I bet old Gerald's got some better bits of kit than this lot of old tat?" He rocked back on the kitchen chair; the legs crunched in protest.

"You've got a nerve Jimmy Benson, there's nothing wrong with this furniture, and stop rocking on that chair!" She glared at him.

"Me an' Ivy will need some bits and pieces Betty, help us get started like. Why not call it our wedding present?" He fixed her with a calculating stare. "You'd only get washers for it if you tried to sell it anyway."

"For God's sake Jimmy, you don't half take the biscuit." Exasperated Betty looked around at the shabby bits and pieces, she knew Jimmy was right, there was nothing there of any value.

"I'll let you have it *all* on one condition."

"Name it?"

"That, if it's a girl, then the baby's middle name is to be Iris, after my mother."

357

"What if it's a boy?"

"If it's a boy then James, after Ivy's father." Betty had a wistful look in her eye as she stated her terms.

Ivy's pregnancy, marriage and her own impending wedding to Gerald had stirred a lot of memories, memories she had buried away deep in her heart. She'd been thinking a lot about her poor mother Iris and James Pugh recently. Where was James now? Was he even alive? Would her mother Iris ever get to see this great-grandchild?

"Done." It was no skin off Jimmy's nose what the baby was called. Leastways it kept Betty happy, and they would have some sticks of furniture. He'd inform Ivy later of the arrangements. *It was all going to plan.... just like clockwork.*

Chapter 34

"Receptionist said ee's down through here now Cappy," Jimmy led the way through the labyrinth of identical hospital corridors.

It was visiting time. The corridors were lively with the clank of tea trolleys rattling through. Nurses with starched bibs and hats fluttered about efficiently, carrying bedpans and sputum dishes from ward to sluice. Cappy gave one pink cheeked nurse a wink as she bustled past.

"I hate these bloody places," Cappy grumbled. "The smell of carbolic and piss fair turns my stomach. If it wasn't for Sean and the occasional pretty nurse I'd never come inside a place like this… and if I was stuck in one for the rest of my days? Blimey I think I'd rather pop my clogs."

"Shut up Cappy! Jimmy was fed up with Cappy's moaning about his dislike of hospitals. He stopped outside a door marked Ward 9 and thrust a paper bag into Cappy's hand. "Take this you, miserable git and try to give it to Sean with a smile on your face."

Sean was now in a ward of six beds. Eileen took each new development as a positive milestone on Sean's road to recovery. The move to this new ward of fitter patients was progress indeed.

"There 'ee is, at the end, with Eileen" Jimmy said. Eileen was sat at Sean's bedside packing away her knitting needles and rolling what looked like a grey sleeve into her bag.

The donkey-grey sleeve was part of a new cardigan for Sean; over the weeks there had been significant progress in the garment. Eileen had spent as many waking hours as she could at Sean's bedside and in the early, dark days, for many a long hour, the only other noise in the side ward was the click of Eileen's needles as she waited for Sean to pull through. As Sean's recovery progressed her knitting dwindled. The more animated he became the less time Eileen had to knit, and she loved him for it. Her time was occupied with other duties such as reading to Sean, helping him to retrieve memories and telling him news of the world outside. It thrilled her that she had so little time to knit now each day. The cardigan could wait.

360

Eileen lifted her face and a sunny smile twinkled in her eyes. "Hello Cappy, Jimmy... look Sean you've got visitors."

Sean gave a half turn of his head presenting his right eye to his visitors. "'lo shimmy, 'lo 'appy" he slurred through half a mouth. Eileen dabbed away the drool that threatened to snake its way down his chin and onto his pyjama top. He stretched out his right hand. Cappy held it and gave it a squeeze. His left arm lay heavy and still on top of the bed spread.

"Good to see you Sean." Cappy took a seat, "me and Jimmy brought you something, just a little treat like," he passed the paper bag to Eileen.

"Oh, my goodness Sean, won't you just look at that!" Eileen held the bag up so that he could see its contents. "Three bananas and two oranges! My goodness what a treat, thank you both." Eileen beamed such a radiant, grateful smile her tired face looked positively beautiful again.

"You're both welcome lass, there's more fruit coming in the docks now, often a bit comes our way, we'll make sure Sean doesn't go short. They say fruit aids the recovery, so we thought we'd bring some." Jimmy gave Eileen a wink.

361

Jimmy had become friendly with the owner of the packing warehouse where Eileen used to work; exotic fruit was a lucrative business. There were plenty of opportunities to make a bit extra when the precious cargoes came into the quayside and Jimmy could often snaffle some choice fruit when no-one was looking.

"We've had some good news this morning, haven't we Sean?" She held his inert hand, her slender fingers rubbing and massaging as she spoke, her thumb looping circles on the palm of Sean's hand. "Dr Cradoc is so pleased with Sean's progress they're moving him to Rookwood hospital on Friday. It's the start of his rehabilitation."

Eileen bent and flexed Sean's fingers on his left arm, each finger stretched and coaxed into life as she spoke. "It's a bit of a bus ride to Llandaff every day but I'm sure we'll manage; they do such good work there." Eileen's fingers worked their subtle magic on Sean's wrist circling and flexing to the left and right easing out the rigidity; it was as if she acted on instinct, like a tic she couldn't control.

Rookwood Hospital had a towering reputation for the work it did with injured soldiers. Sat in glorious gardens, specialized doctors and state of the art equipment mended body and soul. Eileen had high hopes.

"Dr Cradoc says they have huge experience of dealing with trauma and stroke, now Sean has made it this far, Dr Cradoc has hopes of significant improvement if Sean is moved there." She kissed Sean's dull hand and placed it back on the coverlet, she would resume the manipulation tomorrow.

"That is good news Sean. They say those physio therapists can work wonders. Good luck to you." Jimmy said. He cleared his throat; he felt a bit awkward sharing his own news, but now was as good a time as any, he needed to get it out into the open. "Hmm, I've got a bit of good news an all Sean."

Sean looked his way. A tired pallor was creeping over him, it was exhausting trying to concentrate.

"I haven't had a chance to tell you before but I'm moving and all. I'm off to that development in Ely you told me about months ago."

Cappy looked taken aback, Jimmy hadn't said a word to him about moving to Ely on the journey to the hospital.

"I've married a lass, Ivy, and we've got a baby on the way, so

I applied for one of those houses,. I don't know if you remember it like, but it was your idea, and a good one an' all. We filled in the forms and we've been lucky, we move into our new house next week…so thanks Sean."

A tear trickled down Sean's cheek. *All his hopes and dreams. He did remember it.*

Eileen shot Jimmy a fierce look. "I think Sean is getting tired now."

A bell rang in the corridor, visiting time was coming to an end. "We'd best be off Jimmy let Sean to get a bit of rest." Cappy said, furious at the insensitivity of Jimmy's remarks. Cappy knew that Sean had hoped to get married and move to Ely before the accident, it seemed a bit rich for Jimmy to parade his good luck to the poor guy. Cappy never did like Jimmy Benson, he was a cold, insensitive bastard at the best of times, but this took the biscuit…. *Talk about hitting a man when he's down.*

As Eileen watched the two men amble down the ward, she struggled to contain the tears of frustration bubbling to the surface. They'd had those same plans too, and a baby! Since the day of the accident, Eileen had vowed to be cheerful for

Sean, at all times, and she wasn't going to break that vow now by indulging in pathetic self-pity over a house.

Sean was making remarkable progress according to his doctors and there was hope of more to come over the weeks and months ahead. The right side of his body was weak but free of the paralysis, slowly but surely the left side was beginning to co-operate. It remained to be seen how much would come back to him, but they both dared to dream, and to hope. Eileen prayed for them both and was certain God was listening.

Eileen squeezed Sean's hand. "When we get you to Rookwood we must start making plans of our own," she smiled.

"Now you are getting your speech back there's nothing to stop you saying those marriage vows! I know we've got a long road ahead of us but we're walking it together, every step of the way…. Just you remember that! I love you more than life Sean Riley and you're *going* to make an honest woman of me come hell or high water."

She kissed away the tear trickling down his face.

"Luff… you." He croaked.

Through his drooping left eye, Sean could see the most beautiful woman in the whole world smiling back at him.

Chapter 35

"Gareth! Come Yer…. Gareth! Oh, for crying out loud, that child will do for me one day." A buxom, heavily pregnant woman bawled after a small boy running hell for leather up the unmade road towards a mound of soil and rubble. "Gareth!" She ran towards the child, clutching her belly as she went.

The boy was dancing away from her towards a deep hole at the end of the half-finished cul-de-sac. When she reached the lad, she grabbed him firmly by the hand and yanked him back towards her new neighbour Ivy Benson standing outside number twelve.

"Sorry about that Ivy…honestly this child will be the death of me, he's a little tinker, always up to everything 'ee is. I do hope I have a little girl this time, they say girls are easier, well let's put it this way, I'm sure a girl couldn't be any worse!" Norah grinned.

Gareth pulled and squirmed in a determined effort to release his hand, but the woman was resolute. "Stop it now Gareth, or your Da will have something to say when he comes home!"

Norah Ashworth had moved into her smart terraced council home only three weeks earlier. A gregarious good-hearted woman, she made it her business to greet every new arrival into Wilson road. With three children already and a fourth on the way, the Ashworth family had been allocated a three bedroomed end terrace, with a larger sitting room and roomier kitchen to accommodate an expanding brood.

The new houses were laid out in uniform strips of four, with the two bedroomed homes sandwiched in the middle of the other units destined for larger families. Chain link fence separated the gardens back and front with identical flat porch roofs jutting over plain front doors. The regimented pattern of neat, functional boxes repeated itself across the new Taff Ely development, hundreds of decent homes for poor families from the slums of Cardiff sprang up across the once muddy farmland.

The roads were yet to be finished and local children scrambled over idle machinery and drainage holes when the workers went home of an evening, three-year old Gareth was determined to join in the fun. He trailed his big brothers

Lenny and George until they gave him the slip and set off for adventures without him. Not to be outdone, at every opportunity Gareth scampered up the road as fast as his legs would carry him looking for places to explore, holes to jump into.

Ivy and Jimmy had moved into number twelve Wilson road the afternoon before. Through her new net curtains Norah had noticed Ivy's bulging belly and her handsome husband moving in their furniture. She'd told her Jack that she'd go over and introduce herself to the family the following morning; see if they needed any help.

"Stands to reason she'll be needing a friend Jack; the girl looks barely old enough to be married and she's heavily pregnant like me." Norah opined over supper that evening.

"Course she must be old enough Norah. Council were strict about them rules as we well know. She's just one of them sort blessed with a young face." Jack mumbled his mouth full of faggots, boiled potatoes, and peas.

Norah knew better than to take offence. Three boisterous boys in quick succession had taken a toll on her looks and she knew it. Her Jack still told her she was beautiful, still eager to have

369

her body despite its battle scars from having Lenny, George and Gareth. She cleared the plates away.

The new couple were certainly a different age though to her and Jack, the girl looked decades younger than her husband. She'd be sure to find out all the gossip tomorrow.

"Anyway, even though our Gareth's a little divil, I wouldn't be without him," Nora ruffled the boy's mop of golden ringlets. "I'm sure you're going to like it around here Ivy, once they've finished making up the roads and put in the trees they've promised, it will be so pretty next spring." In her mind's eye Norah could imagine the row of pink and white cherry trees looking a picture dotted down the road. She liked blossom trees, they reminded her of the hawthorn bushes in the valleys.

"I can't wait for those bloody trees to be planted, this little monkey makes a bee line for all the holes, it's like a magnet for him. He jumps straight in them and gets himself filthy rotten, don't you Gareth?"

Gareth had the good grace to hang his head and looked down at his mud-stained shorts and grass-streaked knees. Two sorrowful blue eyes peeked out from under his floppy fringe.

370

"I don't imagine you could be angry with him for long," Ivy laughed, "he has got the face of an angel." Ivy admired the handsome child with cherubic features and crystal blue eyes.

Norah brimmed with pride, "Oh aye, he's going to be heart breaker when he's older, I'm sure. My Jack flatters himself that Gareth is the image of him as a lad. But if truth be told he looks the image of my Da as a nipper, but I daren't point it out to my Jack and take the wind out of his sails." Norah joked.

Ivy smiled indulgently. Norah was chatty and amusing and Ivy was keen to make friends. Ever since she announced her pregnancy she'd been cut off from people by Jimmy and Mam, she did everything she was told and didn't rock the boat. Her reward was the smart, little council house Jimmy assured her was a done deal if she played the game. It seems he was right.

When the interesting, fat envelope, addressed to Mr and Mrs Jimmy Benson, had landed on the mat in Bute street Ivy dared to hope for good news. She had left the envelope on the kitchen table for Jimmy to open when he got in from work; she knew better than to open the post.

"Bingo Ivy!" Jimmy cried thrusting his fist in the air

371

triumphantly. The wad of official looking papers lay strewn across the kitchen table. Jimmy's reading skills weren't too good, several complex sheets were discarded in his rush to get to the decision section; but he could figure out enough to see that box marked "Housing Allocation," had a new address- 12 Wilson road Ely and the moving in date written in thick black ink; August 25th.

Jimmy scooped up the documents, put them away to study later. He would go to the council offices tomorrow to get someone to explain all the ins and outs of the decision. His plan had been a success, he'd be celebrating with a round of drinks in the Duke tonight.

Ivy stood washing dishes at the sink. "It's good news then Jimmy," she had dared to ask because she could sense his happiness.

He came over and gave her a big hug. She would always remember that hug, that spontaneous warm gesture lived in her heart and she drew on it on when times were tough.

Norah nattered on. "Well, you were certainly blessed with good weather yesterday for your move Ivy. August can be such a rubbishy month for weather. The month of rain my

Jack says. Still, they say it's good for the garden, not that we've started planting ours yet."

Ivy nodded in agreement. She was under strict instructions from Jimmy not to share personal information. He told her to add two years to her age if anyone asked, and to say they'd been married eight months. Thankfully, Norah steered onto the topic of babies.

"I can see your expecting an all" She pointed to the bump, "I'm due in three weeks but heaven knows none of mine come when they're supposed to. When are you due Ivy?"

"First week of October or there abouts," Ivy felt she was on safe ground.

"And it's your first?"

"Yes."

"How exciting, you must both be thrilled you and…. What did you say your husband's name was?"

"Jimmy Benson," Ivy felt the ground becoming a little rockier.

"My Jack works in the meat packing warehouse on Mermaid

373

quay, he's always up and out early of a morning. And what does Mr Benson do?"

Ivy felt the ground fall away, she was in forbidden territory now. Jimmy didn't tolerate people poking into his affairs. If asked, she was to say he worked labouring at the docks and to say as little as possible.

"He works at the docks Norah, a general labourer; Jimmy takes work when he can get it."

"Oh, Jack might know him already then. It's not such a big place. Anyhow, I'm sure they'll have a good chin wag when we all get to know each other."

"Err yes, I'm sure they will," Ivy looked about her nervously, she was itching to get back indoors.

"Well, I mustn't stand around chatting all day this mucky pup needs to have a bath," she scooped the lad up into her arms and balanced him on her hip. "Come on you dirty tyke…. It's been nice meeting you Ivy. I'm sure we will be the best of friends. First babies are always a bit of a mystery an' all, so I'm more than happy for a chat if you need any advice on that score. Just pop over and give me a knock if you need me, any time; our door is always open."

"Thank you Norah, I will." Ivy smiled a small grateful smile. It felt good to have someone to talk to.

Later that evening as Norah was filling Jack in on all the details of the new family in number 12, she remarked on Ivy's shyness. "She's like a little rabbit, all twitchy and nervy. A nice girl though, only twenty, she said and it's her first baby. I have to say though after I said she could pop over here any time she needed to; she didn't return the offer though."

"Norah, give the girl a chance for heaven's sake!" Jack interrupted. He was used to his wife rabbiting on about this and that, the minutia of other people's lives, but even he had to admit Norah's kindness and gestures of goodwill could sometimes border on nosiness.

Norah looked affronted. They'd had this argument before. How many times had she told Jack; it was just the valley way?

Jack came from Splott, but Norah hailed from Merthyr and saw things rather differently. The old joke was that if Cardiff man sat next to a man from valleys on a bus from Merthyr to

Cardiff by the time they both got to Cardiff the Merthyr man would know everything about his travelling companion including his inside leg measurement; it wasn't nosiness it was just being interested, that was all. It was just the way it was in valleys. Jack begged to differ.

"Mameee.... mameeee George hit me." Gareth wailed at the top of his voice.

"No, I never Mammy! Gareth hit me first didn't he Lenny?" five-year-old George protested in his defence.

"He did Mam and Gareth knocked over my soldiers too," Lenny, the eldest of the lads at six and a half, added to Gareth's crime list.

"No, I never Mammy," Gareth started to sob; fat tears streaked down his face.

Gareth had come in crying that his brothers were being mean to him. In the kerfuffle that followed of claim and counter claim, as she sorted out her three warring boys Norah forgot all about Ivy.

Chapter 36

August fulfilled its soggy reputation and rain pelted the earth in Wilson road for two solid weeks. Children were kept indoors away from the sticky brown ooze that blighted the half-built roads. Persistent drizzle turned the narrow patches of ground front and back of the Wilson road houses into heavy unworkable slop.

From behind her net curtain Ivy watched as more families moved in. Troops of children and scraggy parents arrived; some bringing a few sticks of furniture on the back of a horse and cart, others arriving with barely the clothes they stood up in. Some days a worthy charity would deliver a few chairs and mattresses to the poorer families. Such deliveries were dispensed with quickly, nobody wanted the stigma, of being too poor to have a bed to lie on.

At the crack of dawn, the milkman's horse and cart clopped up the street laden with chinking bottles; with so many

families and pregnant women entitled to free milk the
milkman and his boy dashed up every path dispensing dozens
of bottles. Slowly but surely the street filled up.

There were troops of children everywhere, scrambling around,
yelling and playing from dawn 'til dusk, it was like living in a
hive.

Jimmy and Ivy were rubbing along well enough. He left early
and came home late most days; it was not her place to ask
what he got up to. So long as the house was kept immaculate,
and she managed the meagre housekeeping he was civil; most
times she barely saw him..

Ivy was not allowed any money of her own, only the
housekeeping Jimmy gave her, and she could not go anywhere
other than the trips to the new shopping parade on the Grand
Avenue to buy the groceries; but at least he didn't bother her
at night. Jimmy had taken to sleeping in the other room. He
said it was so she could rest; she knew it was because he
found her pregnant belly disgusting.

One day he caught her washing herself in the upstairs sink,
struggling to bend across her stretched, pink veined belly in
an effort to lather between her legs.

378

"My God Ivy, you look like a frog ready to burst!" He'd said, his horrified face registering disgust.

As a young lad Jimmy and his friends made a sport of hunting down pond frogs in the fields and seeing who could jump on them. The explosive pop and ooze as the fat white and green body lay crushed and wriggling under his boot had filled Jimmy with a joy bordering on hysteria. Jimmy always seemed to catch the most.

Life in Wilson road, day in, day out was the same for Ivy. As her belly grew her love for the baby inside her grew too. She sang lullabies when the kicking and wriggling became intense, she told it stories as her needles clicked; tiny stitches creating lacy garments so small they looked doll sized.

Betty had only visited Wilson road once to see how Ivy was. One Monday morning three weeks after the move; out of the blue, Betty had just turned up unannounced and dripping wet on the doorstep.

"Hello Ivy, I thought I'd pop by and see how you are. Here luv, take my coat and hang it up, there's a good girl, its soaking even though I used Gerald's big umbrella!" Raindrops scattered in an explosive shower on the doorstep as she

379

opened and closed the umbrella several times.

"Hello Mam, this is a nice surprise, come on in."

"Do you know I had to catch two buses to get here from Roath and then walk from that bus stop? It's heck of a long way, I'm parched; I'd love a cup of tea." Her mother removed the grips securing her hat in place and marched into the tiny sitting room carrying a large shopping bag.

The square hall had two doors, one leading to the kitchenette, the other to the tiny sitting room. Sandwiched between the two walls, a steep flight of stairs opposite the front door headed up to two even sized rooms and a small washroom complete with bath and basin. The brick built lav was just outside the backdoor.

Ivy hung her mother's soggy coat on the hooks just inside the hallway. Ivy had no idea her mother would drop by; she wasn't sure Jimmy would like it.

"Goodness me, you are popping out Ivy… Here let me look at you!" Betty gave her daughter a hug. She took in the shabby house coat straining over a pronounced low bump. Ivy looked grey and tired around the eyes, her face pinched and pale. It was hard to believe her daughter was only eighteen.

Ivy couldn't fail to notice how smart Mam looked. Since marrying Gerald, bit by bit, Betty had gradually acquired a subtle, polished gleam rather like the little bronze dragons outside Cardiff market; yellow talons polished to gold by the constant rubbing of children's inquisitive fingers.

"Second thoughts Ivy, why don't you put your feet up and I'll make us that tea, I'm sure I'll soon find everything we need." Brooking no argument, Betty ushered her daughter into the sitting room and set about exploring the kitchen cupboards and pantry.

Betty walked into Ivy's sitting room carrying a tray laden with crockery and the last two Welsh cakes discovered in the pantry. Betty's two old armchairs were artfully arranged in front of the small fireplace, the battered two-seater brown sofa squeezed along the wall. In the small alcove, with a window facing the garden sat Betty's old glass fronted sideboard complete with familiar old crockery and in the corner sat her sitting room lamp on a small trolley.

"Goodness this is like stepping back in time! It's looking very

381

nice Ivy."

Ivy smiled at the compliment. She'd spent hours carefully positioning the furniture to best advantage when they first moved in.

"I've brought us those last two Welsh cakes from the pantry, they looked like they needed eating up" she saw Ivy's nervous look, "that's all right isn't it Ivy?" she handed Ivy the teacup and tea plate.

"Err yes, of course Mam," she knew Jimmy would be cross if the last of the cake was gone. "I won't have mine just yet though, I'll keep it for later if you don't mind."

"Suit yourself. Anyway, I'm pleased to see you've settled in. I came across Jimmy a few times on my travels, and he said you were terribly busy."

Jimmy never mentioned meeting Mam.

Betty glanced around the room and spotted a bag of knitting, "getting ready for the baby I see. I must say now I've got used to the idea; it all seems to have worked out for the best." She hoped Ivy was coming to terms with her situation.

"I'm so excited to meet our new little grandchild Ivy. Gerald loves children, he's looking forward to seeing this little one an' all," she patted Ivy's belly, "or should I say *big* one. Goodness you are large, are you sure it's just the one Ivy?"

Ivy nodded. "The midwife said the same, she said the doctor might insist on an operation because I'm so small," a worried frown crossed Ivy's face. She dreaded the idea of the baby being cut out of her.

"I shouldn't worry too much Ivy, perhaps you've got your dates wrong? Or maybe it's a strapping lad in there, they say you always carry a boy all out front. Try not to think about it love, cross that bridge when you come to it." Betty soothed.

Ivy gave a small smile and cradled her belly.

"I must say it's nice out here Ivy, the roads are a state though, in some places it's like farm tracks, but you can see Ely's going to be much nicer than Bute when it's finished. Have you made any friends yet?"

"Umm... Yes, sort of, I'm getting to know a few neighbours, Norah Ashworth lives opposite in number 7, she's nice. Her fourth baby is due any day now. Norah's been very friendly since the day we moved in. But Jimmy doesn't like people knowing our business, so I don't ask people back."

Betty noted the remark and let it go. It was Gerald who had suggested this visit; said he was worried that Jimmy was keeping Ivy cut off from the world, that it wasn't natural for a girl not to see her mother when she was expecting a baby. On the few occasions Betty had run in to Jimmy she got the impression he was fobbing her off, making excuses for Betty not to visit, so Betty caught the trolley bus to Ely to see for herself.

"I'm pleased you're making friends, but don't let Jimmy bully you Ivy. It's hard having a new baby on your hands; he should let you have company, and you can tell him I said so." She wagged her finger theatrically.

Ivy looked nervous she couldn't discuss Jimmy with anyone, not even Mam.

"Don't worry Mam, I'll be fine," she twiddled her fingers in her lap anxious to move the conversation on.

"You look well Mam, I'm glad you came."

"Apart from wanting to see you of course Ivy, I was on a little errand as well," She started to unpack her shopping bag. "Gerald sent some fruit and vegetables from the shop. I'm sorry this is all I could carry, the bag was cutting my fingers in half, and... I wanted to give you this as a little moving in present."

Betty rummaged in the bag and drew out a shoe box. "Here I wanted you to have this, I've always treasured it; remember I told you it was given to me by my mother?"

Ivy gasped in delight as she unpacked Nanna Patterson's cranberry glass vase and held it up to the light. "Oh, Mam it's so pretty, are you sure you can bear to part with it?"

"Of course, I want you to have it. It would look fine on top of the sideboard, a bit of light from that window would bring it alive. Here let me show you." Betty angled the vase on the oak sideboard to best advantage. "There you are, perfect. Nanna Patterson's vase looks right at home. It's nearly a hundred years old, so careful how you dust Ivy." Betty joked.

"I shall treasure it Mam, thank you."

That evening Jimmy walked through the front door and an appetising aroma of bacon and vegetable soup greeted him.

385

In the warm fug of the kitchen Ivy was scrubbing down the wooden draining board where she'd been skimming off the scum and sorting out the bones before returning the meat into the hot vegetable and stock mixture.

In the afternoon, after Betty left, Ivy had popped down to the butchers on the parade for some bacon bones. Dewar's meat counter had impressive flitches of bacon, smoked and green hanging from large hooks in the ceiling and a jumbled of bacon ribs piled in a bowl on the counter. Ivy had pointed out the bones with the most meat left clinging to them and set off home with her prize wrapped in waxed paper. With the addition of a leek and a few potatoes to add to Gerald's vegetables the smoked bones would help make a delicious pot of cawl.

"Smells good Ivy," Jimmy sniffed appreciatively. He had to admit coming back to his own home with good food waiting for him had its attractions. Betty had taught Ivy well on the housekeeping front and he had to admit Ivy was biddable, didn't back chat him like some snippy lasses. If only there wasn't that hard disgusting belly that shifted about in front of her. He was dreading a baby about the house, wreathes of napkins draped around the place, a nipper bawling and demanding attention.

It was the price he'd paid to fill in that bloody council form.

"Your supper's ready Jimmy; shall I serve it now?" Ivy wiped her hands on the front of her house-coat and returned the pan to the boil. She placed crusty loaf on the bread board for him to help himself.

Jimmy nodded and sat to the kitchen table. She ladled out a steaming bowl of cawl, taking care to ensure Jimmy's portion was full of chunky, meaty shreds. She placed the bowl in front of him, chopped swede, leeks, potatoes and chunky carrots swam in a tasty broth.

"I haven't added any salt because sometimes they over cure the bacon in Dewar's," Ivy stood and waited to see if the soup met with approval."

"Hmm, Jimmy grunted," he sprinkled pepper liberally over the soup before dunking chunks of crusty bread in the bowl.

Ivy took a deep breath "Mam popped over this morning.. I must say it was a surprise, 'specially since it was tipping with rain." She looked at Jimmy, his spoon poised mid mouthful.

"Did she now…. And what did she want?"

"Nothing, well just to see the house really and to bring us these fresh vegetables from Gerald."

"Did she have anything to say for herself?" He'd bumped into Betty several times around the Roath area in the last few weeks, perhaps he shouldn't be surprised she'd turned up. He couldn't have her interfering though.

"No, we just chatted about how I was feeling and the baby, and she gave me a little present; Nanna Patterson's vase."

"I see, well I hope she's not going to make a habit of it." Just remember Ivy we can't have any Tom, Dick or Harry popping in unannounced. I won't stand for it! Is that understood?" The bowl of thick soup laden with chunky vegetables reminded Jimmy that Betty had her uses. *Betty could come two or three times a month, but no more.*

"I don't mind the odd visit, but I can't be doing with the place being turned into Cardiff terminus," he pushed a piece of cartilage to the side of his soup plate.

"Of course, Jimmy."

"That was nice Ivy. I'm off out now for the evening. Make sure you lock that back door before you go up to bed."

She heaved a sigh of relief. *He hadn't asked for a Welsh cake.*

Chapter 37

Two days later as Ivy collected the milk bottles she saw Norah waving furiously at her from across the road, a slimmer, trimmer Norah. Norah had had her baby.

Ivy put the door on the latch and slipped over the road to see her friend.

"It's a girl this time thank the Lord…. Karen Louise." Norah, beamed. Standing in her dressing gown, Norah looked tired but jubilant. "The little angel arrived five o'clock yesterday tea-time, it was all over and done with, in under three hours. She slipped out with no trouble at all; midwife arrived just in time to cut the cord. See I told you girls were easier Ivy!" Norah laughed.

Ivy wondered what cord Norah was talking about, she was clueless about such matters.

"That's wonderful Norah, I'm so pleased for you. And she was early as well, lucky you." Ivy felt more cumbersome, and achy as each day passed." I hope I'm lucky like that."

"The first baby is always the worst Ivy then it gets better, believe you me. Now it's like shelling peas, according to my Jack! I told him if it's *that* easy he can have the next one. This is it for me now... job done! I've got my little girl, so it's no more babies for me, I'm going to enjoy this one."

"I hope I have a little girl an' all, then they could be friends."

"I bet Jimmy wants a boy. All men want a son first time around. My Jack was desperate for a son when I was expecting our Leonard."

"Jimmy hasn't said," Ivy shrugged. It was the most accurate thing Ivy could thing to say; Jimmy didn't talk about the impending arrival of the baby at all.

Jack appeared at the front door carrying a mewling, grizzling bundle swathed in blankets. "Good morning Ivy." He handed the baby to Norah. "Someone is shouting for their breakfast and I've got to get off for work. New baby or no new baby, the foreman will have my guts for garters if I'm late for my shift."

Norah cradled little Karen in the crook of her arm.

Ivy peeked at the scrunched-up face, peeping out from the blanket folds; pink gaping mouth rooting left and right like a baby chick; two fierce slate blue eyes and few whisps of ruffled dark hair.

"She's gorgeous Norah!" Ivy felt a warm rush of joy pass over her. In six weeks, she would be cradling her own precious bundle. She never regretted deciding to keep the baby.

The wailing grew louder.

"Well now, I'd best get this little one inside before she wakes the entire street. With lungs like these, I don't think I shall be getting much sleep any time soon, will I my precious? Pop over later for a cup of tea if you like Ivy, any time. I'm not going anywhere."

Jack re-appeared with Gareth hanging off his trouser leg, clinging on, koala like. "Go see Mammy Gareth there's a good boy; your Da's got to go to work, an' I'm late already." He shook his leg. "Come on you tinker, let go." He peeled away the limpet like grasp. "I can't ride my push bike with you hanging on my leg can I now?" Jack grinned.

He gave Norah a quick kiss on her forehead. "I'll see you later tonight luvvie, try to get a bit of rest, put your feet up…. And *you* be good for Mammy Gareth." He ruffled Gareth's mop of hair.

Norah rolled her eyes as if to say that Jack may as well ask her to fly to the moon as get some rest… or for Gareth to behave himself for that matter!

Karen's lungs suddenly erupted. "Right then let's get you fed before you bust my eardrums young lady."

"Come over later, Ivy." Norah grasped Gareth by the arm, steering the child inside.

"I will Norah, after lunch when I've finished my jobs."

Ivy hurried indoors, Jimmy would be furious to catch her gossiping when the sink was full of washing up and his work shirts still soaking in the bucket from the night before.

At just two o'clock Ivy knocked the door of number 7, just a light rap in case she disturbed the baby.

"Come in Ivy" Norah clicked the door quietly behind her. "Let's go through to the kitchen, Karen's asleep in the sitting room." She ushered Ivy through to the back kitchen. "Take a

393

seat. Here be a love, rub these for me while I put the kettle on."

Norah dumped a pile of stiff, slightly grey nappies on the table in front of Ivy.

Ivy looked clueless. "What do you mean Norah?"

As an only child Ivy had had no experience of motherhood, no siblings to bath or change, no feeds to administer, no little noses to wipe. It was a world as alien as the moon.

"Here like this, haven't you ever seen a nappy before?" Norah joked as she showed Ivy how to raise the nap on the terry squares by rubbing them vigorously between her fingers and knuckles.

"I haven't," Ivy admitted. Ivy had never even held a baby.

"Well blow me down!" As the eldest one of six siblings, raising babies came as naturally to Norah as breathing. The large chaotic families in the terraced streets of Merthyr were awash with children tumbling in and out of each other's houses. Girls learned the craft of motherhood at an early age, carrying around younger siblings on their hips so their Mams could get on.

"Do you know anything about babies Ivy?"

"No." Ivy hung her head.

"Not even how to fold a nappy?"

Ivy shook her head.

"Well, it's about time you learned before that little one comes along. Let's have that cup of tea first then you can learn a few of the basics."

Karen was starting to grumble in the front room.

"Give it ten minutes, you don't pick them up the minute they start, or they'll have you on a bit of string." Norah advised. She looked at the kitchen clock. "Goodness me its nearly quarter past two! She'll soon be bawling her head off soon for her next feed, babies are like clockwork when it comes to feeding."

Norah grabbed one of the softened squares. "Here let me show you how to fold a nappy Ivy." With nimble fingers Norah swiftly folded the square into a kite shape and then tucked the ends in to smaller oblong leaving a thick pad in the middle. "you have to learn to adapt the shape as they grow,

395

but this version does for the tiddlers and then you pop a muslin liner on top."

Ivy watched fascinated. The craft of nappy folding obviously needed practice.

"Have you got your nappies yet?"

Ivy shook her head.

"My Mam gave me these as a present when Lenny was born; a dozen nappies and two buckets," Norah chuckled. "Get the best you can afford Ivy, because they need to last. Mam got these in Merthyr market. A woman there makes them from a roll of terry towelling."

Karen's yelling was rising to a crescendo.

"Back in a tick,"

Norah returned with the bawling Karen, her face the colour of a well ripened strawberry.

"There, there, what a fuss, young lady." Norah unfastened her blouse and flopped out a large swollen breast. Holding the brown, plump nipple between two fingers, Norah guided it into the baby's mouth. The baby sucked greedily, tiny starfish

396

hands flexing with pleasure.

Norah tucked a cushion under her arm to support the baby's head and resumed folding nappies. "I find it easier to fold a pile of nappies in one go, that way you aren't fumbling around in the middle of the night."

Ivy watched the suckling child. She couldn't imagine baring her body like that. "Do you do *that* in front of Jack?" she asked.

"Course I do Ivy, if I have to, it's not like he hasn't seen it all before. I just wear clothes that allow for easy access!" Norah laughed.

Ivy, watched as Karen switched breasts, the second tit already dripping profusely. "Alright little love there's plenty there. Believe me Ivy after you've had a baby or two, you won't find anything embarrassing."

As the baby suckled its little face screwed up. Every so often, wet raspberry sounds reverberated through the nappy.

"It's like night following day, the minute they feed they off load at the other end!" Norah laughed.

"Are we going to give Aunty Ivy a lesson in changing a dirty nappy then?"

Ivy felt she had an awful lot to learn.

Chapter 38

September was glorious in Wilson road. Rich bright
mornings saw wreathes of washing fluttering in the gardens,
clusters of children played hopscotch and skipping; laughing
all day in the street until they were dragged inside at teatime.
The splendid warm weather helped dry out the soggy clay
topsoil; and up and down Wilson men were trying to prepare
the gardens before autumn set in.

Seasoned gardeners reckoned there was still time for a crop
of some root vegetables and over wintering spring cabbage,
others set seedlings on window ledges and prepared the soil
with steaming manure ready for spring planting. Over the
balmy weeks the road was a hive of activity, laughing and
joking neighbours swapping stories and borrowing tools.
Shrieking, squealing, children ran in and out of houses and the
women hung over fences, arms crossed and gossiping at the
end of the day, all enjoying the last of the summer sun.

Jack divided his garden into useful areas for vegetables and soft fruits, he'd even built a generous shed for his tools from scrap materials scavenged from around the estate. The brick, tin and wooden structure even had a small window; the boys instantly commandeered it as a den and troops of children gravitated to play in the Ahsworth's garden.

To please Norah, with the help, or hindrance, from his sons Jack created a small, circular seeded lawn area separated from the vegetable garden by a row of fruit bushes.

Much to Norah's joy, only days after sprinkling the seeds, tiny grass seedlings were beginning to clothe the warm mud; a fuzz of emerald-green shoots soon took over. Karen joined in the late summer bounty by dozing outside in the sunshine watching the flap of nappies on the line as they fluttered in the breeze.

Norah looked forward to having a colourful flower patch outside the back door like her Mam did at home in Merthyr; blowsy snap dragons, bold hydrangeas and clumps of golden rod interspersed with lily of the valley and violets.

The men all bonded over the project, pride was at stake to deliver the prettiest and most productive plots in Wilson Road. Friendships were made as men chatted over fences and smoked on late summer evenings.

Jimmy wasn't interested in growing vegetables; it took too much of his precious time and smacked of hard work. Anyway, Betty could usually be relied on the eke out the Benson larder with a delivery of Gerald's fruit and veg once a fortnight. He saw no need to join in the collective push for gardening in Wilson road.

The back garden of number 12 was long and narrow. Jimmy roughly forked over the heavy topsoil and chucked a sack of grass seed over the lot, back and front; job done. Jimmy's only concession to practical household matters was to plant a row of fruit trees on each side, two apple trees, two plum trees and two pear trees flanked the mud patch. Eventually the fruit trees would shield the garden from nosey neighbours and give Ivy a crop for bottling next Autumn, or even better making alcohol.

Jimmy always had other fish to fry, chewing the fat over the garden fence was not for him. He didn't care what the other men thought, and he didn't want other people poking into his business, ferreting out information. A brief exchange of pleasantries if he met a neighbour in the street was as far as

Jimmy was prepared to go. As the weeks went past the men in Wilson road learned not to waste their breath trying to be chatty and hale-fellow-well-met with surly Jimmy Benson.

Ivy cried a little when other gardens started to take shape. She vowed to create some pretty flower beds in the front garden once the baby arrived, perhaps she could grow some seedlings on the window ledge, ready for spring planting. Norah's Jack had soil filled egg boxes with little plants sprouting up ranged along the kitchen window ledge, perhaps there might be a few spare plants?

Feeling hot, lumpen and awkward Ivy stayed indoors. Apart from the occasional visit to see Norah and the new baby, or the weekly visit from Madeline Spears, her midwife, her days were lonely, devoid of interest; she longed for the baby to come along, a little one to love.

Jimmy didn't allow gossiping over the garden fence. Jimmy only allowed, or tolerated, useful relationships; people who could pass something his way. People he could use. Her mother was coming this afternoon and she was looking forward to the company.

"Here we are Ivy love, some nice fresh veg, to keep you

402

going." Betty tipped the bag out on the table; leeks, apples, beans, tomatoes and carrots tumbled out. Betty thought Ivy needed fattening up before the baby arrived and Gerald was generous with veg from the shop. "There's a glut of runner beans and broad beans about at the moment, and in this bag I've got a nice punnet of raspberries, lovely with a drop of cream from the top of the milk they are. And I've brought this as well." Two yellow labelled cans decorated with fish and strange writing sat on the table. *Snoek.*

"What is that Mam?" Ivy examined the unfamiliar can.

"Snook…it's a fish, a bit like mackerel only…. Well fishier!"

"Fishier?"

"It's a bit of an acquired taste, so they say," Betty had heard some tales about the pungent nature of tinned Snoek. It was highly nutritious and to Betty's mind couldn't be any worse than a dose of the dreaded cod liver oil. "I thought it might be handy to keep in the cupboard; help build yourself up after the baby comes."

"What do I do with it, Mam?"

"You use it in things, fish cakes, fritters, that sort of thing.
403

I've never had it myself; I've always managed to get a cod head from the market. But stuck out here well it's not so easy to get stuff like that I shouldn't wonder."

"Thanks Mam." Ivy knew only too well about preparing cod heads. Regularly the old kitchen in Bute street wreaked of boiled cod's head; next door's cat lurking at the back door for the leavings. Ivy was an expert at flaking off the meat from around the cod's cheeks, hunting out the tasty morsels such as the tongue. When mixed with lots of parsley and fluffy mashed potatoes the resulting fish cakes were a delight. Ivy thought she'd give it a try; it would be a darn sight easier than doing battle with a cod's head.

"I think I'd better try growing some parsley then Mam, and perhaps some other herbs too, maybe some thyme and sage. I reckon a few pots outside the backdoor would do the job." Ivy warmed to her theme of creating a herb garden.

Betty had noticed the miserable strip of mud back and front of the house. On her way from the bus stop she'd seen ordered rows of tilled soil; seedlings protected from pigeons by string. In other gardens, flower beds were taking shape, bushes being planted. It was obvious that the garden of number 12 would be letting the side down when spring came. Betty knew better than to pass comment.

"A useful, little herb garden is a lovely idea Ivy."

The two women sat drinking tea in the kitchen. Ivy was feeling bone tired, her enormous, wriggling bump meant sleeping on her back impossible, the kicking and squirming of the baby kept her awake for hours on end. As Mam chattered on Ivy was struggling to keep her eyes open.

"You do look tired Ivy love. What's that midwife got to say?"

"Mrs Spears said baby is in breech position and even though she's been pushing and prodding me to death, she reckons it's not going to budge now," Ivy grimaced.

"Even if it does turn, she reckons I'm probably going to have to have a caesarean section anyway 'cos my hips are so small." Ivy's bottom lip started to wobble. "I'm so frightened of them cutting me up Mam," Ivy burst into tears.

"Now don't go worrying yourself Ivy," Betty gave her daughter a hug, felt the thin, bony, shoulders under Ivy's dress. She remembered her own fear and how Phoebe had sat up with her all night until this beautiful, perfect creature, this

405

Ivy was placed in her arms.

"It's natural to be anxious Ivy. If they do decide to operate you'll be in the best hands. You will be under anaesthetic, so you won't feel a thing, and it will all be over and done with before you know it." Betty did her best to lift Ivy's spirits.

"Mrs Spears said that the baby should be due in two weeks so they're going to take me in next week, Tuesday I think, and then the doctor will decide when it will come."

"The doctors will know what's best Ivy, no point working yourself up about it. Have you got everything you need for the baby?"

"Yes Mam, I think so." Under Norah's tutelage, Ivy had scraped together her baby things. The top drawer of the chest of drawers was now lined with some soft blankets and re-purposed as a cot ready for its new occupant. A pile of tiny nightdresses had been washed and Mam's gift of nappies sat folded and waiting for use. All Ivy had to do now was wait for the big day to arrive.

"When you go to hospital I could always pop over; maybe stay with Jimmy for a day or two, make sure the house is nice and ready for you to come back home to." Betty suggested.

Ivy grimaced, she couldn't help herself. A bit of help would be wonderful, but she knew Jimmy wouldn't want Betty staying in the house.

"I'm not sure Jimmy would want that Mam. Thank you." She added hastily.

"Psh! We'll see about that!" Betty looked exasperated. "What do you mean Ivy? It's only natural a mother wants to help her daughter at times like these. It's not about what Jimmy wants. I really think…."

"Shh Mam! Jimmy's back early." Ivy started at the click of the front door latch. "Don't make a fuss Mam, please," she whispered.

"Afternoon Betty," Jimmy dumped a small sack of seed potatoes on Ivy's clean kitchen floor, as the sack landed a puff of fine, brown dust sprayed out on to the quarry tiles. "These blighters have nigh on killed me carrying them on my back from the Grand Avenue," he saw the vegetables and the Snoek piled on the table.

"Blimey Snoek! This stuff is God awful," Jimmy examined

the cans. "No wonder they can't sell it. Why have you bought this rubbish Ivy?" He demanded.

Ivy flushed with embarrassment, "I didn't buy it Jimmy, it was a present from Mam."

Betty fixed him with a hard stare; ungrateful sod that he was. Jimmy might have access to all sorts of fiddles down on the docks but for most people decent food was still hard to come by.

"Ivy needs building up Jimmy," Betty said tersely. "It's very nutritious. She'll need plenty of good food after that baby comes."

"Well Ivy's welcome to eat it then Betty, but she won't be serving it to me."

Ivy shot her Mam a *don't say anything* warning glance. For the sake of peace Betty held her tongue and moved onto safer ground.

"So, you're going to be planting some spuds by the look of it, Jimmy."

"Not me Betty. This sack was going wanting down on the

408

quay, so I gave it a new home. Seed potatoes are in high demand around here, I reckon there's good money to be made from neighbours that wants them." Jimmy flashed a cheeky wink.

"How do you plan to get rid of them Jimmy, some people might start asking questions." Betty raised a questioning eyebrow she had no doubt the potatoes were not acquired honestly. Since marrying Gerald, she noticed Jimmy's fiddles more and more.

"Ivy has got nothing to do most days; she can go for a walk and knock on a few doors up and down around here, perhaps take a basketful with her." Jimmy said blithely.

Ivy couldn't believe her ears.

"Ivy can spin some yarn; say we've got some seed potatoes going spare, then she can either take a bit of money for them or goods in kind. One way or another that sack is worth a fair bit. No-one's going to question a pregnant woman about a few spare seed potatoes."

Ivy looked mortified. With a basket of potatoes going from door to door she would feel like a gypsy peddling pegs and heather.

"Why can't we just eat them ourselves Jimmy?" Ivy dared to ask. She dreaded the idea of knocking doors, walking about for hours would play havoc with her back.

"Because you fool, they are all sprouting and chitting ready to plant; they won't keep now, in a week or two they'll be ruined and fit for nothing. They're worth more as a seed potato! Seed potatoes are what's needed around here, and you *will* get out and sell them as soon as possible." Jimmy's word was final, Ivy knew there was no point in arguing.

The only comfort to Ivy was that she could give Norah a few potatoes to repay her for all her kindness over the weeks. Jimmy wouldn't know that a few in the bag hadn't been rotten.

"Yes Jimmy," she mumbled.

Betty was fuming at Jimmy's imperious behaviour. Sending Ivy out selling potatoes when the girl was eight months pregnant...*what was the man thinking of!*

What left Betty speechless was the sight of Jimmy scooping up the small punnet of raspberries she had carried all the way

410

from Roath as a treat for Ivy, then sauntering out of the kitchen positively shovelling the juicy berries in his mouth without so much as a "by your leave." *The man was a selfish pig!*

Chapter 39

Tuesday morning arrived and the midwife called early; she
was not pleased with Ivy.

"Your blood pressure is dangerously high Mrs Benson, and I
can tell by the state of your ankles you have not been resting
as I instructed," Marion Spears prodded at the puffy tissue
surrounding Ivy's bony ankles.

Ivy couldn't tell the midwife her swollen ankles were caused
by spending three days walking around the roads on the Ely
estate trying to hawk potatoes on Jimmy's instructions. She
couldn't say that her gamey leg was troubled by the rutted
unmade Ely roads and that her hip ached from carrying a
laden basket home because so many households wanted to
trade rather than pay for the seed potatoes. The only
consolation was that Ivy's larder was much fuller now than it
was a few weeks ago and she had promises of winter
vegetables to come when the harvest came in. Ivy certainly
couldn't tell Mrs Spears that she ended up planting the

remaining ten potatoes herself in the muddy patch by the backdoor rather than let them go to waste. Jimmy was too busy for the task.

"Sorry Mrs Spears, there's been a lot to do," was the best excuse Ivy could mutter.

"Well Mrs Benson, we are going to put a stop to that. Where is Mr Benson?"

"He's at work."

"When do you expect him home?"

"I'm not sure when he'll be back, Jimmy doesn't usually say." Ivy looked twitchy and anxious, she hated telling people Jimmy's business.

"I see," Mrs Spears was beginning to form a dim view of Mr Benson, he was never around when he was needed. "It seems the Doctor was right Mrs Benson you do need to come into hospital for a week's bed rest and almost certainly a caesarean section."

Ivy moaned. "Are you sure Mrs Spears, I'd rather…"

"I'm *absolutely* sure Mrs Benson and I'm afraid what you'd
413

rather doesn't come into the matter. We need to think about baby now." Marion Spears collected her things in a brusque efficient manner.

Ivy looked crestfallen. "What happens now?"

"I shall go back to the City hospital and fill in the necessary forms. An ambulance will come to collect you at about four o'clock this afternoon. Please bring all your things such as washbag and nightclothes with you."

"But what about Jim...Mr Benson?"

"Your husband will survive perfectly well without you Mrs Benson." Marion Spears said crisply. "I'll leave this card on the table, where he can find it. It contains the telephone number for the hospital ward, and I'll write a little note so that he can know when visiting is allowed. Visiting time finishes at five o'clock today so Mr Benson might not be able to see you until tomorrow morning."

Ivy didn't imagine that Jimmy would spend much time sitting beside her hospital bed. Jimmy always said he hated visiting Sean Riley in the Cardiff Infirmary with the overpowering scent of carbolic and boiled cabbage lingering in the corridors;

414

people weeping and worrying in hallways. Since Sean had been moved to Rookwood Jimmy had only managed to visit once and then only for half an hour. He had no plans to go back to Rookwood soon.

On the plus side Ivy could see that a few days rest from the drudgery of housework with all meals provided had its appeal; she was exhausted.

"Nothing will happen for a few days Mrs Benson; the doctors will want to build your strength up first." She glimpsed Ivy's terrified face; the girl was only eighteen and she looked like a scared rabbit.

"Is there anything else Mrs Benson?"

"Jimmy's not very good at reading Mrs Spears."

"I see. Well, in that case I'll make the note simple, and I'll pop next door to leave a message with the neighbour to be on the safe side. What's your neighbours name Ivy?"

"I'm not sure, I haven't met them yet," Ivy said doubtfully. "But there's always my friend Norah across the road at number 7, I think she would be the best. In fact, I'll do that Mrs Spears as soon as you've left."

415

"Good, that's settled then. The ambulance will be here at four, please make sure you are packed and ready to go. You *will* have some rest Mrs Benson and that's an order!" Marion Spears gave Ivy a motherly smile. The poor girl looked lost and nervy, obviously her husband was not helping at all.

If the caesarean section went ahead then Ivy would be in hospital for at least week or two after the birth, if not longer, and her husband would have to muck in and hold the fort. Marion Spears couldn't have Ivy worrying about a grown man.

"You'll be in good hands Mrs Benson and when you are back home with baby I will pop by to see you every day to check on things." The midwife turned to go. "Just think the next time I see you Mrs Benson you'll have a lovely little boy or girl in your arms, and you will have forgotten all the bad bits… it's nature's way." Marion Spears patted Ivy's hand. The girl was in for a difficult time.

"Now, remember, after you've told your friend the arrangements, you must sit down and put those swollen feet up for the whole afternoon please."

When Jimmy came home that night it was 9pm and dark. At first he thought Ivy must have gone to bed early. The lack of a

416

wife didn't occur to him until there was a sharp rap on the door knocker at 9.15pm; it was Jack Ashworth.

"What's up?" Jimmy said snappily. He couldn't think of a good reason for a neighbour to be hammering on the door.

"I've got a message for you Jimmy" Jack tried to ignore Jimmy's rude tone. "An ambulance came and took Ivy to hospital this afternoon. Norah's been watching out the window for you to come back so we could let you know."

"What's wrong with her? She was alright when I left this morning?" Jimmy sounded more irritated than concerned.

"Ivy told Norah that the midwife didn't like her blood pressure or the position of the baby, so they've taken her in for a bit of bed rest before she has the baby. Ivy had no say in the matter, the midwife insisted on it apparently."

"Harrumph," Jimmy snorted.

Jack couldn't fail to notice the irritation on Jimmy's face, "apparently there's a note for you on the kitchen table with all the details of the ward and visiting hours. Any-way I've given you the message. Goodnight Jimmy." Jack shook his head, *Jimmy Benson was totally selfish, he wasn't concerned about*

417

his poor wife at all.

"Night, "Jimmy muttered, he had the good grace to add a small "thanks Jack." Before shutting the door. In the kitchen Jimmy saw a piece of paper sticking out from under his bottle of stout.

Bugger, soon the house would be filled with a wailing baby and stinking nappies. Ivy had better get out of that ward as quickly as possible, until then he'd be eating down at the Duke.

Chapter 40

In ward six Ivy sat up in bed wearing a floral nightdress waiting for the doctor to come on his rounds, she was hungry and nervous. The lady with the breakfast trolley obeyed the Nil by Mouth notice above Ivy's bed and dutifully clanked past. Dr Morris was expected at 8am; decisions would be made.

That morning at 7 o'clock Ivy had bathed as instructed by matron and put on her best nightdress, the pretty pink and white nightie had been a gift from Aunty Phoebe along with a pink knitted bed jacket. Ivy's old nightdress would have shamed her that morning.

In ward six, seven other women sat waiting to know their fate, Ivy was first on the doctor's list.

A grey-haired, efficient looking Dr Morris strode into the ward. Three young nurses led by Matron struggled to keep up, a nurse closed Ivy's curtains with a chiming swish.

"This is Mrs Benson, Doctor Morris. This is Mrs Benson's first pregnancy; she is thirty-nine weeks now with baby settled in breech position… nurse Jones please lift Mrs Benson's gown for Doctor Morris to examine his patient." Matron ordered.

Ivy felt mortified as the nurse whisked back her nightdress, the shaving of her privates yesterday had come as a shock, now her stubbly pubis was in full view.

"Good morning, Mrs Benson, how are we feeling today," experienced fingers palpated and assessed. The tiny width of hips noted.

"Very well thank you Doctor Morris," embarrassed Ivy looked over the top of his grey head at some point in the distance.

"It seems this baby is determined to be awkward and stay put, so we will be proceeding with a caesarean section this morning as planned. Matron put Mrs Benson first on the operating list and she can have her pre-med now." Dr Morris consulted his notes.

"Yes Dr Morris," Matron gestured for a young nurse to get the elixir from the medicine cart.

Ivy whimpered. "Will it be all right Dr Morris? I've never had an operation before?"

"Mrs Benson, there is no need to worry yourself by midday you will have been delivered of a lovely little baby. Just think, no spending hours and hours in labour like some poor women, it's all over and done with whilst you have a nice little sleep, and you won't feel a thing." He gave her hand a reassuring pat.

"Nurse Jones, get Mrs Benson ready and changed for theatre and then give Mrs Benson her sedative please." Matron instructed.

Nurse Jones selected a white garment and hat for Ivy from the trolley.

"Mrs Benson in about half an hour you will be feeling nice and dozy, and you'll be wheeled down to surgery for the operation. As Dr Morris said you won't feel a thing during the procedure." Matron gave a brief smile, turned smartly on her heels and left for the next patient.

The flap of nursing staff and Doctor Morris moved along to

the next bed leaving Ivy with nurse Jones.

"I'm so nervous" Ivy said to the young nurse. "I know it's being silly but well…" Ivy couldn't voice her fears about not waking up ever again.

"Don't fret Mrs Benson, just remember its baby that matters now; if baby had a difficult birth all sorts of things could go wrong, and we don't want that to happen do we?"

Ivy shook her head and obediently surrendered her best nightgown.

"This is for the best really it is Mrs Benson. It'll soon be over." As nurse Jones soothed and reassured Ivy was dressed in her hospital gown and in a few minutes the emerald-green, viscous liquid sent her drifting deep in to oblivion.

"Hello Ivy love," a disembodied voice dug its way into her brain. She felt groggy and disorientated. The place where she lay was strangely quiet and dim.

"Ivy, its Mam here." Fingers stroked her face. Ivy's eyes felt sticky, and her throat was sore.

"It's all over Ivy; you've had the baby," tears rolled down

422

Betty's face. Matron had told her to be strong for her daughter, but Betty's heart was breaking.

Betty pulled the alarm cord. A bell sounded somewhere in the distance at the nursing station, it was 9pm.

Two pairs of shoes clacked briskly towards Ivy's side room; nursing staff didn't run.

"Good evening Ivy. I'm glad to see you're back with us, that's good news." Matron said smoothly.

A cool hand lifted Ivy's wrist. "Well done, your pulse is normal. Doctor Morris is on his way to explain everything. He'll be here in a minute."

Ivy groaned.

"Try to lie still Ivy, you've had a tough time." Matron gestured for nurse Jones to straighten Ivy's pillow. "I'm sure once Doctor's had a little chat with you we can get you some more medication for the pain…. Ah, here's Dr Morris now."

Betty moved to the corner of the small room; she would not leave Ivy now. Dr Morris gave Betty a nod of acknowledgement.

"Let's have a little look at you Mrs Benson," he shone a light in Ivy's eyes. "Good, good," he muttered.

Ivy started to surface from the depths of sleep, a dark place where in her nightmares she dimly recollected chaos and panic.

"Where's my baby?" she mumbled through dry lips.

"Don't worry baby is being looked after Ivy," Doctor Morris soothed. "I'm afraid I have to tell you that the delivery did not go as well as planned, there were some… er complications."

Betty took a sharp intake of breath and waited for the hammer blow to fall.

"You're going to be fine Ivy when all the stitches are healed, but…. but when we took the baby out you wouldn't stop bleeding." Dr Morris paused to gather himself. "The surgeons did everything they could to stop the bleeding, but I'm afraid you had to be given an emergency hysterectomy."

"What?" She croaked; Ivy didn't understand what the doctor was saying.

"There was no other option. We had to remove *all* of your

womb Mrs Benson. We had to take it away to save your life."
Dr Morris felt sad for the poor girl, she was only eighteen.

Ivy felt befuddled by the words that struggled to penetrate her
consciousness. *The doctor was saying she'd lost a lot of blood
and they'd done something to stop it. Why did it matter?*

"So just to be clear Ivy. I'm very sorry, but this operation
means you can't have any more babies.... ever." Dr Morris
was stroking Ivy's hand.

Ivy felt numb inside. "Where's my baby?" She croaked.

Betty gave Matron a stern glance as if to say don't punish Ivy
anymore tonight, for pity's sake.

"Baby was a bit upset by all the procedures this morning, so
she is spending the night in a special bed where the doctors
can keep an eye on her," Matron explained smoothly.

*She... the woman had said she. Ivy thought. I've had a little
girl.*

"I think Mrs Benson should get some rest now. It's been a
busy day, we can chat some more about the next steps
tomorrow," Doctor Morris advised. "I'll be along in the

425

afternoon Matron after the meeting with the Paediatricians about baby Benson. Goodnight Mrs Williams." Dr Morris left the wreckage of Ivy Benson to be cared for by Nurse Jones and her mother.

Tomorrow was going to be another tough day for Ivy.

"Bye Ivy, I'd best be off love; I don't want to miss my bus. You get some well-earned rest and I'll be back with Jimmy at visiting time, first thing tomorrow afternoon," Betty fought to hold back tears. "Try not to worry love."

"It's a girl Mam," Ivy raised a weak smile.

"Yes I know love." Betty tried not to let on what else she thought she knew; it was not her place to inform Ivy of the situation, anyway things might happen in the night. *In cases like this, these babies often took a turn for the worse or so they say.*

"June…. I'm calling her June. June, Iris, like you wanted Mam." Ivy whispered happily; she could live with the long tight pain on her abdomen swathed under the wad of bandages. She didn't care about any of it, at least the baby was safe and well. She had her precious baby June.

426

"That's a pretty name Ivy, now get some sleep. We can talk about this when Jimmy's here." Betty smiled and kissed her daughter farewell.

Chapter 41

Jimmy was fuming, *two more weeks!* Betty had said Ivy was being kept in hospital at least another two weeks after the operation. What was he supposed to do without his wife doing the chores? He fixed Betty with a fierce glare.

"It's such bad luck Jimmy. The poor girl has had a terrible time. It was a million to one chance nurse Jones said," Betty sniffed into her handkerchief.

"Why on earth did they do that bloody operation on her in the first place; bloody butchery by the sound of it, that's what I want to know?"

"The baby was sat all wrong, it seems there was no choice. Dr Morris explained it to me, they couldn't stop the bleeding. He said we were lucky not to lose her Jimmy." Betty had cried all night at the thought of her poor daughter being mutilated and at death's door. There would be no more babies for Ivy. Ivy's days of motherhood were over before they had barely begun.

"What happens now then Betty?" He paced the kitchen floor smoking his tenth cigarette of the morning.

Betty noticed the pile of greasy, dirty dishes in the sink; fluff and crumbs lay on the floor and the kitchen table was sticky with ring marks.

"We are to attend a meeting with Ivy, the medical team and a baby specialist at two o'clock to decide the next steps to take." Betty tried not to say too much; Dr Morris had been quite firm that baby June was being evaluated and that it was unhelpful to rush to conclusions.

"Why do they need a baby specialist. What's wrong with it?"

"The baby had a pretty difficult time as well; she spent the night in intensive care," Betty cleared her throat, "er, they were a bit concerned June may have problems."

"What sort of problems?" His eyes narrowed; Jimmy didn't like things being kept from him.

"I can't say Jimmy." Betty shook her head.

"Can't or won't!" Jimmy flicked the fag end into the dirty washing up.

429

"I can't," Betty bleated. "All I know is I overheard Matron asking Dr Morris if Ivy should be allowed to see the baby and Dr Morris said she could if she wanted to." She shrugged her shoulders. "I don't know what they meant by that."

"Well, we will soon find out won't we." Jimmy sneered.

"Yes," Betty took a deep breath and gathered her courage, "Ivy is going to need all our support. Try to be kind to her Jimmy," Betty pleaded.

Jimmy shook his head as if to tell Betty to keep her nose out.

"If you want to be kind to her Betty, then I suggest you clear up this kitchen, it'll save her a job when she comes home. We can catch the 1.15pm bus from the grand Avenue so you've got an hour before we leave."

Betty swallowed her fury and set about clearing the kitchen. Umpteen disintegrating fag ends were floating in and amongst greasy dishes and a burnt potato pan looked almost beyond redemption. *You are a pig Jimmy Benson and that's the God's honest truth of it.*

Ivy sat propped up in bed. A mound of crisp, cool pillows helped her to stay in a comfortable position. Nurse Jones had given her a bed bath and tidied her hair, she felt half human.

"Your Mam's in a bit of state, but you're worth every bit of it my precious," Ivy cradled June to her breast as Norah had shown her. A whisp of strawberry blonde hair covered June's tiny head, gossamer strands like spun gold. At every suck Ivy's stitches on her abdomen pulled and stung like they were on fire; a line of barbed wire cutting into her.

Ivy tried not to grimace with pain as the baby rooted around trying to latch on. Tiny fingers scrabbling against her skin. "You'll soon get the hang of this June…. We both will." Ivy winced.

Nurse Jones came in with Matron.

"It seems you are a natural with baby Mrs Benson," Matron said with a kindly smile. "Now baby has had her feed I'd like nurse Jones to take her away for a nappy change and baby can join us when Mr Benson and the Doctors come to talk to you at around 2o'clock. Now you should get some rest Mrs Benson, you need to build your strength."

Ivy was reluctant to let her precious bundle go. "Bye, bye June, Mammy will see you later, and you'll see Daddy and

431

Nanna," Ivy handed June to nurse Jones, Ivy didn't notice the warning glance Matron shot towards the young nurse.

The small side room was crowded. Ivy was helped to sit up by nurse Jones and a chair was placed either side of the high hospital bed for Jimmy and Betty. Nurse Jones was dispatched to collect baby June Benson from the nursery.

"Mr and Mrs Benson, this is Professor Brown our resident specialist in paediatric medicine." Dr Morris effected the introductions with a kindly smile. He consulted his notes. "Unfortunately, due to placenta praevia Mrs Benson was obliged to have a radical hysterectomy at the same time as her baby was delivered. It has been explained to Mrs Benson that this operation was done as a medical necessity, and that as a direct consequence of that procedure she will not be able to have any more babies."

Betty gave a small sob and Matron glared at her. All focus needed to be on Ivy.

Nurse Jones wheeled a crib into the room where June lay fast asleep, tightly swaddled in pink blankets.

"Perhaps Professor Brown you would like to outline June's

432

situation for Mr and Mrs Benson, so that we are all in possession of the full facts." Dr Morris said.

"Thank you Dr Morris. Please pass me the baby, nurse Jones." Professor Brown unwrapped the sleeping baby and June began to squawk. "As you will see baby June has a small head and particularly small ears," he turned the baby on its side, "she also has a short neck."

Ivy looked puzzled, to her June looked perfect.

"So, what are you saying," Jimmy said gruffly, "is she like a runt or something."

"She's beautiful," Ivy wailed, "it doesn't matter if she's small Jimmy…. I'm small."

"What I'm saying Mr and Mrs Benson is that June has some worrying characteristics. Baby has, as you can see, slightly floppy muscle tone, although in her case it's not so pronounced, which is a good sign," Professor Brown manipulated the tiny arms and legs, "and, as you can see, she has distinctive almond shaped eyes, all these characteristics, point to only one diagnosis…. I'm sorry to say that June has a form of genetic mutation. We are in no doubt that June is a

433

Mongol baby."

Betty gasped; Ivy was so young to have such a child.

Ivy was looking bamboozled, her eyes darted from Doctor to Doctor. "But what does it mean?"

"It means she will grow up to be a dribbling idiot Ivy, led around by its parents, probably not speaking right and a burden to us for the rest of our lives. Isn't that the truth Dr Morris" Jimmy snarled.

Dr Morris kept a blank face; parents were often distraught in situations like this, many got upset, demanding answers. Few were as rude as Mr Benson.

"This is why we are here today Mr Benson to discuss baby's future." Professor Brown tried not to show his disgust for the loud-mouthed man who sat next to his poor wife. He hadn't so much as given the poor girl a kiss or a hug.

"As Dr Morris has said this baby will be Mrs Benson's only natural child which is why the decisions you must take will be particularly difficult."

Ivy started to sob; nurse Jones had placed June in her arms.

Ivy looked at the tiny flat face with the gorgeous, uptilted eyes and felt a rush of love for her beautiful, damaged child.

"What are the options Dr Morris?" Betty could see Ivy was in no place to speak.

"Well in situations like these many, but not all, parents choose to leave the baby here with us in hospital…"

"No! I'm not leaving June." Ivy yelled so loudly that June jumped, threw her arms out and started bawling at the top of her voice.

"Nurse Jones, please take baby Benson back to the nursery for a nap. Don't worry Mrs Benson, baby will join us later," Matron lifted June off the bed and gave Ivy a kindly smile.

"If you say we can leave that baby here in hospital Doctor, then that's what we should do Ivy, let them have the problem." Jimmy's face was rigid.

Ivy sat shaking her head.

"It's not that simple Mr Benson, both parents *must* agree to give the baby up and leave it in the care of a council institution. The baby would be signed over legally to the hospital and after that point your role in the matter ceases. This is not a matter to be taken lightly" Dr Morris explained, his tone matter of fact. "The decision doesn't have to be made today of course. Mrs Benson will be in hospital for another two weeks recovering and we can conduct some more tests to try and evaluate how badly affected baby June is."

"I'm not leaving her," Ivy's face was resolute. "She's our baby Jimmy and I will love her and look after her. I'm not leaving her here!"

"Pwah," Jimmy punched the palm of his hand with disgust. Matron shot him a withering glance.

"Ivy love let the Professor explain what it means if you do decide take June home with you." Betty held Ivy's hand. "Gerald and I will support you whatever the decision." She was proud of her daughter battling for little June, her one and only grandchild.

"Hmm," Professor Brown cleared his throat, this was always the most difficult part of the conversation, because there were no absolutes. It was obvious Mr Benson wasn't exactly supportive of his poor wife and Mrs Benson was so young.

"As I said we won't know how badly affected the baby will be, and the spectrum of disability is wide; each baby is different. Only time will tell how much June will accomplish. The sharp reaction baby gave just now when you shouted Mrs Benson, is called the Moro reflex and its presence was actually a good sign." Professor Brown said.

Ivy looked hopeful. Jimmy sat with his head in his hands, raking his fingers through his hair.

"The paediatric team have carried out some tests: we have listened to her heart; we cannot detect any form of abnormality which can sometimes accompany this diagnosis and her eyesight and hearing appear normal for a baby of her age. Mongol children tend to have delayed development, they are slow to learn and, due to malformation of tongue and palate, *some* may never fully master clear speech, but many do. As I have said each child is different."

Ivy listened and felt the list of positives were in June's favour.

"It's not an exact science Mr and Mrs Benson, but we do know that June will have a shorter life expectancy than other children and she will *always* be different. Only time will tell what she will be able to accomplish." Professor Brown took a deep breath. "Usually, in a case like this, I advise parents to leave baby with us and try again but of course that option is not open to you. One route you could always consider is adoption."

"I'm not leaving her!" Ivy's fingers worried at the delicate, silver crucifix dangling at her throat.

"For God's sake shut up Ivy, you sound like a stuck record!" Jimmy snapped.

"Now, now Mr Benson it's only natural a mother wants to protect her baby." Dr Morris chided.

"I don't want to interrupt Dr Morris, but may I ask a question." Betty willed the good-hearted doctor to be on their side; to give them some hope.

"Of course, Mrs Williams, decisions such as these affect the whole family."

"If Ivy and Jimmy *do* decide take baby June home is there any hope that she might lead a fairly happy life."

"Oh yes… In my view Mrs Williams these babies can often bring a lot of joy. As you know many such children are born

438

to older mothers and they can be loving, happy creatures, but they will always need a lot looking after. As they grow up they are often too trusting, always innocent and child-like." He gave a kindly smile.

"This will not be an easy decision Mr and Mrs Benson, but it is one that must be made without delay." Dr Morris gathered his papers.

"If a mother decides that it is best to leave baby with us, then we usually prefer to bottle feed the child in the nursery in order to prevent too much bonding. That is why we try to get a sense of what the parents want early on… to make sure we do the right things for both parents and the baby." Matron advised.

"I'm not leaving my baby and that's my final word on the matter." Ivy refused to countenance any other course of action.

Ivy knew what it was like to be damaged and different with her gamey leg, and all the tormenting that came with that difference. She would shower June with as much love as possible. She would not abandon June.

"I see. In that case, Nurse Jones please bring baby Benson back for her four o'clock feed as normal."

The medical team said their good-byes and left.

"Oh, I'm so sorry Ivy love. It is such a hard decision for you both."

"No, it's not Mam," she looked at Jimmy with a level gaze. "I will look after June and love her… and nobody is going to stop me."

When Jimmy got home the spectacle of Ivy defying him so blatantly sent him into a towering rage. *How dare she decide to shackle him with a useless Mongol? He would be a laughingstock!*

Jimmy stormed into the sitting room, picked up the precious cranberry glass vase and hurled it at the wall; it smashed to smithereens.

Chapter 42

Betty had done her best to get the house ready for Ivy and June's homecoming. She had cleaned top to bottom removing nearly four weeks of grime and mess. Jimmy had kept out of her way, leaving a key under the mat for Betty to let herself in and do the chores.

Phoebe had told Betty that she'd seen Jimmy most nights down on the wharf doing deals in secluded corners or picking up working girls; always choosing the youngest and the freshest. One evening he'd spotted Phoebe staring at him from a doorway. Steely faced he'd pointed in her direction and mimed at Phoebe to keep her mouth zipped up.

Phoebe wouldn't tell Ivy, but she *would* tell Betty what Jimmy was up to when his wife lay suffering in a hospital bed. She'd be keeping her eyes and ears open for any information on Jimmy Benson, Phoebe was watching him like a hawk! Phoebe had friends in Tiger Bay.

Betty filled Ivy's larder with as much as she and Gerald could spare from their own supplies. Bags of onions, carrots and potatoes sat on the larder floor. It would save Ivy carrying heavy things back from the shops.

It was November next week and the weather was turning dark and cold. A crisp dry October was disappearing in a flurry of squally weather and winter was on its way.

Over the weeks as Betty visited the house, she had made friends with Norah opposite. Betty shared her concerns about baby June and Ivy's ability to cope.

"She's so young Norah; Ivy didn't grow up in a family surrounded by youngsters. I just wish I was nearer to take the strain a bit."

"Don't worry about Ivy Mrs Williams, I'll watch out for her." Norah was proving to be a diamond.

"Thank you Norah, and please call me Betty." Betty felt re-assured that Ivy could count on Norah.

"My sister-in -law, Alice, had a little Mongol baby girl called Carol, when she was forty-two, it was the last of her five pregnancies and she kept her an' all. Course everyone told her not to, especially since she had four healthy boys, but she

442

wouldn't dream of leaving Carol in an institution. That was over five years ago now."

Betty's interest was piqued. "How did Alice manage?"

"It was tough to start with, the baby didn't feed or settle well, and she had all those boys to look after and all, but Alice got there in the end, and that's what matters," Norah said firmly. She jiggled Karen on her knee until the baby gave a loud burp. "That's better my luvvie, as I said, little Carol *was* a difficult baby.... But now she is like one of God's little angels, sweet, loving and trusting. Good as gold she is."

Betty smiled as Karen gave a sunny, gummy grin.

"That's a good girl Karen, I think that little smile means there's more to come," Norah kept rubbing Karen's back to encourage a repeat performance. "Mongol babies stay children for ever really, it's a blessing and a curse but what I *do* know is that Alice never once regrets bringing Carol home from hospital. Never!"

"Thank you Norah, that has given me hope. June is a pretty little thing despite…"

Norah interrupted Betty mid flow. "Please don't say "despite"
443

Betty". The one thing we've all learnt from Carol is that she must be treated like any other child, Alice and her husband John insist on it. John is simply marvellous with that little girl; he worships her. Carol is as precious to them as their four boys are. He won't have a word said against her, he says she is their little *blessing*, and God help anyone who tries to tell him otherwise."

"You're right of course, thank you Norah. Ivy will need as much help and support as she can get, and I know you are going to be a good friend to her. It will be Ivy's one and only baby…. Sorry I should say *their* one and only. So, if you could help Ivy and encourage her with tales of little Carol, I would be so grateful."

"I will do Betty. Alice and John live in Swansea now near her family, but when they next come to Cardiff, I'll ask them to bring little Carol to meet Ivy and baby June. Let Ivy see what the future holds. Don't worry Betty I'll keep a good eye on Ivy. Promise."

Betty had gone back to number twelve with hope in her heart. She tucked a small bunch of colourful Dahlias, picked from Gerald's flower bed, in a jam-jar and placed them in the sitting room window for Ivy to see when she got back from hospital.

Betty had cleared the shattered fragments of cranberry glass that littered the sitting room rug; it was obvious the broken glass vase was no accident; no attempt had been made to clear it up. She guessed Jimmy and his temper was to blame for the destruction of the precious vase; for the sake of harmony Betty let it be. Ivy would be disappointed at its loss.

Perhaps Ivy had made the right decision bringing June home? June was one of God's children as much as any other baby. If little Carol was proving to be a joy to her parents, then why shouldn't June be? Betty mused.

The only big difference as far as Betty could see was that June had Jimmy Benson as a father.

Betty would have loved to stay and welcome Ivy and June home, but as instructed Betty left the key under the mat when she left. Jimmy said he did not want his house being *turned into a waiting room just because Ivy's given birth.* Ivy wasn't due home for hours yet, so Betty was under instructions to come back tomorrow.

445

Betty bit her tongue; she could only hope Jimmy's sour temper would improve once he got used to the idea of having a little baby in the house.

Jimmy said that he'd be out this afternoon when Ivy returned home with *it*.... as he referred to the baby. Not her, or June... just *it*.

Honestly Jimmy Benson I could swing for you!

Ivy arrived home in the ambulance with her precious bundle in her arms. Dr Morris had discharge Ivy on the strict instructions that she should take it easy and rest.

"You've had a difficult time Mrs Benson. I know it's an impossible ask but you really mustn't lift things. Under normal circumstances after a hysterectomy, we would ask that you do not lift anything over 3lb.... little June is 6lbs 10oz now, so you really must try to take it easy for another few weeks at least; allow the healing process to happen."

"Yes Dr Morris; I'll try my best, I promise." Ivy knew it was a vain promise. She would get no help from Jimmy; he'd made it quite clear since Ivy had decided to keep June that she would be doing all the caring for the baby. He'd only visited his wife three times in hospital since the decision was made, pleading work and other things that needed doing. Jimmy refused to hold June despite Ivy's urging. He refused to look after a disabled baby that he didn't want.

"June has been doing so well hasn't she Matron?" Ivy gazed proudly at her sleeping baby. The trauma of the delivery melted away whenever June was in Ivy's arms.

"She has Mrs Benson, she's put on 4oz since birth and she's quite an alert little thing too, which is a good sign. Sometimes babies like June struggle to feed, but June has really got the hang of it."

Ivy beamed with pride. "My Mam has offered to help every day until I can manage on my own, so I won't be doing everything, Matron." Unlike Jimmy, Betty had visited Ivy every afternoon. The trauma of June's arrival three weeks ago had drawn mother and daughter together. With Gerald to support her, Betty could afford to relax a little, to leave hard faced calculating Betty behind her and become Ivy's Mam and little June's Nanna.

When the ambulance parked outside Number 12, at ten past three Norah waved through the window. Betty had primed

Norah to expect Ivy's arrival at about three o'clock. Norah gave it ten minutes before rushing over the see Ivy and baby June.

Ivy was thrilled to see her friend running over with Karen tucked in her arms.

"Hello, my lovely," Norah gave Ivy a big hug. "Now let me see this beautiful baby that I've heard so much about her from Nanna Betty."

Norah peeked inside the blanket, June was sucking her fingers, piercing blue eyes glared at Norah. "Oh, she's gorgeous Ivy, a little stunner… and don't let anybody else tell you otherwise." She placed Karen on the sofa. "Here let me have a little hold." Norah cradled June in her arm. "Hello, my darling, I'm sure you're going to be the best of friends with my little Karen. Your Aunty Norah is going to love looking after you an all."

Tears trickled down Ivy's face. "Thank you Norah, you're an angel and such a good friend. Could you do something for me?"

"Of course, Ivy love what is it?"

448

"Post this letter. I wrote it in hospital, it's to my best friend Alice Tranter. I promised I'd let her know when I'd had the baby," Ivy looked a bit sheepish. "I didn't have my stamps with me in hospital and I couldn't really ask Jimmy. And I'm not supposed to be out and about yet." Ivy didn't want to explain that she kept the stamps hidden from Jimmy or that Mam had forbidden her to have anything to do with Alice Tranter. It sounded silly, disloyal and weak.

"If you've put a stamp on it, then I can pop it in the post box when I'm off out in the morning, you don't need to explain to me Ivy. Well, I'd best be off; let the pair of you settle in."

Norah scooped up Karen who was starting to stir. "You can always tell me anything Ivy, remember that. If ever you need a shoulder to cry on or just a chat to get something off your chest please come to me. I'm not a gossip. Leastways not when it's important to keep my mouth shut," Norah laughed. She knew that she had a reputation for chatting and ferreting out secrets, but she meant it. Norah could keep confidences as well.

Chapter 43

Ivy had mastered the art of doing most chores single
handed; cradling June in her left arm whilst performing all
sorts of tasks with her right.

After six weeks Jimmy had forbidden Betty to call every day,
he moaned about feeling like a spare part in his own home.

"For God's sake Ivy can't we have a rest from that mother of
yours. Surely visiting every other day is more than plenty?
Jimmy raged after her Mam left one afternoon. There had
been a few sharp words. In Ivy's defence her Mam had
chipped in her two penn'orth worth, adding fuel to the fire.

"Look Betty, don't *you* have a go at me, it was Ivy who
wanted to bring *it* home with her, so she'll have to get used to
looking after it," he raged. "Just look at the place it's like a
Chinese laundry, bloody nappies everywhere. A man needs to
feel he can relax in his own home, not have his mother-in-law

breathing down his bloody neck all the time. That *thing* has thrown a complete spanner in the works and I'm not standing for it. Every other day for visiting Ivy is plenty and that's final!"

Betty reluctantly conceded defeat. Every other day it would have to be.

Rising early for June's six o'clock feed Ivy struggled with the daily mashing and boiling of soiled nappies on the top of the stove; rinsing and wringing them through the mangle before Jimmy came down for his breakfast. He hated the steamy, thick smell of boiling soap and cotton.

To avoid Jimmy's temper Ivy would lug the steaming pail of nappies out on to the back step, the heavy bucket clashing and bruising her leg. Ivy waited until after Jimmy had left for the day, before stringing them up in the kitchen to dry. She was exhausted.

At least Mam was coming this morning; she might be able to put her feet up for a few minutes whilst Mam held June.

Betty bustled in with laden shopping bags. "How's Nanna's precious girl this morning then?"

451

Betty scooped up June the minute she'd emptied the bags, "my goodness you are a getting a lump June!" Betty laughed. "We need to feed your Mam up a bit young lady, by the looks of it you're getting all the grub."

Ivy was looking painfully thin, breast feeding a demanding baby and running around after Jimmy was taking its toll.

"Ivy, I'll put the kettle on for a cuppa and you can have a sit down. Have you had any breakfast this morning?"

Ivy shook her head.

"I thought as much, well I've brought some nice, buttered slices of homemade Bara Brith with me and I'm going to sit and watch you eat it." Betty said sternly. "If you don't look after yourself Ivy, who is going to look after June?"

Betty plonked two thick slabs of Bara Brith in front or her daughter with a steaming cup of strong tea. "Go on, get this down you Ivy. There's one slice left and I'm going to tuck that behind the tins in the pantry and you can finish it up tomorrow. It's for you mind!" Betty gave Ivy a stern stare.

Betty had noticed Jimmy was sporting quite a paunch lately, it was obvious that Ivy was the one going without. The more

452

Gerald and she helped with provisions, the more Jimmy reduced Ivy's housekeeping and the more he poured down his throat. Betty would have to be devious.

"Thanks Mam," Ivy devoured the moist, fruity cake with relish. She didn't know what she would have done without Mam and Norah's support over the last six weeks. Ivy had been lonely, weepy and bone achingly tired, but at long last June was starting to turn a corner. At ten weeks she was starting to sleep through the night and Ivy felt a glimmer of hope.

It would Christmas next week, their first Christmas as a family. Ivy had gathered some sprigs of holly from bushes on the Grand avenue and a large arrangement of holly laden with red berries decorated the sideboard giving the small parlour a festive air.

"Won't you all come to us for Christmas day lunch Ivy." Betty pleaded. "Gerald has been keeping a chicken in the yard all year and he's planning on having it for Christmas lunch; a big fat thing it is too." Betty stressed the "*all,*" she hoped Jimmy could be agreeable to at least one family gathering.

It was becoming increasingly obvious that apart from gifts of food or offers of assistance with chores or money, Jimmy wanted nothing to do with family life. He shunned all invitations to visit and did little to make Betty feel welcome when she called.

"You can go if you like Ivy if you've finished the chores, but your Mam had better refund your bus fare. I'm not paying for you to go gadding over to Roath just because she fancies a visit." He'd said when Ivy said Mam had invited them to come over for tea one day. It was always the same refrain; Betty could visit on Jimmy's terms, but Ivy was not allowed to be off out gallivanting without permission.

The thought of a whole plump, crispy chicken made Ivy's mouth water, but she knew Jimmy had already put his foot down on the matter of where they would spend Christmas day.

"I'd love to Mam, but Jimmy is insisting he wants to spend Christmas in his own home. Perhaps I could pop over on Boxing day if the buses are running, bring June to see you both." Ivy suggested.

Jimmy would be gone all day; Ivy would not be missed. "I know Jimmy is off to watch a rugby match with his mates from the Duke of Edinburgh on Boxing day, so I'll be on my own most of the day."

Betty tutted with disapproval. *She knew Jimmy might spend the afternoon at a rugby match but a pound to a penny he'd spend the evening in the pub with his mates.*

"I see. So, what will you be having for your Christmas lunch then Ivy?"

"Bob Dewar the butcher on the parade, has promised to keep me a small collar of bacon joint, not too big mind, but I'm going to roast it for Christmas lunch and then we can have any leftovers cold."

Since moving to Wilson road Ivy had put a few pennies each week into the Dewar's Christmas saving club, she was proud she could afford a bacon joint for Christmas day.

"That will be nice Ivy I'm sure. If you can come over on Boxing day you could always take some cold chicken back with you, a whole bird is way too much for Gerald and me, there will be plenty of leftovers."

Betty left the invitation hanging in the air.

When Betty left after helping Ivy with the housework she was not hopeful of a visit from Ivy. Jimmy's word was law. She'd slipped Ivy two crisp ten-shilling notes for her Christmas present, "these are for you from me and Gerald, keep them safe for something special. Buy little June some clothes after Christmas and something for yourself." She gave Ivy a kiss. "It's for *you* mind!" Betty said sternly.

"Thank you Mam. I haven't been able to buy any presents this year what with…well with everything." Ivy never had any money to call her own; she would squirrel this gift away for when she had need of it.

Betty had her suspicions the money would go on groceries when Ivy was short on housekeeping, but at least it wouldn't go down Jimmy Benson's throat on a Saturday night.

"Don't worry about presents Ivy. The only present I want is to see our gorgeous granddaughter on Boxing day." Betty said.

Tuesday was Christmas day; Betty and Gerald passed a pleasant, companionable Christmas day. In the morning Betty went to Mass for the first time in a very long time, and she gave thanks to God for Ivy's recovery and for the precious gift of baby June. After a fine lunch of roast chicken, they toasted

"The King" and raised a glass to baby June's future and swapped gifts.

Betty realised that at long last she was content. Gerald was a good man who cherished his family, every last one of them, and he was good to her. Gerald so wanted to see little June, but Jimmy had made it quite clear that if anyone was visiting Wilson road it would be Betty and only Betty. As far as Jimmy was concerned Gerald was not a family member; he could hardly refuse Betty, but he certainly could refuse Gerald.

I've found a good man in Gerald, if only Ivy could have done the same.

Boxing day came and went without any visitors to Inkerman Street.

Chapter 44

Weeks drifted into months before Betty's visits resumed to Wilson road. Gerald had been ill with bronchitis and Betty had been sickly with flu and a chest infection that raged in her lungs leaving her short of breath and gasping for air; decades of smoking had weakened her chest; she felt old and fragile and in no fit state to be trekking off to Ely to help Ivy with arduous housework tasks.

The Williams household finally struggled into a blustery March feeling battered about by ill health; now Gerald and Betty were on the mend and Betty was aching to see Ivy and June. Betty sent Ivy a note telling her the good news and promised to visit the following week.

"Nana's coming to see us June, now you can show her what a clever girl you are." Ivy was so proud of June. June rewarded Ivy with a sunny smile.

At five months June was holding her head up, and as the health visitor said, at June's check-up. *"It's good news Mrs Benson.... Baby June appears to be meeting her milestones only a fraction later than normal babies. Let's hope she keeps this up."*

Ivy dared to hope that over the coming months and years June would continue to prove everyone wrong, especially Jimmy. *If only Jimmy could learn to love June, if only he would try a little.*

Ivy saw her Mam striding up the path laden with bags; her hair was looking threaded with grey, and she was looking tired around the eyes.

Ivy opened the door "Come in Mam. Look June… its Nanna Betty!"

Ivy wrestled the bags from Mam's tired hands, pink ridged fingers that throbbed from the cutting handles of string shopping bags. "Here Mam give me those. Goodness they are heavy. Here, give me your coat and then you have June and I'll make us both a nice cup of tea." Ivy ushered Betty into the cosy kitchen and shut the kitchen door to keep the warmth in.

459

"Come on in and see June. She's been waiting to see her Grandma for ages, haven't you my angel?"

In the kerfuffle to get Betty, June and the laden bags into the kitchen Ivy didn't notice the front door failed to latch behind her; soon the door drifted open and chilly air flooded into the hall.

"So, what do you think Mam, hasn't June grown?" Ivy beamed proudly.

"She certainly has love. And I never thought I'd say it Ivy but, she looks so normal!"

"I know everyone says that." Ivy said triumphantly. "At her hospital four-month check- up the Doctor said if it wasn't for her eyes and face shape it would be hard to tell she was…. Well, you know" Ivy hated the word Mongol, to her June was just June.

"That's really good news Ivy, Jimmy must be pleased."

Ivy bustled about making the tea and let the comment pass. She dared not tell Betty that Jimmy hadn't so much as picked up June since the day Ivy brought the baby home from hospital. He studiously ignored the child; it was as if June didn't exist. For him June had no purpose, so he ignored her. The only time Jimmy took any notice was when June cried, then he would tell Ivy to shut *it* up or flounce off out to the pub declaring he needed some peace and quiet.

"And how about you Ivy, are you well? We were sorry not to see you on Boxing day." Betty jigged June on her knee; the baby gurgled contentedly. Pink, chubby fingers explored the glittery beads around Betty's neck.

"I know I'm sorry Mam, I couldn't make it," Ivy kept her eyes low as she unpacked the groceries. She would not say that Jimmy had been in a flaming temper and forbidden her to leave the house; or that Jimmy had smashed the vase of holly against the kitchen wall because June had been fractious and grumpy.

"That's a shame, Gerald so wanted to see this little one. Just look at those lovely golden curls, you're going to be a right little blondie June. Your Mam had auburn hair when she was little like you." Betty cooed. "Aunty Phoebe used to say your Mammy looked like a fluffy apricot!"

June gnawed away on her tiny fist "are you starting to get some teeth darling? Honestly they grow up so quickly Ivy.

461

When will you be coming to see Nanna and Grandad my angel?" Betty gave Ivy a long look.

Ivy said nothing.

"Ivy you can't let Jimmy boss you around. We'd love you to visit us; now Spring is on the way it's easy to catch the bus over to Roath, and there's nothing to stop you Ivy. You don't have to account to *him* all the time." Betty said the word *him* with venom.

The two women did not hear the footsteps in the hall.

"Jimmy wouldn't like it Mam," Ivy looked nervous.

"Phwah," her Mam huffed in disgust, "We don't care what Daddy thinks about that do we Junie? You've got to put your foot down Ivy and bring June for a visit! He's not your jailer for crying out loud."

Jimmy listened at the door…. *So, this was what the old witch got up to behind his back, turning Ivy against him, poisoning the well.*

"I mean does he ever help you out around the place?" Betty took in the wreathes of nappies and piles of dishes drying on the wooden draining board.

"You do know Jimmy only got this house because of you don't you?" Betty said archly.

Ivy looked puzzled.

"If it wasn't for you and this baby Ivy, Jimmy couldn't have even applied for this nice new council house. *You* were his passport to this house, he needed *you* Ivy, and I bet it will be just his name he's put on that tenancy agreement." Betty worried that Ivy was probably in a very uncertain position.

"The more I think about it, the more it seems to me that it was incredibly convenient for Jimmy that you fell pregnant when you did. Very convenient indeed." Betty mused running her fingers through June's fine gold curls.

Ivy looked nervous she didn't like where this discussion was going.

"Shush Mam…."

"Jimmy *is* June's father isn't he Ivy?" Betty looked Ivy straight in the eyes. She could read Ivy like a book.

Ivy wrung her hands. She knew she was bound by her

promise to Jimmy never to tell anyone what happened in Bute street. But she hated lying to Mam, Ivy gave an imperceptible nod of the head.

Jimmy burst into the kitchen. "What do you think you're playing at Betty…. Causing trouble again? Poking your nose in where it's not wanted!"

"Jimmy, how did you…?" Ivy looked petrified. Jimmy wasn't usually home now.

"If you're asking me how I got in Ivy, I walked in through the bloody front door; it's wide open; all the heat's gone out and any Tom Dick or Harry could just stroll in off the street and rob us blind. The question is what is *she* doing here?" He jabbed a finger in Betty's direction. His face like thunder.

"I'm visiting my daughter and my grand-child." Betty jutted out her chin in defiance.

"That part is bloody obvious, what I mean is what are you doing trying to turn my Ivy against me?" Jimmy sneered. "I heard you dripping your poison Betty!"

"I'm not doing anything of the sort, I'm just speaking the truth."

464

"I see you're a fan of speaking the truth are you now Betty," Jimmy jibed. "I bet you haven't been quite so honest about who Ivy's father is have you?"

Betty looked purple with rage.

"I bet you haven't told Ivy the half of it… about how you paid the bills over the years by lying on your back with any bloke that would open his wallet!"

June started to wail. Ivy scooped the crying child into her arms. "Shh now June…shh."

"You knew what the deal was Betty at the time, now butt out. Don't get between a man and his wife if you know what's good for you!"

Betty jumped to her feet. "You're a snake Jimmy Benson. A snake and a liar and I rue the day you came through my front door!"

"Get out of *my* house Betty and don't come back!" Jimmy barked.

Ivy started to sob, "please don't Jimmy," Ivy pleaded, her face blotchy with tears. She needed her Mam.

465

"I'm going Jimmy and you'd better be good to my Ivy *and* June or else…."

Betty grabbed her handbag, "always remember people talk Jimmy." She hissed.

Betty gave Ivy and June a kiss. "Come and see me when you can Ivy." She shot Jimmy a defiant look. Ivy looked terrified.

"She'll come when *I* say she can, and not before, now sling your hook Betty."

Betty left with her head held high.

Bloody Jimmy Benson who did he think he was talking to her like that?

Betty knew that Jimmy was a bully, but he also knew which side his bread was buttered on. She reckoned he'd be back when he wanted something.

Betty knew Norah Asworth would keep an eye on Ivy, but it wasn't the same. She'd drop Norah a line to let her know the state of play.

Gerald would be so disappointed not to see June, it had been five months and he still hadn't seen the little girl.

466

Chapter 45

Norah Ashworth was having a difficult morning.

"No Gareth!.... For the umpteenth time Gareth, will you stop being such a pest? Karen doesn't like it!" Norah scolded, she tucked the hapless Karen, who was now bawling her heart out, under her arm and clipped Gareth around the ear for his trouble.

Gareth opened his lungs and screeched at full volume, "Sorry Mammy.... Sorreeee"

"I don't want "sorry" Gareth; I want you to stop doing it! How would you like it if Mammy pushed you over all the time?"

"No, ...no Mammy..." Gareth stuttered, snot running down his lip. Norah wiped his faced with the edge of her pinafore. "Now go upstairs and sit in your room and I'll tell you when you can come down," with a point of Norah's finger Gareth

467

was ordered upstairs.

"I can come back another time if you like," Ivy felt like she was sitting in the midst of a thunderstorm, all bluster, and noise crashing around her.

"Don't be silly Ivy, it's fine. Thank God you've got a little girl, boys can be such a handful, especially ones like our Gareth." She jigged Karen up and down, soothing the mardy face and jutting lip.

"Gareth thinks it's a big joke to push Karen over every time she pulls herself up to stand, the poor angel gets bowled over like a skittle about a dozen times every day." Norah kissed Karen's chubby cheeks and set the child against the sofa. "There we go. Now you show Aunty Ivy how you can walk around the furniture while Mammy makes a cup of tea and Aunty Ivy reads her letter." Norah handed Ivy a small envelope.

Ivy recognized her Mam's writing.

Months had passed without a visit from Betty and still Jimmy wouldn't back down. Betty had taken to sending Ivy notes via Norah's address. After months of secret missives, Jack voiced

468

his concerns about getting embroiled in the Benson family dispute. When another familiar, distinctive little envelope arrived on the mat that morning; Mrs Ivy Benson, c/o Mrs Norah Ashworth…. Jack had put his foot down.

"Look we're not a messenger service Norah. It's not right, us going behind Jimmy's back. Colluding is what it is!"

Norah was surprised that Jack knew words such as *colluding*.

"I can hardly look the man in the face when I see him at the Culver house pub as it is. It's like I'm lying to him, keeping secrets and I don't like it!" Jack's tone was firm. He waved the small envelope in her face.

"Whatever problems the Bensons have got, it's *not* our place to interfere. That's your problem Norah, you always take on other people's problems, always getting involved, being the shoulder to cry on…. Well, I'm saying that this got to stop. You've got to speak to Ivy, and she must tell her Mam to stop sending letters here. If her Mam wants to send Ivy letters then she must send them to Ivy's house."

Jack didn't like Jimmy Benson, but he didn't want to get on the wrong side of him either. Jack worked on the dock

469

warehouses, he'd seen Jimmy about, saw the company he kept, and he knew that Jimmy had a reputation for being a man who ran to meet trouble and smacked it in the face.

Jack didn't want any trouble brought to his doorstep because of Ivy Benson.

Norah had argued and badgered Jack on Ivy's behalf, but Jack stood firm.

"I mean it Norah; I want no part in this deception." Jack didn't shout, but Norah knew the cause was lost. Betty's letter today would have to be the last.

Balanced on wobbling, chubby legs, Karen, her face a picture of concentration, pulled herself across the sofa cushions. June sat on Ivy's knee studying the performance as Ivy read her letter.

Karen made her way around the furniture with a studied look on her face until she arrived at Ivy's knee.

"What a clever girl! Let's give Karen a clap June," Ivy clapped, and June brought her little hands together as well.

"Good girl June, it will be your turn soon," Ivy beamed. June

470

was doing so well, sitting up and crawling, she was like a little ray of sunshine. Jimmy barely noticed June's presence; she was simply part of the furniture, tucked up in bed before he got home at night. Out of sight out of mind.

Norah brought in the tea in her best china. "What's the news from your Mam Ivy."

"Not a lot… she asks after June of course, asks when I can visit, well you know that sort of thing. She also sent me a ten bob note to help out."

"Ha..hmmm," Norah cleared her throat. "Ivy I'm sorry but my Jack has said that your Mam can't keep sending letters here every week. He doesn't feel it's right. I mean when it first started he thought it was just the odd letter until Jimmy calmed down a bit. But it's been six months now and, well things don't seem to have improved. So, Jack says it's got to stop."

Norah saw Ivy's stricken face. "I tried to argue with him Ivy, but he won't have it. I can't fall out with Jack over this Ivy; he says his mind is made up."

Ivy shook her head sadly, she wasn't surprised, but she so

471

looked forward to letters from Mam.

"You'll have to write and tell her Ivy. Jack says that if another letter arrives here then he'll pop it over through your letter box." Norah sipped her tea. "Can't you speak to Jimmy Ivy?"

Ivy shook her head sadly, "Jimmy's mind is made up Norah, he thinks Mam is interfering where she has no business to, and he's taken umbrage. Anyway, thanks for telling me, I'll write to her and tell her not to write here anymore. Tell Jack there's no hard feelings." Ivy gave a small smile; she felt the loss of this little lifeline keenly. She'd have to find other ways to keep in touch.

"It's Karen's first birthday next month, I'm planning a little party for her, just in the garden. Won't that be fun Karen?" Norah enthused, glad to move on to a happier subject.

Ivy had never been to a birthday party.

"I'm going to make a sponge cake and I managed to get a packet of vanilla blancmange to make a white rabbit mould and a tablet of lime jelly for the grass... do say you'll come and bring June."

"That would be lovely if it's not too much trouble."

472

"No trouble at all and my sister in-law Alice will be coming with her daughter Carol." Norah was desperate for Ivy to see little Carol, after all she'd promised Betty that she would bring them together.

Ivy had heard a lot about six-year-old Carol. Ivy had to admit to having mixed feelings about the prospect of meeting Carol. Part of her wasn't entirely sure if she was ready to meet another child with June's problems; a glimpse into June's future, in case it destroyed her hopes. But Norah had painted such a glowing picture of the child that Ivy had to admit she was curious.

"Thank you Norah. We'd love to come wouldn't we June."

June gurgled contentedly.

At home Ivy scrunched up Betty's final letter before tucking it deep under the kindling in the fireplace. Ivy hid the crisp, brown ten-shilling note in a small tobacco box in June's clothes drawer; the one place Jimmy never went. In the box she had amassed her savings of one pound, fifteen shillings and eight pence, it wasn't much but each time Ivy managed to add a three pence or sixpence to the hoard from her house keeping she felt a sense of winning. Each time her Mam gave her money she kept it hidden away from Jimmy's grasp, he would be furious if he knew. But then as she had learned over the years, she was good at keeping secrets.

 This was *her* money, her bit of freedom. She would write to Mam and suggest they meet in Cardiff market instead. The crowded indoor market with its myriad of stalls offered plenty of opportunities to hide in plain sight. If she posted a letter today Ivy could arrange to see Mam next Friday by the wool stall.

 If nothing else Jimmy had taught her to be devious, and Ivy was getting good at it.

Chapter 46

Slowly but surely Betty and Ivy settled on a routine. Once a month on a Friday morning, Ivy and June caught the bus into the city centre and met Mam and sometimes Gerald in Cardiff market. Jimmy wasn't told any lies but then he wasn't told the whole truth either.

After a few months Ivy mentioned casually to Jimmy that she sometimes happened to bump into Mam as she shopped in the market. He merely grunted.

On one occasion in October Ivy said she had met Nanna Betty whilst out shopping and that Nanna Betty insisted on paying for a gift for June's first birthday, Ivy displayed the pretty winter dress as proof. Much to Ivy's surprise Jimmy merely shrugged and said if Betty wanted to waste her money, then it was up to her and it was no skin off his nose. *At least it saved him having to buy it some new clothes.*

Jimmy was too busy with other fish to fry to care about a feud with Mam. Secretive he was. Ivy knew something was up, she rarely saw him now; most days Jimmy left early and came home late.

Sometimes Ivy noticed he had taken money from the pantry jar she kept for the household bills; occasionally a few shillings would be missing from her house-keeping purse. He never said what he did with the money; she would never dare ask. Some days she barely saw him to speak to, he was elusive and secretive. What did he get up to when he was out on business all day?

Of late Jimmy had been rolling back home long after Ivy had already gone to bed. June slept in the same room as Ivy did in the same single bed that had come from Bute street; Ivy would hear him scrambling up the stairs, late at night drunk; laughing and sniggering as he missed a stair tread. She could hear him stumbling about in the next room, as he banged into furniture and struggled to get out of his trousers and into bed.

He frightened her and disgusted her in equal measure.

If it wasn't for little June to love and care for Ivy would be lost.

To Ivy's relief, Jimmy never came near her now; he said her lined, scarred belly and drooping tits disgusted him; shouted for her to go back to her *boyfriend,* the one he knew she'd never had; said he wished he'd never married her. It was as if he enjoyed wounding her.

At night Ivy cried in her loneliness, she didn't want Jimmy, but she so missed having someone to care for her, she missed feeling young.

Sometimes Ivy thought about young Billy Thomas and how different her life could have been if Alice had married George and she had courted Billy. That brief, carefree window when she felt young and pretty listening to Jazz and laughing. She'd almost forgotten how to laugh now.

There were dark, lonely days when Ivy wondered how she could survive if she ran away from Jimmy. But in her heart she knew she couldn't leave; with no money and nowhere to go how could she think of leaving? There was no other option but to stay, for June's sake.

Everything she'd done had been for her baby, she would stay and fight for June every inch of the way. Ivy had made her bed and she would lie on it. She would stand anything so long as it meant June was safe.

The Friday meetings in Cardiff market with Mam were Ivy's lifeline, her oxygen when she was drowning. The colourful market stalls with the happy chatter and bustle; voices calling to customers lifted her spirits. Here was life!

June loved hearing the caged birds or seeing the rabbits and kittens in the pet shop window on the top floor corridor, tiny scraps of fluff; wide eyes pleading for a new home.

"Look June that black and white one is waving to you," Betty pointed to the pretty kitten pawing furiously at the glass. "Say hello to Mr kitten."

June giggled. "' Kiffen," June lisped, her slightly overlarge, tongue sticking out. June was always smiling.

"Shall we look out for Nanna's friend? Here we go young lady…let's look over the balcony."

Ivy's ears pricked up like a nervous faun. Mam had obviously let someone else in on their secret. "Err, who is it Mam?"

"There she is …. It's only Aunty Phoebe Ivy. Wave to Aunty Phoebe, June…. whoo hoo…. up here, Phoebe." Betty gestured to the squat figure below in a brown coat.

Phoebe scurried up to the upper gallery. "Hello Ivy!" She ran towards Ivy and gave her a huge hug. "Ivy my darling, let me look at you and this lovely little daughter of yours." Phoebe's kind face crinkled with concern. Ivy looked tired and worn out. "Are you looking after yourself my girl?" Phoebe oozed concern.

Ivy gave a small nod and shrugged as if to say motherhood was hard.

"Oh, my goodness, what a smile, you're a cheeky one!" Phoebe took off her gloves. June shrieked in delight as Phoebe tickled her under the chin. "Come to your Aunty Phoebe, June, give your Mammy a rest.."

June rewarded Phoebe with a big sloppy kiss.

"Aw there's lovely Junie giving Aunty Phoebe a nice kiss." Betty smiled. "Now, why don't I buy us all a pot of tea from the corner café?" Betty pulled up some chairs. "And then we can all have a good natter. Phoebe has so wanted to see you Ivy, you two can catch up while I get the drinks." Betty aimed for the busy corner café. She needed Phoebe to help her with Ivy.

479

Over the weeks Betty had raged to Phoebe about Jimmy Benson's increasingly unreasonable behaviour. "It's not Fair Phoebe why does he have to be so bloody obstinate? We're heading towards a second Christmas and we still can't get Ivy and June to come for a visit; not even for Christmas lunch!" Betty wailed.

Phoebe rolled her eyes. This controlling behaviour was madness, Ivy was being cut off from her family and for what reason? All because Jimmy Benson wanted to keep Ivy just where he wanted her. Trapped inside Wilson road under his thumb.

"He won't let anyone go to the house; he won't let Ivy come to see me and Gerald; he keeps her short of money and I'm worried he's started hitting her when he's in one of his foul moods. God knows what he gets up to every day. The man is a pig!"

Norah knew *some* of what Jimmy Benson got up to most days and it wasn't good; working girls preferred to take other customers if they could, rather than deal with Jimmy and his demands. People talked to chatty, inoffensive Phoebe Horwat and she kept her ear to the ground; she heard things.

Unlike Betty, Phoebe knew there wouldn't be kind-hearted man like Gerald to her rescue. She had never managed to leave the life of the Tiger Bay behind her; she was held tight in its claws with no prospect of escape. Times were becoming increasingly hard for a fifty-two-year old prostitute with no-one to protect her and no family to turn to.

Phoebe supplemented her income by being the eyes and ears of businessmen such as China Joe and others; powerful men who would pay for the tit bits information she gleaned whilst sitting in bars with her customers. News of a sloppy foreman or a corrupt Captain on the take, or an idle stockman who didn't always lock up securely at night, was worth trading and Phoebe did it to keep a roof over her head.

"Ivy has got a lovely neighbour Phoebe, called Nora Ashworth, and she was letting me send letters to their house; just over the road at number seven, but now her husband Jack has put his foot down, he's worried about Jimmy and his nasty temper and I don't blame him. Jimmy's a vicious sod!" Betty spat.

"Jack Ashworth didn't want any trouble, what with them being in the same street as Jimmy and Jack working down at

481

Mermaid quay. He told Ivy he wanted no more letters coming to his house. Word gets around."

Phoebe stored this nugget of information away. She knew exactly how word got around on the Cardiff quays.

"It seems Jimmy Benson puts the frighteners on everyone. He has turned Ivy into a nervous wreck, she jumps at her own shadow and barely goes out the house; what can I do Phoebe?" Betty looked anxious.

"He's a bad un, Betty and no two ways about it. I warned you he was bad news at the time." Phoebe left the rest unsaid but that day she had acted as witness to the marriage she could see it was an accident waiting to happen. She'd met plenty of men like Jimmy and they always proved to be rotten apples.

The more Phoebe heard from Betty the more she needed find out all she could about Jimmy Benson. Information was power.

"Aunty Phoebe could eat you up my precious, mwamp mwamp mwamp…" Phoebe pretended to munch under June's chin until the child squealed hysterically.

Phoebe never forgot the precious baby girl, Angela, who she

gave away all those years ago. Ivy was courageous keeping June and if there was anything she could do to protect Ivy and baby June then she would.

"Here Ivy," Phoebe passed over a crisp green note across the table, "put this away for when you need it," Phoebe said levelly. "Now no arguing Ivy… I want you to have it."

"Thank you Aunty Phoebe, you're always so good to me," Ivy fingered the little silver cross around her neck that Phoebe gave her at her christening.

"Rubbish, I only do what a Godmother should do, and talking about God parents has this little one been christened yet?"

Ivy shook her head; a christening had been the subject of a huge argument with Jimmy when June was only three months old. Jimmy had hurled hateful reasons for his refusal to get the child christened; he refused to "parade" June in public, he didn't want old Father Leary and his cronies insisting on christening classes, they wouldn't be going along with any ridiculous *mumbo jumbo* as he saw it. No; he forbade it!

"Jimmy won't allow it!" Ivy knew Phoebe, a staunch Catholic, would be horrified.

483

"Won't allow it! What's the matter with the man?" Phoebe was aghast.

"Please Aunty Phoebe, can we drop it?" Ivy pleaded. She couldn't bear to have yet another discussion about the matter, her Mam had raged about it; worried about June's soul, but in the end there was nothing Ivy could do to cross Jimmy.

"All right, Ivy if you say so" Phoebe held her hands up in defeat. "But I'll be praying for this gorgeous little lamb and that husband of yours can't stop that!"

Phoebe made her way back to Splott and started to form a plan. Men like Jimmy were always up to no good it was only a matter of watching and waiting; she would learn something to her advantage and when she did she would use it.

Chapter 47

Ivy's purse was empty. When she checked her
housekeeping jar in the pantry that was empty too. It was only
Wednesday, and Jimmy didn't usually give her house keeping
money until Friday morning; how was she supposed to stretch
her groceries until then? Ivy felt tears gather in her eyes.

He'd taken all the money again. The last time he cleared out
her purse, was a week before Christmas. When she asked
about the lack of money he'd hit her; told her she was an
ungrateful cow, that it was his money and that if he wanted
back then he'd take it… he wouldn't be asking her
permission, told her to ask her trashy Mam for some money.
Call it your Christmas present he'd jeered.

She could hear him through the kitchen ceiling now snoring,
driving them home like a hog. He would not get up for a few
hours and when he did there was no milk for his tea. She
would have to go shopping on the Grand Avenue.

She heard him come in late last night, clumping up the stairs, stumbling on the landing; drunk and mouthy. She heard the sitting room clock chime three o'clock as she lay there shivering in her bed waiting for sleep to return; June's gentle snuffles soft and warm beside her.

The driving January sleet tore at the windows; in the morning glistening frost coated the inside of the windowpanes. The house was freezing. Ivy dared not light the fire that morning with the meagre nuggets of coal that remained in the coal shed. She couldn't afford to pay the coal man if they ran out before the winter was over. It irked Ivy that now she was short on housekeeping she couldn't afford to pay her contribution into Dewar's Christmas meat fund this week.... *Jimmy was a selfish pig using all the money!*

Ivy dug out her little cigar box of savings and took out a precious half crown, she'd plundered this well on more than one occasion, but what else could she do? She and June needed to eat even if Jimmy got his meals elsewhere. Most of all she needed the bus fare into the City centre to meet Mam. She would not miss seeing her Mam this Friday in the market.

It was just so puzzling. Why did he need so much money all

486

of a sudden? Ivy knew she couldn't challenge him on the subject, it would be more than her life's worth, but it worried at her.

She tidied around and got June wrapped up to go out.

"Come on June darling, shall we go to the shops then and see if Mrs Gibbons has got any of yesterday's bread for sale" There was nothing for it she needed to go out early in the biting cold and see what she could buy with her meagre funds.

She tucked June under her pram blankets. "There you are, as snug as a bug in a rug. You'll have nice rosy cheeks this morning June. Just let Mam put her coat on."

Then she found it.

Last night, in his stupor, Jimmy carelessly slung his outdoor coat on the hooks in the hall, covering all the other garments, as Ivy moved it to get to her own coat she registered a heavy, bulky object inside Jimmy's coat pocket.

As carefully as she could she extricated the lumpy object. It was a camera, a box Brownie. What on earth did Jimmy want with a camera? They didn't go anywhere to take snaps and she'd never seen him use it. It was obvious from the scuffs and marks on the leather case the camera *was* used. She tucked it back exactly as she found it. She knew that cameras didn't come cheap, so that was why the house keeping had evaporated, he'd splashed out on a camera and probably film.

But why? She would ask Mam what she thought.

"A camera you say!" Betty and Phoebe were lost for words.

Ivy looked miserable, yesterday Jimmy had raged that there was no food in the house and yet she knew he had frittered away the housekeeping on buying a camera, she had struggled to hold her tongue. He'd be furious if he thought she was snooping.

So far Phoebe hadn't managed to find much out about Jimmy Benson. Her quest kept hitting brick walls. Jimmy's fearsome reputation meant most people were reluctant to indulge in idle gossip or speculation, only some meagre crumbs of information had come her way.

She did know that Jimmy was hanging around with a new crowd; Bill, the landlord of the Rose and Crown had raised a quizzical eyebrow when Phoebe mentioned not seeing Jimmy Benson around the place.

"He don't come in here anymore Phoebe darling, I haven't seen 'im in months," Bill didn't volunteer any more, he didn't want any trouble. She'd had the same response from the pot boy in The Feathers and from the landlord Terry in the Duke of Edinburgh.

"It's just that he's married my niece Ivy Jenkins," Phoebe left that bit of information lie to stew in Terry's mind.

"So, I heard," *Terry rued the day that he'd somehow given Jimmy the idea of marrying that sweet girl.*

"Well, the last time I saw him was weeks ago Phoebe, then it was just a quick in and out. 'Ee handed over a package or something to Donald, the old chap that sits in the corner. Next time I looked Jimmy had left." Phoebe surmised Terry didn't regret the lack of Jimmy's custom.

"I know that Cappy said he hadn't seen Jimmy in ages either, not since Jimmy stopped visiting Sean with him in Rookwood. Cappy's been pretty annoyed about that, called Jimmy a *fair-weather friend.*" Terry said.

Phoebe vowed to track down Sean's friend Cappy; it sounded as if he might know something. According to Terry, Cappy came in for a few drinks in the Duke most Friday nights unless his missus put her foot down. This Friday Phoebe would be waiting for him with a round of drinks to loosen his tongue.

Chapter 48

Phoebe set up a cash tab behind the bar. As a rule, Terry
didn't encourage that sort of thing, too many lads lost count of
who drank what and arguments broke out, so cash up front it
had to be. Phoebe placed two crisp ten bob notes in Terry's
hand and said he could keep the change, what she needed to
do wouldn't take long.

Phoebe picked a discreet cosy booth and waited like a spider
waited for its quarry. Terry's only job was to tip her the wink
when Cappy came into the pub. The rest was up to her.

Terr gave a slight inclination of his head. Cappy came in for
his pint, Phoebe got to her feet and made a big fuss of spotting
Cappy.

"Well look who's here it's Cappy." She gave him a warm
smile.

"Evening Phoebe," he chirped back, everyone knew and liked
Phoebe. Cappy had a new baby at home so he was under strict
instructions from his wife Rita not to be long or she'd have
his guts for garters.

"Let me buy you a drink Cappy, then you can tell me all the news about your new baby, and if you've got any news of your mate Sean Riley." It was smoothly done, within half an hour Cappy was nursing a mellow whiskey and his second pint of ale. He felt a warm glow seep through him, his tongue began to ease. It took a while of wandering a circuitous route of chit chat, but eventually the subject of Jimmy Benson came up.

"Do you and Jimmy still visit Sean in Rookwood then?"

"I do but 'ee doesn't, there's nothing in it for Jimmy is there?" Cappy couldn't conceal his bitterness. "Jimmy always looks after number one; every-one knows that Phoebe."

"That's true," Phoebe looked behind her to check no-one was eavesdropping. "I think my poor niece has quite a time of it, he can be a difficult man, "she shook her head.

"Aye that he can and a nasty one an' all." Cappy sneered.

"Did you know Cappy, Jimmy's only gone and bought himself a camera! My poor niece can barely put food on the table and the man buys a bloody expensive camera what in God's name was he thinking of?" Phoebe said angrily.

492

She was on dangerous ground now… if Jimmy heard she was
running him down.

"Aye, well that will be all part of his new "business"." Cappy
couldn't conceal his annoyance and downed what was left of
his whiskey.

"What business would that be Cappy?" Phoebe gestured to
Terry for another whiskey.

"Mucky pictures so I've heard," Cappy whispered; he
wrinkled his nose in disgust.

"Oh really! What's he doing with that trade then?" Phoebe
knew as well as anyone that selling sex was a routine business
in Tiger bay.

"The *sort* of pictures Jimmy sells he gets a fair old screw for."
Cappy rubbed his thumb and forefinger together. "The dirty
mac brigade will pay big money for the *right* sort of picture."

"The right sort?" Phoebe raised an eyebrow.

"Young girls…. and boys. They say Jimmy goes out and
about looking for opportunities, loiters about places trying to
get them on their own and… well it doesn't bear thinking

493

about. Disgusting, if you ask me!" Cappy couldn't conceal his loathing for what Jimmy Benson was rumoured to be getting up to.

"Oh my God Cappy, you mean he's taking pictures of little children?" Phoebe gasped.

So, they say." Cappy lowered his voice. "You know Old Donald, the chap who usually sits on his own in that corner, he's supposed to be one of Jimmy's customers. He's always been fond of looking at little girls has Donald; the police have even had words with him 'cos of it. Of course, Donald always says he's being friendly; not doing anything wrong, *just looking* is what he says." Cappy snorted in disbelief as if to say what business has an old bloke got looking at children.

"Anyway, the police aren't buying it and Donald's banned from the local parks, so now he buys pictures of kiddies if he can get 'em."

Thoughts were racing through Phoebe's mind... *June.*

"Well, I'd best be off now Phoebe love, or my Rita will skin me alive, thanks again for the drinks." He rose to leave and bent in close to whisper in Phoebe's ear. "Keep away from

Jimmy Benson, he's bad news Phoebe. I pity that poor lass he's married and that little girl of hers, someone needs to watch out for her. There are men, family men, round here who'd string Jimmy up if they knew half of what he gets up to." Cappy gave her a knowing look.

Phoebe's mind was in turmoil; she would have to find a way of dealing with Jimmy Benson.

Chapter 49

"Honestly Jack it just landed on the mat, along with the rest of the post," Norah was shaking with revulsion and rage.

"Give it here, let me see that!" Jack snatched the letter and the pictures. "Says here that our neighbour Jimmy Benson likes taking pictures of kiddies! Says he watches them, gives them presents, tries to trick them into taking their clothes off and sells the pictures!... Says that every child in Wilson road is at risk!" Jack scrutinized the unsigned letter; wonky, scrawling writing and handwritten envelope.

"Who sent us this filth Norah?" Jack's eyes were blazing; in with the letter there were two pictures of little girls on a beach; one pretty in her best summer frock with blonde hair staring directly at the camera, in another shot a young girl, no more than a toddler looking shy and awkward with just her vest and pants on. *What was Jimmy Benson doing with pictures of these young girls?*

"I don't know Jack... do you think it's true?" Norah twisted her hands nervously.

"Where was this picture taken, and why did someone send this muck to us Norah? Has Jimmy been over here sniffing around our lot? Around our Karen?" Jack demanded.

"No Jack! Honest, he hasn't. Jimmy's never so much as set a foot over the doorstep and Ivy says he doesn't allow any visitors in their house neither. She says he won't let anyone in, that's why there was all that business with Ivy's Mam and those letters." Norah racked her brains. "Do you think this is one of those poison-pen letters, you know someone with an axe to grind, stirring up trouble?"

"Could be Norah, but then why pick on us to tell? Why not go straight to the police? It's obviously someone who knows you're close to Ivy."

Norah felt a grip of fear.

"You need to talk to her Norah today, find out what Ivy knows. Then we can decide what to do." Jack grabbed his coat to go to work. "If it's true, then Jimmy Benson's life won't be worth living, around here or anywhere else for that matter... I'll see to that! People who go after kids are no better than scum!"

497

Ivy was coming over later that morning for a cup of tea and a natter. Norah dreaded the task ahead but as Jack said she had to think of the local children, it would be their fault if something happened, and they hadn't done anything about Jimmy, after getting a warning like that.

"Come in have a cup of tea Ivy love, take the weight off your feet." June settled down on the floor by Ivy's feet.

"Ivy, you know I'm fond of you and June," Norah twiddled with her house coat nervously. "But, I have to ask you something. I know this is a strange question Ivy but.... Does Jimmy have a camera?"

Ivy looked startled. "Yes, he does, why?"

"Have you ever seen him use it? I mean does he take pictures of you and June? Perhaps go to the beach with it?"

"No never, I've never been a beach in my life." Ivy wondered where all this was going.

"Here; take a look at this." Norah thrust the envelope in Ivy's hands.

Norah could see Ivy's hands were shaking as she read the

498

hateful letter.

"I'm sorry Ivy but my Jack said I had to ask you, since we'd been sent the letter. I don't want to believe gossip but… well it's just this is *so* serious love. What are we supposed to think?" Norah looked embarrassed, she saw Ivy's face looking pale and pinched.

"And then there's those pictures, where were those taken? Do you know if Jimmy is taking pictures of children?"

Ivy shook her head in despair. She felt sick. *Who could have written the letter, she didn't recognize the writing?*

"I must go now Norah, thank you for telling me." Ivy, her face a picture of misery, gathered June up.

"My Jack said he wouldn't stand it if it was true Ivy," Norah warned "I know I've landed you with a problem Ivy, but you must get to the bottom of this, find out if it's true. As I said to Jack perhaps it was one of them poison pen letters from a troublemaker, but one way or another you've got to know the truth. We can't just ignore this, Ivy."

Norah was sobbing as she watched Ivy cross the road, her slender shoulders slumped as if she was carrying the weight of

499

the whole world on them. Jimmy Benson was a hard man and Ivy was frightened of him... still as Jack said Ivy had to be told.

When Ivy read the letter, she felt her world splinter into a million pieces.

Scales dropped from her eyes. Jimmy had only ever been interested in skinny plain Ivy Jenkins because she *did* look like a young girl when he first strode into 22 Bute street looking for lodgings. She'd never seen him looking at women in all the time she'd known him. He liked them young; that was why he used to visit Ivy's room.

Ivy had heard about the dirty mac men who lurked in the local parks from Alice Tranter; dirty old men, kiddie fiddlers Alice had called them. Men who used to like watching children and worse.

Ivy headed up to Jimmy's room and started to hunt. Carefully she moved his clothes in the chest of drawers; searched the bottom of his wardrobe; hunted under the bed, explored ever cubbyhole and hiding place until she found what she was looking for. There, tucked away at the very bottom of the bedroom ottoman under the spare linen, extra pillows, and

500

sprigs of lavender,... were more pictures.

In a cardboard envelope she found dozens of black and white images of anxious

 little girls she didn't know; some barely dressed. Ivy wept, how could Jimmy explain those away? She pushed them back under the spare linen.

So, it *was* true, the letter writer knew what Jimmy was up to, knew Norah would warn Ivy and knew June was in danger..

She would look him in the eye tonight and tell him about Norah's strange letter, she would not mention the pictures. Jimmy always objected to her going over to see Norah with June; said she was a gossipy cow. He would be incandescent with fury when she challenged him about this.

Ivy had put June to bed early, she waited in the kitchen; resolute. Ivy had turned her opening phrase over and over in her head... the best she could come up with was "Jimmy we've got a problem."

The click of the front door felt like gunshot going off.

The explosion when she told him, was as mighty as she

thought it would be. He called her a fool and a liar; he blamed June for going over to Norah's causing trouble, said people had it in for him; he denied he'd ever gone to any beach taking photographs, called her a lying bitch and a lazy whore and he'd hit her. He hit her because *it was all her fault.*

When he slammed the front door behind him she breathed a sigh of relief. She knew what she must do. Ivy scrambled up the stairs, she did not have long; he would come after her. She gathered the last of her savings and delving to the bottom of the ottoman she retrieved the incriminating pictures. She packed a few things in suitcase and roused the dozing child. There could be no going back now.

"Come on June it's time to get up again."

June grizzled and rubbed sleepy eyes. Drowsy with sleep her arms and legs wriggled and pushed against her clothes.

"Come on put your arm in for Mammy…. that's a good girl, we're going to see Nanna Betty; we've got to get you dressed."

June yawned and grumbled.

"Oh dear, sleepy head, you can sleep on the bus to Nannas."

Ivy willed June to comply, the last thing she needed was a howling child drawing attention.

"Hurry darling, let's go say good-bye to Aunty Norah before we catch our bus." Ivy chattered to the child easing her out of her warm bed and into her clothes and into the street. Ivy had to make it to the bus stop on the corner of Grand Avenue by 8.30, she needed to hurry; to be gone.

Norah looked shocked to find Ivy standing on the doorstep with June tired and heavy in her arms. Ivy stood like a tiny, shivering sparrow.

"Oh, Ivy love, I'm so sorry. Come on in out of the cold." Norah saw the case on the floor; June rubbing her little fist into sleepy eyes. Ivy was leaving Jimmy.

"I can't Norah or I'll miss my bus. I'm going to Mam's." Ivy looked calm and determined. "Whoever sent that letter to you Norah was telling the truth…. I've got more proof." There were no tears in her eyes she would not cry over Jimmy.

"Oh my God!" Norah's hand rushed to her mouth.

"I found *these* hidden in Jimmy's room," She spat the word *these*… "Give them to Jack and tell him I'm going to the

503

police tonight, they will need to see these; there are dozens of them. Jimmy denied ever going to the beach taking pictures; said it was all a pack of lies, but *he's* the liar Norah and I can't live with… with a man like *that*." Ivy didn't have the words to describe the revolting antics of her husband.

Ivy handed over the pictures, she would keep one as proof. She dared not take any other evidence with her in case she met Jimmy whilst waiting for her bus. Jack must keep the evidence safe, without those pictures and the letter Ivy had nothing. She was not out of Jimmy's clutches yet.

"Have you still got that letter Norah?"

Norah nodded.

"Keep it safe Norah, it's important; proof of what Jimmy does, someone else knows what he's up to, I'll tell the police that you've got it and I'll show them this." She tucked the one photograph in her pocket.

Norah couldn't speak she felt so sorry for Ivy.

"He's disgusting Norah,… a monster! Jimmy will pay for this; I'll make certain of that. People need to know who the real Jimmy Benson is!"

504

Ivy stood with her shoulders back, a look of grim determination on her face.

"I've must run now; I need to get June over to my Mam's before I go to the police station. Thank you Norah for everything…. And I mean it *everything*." Ivy fought back tears.

"Good luck," Norah gave her brave friend a hug and a kiss. "Write to me Ivy."

Ivy nodded. "I will. Say goodbye to your Aunty Norah, June," with a sleepy June balanced on her hip Ivy picked up her suitcase and marched as fast as she could out of Wilson road and away from Jimmy Benson. Ivy's heart was pounding as she fled for their lives with June, her most precious possession, cradled in her arms.

In fifteen minutes, Ivy and June would be safe on a bus…. free. With every step she took away from Wilson road her heart felt a little lighter. She would never go back to the monster that was Jimmy Benson. Later that evening Ivy would walk into Roath police station with her head held high and tell them *everything* she knew about Jimmy Benson….

Printed in Great Britain
by Amazon